THE LAST COYOTE

❖ ❖ ❖ ❖ ❖ ❖ ❖ ❖

Michael Connelly

ALLEN&UNWIN

This edition published in Australia and New Zealand by Allen & Unwin in 2007

First published in 1995

Copyright © Hieronymus, Inc., 1995

Allen & Unwin
83 Alexander Street
Crows Nest NSW 2065
Australia
Phone: (61 2) 8425 0100
Fax: (61 2) 9906 2218
Email: info@allenandunwin.com
Web: www.allenandunwin.com

National Library of Australia
Cataloguing-in-Publication entry:

Connelly, Michael, 1956–.
        The last coyote.

        ISBN 9781741753066 (pbk.).

        1. Bosch, Harry (Fictitious character) – Fiction. 2. Police –
        California – Los Angeles – Fiction. 3. Los Angeles (Calif.) –
        Fiction. I. Title.

813.54

Printed in Australia by Griffin Press

10 9 8 7 6 5 4 3 2 1

This is for Marcus Grupa

THE LAST COYOTE

❖❖❖❖❖❖❖❖

'Any thoughts that you'd like to start with?'

'Thoughts on what?'

'Well, on anything. On the incident.'

'On the incident? Yes, I have some thoughts.'

She waited but he didn't continue. He had decided before he even got to Chinatown that this would be the way he would be. He'd make her have to pull every single word out of him.

'Could you share them with me, Detective Bosch?' she finally asked. 'That is the purpose of –'

'My thoughts are that this is bullshit. Total bullshit. That's the purpose. That's all.'

'No, wait. How do you mean, bullshit?'

'I mean, okay, I pushed the guy. I guess I hit him. I'm not sure exactly what happened but I'm not denying anything. So, fine, suspend me, transfer me, take it to a Board of Rights, whatever. But going this way is bullshit. ISL is bullshit. I mean, why do I have to come here three times a week to talk to you like I'm some kind of – you don't even know me, you don't know anything about me. Why do I have to talk to you? Why do you have to sign off on this?'

'Well, the technical answer is right there in your own statement. Rather than discipline you the department wants to treat you. You've been placed on involuntary stress leave, which means –'

'I know what it means and that's what's bullshit. Somebody arbitrarily decides I'm under stress and that gives the department the power to keep me off the job indefinitely, or at least until I jump through enough hoops for you.'

'Nothing about this was arbitrary. It was predicated on your actions, which I think clearly show –'

'What happened had nothing to do with stress. What it was about was … never mind. Like I said, it's bullshit. So why don't we just cut through it and get to the point. What do I have to do to get back to my job?'

He could see the anger flare behind her eyes. His total disavowal of her science and skill cut to her pride. Quickly the anger was gone, though. Dealing with cops all the time, she had to be used to it.

'Can't you see that all of this is for your own welfare? I have to assume the top managers of this department clearly see you as a valued asset or you wouldn't be here. They'd have put you on a disciplinary track and you'd be on your way out. Instead, they are doing what they can to preserve your career and its incumbent value to the department.'

'Valued asset? I'm a cop, not an asset. And when you're out there on the street nobody's thinking about incumbent value. What does that mean, anyway? Am I going to have to listen to words like that in here?'

She cleared her throat before speaking sternly.

'You have a problem, Detective Bosch. And it goes far beyond the incident that resulted in your being placed on leave. That's what these sessions are going to be all about. Do you understand? This incident is not unique. You have had problems before. What I am trying to do, what I have to do before I can sign off on your return to duty in any capacity, is get you to take a look at yourself. What are you doing? What are you about? Why do these problems happen to you? I want these sessions to be an open dialogue where I ask a few questions and you speak your mind, but with a purpose. Not to harass me and my profession or the leadership of the department. But to talk about you. This is about you in here, no one else.'

Harry Bosch just looked at her silently. He wanted a cigarette but would never ask her if he could smoke. He would never acknowledge in front of her that he had the habit. If he did, she might start talking about oral fixations or nicotine crutches. He took a deep breath instead and looked at the woman on the other side of the desk. Carmen Hinojos was a small woman with a friendly face and manner. Bosch knew she wasn't a bad person. He'd actually heard good things about her from others who had been sent to Chinatown. She was just doing her job here and his anger was not really directed at her. He knew she was probably smart enough to know that, too.

'Look, I'm sorry,' she said. 'I should not have started with that kind of open question. I know that this is an emotional subject with you. Let's try to start again. By the way, you can smoke if you'd like.'

'Is that in the file, too?'

'It's not in the file. It didn't need to be. It's your hand, the way you keep bringing it up to your mouth. Have you been trying to quit?'

'No. But it's a city office. You know the rules.'

It was a thin excuse. He violated that law every day at the Hollywood Station.

'That's not the rule in here. I don't want you to think of this as being part of Parker Center or part of the city. That's the chief reason these offices are away from that. There are no rules like that here.'

'Doesn't matter where we are. You're still working for the LAPD.'

'Try to believe that you are away from the Los Angeles Police Department. When you are in here, try to believe

3

that you're just coming to see a friend. To talk. You can say anything here.'

But he knew she could not be seen as a friend. Never. There was too much at stake here. Just the same, he nodded once to please her.

'That's not very convincing.'

He hiked his shoulders as if to say it was the best he could do, and it was.

'By the way, if you want I could hypnotize you, get rid of your dependency on nicotine.'

'If I wanted to quit, I could do it. People are either smokers or they're not. I am.'

'Yes. It's perhaps the most obvious symptom of a self-destructive nature.'

'Excuse me, am I on leave because I smoke? Is that what this is about?'

'I think you know what it's about.'

He said nothing else, remembering his decision to say as little as possible.

'Well, let's continue then,' she said. 'You've been on leave … let's see, Tuesday a week?'

'Right.'

'What have you been doing with your time?'

'Filling out FEMA forms mostly.'

'FEMA?'

'My house was red-tagged.'

'The earthquake was three months ago. Why have you waited?'

'I've been busy. I've been working.'

'I see. Did you have insurance?'

'Don't say "I see," because you don't. You couldn't possibly see things the way I do. The answer is no, no insurance. Like most everybody else, I was living in denial. Isn't that what you people call it? I bet you had insurance.'

'Yes. How bad was your house hit?'

4

'Depends on who you ask. The city inspectors say it's totaled and I can't even go inside. I think it's fine. Just needs some work. They know me by name at Home Depot now. And I've had contractors do some of it. It'll be done soon and I'll appeal the red tag. I've got a lawyer.'

'You're living there still?'

He nodded.

'Now that's denial, Detective Bosch. I don't think you should be doing that.'

'I don't think you have any say about what I do outside my job with the department.'

She raised her hands in a hands-off manner.

'Well, while I don't condone it, I suppose it serves its purpose. I think it's good that you have something to keep you occupied. Though I'd much rather it be a sport or a hobby or maybe plans for a trip out of town, I think it's important to keep busy, to keep your mind off the incident.'

Bosch smirked.

'What?'

'I don't know. Everybody keeps calling it the incident. It kind've reminds me of how people called it the Vietnam conflict, not the war.'

'Then what would you call what happened?'

'I don't know. But incident ... it sounds like ... I don't know. Antiseptic. Listen, Doctor, let's go back a minute. I don't want to take a trip out of town, okay? My job is in homicide. It's what I do. And I'd really like to get back to it. I might be able to do some good, you know.'

'If the department lets you.'

'If you do. You know it's going to be up to you.'

'Perhaps. Do you notice that you speak of your job as if it's a mission of some sort?'

'That's about right. Like the Holy Grail.'

He said it with sarcasm. This was getting intolerable and it was only the first session.

'Is it? Do you believe your mission in life is to solve murders, to put bad people in jail?'

He used the shoulder hike to say he didn't know. He stood up and walked to the window and looked down on Hill Street. The sidewalks were crowded with pedestrians. Every time he had been down here they were crowded. He noticed a couple of Caucasian women walking along. They stood out in the sea of Asian faces like raisins in rice. They passed the window of a Chinese butcher shop and Bosch saw a row of smoked ducks hanging whole, by their necks.

Farther up the road he saw the Hollywood Freeway overpass, the dark windows of the old sheriff's jail and the Criminal Courts building behind it. To the left of that he could see the City Hall tower. Black construction tarps hung around the top floors. It looked like some kind of mourning gesture but he knew the tarps were to hold debris from falling while earthquake repairs were made. Looking past City Hall, Bosch could see the Glass House. Parker Center, police headquarters.

'Tell me what your mission is,' Hinojos said quietly from behind him. 'I'd like to hear you put it in words.'

He sat back down and tried to think of a way to explain himself but finally just shook his head.

'I can't.'

'Well, I want you to think about that. Your mission. What is it really? Think about that.'

'What's your mission, Doctor?'

'That's not our concern here.'

'Of course it is.'

'Look, Detective, this is the only personal question I will answer. These dialogues are not to be about me. They are about you. My mission, I believe, is to help the men and women of this department. That's the narrow focus. And by doing that, on a grander scale I help the community, I help the people of this city. The better the cops are that we have out on the street, the better we all are. The safer we all are. Okay?'

'That's fine. When I think about my mission, do you want me to shorten it to a couple sentences like that and rehearse it to the point that it sounds like I'm reading out of the dictionary?'

'Mr – uh, Detective Bosch, if you want to be cute and contentious the whole time, we are not going to get anywhere, which means you are not going to get back to your job anytime soon. Is that what you're looking for here?'

He raised his hands in surrender. She looked down at the yellow legal pad on the desk. With her eyes off him, he was able to study her. Carmen Hinojos had tiny brown hands she kept on the desk in front of her. No rings on either hand. She held an expensive-looking pen in her right hand. Bosch always thought expensive pens were used by people overly concerned with image. But maybe he was wrong about her. She wore her dark brown hair tied back. She wore glasses with thin tortoiseshell frames. She should have had braces when she was a kid but didn't. She looked up from the pad and their eyes locked.

'I am told this inci – this … situation coincided with or was close to the time of the dissolving of a romantic relationship.'

'Told by who?'

'It's in the background material given to me. The sources of this material are not important.'

'Well, they are important because you've got bad sources. It had nothing to do with what happened. The dissolving, as you call it, was almost three months ago.'

'The pain of these things can last much longer than that.

7

I know this is personal and may be difficult but I think we should talk about this. The reason is that it will help give me a basis for your emotional state at the time the assault took place. Is that a problem?'

Bosch waved her on with his hand.

'How long did this relationship last?'

'About a year.'

'Marriage?'

'No.'

'Was it talked about?'

'No, not really. Never out in the open.'

'Did you live together?'

'Sometimes. We both kept our places.'

'Is the separation final?'

'I think so.'

Saying it out loud seemed to be the first time Bosch acknowledged that Sylvia Moore was gone from his life for good.

'Was this separation by mutual agreement?'

He cleared his throat. He didn't want to talk about this but he wanted it over with.

'I guess you could say it was mutual agreement, but I didn't know about it until she was packed. You know, three months ago we were holding each other in bed while the house was shaking apart on the pad. You could say she was gone before the aftershocks ended.'

'They still haven't.'

'Just a figure of speech.'

'Are you saying the earthquake was the cause of the breakup of this relationship?'

'No, I'm not saying that. All I'm saying is that's when it happened. Right after. She's a teacher up in the Valley and her school got wrecked. The kids were moved to other schools and the district didn't need as many teachers. They offered sabbaticals and she took one. She left town.'

'Was she scared of another earthquake or was she scared of you?'

She looked pointedly at him.

'Why would she be scared of me?'

He knew he sounded a little too defensive.

'I don't know. I'm just asking questions. Did you give her a reason to be scared?'

Bosch hesitated. It was a question he had never really touched on in his private thoughts about the breakup.

'If you mean in a physical way, no, she wasn't scared and I gave her no reason to be.'

Hinojos nodded and wrote something on her pad. It bothered Bosch that she would make a note about this.

'Look, it's got nothing to do with what happened at the station last week.'

'Why did she leave? What was the real reason?'

He looked away. He was angry. This was how it was going to be. She would ask whatever she wanted. Invade him wherever there was an opening.

'I don't know.'

'That answer is not acceptable in here. I think you do know, or at least have your own beliefs as to why she would leave. You must.'

'She found out who I was.'

'She found out who you were, what does that mean?'

'You'd have to ask her. She said it. But she's in Venice. The one in Italy.'

'Well, then what do you think she meant by it?'

'It doesn't matter what I think. She's the one who said it and she's the one who left.'

'Don't fight me, Detective Bosch. Please. There is nothing I want more than for you to get back to your job. As I said, that's my mission. To get you back there if you can go. But you make it difficult by being difficult.'

9

'Maybe that's what she found out. Maybe that's who I am.'

'I doubt the reason is as simplistic as that.'

'Sometimes I don't.'

She looked at her watch and leaned forward, dissatisfaction with the session showing on her face.

'Okay, Detective, I understand how uncomfortable you are. We're going to move on, but I suspect we will have to come back to this issue. I want you to give it some thought. Try to put your feelings into words.'

She waited for him to say something but he didn't.

'Let's try talking about what happened last week again. I understand it stemmed from a case involving the murder of a prostitute.'

'Yes.'

'It was brutal?'

'That's just a word. Means different things to different people.'

'True, but taking its meaning to you, was it a brutal homicide?'

'Yes, it was brutal. I think almost all of them are. Somebody dies, it's brutal. For them.'

'And you took the suspect into custody?'

'Yes, my partner and I. I mean, no. He came in voluntarily to answer questions.'

'Did this case affect you more than, say, other cases have in the past?'

'Maybe, I don't know.'

'Why would that be?'

'You mean why did I care about a prostitute? I didn't. Not more than any other victim. But in homicide there is one rule that I have when it comes to the cases I get.'

'What is that rule?'

'Everybody counts or nobody counts.'

'Explain it.'

'Just what I said. Everybody counts or nobody counts. That's it. It means I bust my ass to make a case whether it's a prostitute or the mayor's wife. That's my rule.'

'I understand. Now, let's go to this specific case. I'm interested in hearing your description of what happened after the arrest and the reasons you may have for your violent actions at the Hollywood Division.'

'Is this being taped?'

'No, Detective, whatever you tell me is protected. At the end of these sessions I will simply make a recommendation to Assistant Chief Irving. The details of the sessions will never be divulged. The recommendations I make are usually less than half a page and contain no details from the dialogues.'

'You wield a lot of power with that half page.'

She didn't respond. Bosch thought for a moment while looking at her. He thought he might be able to trust her but his natural instinct and experience was that he should trust no one. She seemed to know his dilemma and waited him out.

'You want to hear my side of it?'

'Yes, I do.'

'Okay, I'll tell you what happened.'

Bosch smoked along the way home but realized that what he really wanted was not a cigarette, but a drink to deaden his nerves. He looked at his watch and decided it was too early to stop at a bar. He settled for another cigarette and home.

After negotiating the drive up Woodrow Wilson, he parked at the curb a half block from the house and walked back. He could hear gentle piano music, something classical, coming from the home of one of his neighbors but he couldn't tell which house. He didn't really know any of his neighbors or which one might have a piano player in the family. He ducked under the yellow tape strung in front of the property and entered through the door in the carport.

This was his routine, to park down the street and hide the fact that he lived in his own house. The house had been red-tagged as uninhabitable after the earthquake and ordered demolished by a city inspector. But Bosch had ignored both orders, cut the lock on the electric box, and had been living in it for three months.

It was a small house with redwood siding that stood on steel pylons anchored in the sedimentary bedrock folded and formed as the Santa Monica Mountains rose out of the desert during the Mesozoic and Cenozoic eras. The pylons had held true in their moorings during the quake, but the overlying house had shifted atop them, breaking partially free of the pylons and seismic bolts. It slid. All of about two inches. Still, it was enough. Though short on distance the slide was long on damage. Inside, the woodframe house flexed and window and door frames lost their square. The glass shattered, the front door became terminally closed, frozen in a frame that had canted to the north with the rest of the house. If Bosch wanted to open that door, he would probably need to borrow the police tank with the battering ram. As it was, he'd had to use a crowbar to open the carport door. Now that door served as the main entrance to his home.

Bosch had paid a contractor five thousand dollars to jack the house up and then over the two inches it had moved. It was then put down in its proper space and rebolted to the pylons. After that, Bosch was content to work as time allowed on reframing windows and interior doors himself. The glass came first and in the months after that he reframed and rehung the interior doors. He worked from books on carpentry and often had to do individual projects two and three times until he had them reasonably correct. But he found the work enjoyable and even therapeutic. Working with his hands became a respite from his job in homicide. He left the front door as it was, thinking that somehow it was fitting, that it was a salute to the power of nature. And he was content to use the side door.

All of his efforts did not save the house from the city's list of condemned structures. Gowdy, the building inspector who had been assigned to this section of the hills, kept it red-tagged as condemned, despite Bosch's work, and so began the hiding game in which Bosch made his entrances and exits as surreptitiously as a spy's to a foreign embassy. He tacked black plastic tarps over the inside of the front windows so they would emit no telltale light. And he always watched for Gowdy. Gowdy was his nemesis.

In the meantime, Bosch hired a lawyer to appeal the inspector's edict.

The carport door granted entry directly into the kitchen. After he came in, Bosch opened the refrigerator and retrieved a can of Coca-Cola, then stood in the doorway of the aging appliance letting its breath cool him while he studied its contents for something suitable for dinner. He knew exactly what was on the shelves and in the drawers but still he looked. It was as if he hoped for the surprise appearance of a forgotten steak or chicken breast. He followed this routine with the refrigerator often. It was the ritual of a man who was alone. He knew this also.

On the back deck Bosch drank the soda and ate a sandwich consisting of five-day-old bread and slices of meat from plastic packages. He wished he had potato chips to go with it because he would undoubtedly be hungry later after having only the sandwich for dinner.

He stood at the railing looking down at the Hollywood Freeway, near capacity now with the Monday-evening commute. He had gotten out of downtown just before the crest of the rush-hour wave had broken. He would have to guard against going overtime on the sessions with the police psychologist. They were scheduled for 3:30 P.M. on Mondays, Wednesdays and Fridays. Did Carmen Hinojos ever let a session go over? he wondered. Or was hers a nine-to-five mission?

From his vantage on the mountain, he could see almost all northbound lanes of the freeway as it cut through the Cahuenga Pass to the San Fernando Valley. He was reviewing what had been said during the session, trying to decide whether it was a good or bad session, but his focus drifted and he began to watch the point where the freeway came into view as it crested the pass. Absentmindedly, he would choose two cars that came over about even with each other and follow them through the mile-long segment of the freeway that was visible from the deck. He'd pick one or the other and follow the race, unknown to its drivers, until the finish line, which was the Lankershim Boulevard exit.

After a few minutes of this he realized what he was doing and spun around, away from the freeway.

'Jesus,' he said out loud.

He knew then that keeping his hands busy would not be enough while he was away from his job. He went back inside and got a bottle of Henry's from the refrigerator. Right after he opened the beer the phone rang. It was his partner, Jerry Edgar, and the call was a welcome distraction from the silence.

'Harry, how's things in Chinatown?'

Because every cop secretly feared that he or she might one day crack from the pressures of the job and become a candidate for therapy sessions at the department's Behavioral Sciences Section, the unit was rarely spoken of by its formal name. Going to BSS sessions was more often referred to as 'going to Chinatown' because of the unit's location there on Hill Street, several blocks from Parker Center. If it became known about a cop that he was going there, the word would spread that he had the Hill Street blues. The six-story bank building where the BSS was located was known as the 'Fifty-One-Fifty' building. This was not its address. It was the police radio code number for describing a crazy person. Codes like this were part of the protective structure used to belittle and, therefore, more easily contain their own fears.

'Chinatown was great,' Bosch said sarcastically. 'You ought to try it some day. It's got me sitting here counting cars on the freeway.'

'Well, at least you won't run out.'

'Yeah. What's going on with you?'

'Pounds finally did it.'

'Did what?'

'Stuck me with somebody new.'

Bosch was silent a moment. The news gave him a sense of finality. The thought that maybe he would never get his job back began to creep into his mind.

'He did?'

'Yeah, he finally did. I caught a case this morning. So he stuck one of his suckups with me. Burns.'

'Burns? From autos? He's never worked homicide. Has he ever even worked CAPs?'

Detectives usually followed one of two paths in the department. One was property crimes and the other was crimes against persons. The latter included specializing in homicide, rape, assault and robbery. CAPs detectives had the higher-profile cases and usually viewed property crime investigators as paper pushers. There were so many property crimes in the city that the investigators spent most of their time taking reports and processing the occasional arrest. They actually did little detective work. There was no time to.

'He's been a paper guy all the way,' Edgar said. 'But with Pounds that doesn't matter. All he cares about is having somebody on the homicide table who isn't going to give his shit back to him. And Burns is just the guy. He probably started lobbying for the job the minute the word went out about you.'

'Well, fuck him. I'm gonna get back to the table and then he goes back to autos.'

Edgar took his time before answering. It was as if Bosch had said something that made no sense to him.

'You really think that, Harry? Pounds ain't going to stand for you coming back. Not after what you did. I told him when he told me I was with Burns that, you know, no offense but I'd wait until Harry Bosch came back and he

16

said if I wanted to handle it that way, then I'd be waitin' until I was an old man.'

'He said that? Well, fuck him, too. I still got a friend or two in the department.'

'Irving still owes you, doesn't he?'

'I guess maybe I'll find out.'

He didn't go further with it. He wanted to change the subject. Edgar was his partner but they had never gotten to the point where they completely confided in each other. Bosch played the mentor role in the relationship and he trusted Edgar with his life. But that was a bond that held fast on the street. Inside the department was another matter. Bosch had never trusted anyone, never relied on anyone. He wasn't going to start now.

'So, what's the case?' he asked, to divert the conversation.

'Oh, yeah, I wanted to tell you about it. This was weird, man. First the killing's weird, then what happened after. The call out was to a house on Sierra Bonita. This is about five in the A.M. The citizen reports he heard a sound like a gunshot, only muffled-like. He grabs his deer rifle out of the closet and goes outside to take a look. This is a neighborhood that's been picked clean lately by the hypes, you know? Four B and Es on his block alone this month. So, he was ready with the rifle. Anyway, he goes down his driveway with the gun – the garage is in the back – and he sees a pair of legs hanging out of the open door of his car. It was parked in front of the garage.'

'He shoots him?'

'No, that's the crazy thing. He goes up with his gun but the guy in his car is already dead. Stabbed in the chest with a screwdriver.'

Bosch didn't get it. He didn't have enough of the facts. But he said nothing.

'The air bag killed him, Harry.'

'What do you mean, the air bag killed him?'

'The air bag. This goddamn hype was stealing the air bag out of the steering wheel and somehow the thing went off. It inflated instantly, like it was supposed to, and drove the screwdriver right into his heart, man. I've never seen anything like it. He must've been holding the screwdriver backwards or he was using the butt-end to bang on the wheel. We haven't exactly figured out that part yet. We talked to a guy at Chrysler. He says that you take the protective cover off, like this dude had, and even static electricity can set the thing off. Our dead guy was wearing a sweater. I don't know, could've been it. Burns says it's the first death by static cling.'

While Edgar chuckled at his new partner's humor, Bosch thought about the scenario. He remembered a department info bulletin going out on air bag thefts the year before. They had become a hot commodity in the underground market, with thieves getting as much as three hundred dollars apiece for air bags from unscrupulous body shops. The body shops would buy them for three hundred and turn around and charge a customer nine hundred to install one. That was double the profit derived when ordering from the manufacturer.

'So it goes down as accidental?' Bosch asked.

'Yeah, accidental death. But the story ain't over. Both doors of the car were open.'

'The dead guy had a partner.'

'That's what we figure. And so if we find the fucker we can charge him. Under the felony homicide law. So we had SID laser the inside of the car and pull all the prints they could. I took 'em down to Latents and talked one of the techs into scanning them and running them on the AFIS. And bingo.'

'You got the partner?'

'Dead bang. That AFIS computer has got a long reach,

Harry. One of the nets is the US Military Identification Center in St Louis. We got a match on our guy outta there. He was in the Army ten years ago. We got his ID from that, then got an address from the DMV and picked him up today. He copped on the ride in. He's gonna go away for a while.'

'Sounds like a good day, then.'

'Didn't end there, though. I haven't told you the weird part yet.'

'Then tell me.'

'Remember I said we lasered the car and took all the prints?'

'Right.'

'Well, we got another match, too. This one on the crime indexes. A case outta Mississippi. Man, all days should be like this one was.'

'What was the match?' Bosch asked. He was growing impatient with the way Edgar was parceling out the story.

'We matched prints put on the net seven years ago by something called the Southern States Criminal Identification Base. It's like five states that don't add up in population to half of LA. Anyway, one of the prints we put through today matched the doer on a double homicide in Biloxi all the way back in 'seventy-six. Some guy the papers there called the Bicentennial Butcher on account he killed two women on the Fourth of July.'

'The car's owner? The guy with the rifle?'

'Damn right. His fingerprints were on the cleaver left in one girl's skull. He was a bit surprised when we came back to his house this afternoon. We said, "Hey, we caught the partner of the guy who died in your car. And by the way, you're under arrest for a two-bagger, motherfucker." I think it blew his mind, Harry. You shoulda been there.'

Edgar laughed loudly into the phone and Bosch knew,

after only one week of being grounded, how much he missed the job.

'Did he cop?'

'No, he kept quiet. You can't be that stupid and get away with a double murder for almost twenty years. That's a nice run.'

'Yeah, what's he been doing?'

'Looks like he's just been laying low. Owns a hardware on Santa Monica. Married and has a kid and a dog. A total reform case. But he's going back to Biloxi. I hope he likes southern cooking 'cause he won't be coming back here anytime soon.'

Edgar laughed again. Bosch said nothing. The story was depressing because it was a reminder of what he was no longer doing. It also reminded him about what Hinojos had asked about defining his mission.

'Got a couple of Mississippi state troopers comin' out tomorrow,' Edgar said. 'Talked to them a little while ago and they are happy campers.'

Bosch didn't say anything for a while.

'Harry, you still there?'

'Yeah, I was just thinking about something … Well, it sounds like a hell of a day of crime fighting. How's the fearless leader taking it?'

'Pounds? Jesus, he's got a hard-on over this the size of a Louisville slugger. You know what he's doing? He's trying to figure out a way to take credit for all three clearances. He's trying to put the Biloxi cases on our rate.'

It didn't surprise Bosch. It was a widespread practice among department managers and statisticians to add positive credit to crime clearance levels whenever and wherever possible. In the air bag case, there was no actual murder. It was an accident. But because the death occurred during the commission of a crime, California law held that an accomplice to the crime could be charged with his partner's death. Bosch knew that based on the partner's arrest for murder, Pounds intended to add a case to the murder clearance chart. He would not balance this by adding a case to the murder occurrence chart because the death by air bag was an accident. This little statistical two-step would result in a nice little boost for the Hollywood Division's overall homicide clearance rate, which in recent years had continually threatened to dip below fifty percent.

But unsatisfied with the modest jump this accounting deception would provide, Pounds intended to boldly add the two Biloxi murders to the clearance chart as well. After all, it could be argued, his homicide squad did clear two more cases. Adding a total of three cleared cases to one side of the chart without adding any to the other would likely give a tremendous boost to the overall clearance rate – as well as to the image of Pounds as a detective bureau commander. Bosch knew that Pounds was probably delighted with himself and the accomplishments of the day.

'He said our rate would jump six points,' Edgar was saying. 'He was a very pleased man, Harry. And my new partner was very pleased he had pleased his man.'

'I don't want to hear any more.'

'I didn't think so. So what are you doing to keep busy, besides counting cars on the freeway? You must be bored stiff, Harry.'

'Not really,' Bosch lied. 'Last week I finished fixing the deck. This week I'll –'

'Harry, I'm telling you, you're wasting your time and money. The inspectors are going to find you in there and kick you out on your ass. Then they'll tear the place down themselves and hand you the bill. Your deck and the whole house will be in the back of a dump truck then.'

'I hired a lawyer to work on it.'

'What's he gonna do?'

'I don't know. I want to appeal the red tag. He's a land use guy. He said he can work it out.'

'I hope so. I still think you ought to tear it down and start over.'

'I didn't win the lotto yet.'

'The feds've got disaster loans. You could get one and –'

'I've applied, Jerry, but I like my house the way it is.'

'Okay, Harry. I hope your lawyer works it out. Anyway, I gotta go. Burns wants to have a beer over at the Short Stop. He's there waiting.'

The last time Bosch had been at the Short Stop, a hole-in-the-wall cop bar near the academy and Dodger Stadium, it had still had I SUPPORT CHIEF GATES bumper stickers on the wall. For most cops, Gates was a dying ember of the past, but the Short Stop was a place where old-liners went to drink and remember a department that no longer existed.

'Yeah, have fun over there, Jerry.'

'Take care, man.'

Bosch leaned against a counter and drank his beer. He came to the conclusion that Edgar's call had been a cleverly disguised way of telling Bosch that he was choosing sides and cutting him loose. That was okay, Bosch thought. Edgar's first allegiance was to himself, to surviving in a place that could be treacherous. Bosch couldn't hold that against him.

Bosch looked at his reflection in the glass of the oven door. The image was dark but he could see his eyes in the shadow and the line of his jaw. He was forty-four years old and in some ways looked older. He still had a full head of curly brown hair but both the hair and the mustache were going to gray. His black-brown eyes seemed to him tired and used up. His skin had the pallor of a night watchman's. Bosch was still leanly built but sometimes his clothes hung on him as if they had been issued at one of the downtown missions or he had recently been through a bad illness.

He broke away from his reflection and grabbed another beer out of the refrigerator. Outside on the deck, he saw the sky was now brightly lit with the pastels of dusk. It would be dark soon, but the freeway below was a bright river of moving lights, its current never ebbing for a moment.

Looking down on the Monday night commute, he saw the place as an anthill with the workers moving along in lines. Someone or some force would soon come along and kick the hill again. Then the freeways would fall, the houses would collapse and the ants would just rebuild and get in line again.

He was bothered by something but was not quite sure what it was. His thoughts swirled and mixed. He began to see what Edgar had told him about his case in the context of his dialogue with Hinojos. There was some connection there, some bridge, but he couldn't get to it.

He finished his beer and decided that two would be enough. He went to one of the lounge chairs and sat down with his feet up. What he wanted to do was give everything a rest. Mind and body. He looked up and saw the clouds had now been painted orange by the setting sun. They looked like molten lava moving slowly across the sky.

Just before he dozed off a thought pushed through the lava. Everybody counts or nobody counts. And then, in the last moment of clarity before sleep, he knew what the connecting ribbon that had run through his thoughts had been. And he knew what his mission was.

In the morning Bosch dressed without showering so he could immediately begin work on the house and blank out the lingering thoughts from the night before with sweat and concentration.

But clearing the thoughts away was not easy. As he dressed in old lacquer-stained jeans, he caught a glimpse of himself in the cracked mirror over the bureau and saw that his T-shirt was on backward. Printed across his chest on the white shirt was the homicide squad's motto.

OUR DAY BEGINS WHEN YOUR DAY ENDS

It was supposed to be on the back of the shirt. He pulled it off, turned it and put it back on. Now in the mirror he saw what he was supposed to see. A replica of a detective's badge on the left breast of the shirt and the smaller printing that said LAPD HOMICIDE.

He brewed a pot of coffee and took it and a mug out to the deck. Next he lugged out his toolbox and the new door he had bought at Home Depot for the bedroom. When he was finally ready and had the mug filled with steaming black coffee, he sat on the footrest of one of the lounge chairs and placed the door on its side in front of him.

The original door had splintered at the hinges during the quake. He had tried to hang the replacement a few days earlier but it was too large to fit the door jamb. He figured he needed to shave no more than an eighth of an inch off the opening side to make the fit. He set to work with the plane, moving the instrument slowly back and forth along the edge as the wood peels fell away in paper-thin curls. Occasionally he would stop and study his progress and run his hand along the area of his work. He liked being able to see the progress he was making. Few other tasks in life seemed that way to him.

But still, he could not concentrate for long. His focus on the door was interrupted by the same intrusive thought that had haunted him the night before. Everybody counts or nobody counts. It was what he had told Hinojos. It was what he had told her he believed. But did he? What did it mean to him? Was it merely a slogan like the one on the back of his shirt or was it something he lived by? These questions mingled with the echoes of the conversation he'd had the night before with Edgar. And with a deeper thought that he knew he had always had.

He took the plane off the door edge and ran his hand along the smooth wood again. He thought he had it right and carried it inside. Over a drop cloth in an area of the living room he had reserved for woodworking, he ran a sheet of small-grain sandpaper over the door edge until it was perfectly smooth to his touch.

Holding the door vertically and balancing it on a block of wood, he eased it into the hinges and then dropped the pins in. He tapped them home with a hammer and they went in easily. He had oiled the pins and hinges earlier and so the bedroom door opened and closed almost silently. Most important, though, was that it closed evenly in the jamb. He opened and closed it several more times, just staring at it, pleased with his accomplishment.

The glow of his success was short-lived, for having completed the project left his mind open to wander. Back out on the deck the other thoughts came back as he swept the wood shavings into a small pile.

Hinojos had told him to stay busy. Now he knew how he would do it. And in that moment he realized that no matter how many projects he found to take his time, there was one job he still had to do. He leaned the broom against the wall and went inside to get ready.

The LAPD storage facility and aerosquad headquarters known as Piper Tech was on Ramirez Street in downtown, not far from Parker Center. Bosch, in a suit and tie, arrived shortly before eleven at the gate. He held his LAPD identification card out the window and was quickly waved in. The card was all he had. The card, along with his gold badge and gun, had been taken from him when he was placed on leave the week before. But it was later returned so that he could gain entry to the BSS offices for the stress therapy sessions with Carmen Hinojos.

After parking, he walked to the beige-painted storage warehouse that housed the city's history of violence. The quarter-acre building contained the files of all LAPD cases, solved or unsolved. This was where the case files came when nobody cared anymore.

At the front counter a civilian clerk was loading files onto a cart so that they could be wheeled back into the expanse of shelves and forgotten. By the way she studied Bosch, he knew it was rare that anyone ever showed up here in person. It was all done by telephones and city couriers.

'If you're looking for city council minutes, that's building A, across the lot. The one with brown trim.'

Bosch held up his ID card.

'No, I want to pull a case.'

He reached into his coat pocket while she walked up to

the counter and bent forward to read his card. She was a small black woman with graying hair and glasses. The name tag affixed to her blouse said her name was Geneva Beaupre.

'Hollywood,' she said. 'Why didn't you just ask for it to be sent out in dispatch? There ain't no hurry on these cases.'

'I was downtown, over at Parker ... I wanted to see it as soon as I could, anyway.'

'Well, you got a number?'

From his pocket he pulled a piece of notebook paper with the number 61–743 written on it. She bent to study it and then her head jerked up.

'Nineteen sixty-one? You want a case from – I don't know where nineteen sixty-one is.'

'It's here. I've looked at the file before. I guess there was someone else clerking here back then, but it was here.'

'Well, I'll look. You're going to wait?'

'Yeah, I'll wait.'

This seemed to disappoint her but Bosch smiled at her in the most friendly way he could muster. She took the paper with her and disappeared into the stacks. Bosch walked around the small waiting area by the counter for a few minutes and then stepped outside to smoke a cigarette. He was nervous for a reason he could not exactly place. He kept moving, pacing.

'Harry Bosch!'

He turned and saw a man approaching him from the helicopter hangar. He recognized him but couldn't immediately place him. Then it hit him: Captain Dan Washington, a former Hollywood patrol skipper who was now commander of the aerosquadron. They shook hands cordially and Bosch immediately hoped Washington did not know of his ISL situation.

'Howzit going in the 'wood?'

'Same old same old, Captain.'

'You know, I miss that place.'

'You're not missing much. How is it with you?'

'Can't complain. I like the detail but it's more like being an airport manager than a cop, I guess. It's as good a place to lay low as any other.'

Bosch recalled that Washington had gotten into a political scrap with the department weight and taken the transfer as a means of survival. The department had dozens of out-of-the-way jobs like Washington's, where you could lay up and wait for your political fortunes to change.

'What're you doing over here?'

There it was. If Washington knew Bosch was on leave, then admitting he was pulling an old case file would be admitting he was violating the leave order. Still, as his position in the aerosquad attested, Washington was not a straight-line company man. Bosch decided to run the risk.

'I'm just pulling an old case. I got some free time and thought I'd check a few things.'

Washington narrowed his eyes and Bosch knew that he knew.

'Yeah ... well, listen, I gotta run, but hang in there, man. Don't let the book men get you down.'

He winked at Bosch and moved on.

'I won't, Captain. You either.'

Bosch felt reasonably sure Washington wouldn't mention their meeting to anybody. He stepped on his cigarette and went back inside to the counter, privately chastising himself anyway for having gone outside and advertised that he was there. Five minutes later he started hearing a squeaking sound coming from one of the aisles between the stacks. In a moment Geneva Beaupre appeared pushing a cart with a blue three-ring binder on it.

It was a murder book. It was at least two inches thick,

dusty, and with a rubber band around it. The band held an old green checkout card to the binder.

'Found it.'

There was a note of triumph in her voice. It would be the major accomplishment of her day, Bosch guessed.

'Great.'

She dropped the heavy binder on the counter.

'Marjorie Lowe. Homicide, 1961. Now ...' She took the card off the binder and looked at it. 'Yes, you were the last to take this out. Let's see, that was five years ago. You were with Robbery-Homicide then ...'

'Yes. And now I'm in Hollywood. You want me to sign for it again?'

She put the card down in front of him.

'Yes. Put your ID number there, too, please.'

He quickly did as he was told and he could tell she was studying him as he wrote.

'A lefty.'

'Yeah.'

He slid the card back across the counter to her.

'Thanks, Geneva.'

He looked at her, wanting to say something else, but decided it might be a mistake. She looked back at him and a grandmotherly smile formed on her face.

'I don't know what you're doing, Detective Bosch, but I wish you good luck. I can tell it's important, you coming back to this after five years.'

'It's been longer than that, Geneva. A lot longer.'

Bosch cleared all the old mail and carpentry books off the dining room table and placed the binder and his own notebook on top of it. He went to the stereo and loaded a compact disc, 'Clifford Brown with Strings.' He went to the kitchen and got an ashtray, then he sat down in front of the blue murder book and looked at it for a long time without moving. The last time he'd had the file, he had barely looked at it as he skimmed through its many pages. He hadn't been ready then and had returned it to the archives.

This time, he wanted to be sure he was ready before he opened it, so he sat there a long time just studying the cracked plastic cover as if it held some clue to his preparedness. A memory crowded into his mind. A boy of eleven in a swimming pool clinging to the steel ladder at the side, out of breath and crying, the tears disguised by the water that dripped out of his wet hair. The boy felt scared. Alone. He felt as if the pool were an ocean that he must cross.

Brownie was working through 'Willow Weep for Me,' his trumpet as gentle as a portrait painter's brush. Bosch reached for the rubber band he had put around the binder five years earlier and it broke at his touch. He hesitated only another moment before opening the binder and blowing off the dust.

The binder contained the case file on the October 28, 1961, homicide of Marjorie Phillips Lowe. His mother.

The pages of the binder were brownish yellow and stiff with age. As he looked at them and read them, Bosch was initially surprised at how little things had changed in nearly thirty-five years. Many of the investigative forms in the binder were still currently in use. The Preliminary Report and the Investigating Officer's Chronological Record were the same as those presently used, save for word changes made to accommodate court rulings and political correctness. Description Boxes marked NEGRO had sometime along the line been changed to BLACK and then AFRICAN-AMERICAN. The list of motivations on the Preliminary Case Screening chart did not include DOMESTIC VIOLENCE or HATRED/PREJUDICE classifications as they did now. Interview summary sheets did not include boxes to be checked after Miranda warnings had been given.

But aside from those kinds of changes, the reports were the same and Bosch decided that homicide investigation was largely the same now as back then. Of course, there had been incredible technological advances in the past thirty-five years but he believed there were some things that were always the same and always would remain the same. The legwork, the art of interviewing and listening, knowing when to trust an instinct or a hunch. Those were things that didn't change, that couldn't.

The case had been assigned to two investigators on the Hollywood homicide table. Claude Eno and Jake McKittrick. The reports they filed were in chronological order in the binder. On their preliminary reports the victim was referred to by name, indicating she had immediately been identified. A narrative on these pages said the victim was found in an alley behind the north side of Hollywood Boulevard between Vista and Gower. Her skirt and undergarments had been ripped open by her attacker. It was presumed that she had been sexually assaulted and strangled. Her body had been dropped into an open trash bin located next to the rear door of a Hollywood souvenir store called Startime Gifts & Gags. The body was discovered at 7:35 A.M. by a foot patrol officer who walked a beat on the Boulevard and usually checked the back alleys at the beginning of each shift. The victim's purse was not found with her but she was quickly identified because she was known to the beat officer. On the continuation sheet it was made clear why she was known to him.

Victim had a previous history of loitering arrests in the Hollywood. (See AR 55–002, 55–913, 56–111, 59–056, 60–815 and 60–1121) Vice Detective Gilchrist and Stano described victim as a prostitute who periodically worked in the Hollywood area and had been repeatedly warned off. Victim lived at El Rio Efficiency Apts located two blocks northerly of crime scene. It was believed that the victim had been currently involved in call girl prostitution activities. R/O 1906 was able to make identification of the victim because of familiarity of having seen victim in the area in previous years.

Bosch looked at the reporting officer's serial number. He knew that 1906 belonged to a patrolman then who was now one of the most powerful men in the department. Assistant Chief Irvin S. Irving. Once Irving had confided to Bosch that he had known Marjorie Lowe and had been the one who found her.

Bosch lit a cigarette and read on. The reports were sloppily written, perfunctory, and filled with careless misspellings. In reading them, it was clear to Bosch that Eno and McKittrick did not invest much time in the case. A prostitute was dead. It was a risk that came with her job. They had other fish to fry.

33

He noticed on the Death Investigation Report a box for listing the next of kin. It said;

Hieronymus Bosch (Harry), son, age 11, McClaren Youth Hall. Notification made 10/28–1500 hrs. Custody of Department of Public Social Services since 7/60 – UM. (See victim's arrest reports 60–815 and 60–1121) Father unknown. Son remains in custody pending foster placement.

Looking at the report, Bosch could easily decipher all of the abbreviations and translate what was written. UM stood for unfit mother. The irony was not lost on him even after so many years. The boy had been taken from a presumably unfit mother and placed in an equally unfit system of child protection. What he remembered most was the noise of the place. Always loud. Like a prison.

Bosch remembered McKittrick had been the one who came to tell him. It was during the swimming period. The indoor pool was frothing with waves as a hundred boys swam and splashed and yelled. After being pulled from the water, Harry wore a white towel that had been washed and bleached so many times that it felt like cardboard over his shoulders. McKittrick told him the news and he returned to the pool, his screams silenced beneath the waves.

Quickly leafing through the supplemental reports on the victim's prior arrests, Bosch came to the autopsy report. He skipped most of it, not needing the details, and settled on the summary page, where there were a couple of surprises. The time of death was placed at seven to nine hours before discovery. Near midnight. The surprise was in the official cause of death. It was listed as blunt-force trauma to the head. The report described a deep contusion over the right ear with swelling but no laceration that caused fatal bleeding in the brain. The report said the killer might have believed he strangled the victim after knocking

34

her unconscious but it was the coroner's conclusion that she was already dead when the killer wrapped Marjorie Lowe's own belt around her neck and tied it off. The report stated further that while semen was recovered from the vagina there were no other injuries commonly associated with rape.

Rereading the summary with an investigator's eyes, Bosch could see the autopsy conclusions only muddied the waters for the original two detectives. The initial assumption based on the appearance of the body was that Marjorie Lowe was the victim of a sex crime. That raised the specter of a random encounter – as random as the couplings of her profession – leading to her death. But the fact that strangulation occurred after death and that there was no convincing physical evidence of rape raised another possibility as well. They were factors from which it could also be speculated that the victim had been murdered by someone who then attempted to disguise his involvement and motivation in the randomness of a sex crime. Bosch could think of only one reason for such misdirection, if that had been the case. The killer knew the victim. As he moved on, he wondered if McKittrick and Eno had made any of the same conclusions he had made.

There was an eight-by-ten envelope next in the file which was marked as containing crime scene and autopsy photos. Bosch thought about it a long moment and then put the envelope aside. As with the last time he had pulled the murder book out of the archives, he couldn't look.

Next was another envelope with an evidence inventory list stapled to it. It was almost blank.

EVIDENCE RECOVERED
Case 61–743
Latent fingerprints taken from leather belt with silver sea shells.

SID report no. 1114 11/06/61
Murder weapon recovered – black leather belt with
sea shells attached. Property of victim.
Victims clothing, property. Filed w/ evidence
custodian – Locker 73B LAPDHQ
  1 blouse, white – blood stain
  1 black skirt – torn at seam
  1 pair black high heel shoes
  1 pair black sheer stockings, torn
  1 pair undergarments, torn
  1 pair gold colored earrings
  1 gold colored hoop bracelet
  1 gold chain necklace w/cross

That was it. Bosch studied the list for a long time before
jotting the particulars down in his notebook. Something
about it bothered him but he couldn't draw it out. Not
yet. He was taking in too much information and he would
have to let it settle some before the anomalies floated to
the surface.

He dropped it for the moment and opened the evidence
envelope, breaking the seal of a red tape that had cracked
with age. Inside was a yellowed print card on which two
complete fingerprints, from a thumb and an index finger,
and several partials had been taped after being lifted with
black powder from the belt. Also in the envelope was a
pink check card for the victim's clothes, which had been
placed in an evidence locker. The clothes had never been
retrieved because a case had never been made. Bosch put
both items aside, wondering what would have happened
to the clothing. In the mid-sixties Parker Center had
been built and the department moved out of the old head
quarters. It was long gone now, falling to the wrecking
ball. What happened to the evidence from unsolved
cases?

Next in the file was a group of summary reports on interviews conducted during the first days of the investigation. Most of these were of people with peripheral knowledge of the victim or the crime. People like other residents in the El Rio Apartments and other women in the same profession as the victim. There was one short summary that caught Bosch's eye. It was from an interview conducted three days after the murder with a woman named Meredith Roman. She was described in the report as an associate and sometime roommate of the victim. At the time of the report she also lived in the El Rio, one floor up from the victim. The report had been typed up by Eno, who seemed to be the clear-cut winner in illiteracy when comparing the reports of the two investigators assigned to the case.

Meredith Roman (10–9–30) was interviewed at length this date at her apartment in the El Rio Efficiencies where she lived one floor above the victim's apartment. Miss Roman was able to provide this detective with very little useful information in relation to the activities of Marjorie Lowe during the period of the last week of live.

Miss Roman acknowledged that she has engaged in prostitutional acts while in the company of the victim on numrus occassion in the previous eight years but she has no booking record to date. (later confirmed) She told the undersigned detective that such engagements were skeduled by a man named Johnny Fox, (2–2–33) who resides at 1110 Ivar in Hollywood. Fox, age 28, has no records of arrests but vice intelligence confirms he has been a suspect previously in cases of pandering, malicious assault and sales of heroin.

Miss Roman states that the last time she saw the victim was at a party on second floor of the

Roosevelt Hotl on 10/21. Miss Roman did not attend party with victim but saw her there momentarily for a short conversation.

Miss Roman states that she now has plans to retire from the business of prostitution and leave Los Angeles. She stated that she will provide detectives with a forwarding adress and telephone number so that she can be contacted if necessary. Her demenor was corperative with the undersigned.

Bosch immediately looked through the summaries again for the report on Johnny Fox. There was none there. He flipped to the front of the binder to the Chronological Record and looked for an entry that would indicate whether they had even talked to Fox. The CR was just a log of one-line entries with references to other reports. On the second page he found a single notation.

11–3 800–2000 Watched Fox apt. No show.

There was no other mention of Fox in the record. But as Bosch read through the CR to the end, another entry caught his eye.

11–5 940 A. Conklin called to skedule meeting.

Bosch knew the name. Arno Conklin had been a Los Angeles district attorney in the 1960s. As Bosch remembered it, 1961 was too early for Conklin to have been DA, but he would still have been one of the office's top prosecutors. His interest in a prostitute's murder seemed curious to Bosch. But there was nothing in the binder that held an answer. There was no summary report of a meeting with Conklin. Nothing.

He noted that the misspelling of the word *schedule* in the CR entry had been made earlier in the summary of the Roman interview typed by Eno. Bosch concluded from this that Conklin had called Eno to set the meeting.

However, the significance of this, if any, he didn't know. He wrote Conklin's name down at the top of a page in his notebook.

Getting back to Fox, Bosch could not understand why he was not located and interviewed by Eno and McKittrick. It seemed that he was a natural suspect – the victim's pimp. Or, if Fox had been interviewed, Bosch could not understand why there was no report in the murder book on such a key part of the investigation.

Bosch sat back and lit a cigarette. Already, he was tense with the suspicion that things were amiss with the case. He felt the stirring of what he knew was outrage. The more he read the more he believed the case had been mishandled from the start.

He leaned back over the table and continued flipping through the pages of the binder while he smoked. There were more meaningless interview summaries and reports. It was all just filler. Any homicide cop worth his badge could churn out reports like these by the dozens if he wanted to fill a binder and make it look like he'd done a thorough investigation. It appeared that McKittrick and Eno were as skilled at it as the best. But any homicide cop worth his badge could also tell filler when he saw it. And that's what Bosch saw here. The hollow feeling in his stomach grew more pronounced.

Finally, he came to the first Follow-Up Homicide Investigation Report. It was dated one week after the murder and written by McKittrick.

Homicide of Marjorie Phillips Lowe remains open at this time, no suspects identified.

Investigation at this time has determined that victim was engaged in prostitution in the Hollywood area and may have fallen victim to a customer who committed the homicide.

Preliminary suspect John Fox denied involvement

in the incident and has been cleared at this time through fingerprint comparison and confirmation of alibi through witnesses.

No suspects at this time have been identified. John Fox states that on Friday, 11/30 at approximately 2100 hours the victim left her residence at the El Rio Apts to go to an unknown location for the purposes of prostitution. Fox states the arrangement was made by victim and he was not made privy to it. Fox siad it was not unusual practice for victim to make arrangements for liaissons without his knowledge.

Victim's undergarment was found with body in ripped condition. Noted, however, a pair of stockings also belonging to the victim showed no tears and were believed to possibly have been removed voluntarily.

Experience and instinct of investigators leads to the conclusion that the victim met with foul play at the unknown location after voluntarily arriving and possibly removing some clothing. The body was then transported to the trash bin in the alleyway between Vista and Gower, where it was discovered the following morning.

Witness Meredith Roman was reinterviewed this date and asked to amend her earlier statement. Roman informed this investigator that it was her belief that the victim had gone to a party in Hancock Park the night previous to the discovery of her body. She could provide no address or name of party at the location. Miss Roman said her plan was to attend with victim but on the previous evening she was assaulted by John Fox in a dispute over money. She could not attend the party because she believed a bruise on her face made her unpresentable. (Fox readily acknowledged striking Roman in subsequent telephone interview. Roman refused charges.)

Investigation is termed at standstill as no further leads have been provided at this time. Investigators are currently seeking the aid of vice section officers in regard to knowledge of similar incidents and/or possible suspects.

Bosch read the page again and tried to interpret what was really being said about the case. One thing that was clear from it was that regardless of whether there was an interview summary report in the binder, Johnny Fox had obviously been interviewed by Eno and McKittrick. He had been cleared. The question Bosch now had was, why did they not type up a summary report, or had it been typed up and later removed from the murder book? And if so, who removed it and why?

Lastly, Bosch was curious about the lack of any mention of Arno Conklin in the summary or any other report save for the investigative chronology. Maybe, Bosch thought, more than just the Fox interview summary had been lifted from the binder.

Bosch got up and went to his briefcase, which he kept on the counter near the kitchen door. From it he took his personal phone book. He didn't have a number for LAPD archives so he called the regular records number and was transferred. A woman answered after nine rings.

'Uh, Mrs Beaupre? Geneva?'

'Yes?'

'Hello, this is Harry Bosch. I was there earlier today to pick up a file.'

'Yes, from Hollywood. The old case.'

'Yes. Could you tell me, do you still have the checkout card there at the counter?'

'Hold the line. I already filed it.'

A moment later she was back.

'Yes, I have it here.'

'Could you tell me, who else has checked this binder out in the past?'

'Why would you need to know that?'

'There are pages missing from the file, Mrs Beaupre. I'd like to know who might have them.'

'Well, you checked it out last. I mentioned that be –'

'Yes, I know. About five years ago. Is there any listing of it being taken out before that or since then? I didn't notice when I signed the card today.'

'Well, hold the line and let me see.' He waited and she was back quickly. 'Okay, I've got it. According to this card, the only other time that file was ever taken out was in 1972. You're talking way back.'

'Who checked it out back then?'

'It's scribbled here. I can't – it looks like maybe Jack … uh, Jack McKillick.'

'Jake McKittrick.'

'Could be.'

Bosch didn't know what to think. McKittrick had the file last but that was more than ten years after the murder. What did it mean? Bosch felt confusion ambush him. He didn't know what he had been expecting but he'd hoped there would have been something other than a name scribbled more than twenty years ago.

'Okay, Mrs Beaupre, thanks very much.'

'Well, if you've got missing pages I'm going to have to make a report and give it to Mr Aguilar.'

'I don't think that will be necessary, ma'am. I may be wrong about the missing pages. I mean, how could there be missing pages if nobody's looked at it since the last time I had it?'

He thanked her again and hung up, hoping his attempt at good humor would persuade her to do nothing about his call. He opened the refrigerator and looked inside while he thought about the case, then closed it and went back out to the table.

The last pages in the murder book were a due diligence report dated November 3, 1962. The department's homicide procedures called for all unsolved cases to be reviewed after a year by a new set of detectives with an eye toward looking for something that the first set of investigators might have missed. But, in practice, it was a rubber stamp process. Detectives didn't relish the idea of finding the mistakes of their colleagues. Additionally, they had their own case loads to worry about. When assigned DDs, as they were called, they usually did little more than read through the file, make a few calls to witnesses and then send the binder to archives.

In this case, the DD report by the new detectives, named Roberts and Jordan, drew the same conclusions as the reports by Eno and McKittrick. After two pages detailing the same evidence and interviews already conducted by the original investigators, the DD report concluded that there were no workable leads and the prognosis for 'successful conclusion' of the case was hopeless. So much for due diligence.

Bosch closed the murder book. He knew that after Roberts and Jordan had filed their report, the binder had been shipped to archives as a dead case. It had gathered dust there until, according to the checkout card, McKittrick pulled it out for unknown reasons in 1972. Bosch wrote McKittrick's name under Conklin's on the page in the notebook. Then he wrote the names of others he thought it would be useful to interview. If they were still alive and could be found.

Bosch leaned back in his chair, realizing that the music had stopped and he hadn't even noticed. He checked his watch. It was two-thirty. He still had most of the afternoon but he wasn't sure what to do with it.

He went to the bedroom closet and took the shoebox off the shelf. It was his correspondence box, filled with letters and cards and photos he had wished to keep over the course of his life. It contained objects dated as far back as his time in Vietnam. He rarely looked in the box but his mind kept an almost perfect inventory of what was in it. Each piece had a reason for being saved.

On top was the latest addition to the box. A postcard from Venice. From Sylvia. It depicted a painting she had seen in the Palace of the Doges. Hieronymus Bosch's 'The Blessed and the Damned.' It showed an angel escorting one of the blessed through a tunnel to the light of heaven. They both floated skyward. The card was the last he had heard from her. He read the back.

Harry, thought you'd be interested in this piece of your namesake's work. I saw it in the Palace. It's beautiful. By the way, I love Venice! I think I could stay forever! S.

But you don't love me, Bosch thought as he put the card aside and began to dig through the other pieces in the box. He wasn't distracted again. About halfway through the box he found what he was looking for.

The midday drive out to Santa Monica was long. Bosch had to take the long way, the 101 to the 405 and then down, because the 10 was still a week away from being reopened. By the time he got into Sunset Park it was after three. The house he was looking for was on Pier Street. It was a small Craftsman bungalow set on the crest of a hill. It had a full porch with red bougainvillea running along the railing. He checked the address painted on the mailbox against the envelope that contained the old Christmas card on the seat next to him. He parked at the curb and looked at the card once more. It had been addressed to him five years earlier, care of the LAPD. He had never responded to it. Not until now.

As he got out he could smell the sea and guessed that there might be a limited ocean view from the house's western windows. It was about ten degrees cooler than it had been at his home and so he reached back into his car for the sport coat. He walked to the front porch while putting it on.

The woman who answered the white door after one knock was in her mid-sixties and looked it. She was thin, with dark hair, but the gray roots were beginning to show and she was ready for another dye job. She wore thick red lipstick, a white silk blouse with blue seahorses on it over navy blue slacks. She readily smiled a greeting and Bosch recognized her, but he could see that his own image was completely alien to her. It had been almost thirty-five years since she had seen him. He smiled back anyway.

'Meredith Roman?'

She lost her smile as quickly as she had found it before.

'That's not my name,' she said in a clipped tone. 'You have the wrong place.'

She moved to close the door but Bosch put his hand on it to stop her. He tried to be as unthreatening about it as he could. But he could see panic starting in her eyes.

'It's Harry Bosch?' he said quickly.

She froze and looked Bosch in the eyes. He saw the panic go away. Recognition and memories flooded her eyes like tears. The smile came back.

'Harry? Little Harry?'

He nodded.

'Oh, darling, c'mere.' She drew him into a tight hug and talked in his ear. 'Oh, so good to see you after – let me look at you.'

She pushed him back and held her hands wide as if appraising a roomful of paintings at once. Her eyes were animated and sincere. It made Bosch feel good and sad at the same time. He shouldn't have waited so long. He should have visited for reasons other than the one that brought him here now.

'Oh, come in, Harry. Come in.'

Bosch entered a nicely furnished living room. The floor was red oak and the stucco walls were clean and white. The furniture was mostly matching white rattan. The place was light and bright but Bosch knew he was there to bring darkness.

'Meredith is no longer your name?'

'No, Harry, not for a long time.'

'What do I call you?'

'My name is Katherine. With a K. Katherine Register. Spelled like the cash register but you pronounce it *ree* as in reefer. That's what my husband used to say. Boy, he was so straight. Outside of me the closest that man ever came to something illegal was to say the word.'

'He *used* to say that?'

'Have a seat, Harry, for crying out loud. Yes, used to. He passed away five years ago last Thanksgiving.'

Bosch sat down on the couch and she took the chair across the glass coffee table.

'I'm sorry.'

'It's okay, you didn't know. You never even knew him and I've been a different person for a long time. Can I get you something? Some coffee or maybe something stronger?'

It occurred to him that she had sent him the card on the Christmas soon after her husband's death. He was hit with another wave of guilt for not having responded.

'Harry?'

'Oh, uh, no, I'm fine. I … do you want me to call you by your new name?'

She started laughing at the ridiculousness of the situation and he joined in.

'Call me any damn thing you want.' She laughed girlishly, a laugh he remembered from a long time before. 'It's great to see you. You know, to see how, uh …'

'I turned out?'

She laughed again.

'I guess so. You know, I knew you were with the police because I had read your name in some of the news stories.'

'I know you knew. I got the Christmas card you sent to the station. That must have been right after your husband died. I, uh, I'm sorry I never wrote back or visited. I should have.'

'That's okay, Harry, I know you're busy with the job and a career and all … I'm glad you got my card. Do you have a family?'

'Uh, no. How about you? Any children?'

'Oh, no. No children. You have a wife, don't you, a handsome man like you?'

'No, I'm alone right now.'

She nodded, seeming to sense that he wasn't here to reveal his personal history to her anyway. For a long moment they just both looked at each other and Bosch wondered what she really thought of his being a cop. The initial delight in seeing each other was descending into the uneasiness that comes when old secrets come close to the surface.

'I guess …'

He didn't finish the thought. He was grappling for a way into the conversation. His interviewing skills had deserted him.

'You know, if it's not too much trouble, I'd take a glass of water.'

It was all he could think of.

'Be right back.'

She got up quickly and went to the kitchen. He heard her getting ice out of a tray. It gave him time to think. It had taken him an hour to drive to her house but he hadn't given one thought to what this would be like or how he would get to what he wanted to say and ask. She came back in a few minutes with a glass of ice water. She handed it to him and put a round coaster made of cork on the glass-topped coffee table in front of him.

'If you're hungry, I can bring out some crackers and cheese. I just didn't know how much time you –'

'No, I'm fine. This is great, thanks.'

He saluted her with the glass and drank half of it, then put it down on the table.

'Harry, use the coaster. Getting rings out of the glass is murder.'

Bosch looked down at what he had done.

'Oh, sorry.'

He corrected the placement of his glass.

'You're a detective.'

'Yes. I work in Hollywood now … Uh, but I'm not really working right now. I'm on sort of a vacation.'

'Oh, that must be nice.'

Her spirits seemed to lift, as if she knew there was a chance he was not here on business. Bosch knew it was time to get to the point.

'Uh, Mer – uh, Katherine, I need to ask you about something.'

'What is it, Harry?'

'I look around here and I see you have a very nice home, a different name, a different life. You're no longer Meredith Roman and I know you don't need me to tell you that. You've got … I think what I'm saying is the past may be a difficult thing to talk about. I know it is for me. And, believe me, I don't want to hurt you in any way.'

'You're here to talk about your mother.'

He nodded and looked down at the glass on the cork coaster.

'Your mother and I were best friends. Sometimes I think I had almost as much a hand in raising you as she did. Until they took you away from her. From us.'

He looked back up at her. Her eyes were looking hard at distant memories.

'I don't think a day goes by that I don't think about her. We were just kids. Having a good time, you know. We never thought either of us could get hurt.'

She suddenly stood up.

'Harry, come here. I want to show you something.'

He followed her down a carpeted hallway and into a bedroom. There was a four-poster bed with light blue coverings, an oak bureau and matching bedside tables. Katherine Register pointed to the bureau. There were several photos in ornate stand-up frames on top. Most of them were of Katherine and a man who seemed much older than she was in the photos. Her husband, Bosch guessed. But she pointed to one that was to the right side of the grouping. The photo was old, its color faded. It was a picture of two young women with a tiny boy of three or four.

'I've always had that there, Harry. Even when my husband was alive. He knew my past. I told him. It didn't matter. We had twenty-three great years together. You see, the past is what you make of it. You can use it to hurt yourself or others or you can use it to make yourself strong. I'm strong, Harry. Now, tell me why you came to visit me today.'

Bosch reached for the framed photo and picked it up.

'I want ...' He looked up from the photo to her. 'I'm going to find out who killed her.'

An undecipherable look froze on her face for a moment and then she wordlessly took the frame out of his hands and put it back on the bureau. Then she pulled him into another deep embrace, her head against his chest. He could see himself holding her in the mirror over the bureau. When she pulled back and looked up at him he saw the tears were already down her cheeks. There was a slight tremor in her lower lip.

'Let's go sit down,' he said.

She pulled two tissues out of a box on the bureau and he led her back to the living room and to her chair.

'Do you want me to get you some water?'

'No, I'm fine. I'll stop crying, I'm sorry.'

She wiped at her eyes with the tissues. He sat back down on the couch.

'We used to say we were the two musketeers, both for one and one for both. It was stupid, but it was because we were so young and so close.'

'I'm starting from scratch with it, Katherine. I pulled the old files on the investigation. It –'

She made a dismissing sound and shook her head.

'There was no investigation. It was a joke.'

'That's my sense of it, too, but I don't understand why.'

'Look, Harry, you know what your mother was.' He nodded and she continued. 'She was a party girl. We both were. I'm sure you know that's the polite way of saying it. And the cops really didn't care that one of us ended up dead. They just wrote the whole damn thing off. I know you're a policeman now, but that's the way it was then. They just didn't care about her.'

'I understand. Things probably are not too much different now, believe it or not. But there has to have been more to it than that.'

'Harry, I don't know how much you want to know about your mother.'

He looked at her.

'The past made me strong, too. I can handle it.'

'I'm sure it did ... I remember that place where they put you. McEvoy or something like –'

'McClaren.'

'That's it, McClaren. What a depressing place. Your mother would come home from visiting you and just sit down and cry her eyes out.'

'Don't change the subject, Katherine. What is it I should know about her?'

She nodded but hesitated for a moment before continuing.

'Mar knew some policemen. You understand?'

He nodded.

'We both did. It was the way it worked. You had to get along to go along. That's what we called it anyway. And when you have that situation and she ends up dead, it's usually best for the cops to just sweep it under the rug. Let sleeping dogs lie, as they say. You pick the cliché. They just didn't want anyone embarrassed.'

'Are you saying you think it was a cop?'

'No. I'm not saying that at all. I have no idea who did it, Harry. I'm sorry. I wish I did. But what I'm saying is, I think those two detectives that were assigned to investigate this knew where it could lead. And they weren't going to go that way because they knew what was good for them in the department. They weren't stupid in that way and like I said, she was a party girl. They didn't care. Nobody did. She got killed and that was that.'

Bosch looked around the room, not sure what to ask next.

'Do you know who the policemen she knew were?'

'It was a long time ago.'

'You knew some of the same policemen, didn't you?'

'Yes. I had to. That was the way it worked. You used your contacts to keep you out of jail. Everybody was for sale. Back then, at least. Different people wanted different forms of payment. Some of them, money. Some of them, other things.'

'It said in the mur – the file that you never had a record.'

'Yes, I was lucky. I was picked up a few times but never booked once. They always turned me loose once I could make a call. I kept a clean record because I knew a lot of policemen, honey. You understand?'

'Yes, I understand.'

She didn't look away when she said it. All these years in the straight life and she still had a whore's pride. She could talk about the low points of her life without flinching or batting an eye. It was because she had made it through and there was dignity in that. Enough to last the rest of her life.

'Do you mind if I smoke, Harry?'

'No, not if I can.'

They took out cigarettes and Bosch got up to light them.

'You can use that ashtray on the side table. Try not to get ashes on the rug.'

She pointed to a small glass bowl on the table at the other end of the couch. Bosch reached over for it and then held it with one hand while he smoked with the other. He looked down into it as he spoke.

'The policemen you knew,' he said, 'and who she probably knew, you don't remember any names?'

'I said it was a long time ago. And I doubt they had anything to do with this, with what happened to your mother.'

'Irvin S. Irving. Do you remember that name?'

She hesitated a moment as the name rolled around in her mind.

'I knew him. I think she did, too. He was on the beat on the Boulevard. I think it would have been hard for her not to know him ... but I don't know. I could be wrong.'

Bosch nodded.

'He was the one who found her.'

She hiked her shoulders in a what's-that-prove gesture.

'Well, somebody had to find her. She was left out there in the open like that.'

'What about a couple of vice guys, Gilchrist and Stano?'

She hesitated before answering.

'Yes, I knew them ... they were mean men.'

'Would my mother have known them? In that way?'

She nodded.

'What do you mean that they were mean? In what way?'

'They just ... they just didn't care about us. If they wanted something, whether it was a little piece of information you might have picked up on a date or

53

something more … personal, they just came and took it. They could be rough. I hated them.'

'Did they –'

'But could they have been killers? My feeling at the time, and now, is no. They weren't killers, Harry. They were cops. True, they were bought and paid for, but it seemed everybody was. But it wasn't like it is today where you read the paper and you see some cop on trial for killing or beating or whatever. It's – sorry.'

'It's okay. Anybody else you can think of?'

'No.'

'No names?'

'I put that all out of my mind a long time ago.'

'Okay.'

Bosch wanted to take out his notebook but he didn't want to make this seem like an interview. He tried to remember what else he had read in the murder book that he could ask about.

'What about this guy Johnny Fox?'

'Yes, I told those detectives about him. They got all excited but then nothing ever happened. He was never arrested.'

'I think he was. But then he was let go. His fingerprints didn't match the killer's.'

She raised her eyebrows.

'Well, that's news to me. They never told me anything about any fingerprints.'

'On your second interview – with McKittrick, you remember him?'

'Not really. I just remember that there were police, you know? Two detectives. One was smarter than the other, that's what I remember. But I don't remember which one was which. It seemed like the dumber one was in charge and that was par for the course in those days.'

'Well, anyway, McKittrick talked to you the second

time. In his report he said you changed your story and you told about this party in Hancock Park.'

'Yes, the party. I didn't go because that ... Johnny Fox hit me the night before and I had a bruise on my cheek. It was gorgeous. I played around with makeup but I couldn't do anything about the swelling. Believe me there wasn't much business in Hancock Park for a party girl with a knot on her face.'

'Who was having the party?'

'I don't remember. I don't know if I even knew whose party it was.'

Something about the way she answered bothered Bosch. Her tone had changed and it came across as almost a rehearsed answer.

'Are you sure you don't remember?'

'Of course, I'm sure.' Katherine stood up. 'I think I'm going to get some water now.'

She took his glass to refill and left the room again. Bosch realized that his familiarity with the woman, his emotion in seeing her again after so long, had blocked most of his investigative instincts. He had no feel for the truth. He could not tell whether there was more to what she was telling him or not. He decided he had to somehow steer the conversation back to the party. He thought she knew more than she had said all those years ago.

She came back with two glasses filled with ice water and placed his back down on the cork coaster. Something about the way she was so careful about putting the glass down gave him a knowledge about her that had not come through in her spoken words. It was simply that she had worked hard to attain the level she was at in life. That position and the material things it brought with it − like glass coffee tables and plush carpets − meant a lot to her and were to be taken care of.

She took a long drink from her glass after sitting down.

'Let me tell you something, Harry,' she said. 'I didn't tell them everything. I didn't lie, but I didn't tell them everything. I was afraid.'

'Afraid of what?'

'I became afraid on the day they found her. You see, I'd gotten a call that morning. Before I even knew what had happened to her. It was a man, but a voice I didn't recognize. He told me if I said anything I would be next. I remember, he said, "My advice to you, little lady, is to get the hell out of Dodge." Then, of course, I heard the police were in the building and had gone to her apartment. Then I heard she was dead. So I did what I was told. I left. I waited about a week until the police said they were done with me, then I moved to Long Beach. I changed my name, changed my life. I met my husband down there and then years later we moved here. ... You know, I've never been back to Hollywood, not even to drive through. It's an awful place.'

'What was it that you didn't tell Eno and McKittrick?'

Katherine looked down at her hands as she spoke.

'I was afraid, you see, so I didn't tell everything ... but I knew who she was going to see there, at the party. We were like sisters. Lived in the same building, shared clothes, secrets, everything. We talked every morning, had our coffee together. We had no secrets between us. And we were going to go to the party together. Of course, after that ... after Johnny hit me, she had to go alone.'

'Who was she going to meet there, Katherine?' Bosch prompted.

'You see that is the right question but the detectives never asked that. They only wanted to know whose party it was and where it was. That didn't matter. What was important was who was she going to meet there and they never asked that.'

'Who was it?'

She looked away from her hands and to the fireplace. She stared at the cold, blackened logs left from an old fire the way some people stare mesmerized by a burning fire.

'It was a man named Arno Conklin. He was a very important man in the –'

'I know who he was.'

'You do?'

'His name came up in the records. But not that way. How could you not tell the cops this?'

She turned and looked at him sharply.

'Don't you look at me that way. I told you I was scared. I'd been threatened. And they wouldn't have done anything with it anyway. They were bought and paid for by Conklin. They wouldn't go near him on just the word of a ... call girl who didn't see anything but knew a name. I had to think of myself. Your mother was dead, Harry. There was nothing I could do about it.'

He could see the sharp edges of anger in her eyes. He knew it was directed at him but more toward herself. She could list all her reasons out loud but inside Bosch thought she paid a price every day for not having done the right thing.

'You think Conklin did it?'

'I don't know. All I know is that she'd been with him before and there was never anything violent. I don't know the answer to that.'

'Any idea now who called you?'

'No, none.'

'Conklin?'

'I don't know. I didn't know his voice anyway.'

'Did you ever see them together, my mother and him?'

'Once, at a dance at the Masonic. I think it was the night they met. Johnny Fox introduced them. I don't think Arno knew ... anything about her. At least, then.'

'Could it have been Fox who called you?'

'No. I would've recognized his voice.'

Bosch thought a moment.

'Did you ever see Fox again after that morning?'

'No. I avoided him for a week. It was easy because I think he was hiding from the cops. But after that I was gone. Whoever called me, he put the fear of God in me. I left town for Long Beach the day the cops said they were done with me. Packed one suitcase and took the bus … I remember, your mother had some of my clothes in her apartment. Things that she had borrowed. I didn't even bother to try to get them. I just took what I had and left.'

Bosch was silent. He had nothing else to ask.

'I think about those days a lot, you know,' Katherine said. 'We were in the gutter, your mother and I, but we were good friends and we had fun in spite of it all.'

'You know, all my memories … you're in a lot of them. You were always there with her.'

'We had a lot of laughs in spite of everything,' she said wistfully. 'And you, you were the highlight of it all. You know, when they took you away from her, it nearly killed her right then … She never stopped trying to get you back, Harry. I hope you know that. She loved you. I loved you.'

'Yes, I know that.'

'But after you were gone, she wasn't the same. Sometimes I think what happened to her was sort of inevitable. Sometimes I think it was like she had been heading toward that alley for a long time beforehand.'

Bosch stood up, looking at the sorrow in her eyes.

'I better go. I'll let you know what happens.'

'I'd like that. I'd like to stay in touch.'

'I'd like that, too.'

He headed toward the door knowing that they wouldn't stay in touch. Time had eroded the bond between them. They were strangers who shared the same story. On the outside step he turned and looked back at her.

'The Christmas card you sent. You wanted me to look into this back then, didn't you?'

She brought out the faraway smile again.

'I don't know. My husband had just died and I was taking stock, you know? I thought about her. And you. I'm proud of how I turned out, Little Harry. So I think about what there could have been for her and you. I'm still mad. Whoever did this should ...'

She didn't finish but Bosch nodded.

'Good-bye, Harry.'

'You know, my mother, she had a good friend.'

'I hope so.'

Back in his car Bosch took his notebook out and looked at the list.

> Conklin
> McKittrick & Eno
> Meredith Roman
> Johnny Fox

He drew a line through Meredith Roman's name and studied those left on it. He knew that the way he had ordered the names was not the same order in which he would attempt to interview them. He knew that before he could approach Conklin, or even McKittrick and Eno, he needed more information.

He took his phone book out of his coat pocket and his portable from his briefcase. He dialed the Department of Motor Vehicles law enforcement line in Sacramento and identified himself to the clerk as Lieutenant Harvey Pounds. He gave Pounds's serial number and asked for a license check on Johnny Fox. After checking his notebook, he gave the appropriate date of birth. As he did this he ran the numbers and figured that Fox was now sixty-one years old.

As he continued to wait he smiled because Pounds would have some explaining to do in about a month. The department had recently begun to audit use of the DMV trace service. Because the *Daily News* had reported that cops all over the department were secretly doing the traces for friendly reporters and private detectives with liberal expense accounts, the new chief had cracked down by requiring all calls and computer link-ups to DMV to be documented on the newly implemented DMVT form, which required attribution of traces to a specific case or purpose. The forms were sent to Parker Center and then audited against the list of traces provided each month by the DMV. When the lieutenant's name showed up on the DMV list in the next audit and there was no corresponding DMVT form, he'd get a call from the auditors.

Bosch had gotten the lieutenant's serial number off his ID card one day when Pounds had left it clipped to his jacket on the coatrack outside his office. He'd written it down in his phone book on a hunch that one day it would come in handy.

The DMV clerk finally came back on the line and said there was no driver's license presently issued to a Johnny Fox with the birth date Bosch had provided.

'Anything close?'

'No, honey.'

'That's Lieutenant, miss,' Bosch said sternly. 'Lieutenant Pounds.'

'That's Ms, Lieutenant. Ms Sharp.'

'And I bet you are. Tell me, Ms Sharp, how far back does that computer run go?'

'Seven years. Anything else?'

'How do I check the years before that?'

'You don't. If you want a hand records search you drop us a letter, Loo-ten-ANT. It will take ten to fourteen days. In your case, count on the fourteen. Anything else?'

'No, but I don't like your demeanor.'

'That makes us even. Good-bye.'

Bosch laughed out loud after flipping the phone closed. He was sure now that trace wouldn't get lost in the process. Ms. Sharp would see to that. The name Pounds would probably be on the top of the list when it came in to Parker Center. He dialed Edgar's number on the homicide table next and caught him before he had left the bureau for the day.

'Harry, what's up?'

'You busy?'

'No. Nothing new.'

'Can you run a name for me? I already did DMV but I need somebody to do the computer.'

'Uh …'

'Look, can you or can't you? If you're worried about Pounds, then –'

'Hey, Harry, cool it. What's wrong with you, man? I didn't say I couldn't do it. Just give me the name.'

Bosch couldn't understand why Edgar's attitude enraged him. He took a breath and tried to calm down.

'The name's John Fox. Johnny Fox.'

'Shit, there's going to be a hundred John Foxes. You got a DOB?'

'Yeah, I got a DOB.'

Bosch checked his notebook again and gave it to him.

'What'd he do to you? Say, how you doing?'

'Funny. I'll tell you later. You going to run it?'

'Yes, I said I'll do it.'

'Okay, you got my portable number. If you can't get through, leave me a message at home.'

'When I can get to it, Harry.'

'What, you said nothing's happening.'

'Nothing is, but I'm working, man. I can't be running around doing shit for you all the time.'

Bosch was stunned into a short moment of silence.

'Hey, Jerry, fuck you, I'll do it myself.'

'Look, Harry, I'm not saying I'm –'

'No, I mean it. Never mind. I don't want to compromise you with your new partner or your fearless leader. I mean after all, that's what it's about, isn't it? So don't give me this shit about working. You're not working. You're about to go out the door for home and you know it. Or wait a minute, maybe it's drinks with Burnsie again tonight.'

'Harry –'

'Take care, man.'

Bosch flipped the phone closed and sat there letting the anger work out of him like heat from the grill of a radiator. The phone rang while it was still in his hand and he immediately felt better. He flipped it open.

'Look, I'm sorry, okay?' he said. 'Forget it.'

There was a long silence.

'Hello?'

It was a woman's voice. Bosch felt immediately embarrassed.

'Yes?'

'Detective Bosch?'

'Yes, I'm sorry, I thought it was someone else.'

'Like who?'

'Who is this?'

'It's Dr Hinojos.'

'Oh.' Bosch closed his eyes and the anger came back. 'What can I do for you?'

'I was just calling to remind you that we have a session tomorrow. Three-thirty. You will be there?'

'I don't have a choice, remember? And you don't have to call to remind me about our sessions. Believe it or not, I have an appointment calendar, a watch, an alarm clock, all of that stuff now.'

He immediately thought he had gone over the top with the sarcasm.

'Sounds like I caught you at a bad time. I'll let –'

63

'You did.'

'– you go. See you tomorrow, Detective Bosch.'

'Good-bye.'

He snapped the phone closed again and dropped it on the seat. He started the car. He took Ocean Park out to Bundy and then up toward the 10. As he approached the freeway overpass he saw the eastbound cars on top weren't moving and the on ramp was jammed with cars waiting to wait.

'Fuck it,' he said out loud.

He went by the freeway ramp without turning and then under the overpass. He took Bundy up to Wilshire and then headed west into downtown Santa Monica. It took him fifteen minutes to find street parking near the Third Street Promenade. He had been avoiding multilevel parking garages since the quake and didn't want to start using them now.

What a walking contradiction, Bosch thought as he prowled for a parking spot along the curb. You live in a condemned house the inspectors claim is ready to slide down the hill but you won't go into a parking garage. He finally found a spot across from the porno theater about a block from the Promenade.

Bosch spent the rush hours walking up and down the three-block stretch of outdoor restaurants, movie theaters and shops. He went into the King George on Santa Monica, which he knew was a hangout for some of the detectives out of West LA Division, but didn't see anybody he knew. After that, he ate pizza from a to-go joint and people-watched. He saw a street performer juggling five butcher knives at once. And he thought he might know something about how the man felt.

He sat on a bench and watched the droves of people pass him by. The only ones who stopped and paid attention to him were the homeless, and soon he had no change or dollar bills left to give them. Bosch felt alone. He thought about Katherine Register and what she had said about the past. She had said she was strong but he knew that comfort and strength could come from sadness. That was what she had.

He thought about what she had done five years ago. Her husband dead, she had taken stock of her life and found the hole in her memories. The pain. She had sent him the card in hopes he might do something then. And it had almost worked. He had pulled the murder book from the archives but hadn't had the strength, or maybe it was the weakness, to look at it.

After it got dark he walked down Broadway to Mr B's, found a stool at the bar and ordered a draft with a Jack Daniels depth charge. There was a quintet playing on the small stage in the back, the lead on tenor saxophone. They were finishing up 'Do Nothing Till You Hear from Me' and Bosch got the idea he had come in at the end of a long set. The sax was draggy. It wasn't a clean sound.

Disappointed, he looked away from the group and took a large swallow of beer. He checked his watch and knew he'd have clear driving if he left now. But he stayed. He picked the shot up and dropped it into the mug and drank deeply from the brutal mix. The group moved into 'What a Wonderful World.' No one in the band stepped up to sing the words but, of course, nobody could touch Louis Armstrong's vocals if they tried. It was okay, though. Bosch knew the words.

> I see trees of green
> Red roses, too
> I see them bloom
> For me and you
> And I think to myself
> What a wonderful world

The song made him feel lonely and sad but that was okay. Loneliness had been the trash can fire he huddled around for most of his life. He was just getting used to it again. It had been that way for him before Sylvia and it could be that way again. It would just take time and the pain of letting her go.

In the three months since she had left, there had been the one postcard and nothing else. Her absence had fractured the sense of continuity in his life. Before her, his job had always been the iron rails, as dependable as the sunset over the Pacific. But with her he had attempted to switch tracks, the bravest jump he had ever made. But somehow he had failed. It wasn't enough to keep her and she was gone. And now he felt he had run clear off the tracks. Inside, he felt as fragmented as his city. Broken, it seemed at times, at every level.

He heard a female voice from nearby singing the words of the song. He turned to see a young woman a few stools away, her eyes closed as she sang very softly. She sang only to herself but Bosch could hear.

> I see skies of blue
> And clouds of white
> The bright blessed day
> The dark sacred night
> And I think to myself
> What a wonderful world

She wore a short white skirt, a T-shirt and a brightly colored vest. Bosch guessed she wasn't older than twenty-five and he liked the idea that she even knew the song. She sat straight, her legs crossed. Her back swayed with the music of the saxophone. Her face was framed by brown hair and was turned upward, her lips slightly apart, almost angelic. Bosch thought she was quite beautiful, so totally lost in the majesty of the music. Clean or not, the sound took her away and he admired her for letting it. He knew that what he saw in her face was what a man would see if he made love to her. She had what other cops called a getaway face. So beautiful it would always be a shield. No matter what she did or what was done to her, her face would be her ticket. It would open doors in front of her, close them behind her. It would let her get away.

The song ended and she opened her eyes and clapped. No one else had applauded until she began. Then everyone in the bar, Bosch included, joined in. Such was the power of the getaway face. Bosch turned and flagged the bartender for another shot and beer. When it was down in front of him he took a glance over at the woman, but she was gone. He turned and checked the bar's door and saw it closing. He'd missed her.

On the way home he worked his way up to Sunset and took that all the way into the city. Traffic was sparse. He had stayed out later than he had planned. He smoked and listened to the all-news channel on the radio. There was a report about Grant High finally reopening in the Valley. It was where Sylvia had taught. Before going to Venice.

Bosch was tired and guessed that he probably wouldn't pass a breath test if stopped. He dropped his speed to below the limit as Sunset cut through Beverly Hills. He knew the cops in BH wouldn't cut him a break and that would be all he'd need on top of the involuntary stress leave.

He turned left at Laurel Canyon and took the winding road up the hill. At Mulholland he was about to turn right on red when he checked the traffic from the left and froze. He saw a coyote step out of the brush of the arroyo to the left of the roadway and take a tentative look around the intersection. There were no other cars. Only Bosch saw this.

The animal was thin and ragged, worn by the struggle to sustain itself in the urban hills. The mist rising from the arroyo caught the reflection of the street lights and cast the coyote in almost a dim blue light. And it seemed to study Bosch's car for a moment, its eyes catching the reflection of the stoplight and glowing. For just a moment Bosch believed that the coyote might be looking directly at him. Then the animal turned and moved back into the blue mist.

A car came up behind him and honked. Bosch had the green light. He waved and made the turn onto Mulholland. But then he pulled to the side. He put the car in park and got out.

It was a cool evening and he felt a chill as he walked across the intersection to the spot where he had seen the blue coyote. He wasn't sure what he was doing but he wasn't afraid. He just wanted to see the animal again. He stopped at the edge of the drop-off and looked down into the darkness below. The blue mist was all around him now. A car passed behind him and when the noise receded he listened and looked intently. But there was nothing. The coyote was gone. He walked back to his car and drove on Mulholland to Woodrow Wilson Drive to home.

Later, as he lay in his bed after more drinks and with the light still on, he smoked the last cigarette of the night and stared up at the ceiling. He'd left the light on but his thoughts were of the dark, sacred night. And the blue coyote. And the woman with the getaway face. Soon all of those thoughts disappeared with him into the dark.

Bosch got little sleep and was up before the sun. The last cigarette of the night before had nearly been his last for all time. He had fallen asleep with it between his fingers, only to be jolted awake by the searing pain of the burn. He dressed the wounds on two fingers and tried to return to sleep, but it wouldn't take him. His fingers throbbed and all he could think of was how many times he had investigated the deaths of hapless drunks who had fallen asleep and self-immolated. All he could think of was what Carmen Hinojos would have to say about such a stunt. How was that for a symptom of self-destruction?

Finally, as dawn's light began to leak into the room he gave up on sleep and got up. While coffee brewed in the kitchen he went into the bathroom and rebandaged the burns on his fingers. As he taped the fresh gauze on, he glanced at himself in the mirror and saw the deep lines under his eyes.

'Shit,' he said to himself. 'What's going on?'

He had black coffee on the back deck while watching the silent city come awake. There was a crisp chill in the air and the earthy smell of eucalyptus was rising from the tall trees down in the pass. The marine fog layer had filled the pass and the hills were just mysterious silhouettes in the mist. He watched the morning begin for nearly an hour, fascinated by the show he had from his deck.

It wasn't until he went back inside for a second cup that

he noticed the red light flashing on his phone machine. He had two messages that had probably been left the day before and that he hadn't noticed after coming in last night. He pressed the play button.

'Bosch, this is Lieutenant Pounds calling on Tuesday at three thirty-five. I have to inform you that while you are on leave and until your, uh, status with the department is decided, you will be required to return your vehicle to the Hollywood Division garage. I have here that it is a four-year-old Chevrolet Caprice, tag number one-adam-adam-three-four-zero-two. Please make arrangements immediately to have the car turned in and checked out. This order is per *Standard Practices Manual* citation three dash thirteen. Violation could result in suspension and/or dismissal. Again, this is an order from Lieutenant Pounds, now three thirty-six on Tuesday. If there is any part of this message that you do not understand, feel free to contact me at the office.'

The machine reported the message had actually been left at 4 P.M. Tuesday, probably right before Pounds had gone home for the day. Fuck him, Bosch thought. The car's a piece of shit anyway. He can have it.

The second message was from Edgar.

'Harry, you there? It's Edgar … Okay, listen, let's forget about today, okay? I mean it. Let's just say I was a prick and you were a prick and we're both pricks and forget it. Whether it turns out you are my partner or you were my partner, I owe you a lot, man. And if I ever act like I forgot that, hit me alongside the head like you did today. Now, to the bad news. I checked everything on this Johnny Fox. I got exactly nothing, man. That's from the NCIC, DOJ, DPP, Corrections, National Warrants, everything. I ran the works on him. Looks like this guy is clean, if he's alive. You say he doesn't even have a DL so that makes me think maybe you got a phony name there or maybe this guy ain't among the living. So, that's that. I don't know what you're up to but if you want anything else, give a call … Oh, and hang in there, buddy. I'm ten-seven after this so you can reach me at home if –'

The message cut off. Edgar had run out of time. Bosch rewound the tape and poured his coffee. Back on the deck he mulled over the whereabouts of Johnny Fox. When he had gotten nothing on the DMV trace, Bosch had assumed Fox might be in prison, where driver's licenses weren't issued or needed. But Edgar had not found him there nor had he found his name on any national computer that tracks criminals. Now Bosch guessed that Johnny Fox had either gone straight or, as Edgar had suggested, was dead. If Bosch was betting, he'd take the latter. Men like Johnny Fox didn't go straight.

Bosch's alternative was to go down to the Los Angeles County Hall of Records and look for a death certificate but without a date of death it would be a needle in the haystack search. It might take him days. Before he'd do that, he decided, he'd try an easier way, the *LA Times*.

He went back inside to the phone and dialed a reporter named Keisha Russell. She was new on the cop beat and still struggling to find her way. She had made a subtle attempt to recruit Bosch as a source a few months earlier. The way reporters usually did that was to write an inordinate number of stories on a crime that did not merit such intense attention. But the process put them in constant contact with the detectives on the case and that allowed them the chance to ingratiate themselves and hopefully procure the investigators as future sources.

Russell had written five stories in a week about one of Bosch's cases. It was a domestic violence case in which a husband had disregarded a temporary restraining order and gone to his separated wife's new apartment on Franklin. He carried her to the fifth-floor balcony and threw her off.

He went over next. Russell had talked to Bosch repeatedly during the stretch of stories. The resultant dispatches were thorough and complete. It was good work and she began to earn Bosch's respect. Still, he knew that she hoped that the stories and her attention would be the building blocks of a long reporter/investigator relationship. Since then not a week had gone by that she didn't call Bosch once or twice to bullshit, pass along departmental gossip she had picked up from other sources, and ask the one question all reporters live and die by: 'Anything going on?'

She answered on the first ring and Bosch was a little surprised she was in so early. He was planning on leaving a message on her voice mail.

'Keisha, it's Bosch.'

'Hey, Bosch, how you doing?'

'Okay, I guess. I guess you heard about me.'

'Not everything, but I heard you went on temporary leave. But nobody would tell me why. You want to talk about it?'

'No, not really. I mean, not now. I have a favor to ask. If it works out, I'll give you the story. That's the deal I've made in the past with other reporters.'

'What do I have to do?'

'Just walk over to the morgue.'

She groaned.

'I mean the newspaper morgue, right there at the Times.'

'Oh, that's better. What do you need?'

'I've got a name. It's old. I know the guy was a dirtbag in the fifties and at least the early sixties. But I've lost track of him after that. Thing is, my hunch is that he's dead.'

'You want an obit?'

'Well, I don't know if this is the type of guy the Times would write an obituary on. He was strictly small time, near as I can tell. I was thinking that there might be a story, you know, if his death was sort of untimely.'

'You mean like if he got his shit blown away.'

'You got it.'

'Okay, I'll take a look.'

She seemed eager, Bosch sensed. He knew that she thought that by doing this favor she would be cementing their relationship in place and it would only pay dividends in the future. He said nothing that would dissuade her of this.

'What's the name?'

'His name is John Fox. He went by Johnny. Last I have a trace on him is 1961. He was a pimp, general piece of trash.'

'White, black, yellow or brown?'

'General piece of white trash, you could say.'

'You have a birth date? It will help narrow it down if there's more than one Johnny Fox in the clips.'

He gave it to her.

'Okay, where you going to be?'

Bosch gave her his portable phone number. He knew that would set the hook. The number would go right onto the source list she kept in her computer like gold earrings in a jewelry box. Having the number where he could be reached at almost any time was worth the search in the morgue.

'Okay, listen, I've got a meeting with my editor – that's the only reason I'm in this early. But after, I'll go take a look. I'll call you as soon as I have something.'

'If there is something.'

'Right.'

After Bosch hung up he ate some Frosted Flakes from a box he took out of the refrigerator and turned on the news radio. He had discontinued the newspaper after the earthquake in case Gowdy, the building inspector, happened by early and saw it out front, a clue that someone was inhabiting the uninhabitable. There was nothing much in the top of the news summary that interested him. No homicides in Hollywood, at least. He wasn't missing out on anything.

There was one story after the traffic report that caught his attention. An octopus on display at a city aquarium in San Pedro had apparently killed itself by pulling a water circulation tube out of its tank fitting with one of its tentacles. The tank emptied and the octopus died. Environmental groups were calling it suicide, a desperate protest by the octopus against its captivity. Only in LA, Bosch thought as he turned the radio off. A place so desperate even the marine life was killing itself.

He took a long shower, closing his eyes and holding his head directly under the spray. As he was shaving in front of the mirror after, he couldn't help but study the circles under his eyes again. They seemed even more pronounced than earlier and fit nicely with the eyes cracked with red from his drinking the night before.

He put the razor down on the edge of the sink and leaned closer to the mirror. His skin was as pale as a recycled paper plate. As he appraised himself, the thought he had was that he had once been considered a handsome man. Not anymore. He looked beaten. It seemed that age was gripping him, beating him down. He thought that he resembled some of the old men he'd seen after they were found dead in their beds. The ones in the rooming houses. The ones living in refrigerator boxes. He reminded himself more of the dead than the living.

He opened the medicine cabinet so the reflection would go away. He looked among the various items on the glass shelves and chose a squeeze bottle of Murine. He put in a heavy dose of the eye drops, wiped the excess spill off his

75

face with a towel and left the bathroom without closing the cabinet and having to look at himself again.

He put on his best clean suit, a gray two-piece, and a white button-down shirt. He added his maroon tie with gladiator helmets on it. It was his favorite tie. And his oldest. One edge of it was fraying but he wore it two or three times a week. He'd bought it ten years earlier when he was first assigned to homicide. He pegged it in place on his shirt with a gold tie tack that formed the number 187 – the California penal code for homicide. As he did this, he felt a measure of control come back to him. He began to feel good and whole again, and to feel angry. He was ready to go out into the world, whether or not it was ready for him.

B osch pulled the knot of his tie tight against his throat
before pulling open the back door of the station. He
took the hallway to the rear of the detective bureau
and then the aisle between the tables toward the front,
where Pounds sat in his office behind the glass windows
that separated him from the detectives he commanded.
Heads at the burglary table bobbed up as he was noticed,
then at the robbery and homicide tables. Bosch did not
acknowledge anyone, though he almost lost a step when
he saw someone sitting in his seat at the homicide table.
Burns. Edgar was there at his own spot, but his back was to
Bosch's path and he didn't see Harry coming through the
room.

But Pounds did. Through the glass wall he saw Bosch's
approach to his office and he stood up behind his desk.

The first thing Bosch noticed as he got closer was that
the glass panel that he had broken just a week before in the
office had already been replaced. He thought it was strange
that this could happen so quickly in a department where
more vital repairs – such as replacing the bullet-riddled
windshield of a patrol car – normally took a month of red
tape and paper pushing. But those were the priorities of
this department.

'Henry!' Pounds barked. 'Come in here.'

An old man who sat at the front counter and took calls
on the public line and gave general directions jumped up

and doddered into the glass office. He was a civilian volunteer, one of several who worked in the station, mainly retirees that most cops referred to collectively as members of the Nod Squad.

Bosch followed the old man in and put his briefcase down on the floor.

'Bosch!' Pounds yelped. 'There's a witness here.'

He pointed to old Henry, then out through the glass. 'Witnesses out there as well.'

Bosch could see that Pounds still had deep purple remnants of broken capillaries under each eye. The swelling was gone, though. Bosch walked up to the desk and reached into the pocket of his coat.

'Witnesses to what?'

'To whatever you're doing here.'

Bosch turned to look at Henry.

'Henry, you can leave now. I'm just going to talk to the lieutenant.'

'Henry, you stay,' Pounds commanded. 'I want you to hear this.'

'How do you know he'll remember it, Pounds? He can't even transfer a call to the right table.'

Bosch looked back at Henry again and fixed him with a stare that left no doubt who was in charge in the glass room.

'Close the door on your way out.'

Henry made a timid glance back at Pounds but then quickly headed out the door, closing it as instructed. Bosch turned back to Pounds.

The lieutenant slowly, like a cat sneaking past a dog, lowered himself into his seat, perhaps thinking or knowing from experience that there might be more safety in not being at a face-to-face level with Bosch. Harry looked down and saw that there was a book open on the desk. He reached down and turned the cover to see what it was.

'Studying for the captain's exam, Lieutenant?'

Pounds shrank back from Bosch's reach. Bosch saw it was not the captain's exam manual but a book on creating and honing motivational skills in employees. It had been written by a professional basketball coach. Bosch had to laugh and shake his head.

'Pounds, you know, you're really something. I mean, at least you're entertaining. I gotta give you that.'

Pounds grabbed the book back and shoved it in a drawer.

'What do you want, Bosch? You know you're not supposed to be in here. You're on leave.'

'But you called me in, remember?'

'I did not.'

'The car. You said you wanted the car.'

'I said turn it in at the garage. I didn't say come in here. Now get out!'

Bosch could see the rosy spread of anger on the other man's face. Bosch remained cool and took that as a sign of a declining level of stress. He brought his hand out of his pocket with the car keys in them. He dropped them on the desk in front of Pounds.

'It's parked out by the drunk tank door. You want it back, you can have it. But you take it through the checkout at the garage. That's not a cop's job. That's a job for a bureaucrat.'

Bosch turned to leave and picked up his briefcase. He then opened the door to the office with such force that it swung around and banged against one of the glass panels of the office. The whole office shook but nothing broke. He walked around the counter, saying, 'Sorry about that, Henry,' without looking at the old man, and then headed down the front hall.

A few minutes later he was standing on the curb on Wilcox, in front of the station, waiting for the cab he had called with his portable. A gray Caprice, almost a duplicate of the car he had just turned in, pulled up in front of him and he bent down to look in. It was Edgar. He was smiling. The window glided down.

'You need a ride, tough guy?'

Bosch got in.

'There's a Hertz on La Brea near the Boulevard.'

'Yeah, I know it.'

They drove in silence for a few minutes, then Edgar laughed and shook his head.

'What?'

'Nothing … Burns, man. I think he was about to shit his pants when you were in there with Pounds. He thought you were gonna come outta there and throw his ass outta your chair at the table. He was pitiful.'

'Shit. I should've. I didn't think of it.'

Silence came back again. They were on Sunset coming up to La Brea.

'Harry, you just can't help yourself, can you?'

'I guess not.'

'What happened to your hand?'

Bosch held it up and studied the bandage.

'Ah, I hit it last week when I was working on the deck. Hurt like a son of a bitch.'

'Yeah, you better be careful or Pounds is going to be on you like a son of a bitch.'

'He already is.'

'Man, he's nothing but a bean counter, a punk. Why can't you just leave it alone? You know you're just –'

'You know, you're beginning to sound like the shrink they're sending me to. Maybe I should just sit with you for an hour today, what you say?'

'Maybe she's talking some sense to you.'

'Maybe I should've taken the cab.'

'I think you should figure out who your friends are and listen to them for once.'

'Here it is.'

Edgar slowed in front of the rental car agency. Bosch got out before the car was even stopped.

'Harry, wait a minute.'

Bosch looked back in at him.

'What's going on with this Fox thing? Who is the guy?'

'I can't tell you now, Jerry. It's just better this way.'

'You sure?'

Bosch heard the phone in his briefcase start to ring. He looked down at it and then back at Edgar.

'Thanks for the ride.'

He closed the car door.

The call was from Keisha Russell at the *Times*. She said she'd found one small story in the morgue under Fox's name but she wanted to meet with Bosch to give it to him. He knew it was part of the game, part of making the pact. He looked at his watch. He could wait to see what the story said. He told her he'd buy her lunch at the Pantry in downtown.

Forty minutes later she was already in a booth near the cashier's cage when he got there. He slipped into the opposite side of the booth.

'You're late,' she said.

'Sorry, I was renting a car.'

'They took your car, huh? Must be serious.'

'We're not going to talk about that.'

'I know. You know who owns this place?'

'Yeah, the mayor. Doesn't make the food bad.'

She curled her lip and looked around as if the place were crawling with ants. The mayor was a Republican. The *Times* had gone with the Democrat. What was worse, for her, at least, was that the mayor was a supporter of the Police Department. Reporters didn't like that. That was boring. They wanted City Hall infighting, controversy, scandal. It made things more interesting.

'Sorry,' he said. 'I guess I could've suggested Gorky's or some more liberal establishment.'

'Don't worry about it, Bosch. I'm just funnin' with ya.'

She wasn't more than twenty-five, he guessed. She was a dark-complected black woman who had a beautiful grace about her. Bosch had no idea where she was from but he didn't think it was LA. She had the touch of an accent, a Caribbean lilt, that maybe she had worked on smoothing out. It was still there, though. He liked the way she said his name. In her mouth, it sounded exotic, like a wave breaking. He didn't mind that she was little more than half his age and addressed him only by his last name.

'Where you from, Keisha?'

'Why?'

'Why? Because I'm interested is all. You're on the beat. I wanna know who I'm dealing with.'

'I'm from right here, Bosch. I came from Jamaica when I was five years old. I went to USC. Where are you from?'

'Right here. Been here all my life.'

He decided not to mention the fifteen months he spent fighting in the tunnels in Vietnam and the nine in North Carolina training for it.

'What happened to your hand?'

'Cut it working on my house. Been doing odd jobs while I'm off. So, what's it been like taking Bremmer's place on the cop beat? He'd been there a long time.'

'Yeah, I know. It's been difficult. But I'm making my way. Slowly. I'm making friends. I hope you'll be one of my friends, Bosch.'

'I'll be your friend. When I can. Let's see what you got.'

She brought a manila file up onto the table but the waiter, an old bald man with a waxed mustache, arrived before she could open it. She ordered an egg salad sandwich. He ordered a well-done hamburger and fries. She frowned and he guessed why.

'You're vegetarian, right?'

'Yes.'

'Sorry. Next time you pick the place.'

83

'I will.'

She opened the file and he noticed she had several bracelets on her left wrist. They were made of braided thread in many bright colors. He looked in the file and saw a photocopy of a small newspaper clipping. Bosch could tell by the size of the clip that it was one of the stories that gets buried in the back of the paper. She passed it over to him.

'I think this is your Johnny Fox. The age is right but it does not describe him like you did. White trash, you said.'

Bosch read the story. It was dated September 30, 1962.

CAMPAIGN WORKER VICTIM OF HIT AND RUN
By Monte Kim, *Times* Staff Writer

A 29-year-old campaign worker for a candidate for the district attorney's office was killed Saturday when he was struck by a speeding car in Hollywood, the Los Angeles police reported.

The victim was identified as Johnny Fox, who lived in an apartment on Ivar Street in Hollywood. Police said Fox had been distributing campaign literature supporting district attorney hopeful Arno Conklin at the corner of Hollywood Boulevard and La Brea Avenue when he was cut down by the speeding car as he crossed the street.

Fox was crossing the southbound lanes of La Brea about 2 P.M. when the car struck him. Police said it appeared Fox was killed on impact and his body was dragged for several yards by the car.

The car that hit Fox slowed momentarily after the collision but then sped away, police said. Witnesses told investigators the car proceeded south on La Brea at a high rate of speed. Police have not located the vehicle and witnesses could not provide a clear description of the make and model year. Police said an investigation is continuing.

Conklin campaign manager Gordon Mittel said Fox had

joined the campaign only a week ago.

Reached at the district attorney's office, where he is in charge of the special investigation branch under retiring DA John Charles Stock, Conklin said he had not yet met Fox but regretted the death of the man working for his election. The candidate declined further comment.

Bosch studied the clip for a long moment after reading it. 'This Monte Kim, is he still at the paper?'

'Are you kidding? That's like a millennium ago. Back then the newsroom was a bunch of white guys sitting around in white shirts and ties.'

Bosch looked down at his own shirt, then at her.

'Sorry,' she said. 'Anyway, he's not around. And I don't know about Conklin. A little before my time. Did he win?'

'Yeah. I think he had two terms, then I think he ran for attorney general or something and got his ass handed to him. Something like that. I wasn't here then.'

'I thought you said you've been here all your life.'

'I went away for a while.'

'Vietnam, right?'

'Right.'

'Yeah, a lot of cops your age were there. Must've been a trip. Is that why you all became cops? So you could keep carrying guns?'

'Something like that.'

'Anyway, if Conklin's still alive, he's probably an old man. But Mittel's still around. Obviously, you know that. He's probably in one of these booths eating with the mayor.'

She smiled and he ignored it.

'Yeah, he's a big shot. What's the story on him?'

'Mittel? I don't know. First name on a big downtown

law firm, friend of governors and senators and other powerful people. Last I heard, he's running the financing behind Robert Shepherd.'

'Robert Shepherd? You mean that computer guy?'

'More like computer magnate. Yeah, don't you read the paper? Shepherd wants to run but doesn't want to use up his own money. Mittel is doing the fund-raising for an exploratory campaign.'

'Run for what?'

'Jesus, Bosch, you don't read the paper or watch TV.'

'I've been busy. Run for what?'

'Well, like any egomaniac I guess he wants to run for president. But for now he's looking at the Senate. Shepherd wants to be a third-party candidate. Says the Republicans are too far right and the Democrats too left. He's right down the middle. And from what I hear, if anybody can get the money together for him to do the third-candidate dance, it's Mittel.'

'So Mittel wants to make himself a president.'

'I guess. But what are you asking me about him for anyway? I'm a cop reporter. You're a cop. What's this have to do with Gordon Mittel?'

She pointed to the photocopy. Bosch became aware that he might have asked too many questions.

'I'm just trying to catch up,' he said. 'Like you said, I don't read the papers.'

'That's *paper,* not papers,' she said smiling. 'I better not catch you reading or talking to the *Daily Snews.*'

'Hell hath no fury like a reporter scorned, right?'

'Something like that.'

He felt assured that he had deflected her suspicions. He held up the photocopy.

'There was no follow-up to this? They never caught anybody?'

'I guess not or there would be a story.'

'Can I keep this?'

'Sure.'

'You feel like taking another walk back to the morgue?'

'For what?'

'Stories about Conklin.'

'There will be hundreds, Bosch. You said he was DA for two terms.'

'I only want stories from before he was elected. And if you have the time, throw in stories on Mittel, too.'

'You know, you're asking a lot. I could get in trouble if they knew I was doing clip searches for a cop.'

She put on a fake pout and he ignored that, too. He knew what she was driving at.

'You want to tell me what this is about, Bosch?'

He still didn't say anything.

'I didn't think so. Well, look, I've got two interviews to do this afternoon. I'm going to be gone. What I can do is get an intern to get the clips together and leave it all for you with the guard in the globe lobby. It will be in an envelope so nobody will know what it is. Would that be okay?'

He nodded. He'd been to Times Square before on a handful of occasions, usually meetings with reporters. It was a block-sized building with two lobbies. The center-piece of the lobby at the First and Spring entrance was a huge globe that never stopped rotating, just as the news never stopped happening.

'You'll just leave it under my name? Won't that get you in trouble? You know, like you said, being too friendly with a cop. That's got to be against the rules over there.'

She smiled at his sarcasm.

'Don't worry. If an editor or somebody asks, I'll just say it's an investment in the future. You better remember that, Bosch. Friendship is a two-way street.'

'Don't worry. I never forget that.'

He leaned forward across the table so he was up close to her face.

'I want you to remember something, too. One of the reasons I'm not telling you why I need this stuff is because I'm not sure what it means. If anything. But don't you get too curious. Don't you go making any calls. You do that, and you might mess things up. I might get hurt. You might get hurt. Got it?'

'Got it.'

The man with the waxed mustache appeared at the side of the table with their plates.

'I noticed you arrived early today. Am I to take that as a sign that you want to be here?'

'Not especially. I was downtown having lunch with a friend, so I just came over.'

'Well, it's good to hear you were out with a friend. I think that is good.'

Carmen Hinojos was behind her desk. The notebook was out and open but she sat with her hands clasped together in front of her. It was as if she was going out of her way to make no move that could be construed as threatening to the dialogue.

'What happened to your hand?'

Bosch held it up and looked at the bandages on his fingers.

'I hit it with a hammer. I was working on my house.'

'That's too bad. I hope it's okay.'

'I'll live.'

'Why are you so dressed up? I hope you don't feel you have to do that for these sessions.'

'No. I … I just like following my routine. Even if I'm not going to work, I got dressed like I was.'

'I understand.'

After she made an offer of coffee or water and Bosch declined, she got the session going.

'Tell me, what would you like to talk about today?'

'I don't care. You're the boss.'

'I'd rather that you not look at the relationship in that way. I'm not your boss, Detective Bosch. I'm just a facilitator, someone to help you talk about whatever you want, whatever you want to get off your chest.'

Bosch was silent. He couldn't think of anything to volunteer. Carmen Hinojos drummed her pencil on her yellow tablet for a few moments before taking up the slack.

'Nothing at all, huh?'

'Nothing comes to mind.'

'Then why don't we talk about yesterday. When I called you, to remind you of our session today, you obviously seemed upset about something. Was that when you hit your hand?'

'No, that wasn't it.'

He stopped but she said nothing and he decided to give in a little bit. He had to admit to himself that there was something about her that he liked. She was not threatening and he believed she was telling the truth when she said she was there only to help him.

'What happened when you called was that I had found out earlier that my partner, you know, my partner before all of this, had been paired up with a new man. I've been replaced already.'

'And how'd that make you feel?'

'You heard how I was. I was mad about it. I think anybody would be. Then I called my partner up later and he treated me like yesterday's news. I taught that guy a lot and …'

'And what?'

'I don't know. It hurt, I guess.'

'I see.'

'No, I don't think you do. You'd have to be me to see it the way I did.'

'I guess that's true. But I can sympathize. Let's leave it at that. Let me ask you this. Shouldn't you have expected your partner to be paired up again? After all, isn't it a department rule that detectives work in pairs? You are on leave for a so-far-unknown period of time. Wasn't it a given that he'd get a new partner, whether permanent or otherwise?'

'I suppose.'

'Isn't it safer to work in pairs?'

'I suppose.'

'What is your own experience? Did you feel safer the times you were with a partner on the job as opposed to those times when you were alone?'

'Yes, I felt safer.'

'So what happened was inevitable and inarguable, yet still it made you angry.'

'It wasn't that it happened that brought it on. I don't know, it was the way he told me and then the way he acted when I called. I really felt left out. I asked him for a favor and he … I don't know.'

'He what?'

'He hesitated. Partners don't do that. Not with each other. They're supposed be there for each other. It's supposedly a lot like a marriage, but I've never been married.'

She paused to write some notes, which made Bosch wonder what had just been said that was so important.

'You seem,' she said while still writing, 'to have a low threshold for the toleration of frustrations.'

Her statement immediately made him angry but he knew that if he showed it then he would be confirming her statement. He thought maybe it was a trick designed to elicit such a response. He tried to calm himself.

'Doesn't everybody?' he said in a controlled voice.

'I suppose, to a degree. When I reviewed your records I saw that you were in the Army during the Vietnam War. Did you see any combat?'

'Did I *see* any combat? Yes, I saw combat. I was in the middle of combat, too. I was even under it. Why do people always ask, did you *see* combat, like it was a goddamn movie they took you to over there?'

She was quiet for a long time, holding the pen but doing no writing. It seemed like she was simply waiting for the sails of his anger to lose the wind. He waved his hand in a gesture he hoped told her that he was sorry, that it was behind him, that they should move on.

'Sorry,' he said, just to make sure.

She still didn't say anything and her stare was beginning to weigh on him. He looked away from her to the bookshelves along one wall of the office. They were filled with heavy, leather-bound psychiatry texts.

'I am sorry to intrude on such an emotionally sensitive area,' she finally said. 'The reason –'

'But that's what this is all about, right? What you have is a license to intrude and I can't do anything about it.'

'So, then, accept it,' she said sternly. 'We've been over this before. To help you we have to talk about you. Accept it and maybe we can move on. Now, as I was saying, the reason I mentioned the war was that I wanted to ask you if you are familiar with post-traumatic stress syndrome. Have you ever heard of it?'

He looked back at her. He knew what was coming.

'Yes, of course. I've heard of it.'

'Well, Detective, in the past it's primarily been associated with servicemen returning from the war but it's not just a war or post-war problem. It can happen in any kind of stressful environment. Any kind. And I have to say I think that you are a walking, talking example of this disorder's symptoms.'

'Jesus ... ,' he said, shaking his head. He turned in his seat so he wasn't looking at her or her bookcase. He stared at the sky through the window. It was cloudless. 'You people sit up here in these offices and have no idea ...'

He didn't finish. He just shook his head. He reached to his neck and loosened his tie. It was like he couldn't get enough air into his chest.

'Hear me out, Detective, okay? Just look at the facts here. Can you think of anything more stressful to be in this city during the last few years than a police officer? Between Rodney King and the scrutiny and villainy that brought, the riots, fires, floods and earthquakes, each officer on this force has had to write the book on stress management and, of course, mismanagement.'

'You left out killer bees.'

'I'm being serious.'

'So am I. It was on the news.'

'With all that's happened and gone on in this city, with every one of these calamities, who is in the middle every time? The police officers. The ones who have to respond. The ones who can't stay at home, duck down and wait until it's over. So let's go from that generalization to the individual. You, Detective. You have been a front-line contender with all of these crises. At the same time you've had your real job to contend with. Homicide. It's one of the highest-stress jobs in the department. Tell me, how many murders have you investigated in the last three years?'

'Look, I'm not looking for an excuse. I told you before that I did what I did because I wanted to. It had nothing to do with riots or –'

'How many dead bodies have you looked at? Just answer my question, please. How many dead bodies? How many widows did you break the news to? How many mothers did you tell about their dead children?'

He brought his hands up and rubbed his face. All he knew was that he wanted to hide from her.

'A lot,' he finally whispered.

'More than a lot ...'

He exhaled loudly.

'Thank you for answering. I'm not trying to corner you. The point of my questions and the treatise on the social, cultural and even geologic fragmentation of this city is that what I'm saying here is that you've been through more than most, okay? And this doesn't even include the baggage you might still have from Vietnam or the loss of the romantic relationship. But whatever the reasons, the symptoms of stress are showing. They are there, plain as day. Your intolerance, your inability to sublimate frustrations, most of all your assault on your commanding officer.'

She paused but Bosch didn't say anything. He had a feeling she wasn't finished. She wasn't.

'There are other signs as well,' she continued. 'Your refusal to leave your damaged home can be perceived as a form of denial of what is happening around you. There are physical symptoms. Have you looked at yourself in the mirror lately? I don't think I need to ask to know that you're drinking too much. And your hand. You didn't hurt yourself with a hammer. You fell asleep with a cigarette in your hand. That is a burn and I'd bet my state license on it.'

She opened a drawer and took out two plastic cups and a bottle of water. She filled the cups and pushed one across the desk to him. A peace offering. He watched her silently. He felt exhausted, unrepairable. He also couldn't help but be amazed by her at the same time she was so expertly cutting him open. After she took a sip of water she continued.

'These things are all indicative of a diagnosis of post-traumatic stress syndrome. However, we have one problem with that. The word *post* when used in such a diagnosis indicates the time of stress has passed. That's not the case here. Not in LA. Not with your job. Harry, you are in a nonstop pressure cooker. You owe yourself some breathing room. That's what this leave is all about. Breathing room. Time to recoup and recover. So don't fight it. Grab it. That's the best advice I can give you. Grab it and use it. To save yourself.'

Bosch breathed out heavily and held up his bandaged hand.

'You can keep your state license.'

'Thank you.'

They rested a moment until she continued in a voice meant to soothe him.

'You also have to know you are not alone. This is nothing to be embarrassed about. There has been a sharp increase in incidents of officer stress in the last three years. Behavioral Sciences Services just made a request to the City Council for five more psychologists. Our caseload went from eighteen hundred counseling sessions in 1990 to more than double that last year. We've even got a name for what's going on here. The blue angst. And you have it, Harry.'

Bosch smiled and shook his head, still clinging to what denial he had left.

'The blue angst. Sounds like the name of a Wambaugh novel, doesn't it?'

She didn't answer.

'So what you're saying is that I'm not going to get my job back.'

'No, I'm not saying that at all. All I am saying is that we have a lot of work ahead of us.'

'I feel like I've been broken down by the world champ. You mind if I call you sometime when I'm trying to get a confession out of a hump who won't talk to me?'

'Believe me, just saying that is a start.'

'What do you want me to do?'

'I want you to want to come here. That's all. Don't look at it as a punishment. I want you to work with me, not against me. When we talk I want you to talk about everything and nothing. Anything that comes to mind. Hold back nothing. And one other thing. I'm not telling you to completely cut it out, but you have to cut back on the drinking. You have to have a clear mind. As you obviously know, the effects of alcohol stay with an individual long after the night they were consumed.'

'I'll try. All of it. I'll try.'

'That's all I ask. And since you suddenly seem so willing, I have another thought. I have a cancelation of a session tomorrow at three. Can you make it?'

Bosch hesitated, didn't say anything.

'We seem to finally be working well and I think it will help. The sooner we get through with our work, the sooner you should be able to get back to your work. What do you say?'

'Three?'

'Yes.'

'Okay, I'll be here.'

'Good. Let's get back to our dialogue. Why don't you start? Whatever you want to talk about.'

He leaned forward and reached for the cup of water. He looked at her as he drank from it, then put the cup back on the desk.

'Just say anything?'

'Anything. Whatever is happening in your life or mind that you want to talk about.'

He thought for a long moment.

'I saw a coyote last night. Near my house. I ... I was drunk, I guess, but I know I saw him.'

'Why was that significant to you?'

He tried to compose the proper answer.

'I'm not sure … I guess there's not too many left in the hills in the city – least near where I live. So whenever I see one, I get this feeling that it might be the last one left out there. You know? The last coyote. And I guess that would bother me if it ever turned out to be true, if I never saw one again.'

She nodded as if he had scored some point in a game he wasn't sure how to play.

'There used to be one that lived in the canyon below my house. I'd see him down there and –'

'How do you know it was a he? And I think you called the one you saw last night a he. How are you sure?'

'I'm not sure. I guess I don't even know. It's just a guess.'

'Okay. Go on.'

'Um, he – it – lived down there below my house and I used to see him from time to time. After the earthquake it was gone. I don't know what happened to it. Then I saw this one last night. Something about the mist and the light out there … it looked like its coat was blue. He looked hungry. There is something … they're kind of sad and threatening at the same time. You know?'

'Yes, I do.'

'Anyway, I thought about him when I got in bed after I got home. That was when I burned my hand. I fell asleep with the cigarette. But before I woke up I had this dream. I mean, I think it was a dream. Maybe like a daydream, like I was still kind of awake. And in it, whatever it was, the coyote was there again. But it was with me. And we were in the canyon or on a hill or something and I wasn't really sure.'

He held up his hand.

'And then I felt the fire.'

She nodded but didn't say anything.

'So what do you think?' he asked.

'Well, interpretation of dreams is not something I do often. Frankly, I'm not sure of its value. The real value I think I see in what you just told me was the willingness to tell me. It shows me a one-eighty-degree turn in your approach to these sessions. For what it's worth, I think it's clear you identify with the coyote. Perhaps, there are not many policemen like you left and you feel the same threat to your existence or your mission. I don't really know. But look at your own words. You called them sad and threatening at the same time. Could that be you also?'

He drank from his cup before answering.

'I've been sad before. But I've found comfort in it.'

They sat in silence for a while, digesting what had been said. She looked at her watch.

'We still have some time. Is there anything else you want to talk about? Maybe something related to this story?'

He contemplated the question for a while and took out a cigarette.

'How much time do we have?'

'As long as you want. Don't worry about the time. I want to do this.'

'You've talked about my mission. You told me to think about my mission. And you said the word again just a minute ago.'

'Yes.'

He hesitated.

'What I say here is protected, right?'

She furrowed her brow.

'I'm not talking about anything illegal. What I mean is, whatever I tell you in here, you're not going to tell people, right? It won't get back to Irving.'

'No. What you tell me stays right here. That's an absolute. I told you, I make a single, narrowly focused recommendation for or against return to duty that I give to Assistant Chief Irving. That's it.'

He nodded, hesitated again and then made his decision. He would tell her.

'Well, you were talking about my mission and your mission and so on and, well, I think I've had a mission for a long time. Only I didn't know it, or I mean … I didn't accept it. I didn't acknowledge it. I don't know how to explain it right. Maybe I was afraid or something. I put it off. For a lot of years. Anyway, what I'm telling you is that I've accepted it now.'

'I'm not sure I'm following you. Harry, you have to come out and tell me what you're talking about.'

He looked down at the gray rug in front of him. He spoke to it because he didn't know how to say it to her face.

'I'm an orphan … I never knew my father and my mother was murdered in Hollywood when I was a kid. Nobody … there never was any arrest made.'

'You're looking for her killer, aren't you?'

He looked up at her and nodded.

'That's my mission right now.'

She showed no shock on her face, which in turn surprised him. It was as if she expected him to say what he had just said.

'Tell me about it.'

Bosch sat at his dining room table with his notebook out and the newspaper clips that Keisha Russell had had a *Times* intern gather for him sitting in front of him in two separate stacks. One stack for Conklin stories and one for Mittel stories. There was a bottle of Henry's on the table and through the evening he had been nursing it like cough syrup. The one beer was all he would allow himself. The ashtray, however, was loaded and there was a pall of blue smoke around the table. He had placed no limit on cigarettes. Hinojos had said nothing about smoking.

She'd had plenty to say about his mission, though. She'd flatly counseled him to stop until he was better emotionally prepared to face what he might find. He told her that he was too far down the road to stop. Then she said something that he kept thinking about as he drove home and it intruded even now.

'You better think about this and make sure it's what you want,' she said. 'Subconsciously or not, you may have been working toward this all your life. It could be the reason you are who you are. A policeman, a homicide investigator. Resolving your mother's death could also resolve your need to be a policeman. It could take your drive, your mission, away from you. You have to be prepared for that or you should turn back.'

Bosch considered what she had said to be true. He

knew that all his life it had been there. What had happened to his mother had helped define everything he did after. And it was always there in the dark recesses of his mind. A promise to find out. A promise to avenge. It was never anything that had been spoken aloud or even thought about with much focus. For to have done that was to plan and this was no part of a grand agenda. Still, he was crowded with the feeling that what he was doing was inevitable, something scheduled by an unseen hand a long time ago.

His mind put Hinojos aside and focused on a memory. He was under the surface of the water, eyes open and looking up toward the light above the pool. Then, the light was eclipsed by a figure standing above, the image murky, a dark angel hovering above. Bosch kicked off the bottom and moved toward the figure.

Bosch picked up the bottle of beer and finished it in one pull. He tried to concentrate again on the newspaper clips in front of him.

He had initially been surprised at how many stories there were about Arno Conklin prior to his ascendance to the throne of the district attorney's office. But as he started to read through them he saw most of the stories were mundane dispatches from trials in which Conklin was the prosecuting attorney. Still, Bosch got somewhat of a feel for the man through the cases he tried and his style as a prosecutor. It was clear that his star rose both in the office and the public's eyes with a series of highly publicized cases.

The stories were in chronological order and the first dealt with the successful prosecution in 1953 of a woman who poisoned both her parents and then stored their bodies in trunks in the garage until neighbors complained about the smell to the police a month later. Conklin was quoted at length in several articles on the case. One time he was described as the 'dashing deputy district attorney.' The case was one of the early forerunners of the insanity defense. The woman claimed diminished capacity. But judging by the number of articles, there was a public furor over the case and the jury only took a half hour to convict. The defendant received the death penalty and Conklin's place in the public arena as a champion of public safety, a seeker of justice, was secured. There was a photo of him talking to the reporters after the verdict. The paper's earlier description of him had him down perfectly. He was a dashing man. He wore a dark three-piece suit, had short blond hair and was cleanshaven. He was lean and tall and had the ruddy, All-American look that actors pay surgeons thousands for. Arno was a star in his own right.

There were more stories about more murder cases in the clips after that first one. Conklin won every one of them. And he always asked for – and got – the death penalty. Bosch noticed that in the stories from the later fifties, he had been elevated in title to senior deputy district attorney and then by the end of the decade to assistant, one of the top jobs in the office. It was a meteoric rise to have taken place in only a decade.

There was one report on a press conference in which DA John Charles Stock announced he was placing Conklin in charge of the Special Investigations Unit and charging him with cleaning up the myriad vice problems that threatened the social fabric of Los Angeles County.

'I've always gone to Arno Conklin with the toughest jobs,' the DA said. 'And I go to him again. The people of the Los Angeles community want a clean community and, by God, we will have it. To those who know we are coming for you, my advice is, move out. San Francisco will have you. San Diego will have you. But the City of Angels won't have you!'

Following that there were several stories spread over a

couple of years with splashy headlines about crackdowns on gambling parlors, pipe dens, whorehouses and the street prostitution trade. Conklin worked with a task force of forty cops comprised of loaners from all departments in the county. Hollywood was the main target of 'Conklin's Commandos,' as the *Times* dubbed the squad, but the scourge of the law came down on wrongdoers all over the county. From Long Beach to the desert, all those who labored for the wages of sin were running scared – at least according to the newspaper articles. Bosch had no doubt that the vice lords Conklin's Commandos were targeting operated business as usual and that it was only the bottom feeders, the replaceable employees, that were getting the hook.

The last Conklin story in the stack was on his February 1, 1962, announcement that he would run for the top spot in the district attorney's office on a campaign of renewed emphasis on ridding the county of the vices that threatened any great society. Bosch noted that part of the stately speech he delivered on the steps of the old downtown courthouse was a well-known police philosophy that Conklin, or his speechwriter, had apparently appropriated as original thought.

People sometimes say to me, 'What's the big deal, Arno? These are victimless crimes. If a man wants to place a bet or sleep with a woman for money, what's wrong with that? Where's the victim?' Well, my friends, I'll tell you what's wrong with that and who the victim is. We're the victim. All of us. When we allow this kind of activity to occur, when we simply look the other way, then it weakens us all. Every one of us.

I look at it this way. These so-called little crimes are each like a broken window in an abandoned house. Doesn't seem like a big problem, right?

Wrong. If nobody fixes that window, pretty soon kids come along and think nobody cares. So they throw a few rocks and break a few more windows. Next, the burglar drives down the street and sees the house and thinks nobody around there cares. So he sets up shop and starts breaking into houses while the owners are at work.

Next thing you know, another miscreant comes along and steals cars right off the street. And so on and so on. The residents start to see their own neighborhood with different eyes then. They think, Nobody cares anymore, so why should I? They wait an extra month before cutting the grass. They don't tell the boys hanging on the corner to put the cigarettes out and go back to school. It's gradual decay, my friends. It happens all across this great country of ours. It sneaks in like weeds in our yard. Well, when I'm district attorney the weeds are coming out by the roots.

The story ended by reporting that Conklin had chosen a young 'firebrand' from his office to manage his campaign. He said that Gordon Mittel would resign from the DA's office and begin work immediately. Bosch reread the story and immediately became transfixed by something that hadn't registered during his first read. It was in the second paragraph.

For the well-known and not-press-shy Conklin, it will be his first run for public office. The 35-year-old bachelor and Hancock Park resident said he has planned the run for a long time and has the backing of retiring DA John Charles Stock, who also appeared at the press conference.

Bosch turned the pages of his notebook back to the list of names he had written before and wrote 'Hancock Park' after Conklin's name. It wasn't much but it was a little piece of verification of Katherine Register's story. And it was enough to get Bosch's juices going. It made him feel that at least he had a line in the water.

'Fucking hypocrite,' he whispered to himself.

He drew a circle around Conklin's name in the notebook. He absentmindedly kept circling it as he tried to decide what he should do next.

Marjorie Lowe's last known destination was a party in Hancock Park. According to Katherine Register, she was more specifically going to meet Conklin. After she was dead, Conklin had called the detectives on the case to make an appointment but any record of the interview, if any occurred, was missing. Bosch knew it was all a general correlation of facts but it served to deepen and solidify the suspicion he had felt from the night he had first looked through the murder book. Something was not right about the case. Something didn't fit. And the more he thought about it, the more he believed Conklin was the wrong piece.

He reached into his jacket, which was on the chairback behind him, and took out his small phone book. He took it into the kitchen, where he dialed the home line of Deputy District Attorney Roger Goff.

Goff was a friend who shared Bosch's affection for the tenor saxophone. They'd spent many days in court sitting side by side during trials and many nights in jazz bars side by side on stools. Goff was an old-line prosecutor who had been with the office nearly thirty years. He had no political aspirations inside or outside of the office. He just liked his job. He was a rarity because he never tired of it. A thousand deputies had come in, burned out, and gone on to corporate America during Goff's watch, but he stayed. He now labored in the criminal courts building with prosecutors and public defenders twenty years his junior.

But he was still good at it and, more important, still had the fire in his voice when he stood before a jury and called down the outrage of God and society against those in the defendant's chair. His mixture of tenacity and plain fairness had made him a legend in downtown legal and law enforcement circles. And he was one of the few prosecutors Bosch had unconditional respect for.

'Roger, Harry Bosch.'

'Hey, goddamnit, how you doing?'

'I'm fine. What are you up to?'

'Watching the tube like everybody else. What're you doing?'

'Nothing. I was just thinking, you remember Gloria Jeffries?'

'Glo – shit, of course I do. Let's see. She's ... yeah, she's the one with the husband got quaded in the motorcycle accident, right?'

Recalling the case, it sounded as if he were reading it off one of his yellow tablets.

'She got tired of caring for him. So one morning he's in bed and she sits on his face until she smothers him. It was about to go by as a natural but a suspicious detective named Harry Bosch wouldn't let it go. He came up with a witness who Gloria had told everything to. The clincher, the thing that got the jury, was that she told the wit that when she smothered him, it was the first orgasm the poor devil had ever been able to give her. How is that for a memory?'

'Damn, you're good.'

'So what about her?'

'She's raising up at Frontera. Getting ready to. I was wondering if you'd have time to write a letter.'

'Fuck, already? What was that, three, four years ago?'

'Almost five. I hear she's got the book now and goes to

the board next month. I'll write a letter but it'd be good if there was one from the prosecutor, too.'

'Don't worry about it, I got a standard in my computer. All I do is change the name and the crime, throw in a few of the gruesome details. The basic line is that the crime was too heinous for parole to be considered at this time. It's a good letter. I'll send it out tomorrow. It usually works charms.'

'Good. Thanks.'

'You know, they gotta stop giving the book to those women. They all get religion when they're coming up. You ever go to one of those hearings?'

'A couple.'

'Yeah, sit through a half a day of them if you have the time and aren't feeling particularly suicidal sometime. They sent me out to Frontera once when one of the Manson girls was up. See, with the big ones like that they send a body out instead of a letter. So, I went out and I sat through about ten of these things waiting for my girl to come up. And let me tell you, everybody's quoting Corinthians, they're quoting Revelations, Matthew, Paul, John three-sixteen, John this, John that. And it works! It goddamn works. These old guys on the board eat that shit up. Plus I guess they're all sitting up there getting thick in their pants having all these women groveling in front of them. Anyway, you got me started, Harry. It's your fault, not mine.'

'Sorry about that.'

'It's okay. So what else is new? Haven't seen you in the building. You got anything coming my way?'

It was the question Bosch had been waiting for Goff to get to so he could nonchalantly steer the conversation toward Arno Conklin.

'Ah, nothing much. It's been slow. But, hey, let me ask you, did you know Arno Conklin?'

'Arno Conklin? Sure, I knew him. He hired me. What are you asking about him for?'

'Nothing. I was going through some old files, making room in one of the cabinets, and I came across some old newspapers. They were pushed into the back. There were some stories about him and I thought of you, thought it was about when you started.'

'Yeah, Arno, tried to be a good man. A little high and mighty for my taste, but I think he was a decent man overall. Especially considering he was both a politician and a lawyer.'

Goff laughed at his own line but Bosch was silent. Goff had used the past tense. Bosch felt a heavy presence push into his chest and he only realized then how strong the desire to avenge could be.

'He's dead?'

He closed his eyes. He hoped Goff wouldn't detect the urgency he had let slip into his voice.

'Oh, no, he's not dead. I meant, you know, when I knew him. He was a good man then.'

'He's still practicing law somewhere?'

'Oh, no. He's an old man. Retired. Once a year they wheel him out at the annual prosecutors banquet. He personally hands out the Arno Conklin Award.'

'What's that?'

'Some piece of wood with a brass plate on it that goes to the administrative prosecutor of the year, if you can believe that. That's the guy's legacy, an annual award to a so-called prosecutor who doesn't set foot inside a court-room all year. It always goes to one of the division heads. I don't know how they decide which one. Prob'ly whoever got his or her nose farthest up the DA's ass that year.'

Bosch laughed. The line wasn't that funny but he was also feeling the relief of learning that Conklin was still alive.

'It's not funny, Bosch. It's fucking sad. Administrative prosecutor, whoever heard of such a thing? An oxymoron. Like Andrew and his screenplays. He deals with these studio people called, get this, creative executives. There's your classic contradiction. Well, there you go, Bosch, you got me going again.'

Bosch knew Andrew was Goff's roommate but he had never met him.

'Sorry, Roger. Anyway, what do you mean, they wheel him out?'

'Arno? Well, I mean they wheel him out. He's in a chair. I told you, he's an old man. Last I heard he was in some full-care retirement home. One of the classy ones in Park La Brea. I keep saying I'm going to see him one day, thank him for hiring me way back when. Who knows, maybe I could put in a word for that award or something.'

'Funny guy. You know, I heard that Gordon Mittel used to be his frontman.'

'Oh, yeah, he was the bulldog outside the door. Ran his campaigns. That's how Mittel got started. Now that's one mean – I'm glad he got out of criminal law and into politics, he'd be a motherfucker to come up against in court.'

'Yeah, I've heard,' Bosch said.

'Whatever you've heard, you can double it.'

'You know him?'

'Not now and not then. I just knew to keep clear. He was already out of the office by the time I came in. But there were stories. Supposedly in those early days, when Arno was the heir apparent and everybody knew it, there was a lot of maneuvering. You know, to get next to him. There was one guy, Sinclair I think his name was, that was set to run Arno's campaign. Then one night the cleaning lady found some porno shots under his blotter. There was an internal investigation and the photos proved to be stolen from another prosecutor's case files. Sinclair was dumped. He always claimed he was set up by Mittel.'

'Think he was?'

'Yes. It was Mittel's style ... But who knows.'

Bosch sensed that he had said and asked enough to pass it off as conversation and gossip. Anything further and Goff might get suspicious about the call.

'So what's the deal?' he asked. 'You zipped up for the night or you want to go by the Catalina? I heard Redman's in town to do Leno. I'd bet you the cover charge that he and Branford drop by to sit in on the late set.'

'Sounds tempting, Harry, but Andrew's making a late dinner now and I think we're just going to stay at home tonight. He's counting on it. You mind?'

'Not at all. Anyway, I'm trying not to bend the elbow so much lately. I need to give it a rest.'

'Now that, sir, is quite admirable. I think you deserve a piece of wood with a brass plate on it.'

'Or a shot of whiskey.'

After hanging up Bosch sat back down at the desk and wrote notes on the highlights of the conversation with Goff into his notebook. Next he pulled the stack of clips on Mittel in front of him. These were more recent clips than those on Conklin because Mittel had not made a name for himself until much later. Conklin had been his first step up the ladder.

Most of the stories were just mentions of Mittel as being in attendance at various galas in Beverly Hills or as host of various campaign or charity dinners. From the start he was a money man, a man politicians and charities went to when they wanted to cast their nets into the rich enclaves of the Westside. He worked both sides, Republican, Democrat, it didn't seem to matter. His profile grew, though, when he started working for candidates on a larger scale. The current governor was a client. So, too, were a handful of congressman and senators from other western states.

A profile written several years earlier – and apparently without his cooperation – ran under the headline THE PRESIDENT'S MAIN MONEY MAN. It said Mittel had been tapped to round up California contributors for the president's reelection war chest. It said the state was one of the cornerstones of the national campaign's funding plan.

The story also noted the irony that Mittel was a recluse in the high-profile world of politics. He was a backstage man who abhorred the spotlight. So much so that he had repeatedly turned down patronage jobs from those he'd helped elect.

Instead, Mittel elected to stay in Los Angeles, where he was the founding partner of a powerful financial district law firm, Mittel, Anderson, Jennings & Rountree. Still, it seemed to Bosch that what this Yale-educated lawyer did had little to do with law as Bosch knew it. He doubted Mittel had been inside a courtroom in years. That made Harry think of the Conklin award and he smiled. Too bad Mittel had quit the DA's office. He might've been in line for it someday.

There was a photo that ran with the profile. It showed Mittel at the bottom of the steps of Air Force One greeting the then president at LAX. Though the article had been published years earlier, Bosch was nevertheless startled by how young Mittel was in the photo. He looked at the story again and checked the man's age. Doing the arithmetic, he realized that currently Mittel was barely sixty years old.

Bosch pushed the newspaper clips aside and got up. For a long time he stood at the sliding glass door to the deck and stared at the lights across the pass. He began to consider what he knew about circumstances thirty-three years old. Conklin, according to Katherine Register, knew

Marjorie Lowe. It was clear from the murder book that he had somehow reached into the investigation of her death for reasons unknown. His reach was then apparently covered up for reasons unknown. This had occurred only three months before he announced his candidacy for district attorney and less than a year before a key figure in the investigation, Johnny Fox, died while in his political employ.

Bosch thought that it was obvious that Fox would have been known to Mittel, the campaign manager. Therefore, he further concluded, whatever it was that Conklin did or knew, it was likely that Mittel, his frontman and the architect of his political run, had knowledge of it as well.

Bosch went back to the table and turned to the list of names in his notebook. Now he picked up the pen and circled Mittel's name as well. He felt like having another beer but he settled for a cigarette.

I n the morning Bosch called the LAPD personnel office and asked them to check whether Eno and McKittrick were still current. He doubted they were still around but knew he had to make the check. It would be embarrassing if he went through a search for them only to find one or both still on the payroll. The clerk checked the roll and told him no such officers were currently on the force.

He decided he would have to put on his Harvey Pounds pose after that. He dialed the DMV in Sacramento, gave the lieutenant's name and asked for Ms Sharp again. By the tone she inflected in the single word 'Hello' after picking up the phone, Bosch had no doubt that she remembered him.

'Is this Ms Sharp?'

'That's who you asked for, isn't it?'

'I did, indeed.'

'Then it's Ms Sharp. What can I do for you?'

'Well, I wanted to mend our fences, so to speak. I have a few more names I need driver's license addresses for and I thought that directly working with you would expedite the matter and perhaps repair our working relationship.'

'Honey, we don't have a working relationship. Hold the line, please.'

She punched the button before he could say anything. The line was dead for so long that he began to believe his scam to burn Pounds wasn't worth it. Finally, a different clerk picked up and said Ms Sharp had instructed her to help. Bosch gave her Pounds's serial number and then the names Gordon Mittel, Arno Conklin, Claude Eno and Jake McKittrick. He said he needed the home addresses on their licenses.

He was put on hold again. During the time he waited he held the phone to his ear with his shoulder and fried an egg over easy in a pan on the stove. He made a sandwich out of it with two slices of white toast and cold salsa from a jar he kept in the refrigerator. He ate the dripping sandwich while leaning over the sink. He had just wiped his mouth and poured himself a second cup of coffee when the clerk finally picked back up.

'Sorry it took so long.'

'No problem.'

He then remembered he was Pounds and wished he hadn't said that.

The clerk explained that she had no addresses or license information on Eno or McKittrick, then gave him addresses for Conklin and Mittel. Goff had been right. Conklin lived in Park La Brea. Mittel lived above Hollywood on Hercules Drive in a development called Mount Olympus.

Bosch was too preoccupied at that point to continue the Pounds charade. He thanked the clerk without further confrontation and hung up. He thought about what his next move should be. Eno and McKittrick were either dead or out of state. He knew he could get their addresses through the department's personnel office but that might take all day. He picked up the phone again and called Robbery-Homicide, asking for Detective Leroy Ruben. Ruben had put nearly forty years in on the department, half of it in RHD. He might know something about Eno

114

and McKittrick. He might also know Bosch was on stress leave.

'Ruben, can I help you?'

'Leroy, it's Harry Bosch. What do you know?'

'Not much, Harry. Enjoying the good life?'

Right away he was telling Bosch he knew of his situation. Bosch knew now that his only alternative was to be straight with him. To a point.

'It ain't bad. But I'm not sleeping late every day.'

'No? What're you getting up for?'

'I'm kind've freelancing on an old case, Leroy. That's why I called. I want to try to track down a couple of old dicks. Thought maybe you'd know of them. They were out of Hollywood.'

'Who are they?'

'Claude Eno and Jake McKittrick. Remember them?'

'Eno and McKittrick. No … I mean, yeah, I think I remember McKittrick. He checked out … it must've been ten, fifteen years ago. He went back to Florida, I think. Yeah, Florida. He was here in RHD for a year or so. At the end there. The other one, Eno, I don't remember any Eno.'

'Well, it was worth a try. I'll see what I can find in Florida. Thanks, Leroy.'

'Hey, Harry, what gives anyway?'

'It's just an old case I had in my desk. It's giving me something to do while I see what happens.'

'Any word?'

'Not yet. They got me talking to the shrink. If I can talk my way past her, I'll get back to the table. We'll see.'

'Okay, well, good luck. You know, me and some of the boys here, when we heard that story we laughed our asses off. We heard about that guy Pounds. He's an asshole. You done good, kid.'

'Well, let's hope I didn't do so good that I lost my job.'

'Ah, you'll be all right. They send you to Chinatown a few times, brush you off and send you back into the ring. You'll be okay.'

'Thanks, Leroy.'

After hanging up, Bosch got dressed for the day, putting on a fresh shirt and the same suit as the day before.

He headed downtown in his rented Mustang and spent the next two hours in a bureaucratic maze. He first went to the Personnel Office at Parker Center, told a clerk what he wanted and then waited half an hour for a supervisor to tell him all over again. The supervisor told him he had wasted his time and that the information he sought was at City Hall.

He walked across the street to the City Hall annex, took the stairs up and then crossed on the tramway over Main Street into the white obelisk of City Hall. He took the elevator up to the Finance Department, on nine, showed his ID card to another counter clerk and told her that, in the interest of streamlining the process, maybe he should talk to a supervisor first.

He waited on a plastic chair in a hallway for twenty minutes before he was ushered into a small office cramped with two desks, four file cabinets and several boxes on the floor. An obese woman with pale skin and black hair, sideburns and the slight hint of a mustache sat behind one of the desks. On her calendar blotter Bosch noticed a food stain from some prior mishap. There was also a reusable plastic quart soda container with a screw-on top and straw on her desk. A plastic name plate on the desk said Mona Tozzi.

'I'm Carla's supervisor. She said you are a police officer?'

'Detective.'

He pulled the chair away from the empty desk and sat down in front of the fat woman.

'Excuse me, but Cassidy is probably going to need her chair when she gets back. That's her desk.'

'When's she coming back?'

'Anytime. She went up for coffee.'

'Well, maybe if we hurry we'll be done by then and I'll be out of here.'

She gave a short who-do-you-think-you-are laugh that sounded more like a snort. She said nothing.

'I've spent the last hour and a half trying to get just a couple addresses from the city and all I get are a bunch of people who want to send me to someone else or make me wait out in the hall. And what's funny about that is that I work for the city myself and I'm trying to do a job for the city and the city isn't giving me the time of day. And, you know, my shrink tells me I've got this post-traumatic stress stuff and should take life easier. But, Mona, I gotta tell you, I'm getting pretty fucking frustrated with this.'

She stared at him a moment, probably wondering if she could possibly make it out the door if he decided to go nuts on her. She then pursed her lips, which served to change her mustache from a hint to an announcement, and took a hard pull on the straw of her soda container. Bosch saw a liquid the color of blood go up through the straw into her mouth. She cleared her throat before talking in a comforting tone.

'Tell you what, Detective, why don't you tell me what it is you are trying to find?'

Bosch put on his hopeful face.

'Great. I knew there was somebody who cared. I need to get the addresses where pension checks for two different retired officers are sent each month.'

Her eyebrows mated as she frowned.

'I'm sorry, but those addresses are strictly confidential. Even within the city. I couldn't give –'

'Mona, let me explain something. I'm a homicide

investigator. Like you, I work for the city. I have leads on an old unsolved murder that I am following up on. I need to confer with the original case detectives. We're talking about a case more than thirty years old. A woman was killed, Mona. I can't find the two detectives that originally worked the case and the police personnel people sent me over here. I need the pension addresses. Are you going to help me?'

'Detective – is it Borsch?'

'Bosch.'

'Detective Bosch, let me explain something to you. Just because you work for the city does not give you access to confidential files. I work for the city but I don't go over to Parker Center and say let me see this or let me see that. People have a right to privacy. Now, this is what I can do. And it is all I can do. If you give me the two names, I will send a letter to each person asking them to call you. That way, you get your information, I protect the files. Would that work for you? They'll go out in the mail today. I promise.'

She smiled but it was the phoniest smile Bosch had seen in days.

'No, that wouldn't work at all, Mona. You know, I'm really disappointed.'

'I can't help that.'

'But you can, don't you see?'

'I have work to do, Detective. If you want me to send the letter, give me the names. If not, that's your decision.'

He nodded that he understood and brought his briefcase up from the floor to his lap. He saw her jump when he angrily unsnapped the locks. He opened it and took out his phone. He flipped it open and dialed his home number, then waited for the machine to pick up.

Mona looked annoyed.

'What are you doing?'

He held his hand up for silence.

'Yes, can you transfer me to Whitey Springer?' he said to his tape.

He watched her reaction while acting like he wasn't. He could tell, she knew the name. Springer was the City Hall columnist for the *Times*. His specialty was writing about the small bureaucratic nightmares, the little guy against the system. Bureaucrats could largely create these nightmares with impunity, thanks to civil service protections, but politicians read Springer's column and they wielded tremendous power when it came to patronage jobs, transfers and demotions at City Hall. A bureaucrat vilified in print by Springer might be safe in his or her job but there likely would never be advancement, and there was nothing stopping a city council member from calling for an audit on an office or a council observer to sit in the corner. The word to the wise was to stay out of Springer's column. Everybody knew that, including Mona.

'Yeah, I can hold,' Bosch said into the phone. Then to Mona, he said, 'He's gonna love this one. He's got a guy trying to solve a murder, the victim's family waiting for thirty-three years to know who killed her, and some bureaucrat sitting in her office sucking on a quart of fruit punch isn't giving him the addresses he needs just to talk to the other cops who worked the case. I'm not a newspaper man but I think that's a column. He'll love it. What do you think?'

He smiled and watched her face flush almost as red as her fruit punch. He knew it was going to work.

'Okay, hang up the phone,' she said.

'What? Why?'

'HANG UP! Hang up and I'll get the information.'

Bosch flipped the phone closed.

'Give me the names.'

He gave her the names and she got up angrily and

silently to leave the room. She could barely fit around the desk but made the maneuver like a ballerina, the pattern instilled in her body's memory by repeated practice.

'How long will this take?' he asked.

'As long as it takes,' she answered, regaining some of her bureaucratic bluster at the door.

'No, Mona, you got ten minutes. That's all. After that, you better not come back 'cause Whitey's gonna be sitting here waiting for you.'

She stopped and looked at him. He winked.

After she left he got up and went around the side of the desk. He pushed it about two inches closer to the opposite wall, narrowing her path back to her chair.

She was back in seven minutes, carrying a piece of paper. But Bosch could see it was trouble. She had a triumphant look on her face. He thought of that woman who had been tried a while back for cutting off her husband's penis. Maybe it was the same face she had when she ran out the door with it.

'Well, Detective Borsch, you've got a little problem.'

'What is it?'

She started around the desk and immediately rammed her thick thigh into its Formica-topped corner. It looked more embarrassing than painful. She had to flail her arms for balance and the impact of the collision shook the desk and knocked her container over. The red liquid began leaking out of the straw onto the blotter.

'Shit!'

She quickly moved the rest of the way around the desk and righted the container. Before sitting down she looked at the desk, suspicious that it had been moved.

'Are you all right?' Bosch asked. 'What is the problem with the addresses?'

She ignored his first question, forgot her embarrassment and looked at Bosch and smiled. She sat down. She spoke as she opened a desk drawer and took out a wad of napkins stolen from the cafeteria.

'Well, the problem is you won't be talking to former detective Claude Eno anytime soon. At least, I don't think you will.'

'He's dead.'

She started wiping up the spill.

'Yes. The checks go to his widow.'

'What about McKittrick?'

'Now McKittrick is a possibility. I have his address here. He's over in Venice.'

'Venice? So what's the problem with that?'

'That's Venice, Florida.'

She smiled, delighted with herself.

'Florida,' Bosch repeated.

He had no idea there was a Venice in Florida.

'It's a state, over on the other side of the country.'

'I know where it is.'

'Oh, and one other thing. The address I have is only a P.O. box. Sorry about that.'

'Yeah, I bet. What about a phone?'

She tossed the wet napkins into a trash can in the corner of the room.

'We have no phone number. Try information.'

'I will. Does it say there when he retired?'

'You didn't ask me to get that.'

'Then give me what you've got.'

Bosch knew he could get more, that they'd have to have a phone number somewhere, but he was handicapped because this was an unauthorized investigation. If he pushed things too far, then he'd only succeed in having his activities discovered and then halted.

She floated the paper across the desk to him. He looked at it. It had two addresses on it, the P.O. box for

McKittrick and the street address in Las Vegas for Eno's widow. Her name was Olive.

Bosch thought of something.

'When do the checks go out?'

'Funny you should ask.'

'Why?'

'Because today's the last day of the month. They always go out the last day of the month.'

That was a break and he felt like he deserved it, that he had worked for it. He picked up the paper she had given him and slipped it into his briefcase, then he stood up.

'Always a pleasure to do work with the public servants of the city.'

'Likewise. And, uh, Detective? Could you return the chair to the place you found it? As I said, Cassidy will need it.'

'Of course, Mona. Pardon my forgetfulness.'

After the bout with bureaucratic claustrophobia, Bosch decided he needed some air to recover. He took the elevator down to the lobby and out the main doors to Spring Street. As he walked out, he was directed by a security officer to walk down the right side of the wide-staired entrance to the great building because there was a film location shoot taking place on the left side. Bosch watched what they were doing as he stepped down the stairs and then decided to take a break and have a smoke.

He sat down on one of the concrete sidings along the stairs and lit a cigarette. The film shoot involved a group of actors posing as reporters who rushed down the stairs of City Hall to meet and question two men getting out of a car at the curb. They rehearsed it twice and then shot it twice while Bosch sat there and smoked two cigarettes. Each time, the reporters all yelled the same thing at the two men.

'Mr Barrs, Mr Barrs, did you do it? Did you do it?'

The two men refused to answer and pushed through the pack and up the stairs with the reporters backtracking. On one of the takes one of the reporters stumbled as he moved backwards, fell on his back on the stairs and was partially trampled by the others. The director kept the scene going, perhaps thinking that the fall added a touch of realism to the scene.

Bosch figured that the filmmakers were using the steps

and front facade of City Hall as a courthouse setting. The men coming from the car were the defendant and his high-priced lawyer. He knew that City Hall was frequently used for such shots because it actually looked more like a courthouse than any real courthouse in the city.

Bosch was bored after the second take, though he guessed there would be many more. He got up and walked down to First and then over to Los Angeles Street. He took that back to Parker Center. Along the way he was asked for spare change only four times, which he thought was a low count for downtown and possibly a sign of improving economic times. In the lobby of the police building he passed the bank of pay phones and on a whim stopped, picked one of the phones off the hook and dialed 305-555-1212. He had dealt with Metro-Dade Police in Miami several times over the years and 305 was the only Florida area code that readily came to mind. When the operator came on he asked for Venice and she informed him that 813 was the proper area code.

He then redialed and got information in Venice. First he asked the operator what the nearest large city to Venice was. She told him that was Sarasota and he asked what the nearest large city was to that. When she said St Petersburg, he finally started getting his bearings. He knew where St Petersburg was on a map – the west coast of Florida – because he knew the Dodgers occasionally played spring training games there and he had looked it up once.

He finally gave the operator McKittrick's name and promptly got a tape recording saying the number was unlisted at the customer's request. He wondered if any of the detectives he had dealt with by phone at Metro-Dade could get the number for him. He still had no idea exactly where Venice was or how far it was from Miami. Then he decided to leave it alone. McKittrick had taken steps to make it difficult to be contacted. He used a P.O. box and had an unlisted phone. Bosch didn't know why a retired cop would take such steps in a state three thousand miles away from where he had worked but he felt sure that the best approach to McKittrick was going to have to be in person. A telephone call, even if Bosch got the number, was easy to avoid. Someone standing right at your door was different. Besides, Bosch had caught a break; he knew McKittrick's pension check was in the mail to his P.O. box. He was sure he could use it to find the old cop.

He clipped his ID card to his suit and went up to the Scientific Investigation Division. He told the woman behind the counter that he had to talk to someone in Latent Prints and pushed through the half door and down the hall to the print lab like he always did, without waiting for her go-ahead.

The lab was a large room with two rows of work tables with overhead fluorescent lights. At the end of the room were two desks with AFIS computer terminals on them. Behind them was a glass-walled room with the mainframes inside. There was condensation on the glass because the mainframe room was kept cooler than the rest of the lab.

Because it was lunch time there was only one technician in the lab and Bosch didn't know him. He was tempted to turn around and come back later when someone else might be there, but the tech looked up from one of the computer terminals and saw him. He was a tall, skinny man with glasses and a face that had been ravaged by acne when he was younger. The damage gave him a permanently sullen expression.

'Yes?'

'Yeah, hi, howya doin'?'

'I'm doing fine. What can I do for you?'

'Harry Bosch, Hollywood Division.'

He put out his hand and the other man hesitated, then shook it tentatively.

125

'Brad Hirsch.'

'Yeah, I think I've heard your name. We've never worked together but that probably won't last. I work homicide so it seems I basically get around to working with everybody in here eventually.'

'Probably.'

Bosch sat down on a chair to the side of the computer module and pulled his briefcase onto his lap. He noticed that Hirsch was looking into his blue computer screen. He seemed more comfortable looking there than at Bosch.

'Reason I'm here is, at the moment, it's kind of slow out in Tinseltown. And so I've been going through some old cases. I came across this one from nineteen sixty-one.'

'Nineteen sixty-one?'

'Yeah, it's old. A female ... cause of death blunt force trauma, then he made it look like a strangulation, a sex crime. Anyway, nobody was ever popped for it. It never went anywhere. In fact, I don't think anyone's really looked at it since the due diligence in sixty-two. A long time. Anyway, the thing is, the reason I'm here, is that back then the cops on this pulled a decent set of prints at the crime scene. They got a bunch of partials and some full rounds. And I've got them here.'

Bosch took the yellowed print card out of the briefcase and held it out to the man. Hirsch looked at it but didn't take it. He looked back at the computer screen and Bosch placed the print card down on the keyboard in front of him.

'And, well, as you know, that was before we had these fancy computers and all of this technology you got here. All they did with this back then was use it to compare these to a suspect's prints. They got no match, they let the guy go and then they just shoved these in an envelope. They've been sitting in the case file ever since. So what I was thinking was, we could –'

'You want to run them through AFIS.'

'Yeah, right. You know, take a shot at it. Spin the dice, maybe we get lucky and pick up a hitchhiker on the information highway. It's happened before. Edgar and Burns out on the Hollywood table nailed an old one this week with an AFIS run. I was talking to Edgar and he said one of you guys down here – I think it was Donovan – said the computer has access to millions of prints from all across the country.'

Hirsch nodded unenthusiastically.

'And that's not just criminal print files, right?' Bosch asked. 'You've got military, law enforcement, civil service, everything. That right?'

'Yes, that's right. But, look, Detective Bosch, we –'

'Harry.'

'Okay, Harry. This is a great tool that's getting better all the time. You're correct about that but there still are human and time elements here. The comparison prints have to be scanned and coded and then those codes have to be entered into the computer. And right now we have a backup that's running twelve days.'

He pointed to the wall above the computer. There was a sign with changeable numbers on it. Like the signs in the union office that said X number of days since the last death in the line of duty.

AUTOMATED FINGERPRINT IDENTIFICATION SYSTEM
Search Requests Will Take 12 Days To Process
No Exception!

'So, you see, we can't take everybody who walks in here and put them at the front of the pack, okay? Now if you want to fill out a search request form, I can –'

'Look, I know there are exceptions. Especially in homicide cases. Somebody made that run for Burns and Edgar the other day. They didn't wait twelve days. They were put through right away and they cleared three homicides just like that.'

Bosch snapped his fingers. Hirsch looked at him and then back to the computer.

'Yes, there are exceptions. But that comes from on high. If you want to talk to Captain LeValley, maybe she'll approve it. If you –'

'Burns and Edgar didn't talk to her. Somebody just did it for them.'

'Well, then that was against the rules. They must have known somebody who did it for them.'

'Well, I know you, Hirsch.'

'Why don't you just fill out a request and I'll see what –'

'I mean, what's it take, ten minutes?'

'No. In your case much longer. This print card you have is an antique. It's obsolete. I'd have to run it through the Livescan machine, which would then assign codes to the prints. Then I'd have to hand-enter the codes it gives me. Then depending on the restrictions on the run you want, it could take –'

'I don't want any restrictions. I want it compared to all data bases.'

'Then the computer time can run as long as thirty, forty minutes.'

With a finger Hirsch punched his glasses back up his nose as if punctuating his resolve not to break the rules.

'Well, Brad,' Bosch said, 'the problem is I don't know how much time I've got on this. Certainly not twelve days. No way. I'm working on it now because I have the time, but the next time I get a fresh call that will be it, I'll be off it. That's the nature of homicide, you know? So, are you sure there isn't something we can do right now?'

Hirsch didn't move. He just stared at the blue screen. It reminded Bosch of the youth hall, when kids would literally shut down like a computer on standby when the bullies taunted them.

'What are you doing now, Hirsch? We could do it right now.'

Hirsch looked at him for a long moment before talking.

'I'm busy. And look, Bosch, I know who you are, okay? That's an interesting story about pulling old cases but I know it's a lie. I know you're on a stress leave. The story's getting around. And you shouldn't even be here and I shouldn't be talking to you. So, could you please leave me alone? I don't want to get into trouble. I don't want people to get the wrong idea, you know?'

Bosch looked at him but Hirsch's eyes had moved back onto the computer screen.

'Okay, Hirsch, let me tell you a real story. One –'

'I really don't want any more stories, Bosch. Why don't you just –'

'I'm going to tell you this story, then I'm leaving, okay? Just this one story.'

'Okay, Bosch, okay. You tell the story.'

Bosch looked at him silently and waited for Hirsch to make eye contact but the latent print technician's eyes remained on the computer screen as if it were his security blanket. Bosch told the story anyway.

'One time, a long time ago, I was almost twelve and I'm swimming in this pool, you see, and I'm under the water but I've got my eyes open. And I look up and I see up through the water up to the edge of the pool. I see this dark figure. You know, it was hard to figure out what it was, all wavy and all. But I could tell it was a man and there wasn't supposed to be a man up there. So I came up for air at the side of the pool and I was right. It was a man. He was wearing this dark suit. And he reached down and grabbed me by the wrist. I was just a scrawny little runt. It was easy for him to do. He pulled me out and he gave me this towel to put on my shoulders and he led me over to a chair and he told me … he told me that my mother was dead. Murdered. He said they didn't know who did it, but whoever he was, he left his fingerprints. He said, "Don't worry, son, we got the fingerprints and they're as good as gold. We'll get him." I remember those words exactly. "We'll get him." Only they never did. And now I'm going to. That's my story, Hirsch.'

Hirsch's eyes dropped down to the yellowed print card on the keyboard.

'Look, man, it's a bad story, but I can't be doing this. I'm sorry.'

Bosch stared at him a moment and then slowly stood up.

'Don't forget the card,' Hirsch said.

He picked it up and held it up to Bosch.

'I'll leave it here. You're going to do the right thing, Hirsch. I can tell.'

'No, don't. I can't do –'

'*I'm leaving it here!*'

The power of his voice shocked even Bosch and it seemed to have scared Hirsch. The print tech replaced the card on the keyboard. After a few seconds of silence Bosch leaned down and spoke quietly.

'Everybody wants the chance to do the right thing, Hirsch. It makes them feel good inside. Even if doing it doesn't exactly fit inside the rules, sometimes you have to rely on the voice inside that tells you what to do.'

Bosch stood back up and took out his wallet and a pen. He pulled out a business card and wrote some numbers on it. He put it down on the keyboard next to the print card.

'That's got my portable and my home on it. Don't bother calling the office, you know I won't be there. I'll be waiting to hear from you, Hirsch.'

He walked slowly out of the lab.

W aiting for the elevator, Bosch guessed that his effort to persuade Hirsch had fallen on deaf ears. Hirsch was the type of guy whose exterior scars masked deeper interior wounds. There were a lot in the department like him. Hirsch had grown up intimidated by his own face. He'd probably be the last person to dare go outside the bounds of his job or the rules. Another department automaton. For him, doing the right thing was ignoring Bosch. Or turning him in.

He punched at the elevator button with his finger again and contemplated what else he could do. The AFIS search was a long shot but he still wanted it done. It was a loose end and any thorough investigation took care of loose ends. He decided he would give Hirsch a day and then he'd make another run at him. If that didn't work, he'd try another tech. He'd try them all until he got the killer's prints into that machine.

The elevator finally opened and he squeezed on. That was one of the only things you could rely on inside Parker Center. Cops would come and go, chiefs, even political power structures, but the elevators would always move slowly and always be crowded when they got to you. Bosch pushed the unlighted button marked B as the doors slowly closed and the square room started to descend. While everyone stood and stared blankly at the lighted numbers over the door, Bosch looked down at his briefcase. No one in the small space spoke. Until, as the car slowed to its next stop, Bosch heard his first name spoken from behind. He turned his head slightly, not sure if it had been someone speaking to him or the name had been directed toward someone else.

His eyes fell on Assistant Chief Irvin S. Irving standing in the rear of the elevator. They exchanged nods just as the doors opened on the first floor. Bosch wondered if Irving had seen him push the button for the basement. There was no reason for a man on involuntary stress leave to be going to the basement.

Bosch decided the car was too crowded for Irving to have seen what button he had pushed. He stepped off the elevator into the alcove off the main lobby and Irving followed him out and caught up with him.

'Chief.'

'What brings you all the way in, Harry?'

It was said casually but the question signaled that there was more than passing interest from Irving. They started walking toward the exit, Bosch quickly putting a story together.

'I have to go over to Chinatown anyway, so I dropped by to go to payroll. I wanted to see about them sending my check to my house instead of out to Hollywood, since I'm not sure when I'll be back.'

Irving nodded and Bosch was pretty sure he had bought it. He was about Bosch's size but had the stand-out feature of a completely shaved head. That feature and his reputation for intolerance for corrupt cops got him the nickname within the department of Mr Clean.

'You're in Chinatown today? I thought you were Monday, Wednesday, Friday. That was the schedule I approved.'

'Yes, that's the schedule. But she had an opening come up today and wanted me to come in.'

'Well, I'm glad to hear you being so cooperative. What happened to your hand?'

'Oh, this?' Bosch held up his hand as if it were someone else's that he had just noticed at the end of his arm. 'I've been using some of my free time to do some work around the house and I cut it on a piece of broken glass. I'm still doing clean-up from the quake.'

'I see.'

Bosch guessed that he didn't buy that one. But he didn't really care.

'I'm getting a quick lunch in the federal plaza,' Irving said. 'You want to come along?'

'Thanks just the same, Chief. I already ate.'

'Okay, well, take care of yourself. I mean that.'

'I will. Thanks.'

Irving started off and then stopped.

'You know, we're handling this situation with you a little differently because I hope to get you back in there at Hollywood homicide without any change in grade or position. I'm waiting to hear from Dr Hinojos but I understand it will be a few more weeks, at least.'

'That's what she tells me.'

'You know, if you're willing to do it, an apology in the form of a letter to Lieutenant Pounds could be beneficial. When push comes to shove, I'm going to have to sell him on letting you back in there. That will be the hard part. I think getting you a clean bill from the doctor won't be a problem. I can simply issue the order and Lieutenant Pounds will have to accept it, but that won't ease the pressure there. I would rather work it that he accepts your return and everybody's happy.'

'Well, I heard he already's got a replacement for me.'

'Pounds?'

'He paired my partner with somebody off autos.

133

Doesn't sound to me like he's expecting or planning on me coming back, Chief.'

'Well, that's news to me. I'll talk to him about that. What do you think about this letter? It could go a long way toward helping your situation.'

Bosch hesitated before answering. He knew Irving wanted to help him. The two of them shared an unspoken bond. Once they had been complete enemies in the department. But contempt had eroded into a truce which now was more a line of wary mutual respect.

'I'll think about the letter, Chief,' Bosch finally said. 'I'll let you know.'

'Very well. You know, Harry, pride gets in the way of a lot of the right decisions. Don't let that happen to you.'

'I'll think about it.'

Bosch watched him bound off around the fountain memorial to officers killed in the line of duty. He watched until Irving got to Temple and started to cross Los Angeles Street to the federal plaza, where there was an array of fast-food emporiums. Then Bosch figured it was safe and turned to go back inside.

He skipped waiting for the elevator again and went down the stairs to the basement.

Most of the underground floor of Parker Center was taken up by the Evidence Storage Division. There were a few other offices, like the Fugitives Division, but it was generally a quiet floor. Bosch found no pedestrian traffic on the long yellow linoleum hallway and was able to get to the steel double doors of ESD without running into anyone else he knew.

The police department held physical evidence on investigations that had not yet gone to the district attorney or city attorney for filing. Once that happened, the evidence usually stayed with the prosecutor's office.

Essentially, that made ESD the city's temple of failure.

What was behind the steel doors Bosch opened was the physical evidence from thousands of unsolved crimes. Crimes that had never resulted in prosecution. It even smelled of failure. Because it was in the basement of the building, there was a damp odor here that Bosch always believed was the rank stink of neglect and decay. Of hopelessness.

Bosch stepped into a small room that was essentially a wire-mesh cage. There was another door on the other side but there was a sign on it that said ESD STAFF ONLY. There were two windows cut in the mesh. One was closed and a uniform officer sat behind the other working on a crossword puzzle. Between the two windows was another sign that said DO NOT STORE LOADED FIREARMS. Bosch walked up to the open window and leaned on the counter. The officer looked up after filling in a word on the puzzle. Bosch saw the name tag on his uniform said Nelson. Nelson read Bosch's ID card so Bosch didn't have to bother to introduce himself, either. It worked out nicely.

'Her ... on – how you say that?'

'Hieronymus. Rhymes with anonymous.'

'Hieronymus. Isn't there a rock and roll band named that?'

'Maybe.'

'What can I do for you, Hieronymus from Hollywood?'

'I got a question.'

'Shoot.'

Bosch put the pink evidence check slip on the counter.

'I want to pull the box on this case. It's pretty old. Would it still be around anywhere?'

The cop took the slip, looked at it and whistled when he saw the year. While writing the case number down on a request log, he said, 'Should be here. Don't see why not. Nothing gets tossed, you know. You want to look at the

135

Black Dahlia case, we got that. That's what, fifty-something years old. We got 'em going back even further. If it ain't solved, it's here.'

He looked up at Bosch and winked.

'Be right back. Why don't you fill out the form.'

Nelson pointed with his pen out the window to a counter on the back wall where the standard request forms were. He got up and disappeared from the window. Bosch heard him yell to someone else in the back.

'Charlie! Hey, Char-LEE!'

A voice from somewhere in the back yelled a response that was unintelligible.

'Take the window,' Nelson called back. 'I'm taking the time machine.'

Bosch had heard about the time machine. It was a golf cart they used to get back to the deep recesses of the storage facility. The older the case, the farther back in time it went, the farther away it was from the front windows. The time machine got the window cops back there.

Bosch walked over to the counter and filled out a request form, then reached in the window and put it on the crossword puzzle. While he was waiting, he looked around and noticed another sign on the back wall. NARCOTICS EVIDENCE NOT RELEASED WITHOUT 492 FORM. Bosch had no idea what that form was. Somebody came through the steel doors then carrying a murder book. A detective, but Bosch didn't recognize him. He opened it on the counter, got a case number and then filled out a form. He then went to the window. There was no sign of Charlie. After a few minutes, the detective turned to Bosch.

'Anybody working back there?'

'Yeah, one guy went to get me a box. He told another guy to watch. I don't know where he is.'

'Shit.'

He rapped sharply with his knuckles on the counter. In a few minutes another uniform cop came to the window. He was an old horse, with white hair and a pear shape. Bosch guessed he'd been working in the basement for years. His skin was as white as a vampire's. He took the other detective's evidence request slip and was gone. Then both Bosch and the other detective were left waiting. Bosch could tell the other man had started looking at him but was acting like he wasn't.

'You're Bosch, right?' he finally asked. 'From Hollywood?'

Bosch nodded. The other man put out his hand and smiled.

'Tom North, Pacific. We've never met.'

'No.'

Bosch shook his hand but didn't act enthusiastic about the introduction.

'We never met but listen, I worked Devonshire burglary for six years before I got my homicide gig in Pacific. Know who my CO was up there back then?'

Bosch shook his head. He didn't know and he didn't care but North didn't seem to realize that.

'Pounds. Lieutenant Harvey "Ninety-eight" Pounds. The fuck. He was my CO. So, anyway, I heard through the network, you know, what you did to his ass. Put his face right through the fuckin' window. That's great, man, fuckin' great. More power to you. I laughed my ass off when I heard that.'

'Well, I'm glad it entertained you.'

'No, really, I know you're getting piped for it. I heard about that, too. But I just wanted to let you know you made my day and a lot of people are with you, man.'

'Thanks.'

'So what are you doing down here? I heard they had you on the Fifty-One-Fifty list.'

It annoyed Bosch to realize that there were those in the department whom he didn't even know who knew what had happened to him and what his situation was. He tried to keep calm.

'Listen, I –'

'Bosch! You gotta box!'

It was the time traveler, Nelson. He was at the window, pushing a light blue box through the opening. It was about the size of a boot box and was held closed with red tape that was cracking with age. It looked like the box was powdered with dust. Bosch didn't bother finishing his sentence. He waved off North and went to the box.

'Sign here,' Nelson said.

He put a yellow slip down on top of the box. It kicked up a small dust cloud, which he waved away with his hand. Bosch signed the paper and took the box in two hands. He turned and saw North looking at him. North just nodded once. He seemed to know it wasn't the right time to ask questions. Bosch nodded back and headed to the door.

'Uh, Bosch?' North said. 'I didn't mean anything about what I said. About the list. No offense, okay?'

Bosch stared at him as he pushed through the door with his back. But he didn't say anything. He then proceeded down the hall carrying the box with two hands, as if it contained something precious.

Carmen Hinojos was in her waiting room when Bosch got there a few minutes late. She ushered him in and waved off his apology for lateness as if it was unnecessary. She wore a dark blue suit and as he passed her in the doorway he smelled a light soapy fragrance. He took the seat on the right side of the desk near the window again.

Hinojos smiled and Bosch wondered why. There were two chairs on the other side of the desk from her. So far, in three meetings, he had taken the same one each time. The one closest to the window. He wondered if she had taken note of this and what, if anything, it meant.

'Are you tired?' she asked. 'You don't look like you got much sleep last night.'

'I guess I didn't. But I'm fine.'

'Have you changed your mind about anything we discussed yesterday?'

'No, not really.'

'You are continuing this private investigation?'

'For now.'

She nodded in a way that told him she expected his reply.

'I want to talk about your mother today.'

'Why? It's got nothing to do with why I'm here, why I'm on leave.'

'I think it's important. I think it will help us get to what

139

is happening with you, what has made you take on this private investigation of yours. It might explain a lot about your recent actions.'

'I doubt it. What do you want to know?'

'When you spoke yesterday, you made several references to her lifestyle, but you never really came out and said what she did, what she was. Thinking about it after the session, I was wondering if you have trouble accepting what she was. To the point of not being able to say she –'

'Was a prostitute? There, I said it. She was a prostitute. I'm a grown man, Doctor. I accept the truth. I accept the truth in anything as long as it's the truth. I think you're going far afield here.'

'Perhaps. What do you feel about her now?'

'What do you mean?'

'Anger? Hatred? Love?'

'I don't think about it. Certainly not hate. I loved her at the time. After she was gone that didn't change.'

'What about abandonment?'

'I'm too old for that.'

'What about back then? Back when it happened.'

Bosch thought a moment.

'I'm sure there was some of that. Her lifestyle, her line of work, got her killed. And I was left behind the fence. I guess I was mad about that and felt abandoned. I was also hurt. The hurt was the worst part. She loved me.'

'What do you mean, left behind the fence?'

'I told you yesterday. I was in McClaren, the youth hall.'

'Right. So her death prevented you from leaving there, correct?'

'For a while.'

'How long?'

'I was there on and off until I was sixteen. I lived a few months two different times with some fosters but I always got sent back. Then, when I was sixteen, another couple took me. I was with them until I was seventeen. I found out later that they kept getting the DPSS checks for a year after I'd split.'

'DPSS?'

'Department of Public Social Services. Now they call it the Division of Youth Services. Anyway, when you took a kid into your home as foster parents, you got a monthly support payment. A lot of people took kids in just for those checks. I'm not saying these people did, but they never told DPSS I wasn't in their home anymore after I left.'

'I understand. Where were you?'

'Vietnam.'

'Wait a minute, let's go back. You said that two different times before this you lived with foster parents but were then sent back. What happened? Why were you sent back?'

'I don't know. They didn't like me. They said it wasn't working out. I went back into the dorms behind the fence and waited. I think getting rid of a teenage boy was about as easy as selling a car with no wheels. The fosters always wanted the younger ones.'

'Did you ever run away from the hall?'

'A couple times. I always got caught in Hollywood.'

'If placing teenagers was so difficult, how did it happen to you the third time, when you were even older, sixteen?'

Bosch laughed falsely and shook his head.

'You'll get a kick out of this. I was chosen by this guy and his wife because I was left-handed.'

'Left-handed? I don't follow.'

'I was a lefty and I could throw a pretty good fastball.'

'What do you mean?'

'Ah, Jesus, it was – see, Sandy Koufax was with the Dodgers then. He was a lefty and I guess they were paying him about a zillion bucks a year to pitch. This guy, the foster, his name was Earl Morse, he had played semipro baseball or something and never really made it. So, he wanted to *create* a left-handed major league prospect. Good left-handers were pretty rare back then, I guess. Or he thought that. Anyway, they were the hot commodity. Earl thought he'd grab some kid with some potential, slap him into shape and then be his manager or agent or something when it came to contract time. He saw it as his way back into the game. It was crazy. But I guess he'd seen his own big league dream crash and burn. So he came out to McClaren and took a bunch of us into the field for a catch. We had a team, we played other halls, sometimes the schools in the Valley let us play them. Anyway, Earl took us out to throw the ball around and it was a tryout but none of us knew it at the time. It didn't even enter my mind what was going on until later. Anyway, he glommed on to me when he saw I was a lefty and could throw. He forgot the others like they were last season's program.'

Bosch shook his head again at the memory.

'What happened? You went with him?'

'Yeah. I went with him. There was a wife, too. She never said much to me or him. He used to make me throw a hundred balls a day at a tire hanging in the backyard. Then every night he'd have these coaching sessions. I put up with it for about a year and then I split.'

'You ran away?'

'Sort of. I joined the Army. I had to get Earl to sign for me, though. At first he wouldn't do it. He had major league plans for me. But then I told him I was never going to pick up another baseball as long as I lived. He signed. Then he and the wife kept cashing those DPSS checks while I was overseas. I guess the extra money helped make up for losing the prospect.'

She was quiet for a long time. It looked to Bosch like

142

she was reading her notes but he had not seen her write anything during this session.

'You know,' he said into the silence, 'about ten years later, when I was still in patrol, I pulled over a drunk driver coming off the Hollywood Freeway onto Sunset. He was all over the place. When I finally got him over and got up there to the window, I bent over to look in and it was Earl. It was a Sunday. He was coming home from the Dodgers. I saw the program on the seat.'

She looked at him but didn't say anything. He was looking at the memory still.

'I guess he'd never found that lefty he was looking for ... Anyway, he was so drunk he didn't recognize me.'

'What did you do?'

'Took his keys and called his wife ... I guess it was the only break I ever gave the guy.'

She looked back down at the pad while asking her next question.

'What about your real father?'

'What about him?'

'Did you ever know who he was? Did you have any relationship at all?'

'I met him once. I was never curious about it until I came back from overseas. Then I traced it down. Turned out he was my mother's lawyer. He had a family and all of that. He was dying when I met him, looked like a skeleton ... So I never really knew him.'

'His name was Bosch?'

'No. My name was just something she came up with. The painter, you know. She thought LA was a lot like his paintings. All the paranoia, the fear. Once she gave me a book that had his paintings in it.'

More silence followed as she thought about this one, too.

'These stories, Harry,' she finally said, 'these stories that you tell are heartbreaking in their own way. It makes me see the boy who became the man. It makes me see the depth of the hole left by your mother's death. You know, you would have a lot to blame her for and no one would blame you for doing it.'

He looked at her pointedly while composing a response.

'I don't blame her for anything. I blame the man who took her from me. See, these are stories about me. Not her. You can't get the feel for her. You can't know her like I did. All I know is that she did all she could to get me out of there. She never stopped telling me that. She never stopped trying. She just ran out of time.'

She nodded, accepting his answer. A few moments passed.

'Did there come a time when she told you what she did … for a living?'

'Not really.'

'How did you know?'

'I can't remember. I think I really didn't know for sure what she did until she was gone and I was older. I was ten when they took me away. I didn't really know why.'

'Did she have men stay with her while you were together?'

'No, that never happened.'

'But you must have had some idea about this life she was leading, that you both were leading.'

'She told me she was a waitress. She worked nights. She used to leave me with a lady who had a room at the hotel. Mrs DeTorre. She watched four or five kids whose mothers were doing the same thing. None of us knew.'

He finished there but she didn't say anything and he knew he was expected to continue.

'One night I snuck out when the old lady fell asleep and I walked down to the Boulevard to the coffee shop where she said she worked. She wasn't in there. I asked and they didn't know what I was talking about ...'

'Did you ask your mother about it?'

'No ... The next night I followed her. She left in her waitress uniform and I followed her. She went to her best friend's place upstairs. Meredith Roman. When they came out, they were both wearing dresses, makeup, the whole thing. Then they both left in a cab and I couldn't follow them.'

'But you knew.'

'I knew something. But I was like nine or something. How much could I know?'

'What about the charade she followed, dressing every night like a waitress, did that anger you?'

'No. The opposite. I thought that was ... I don't know, there was something noble about her doing that for me. She was protecting me, in a way.'

Hinojos nodded that she saw his point.

'Close your eyes.'

'Close my eyes?'

'Yes, I want you to close your eyes and think back to when you were a boy. Go ahead.'

'What is this?'

'Indulge me. Please.'

Bosch shook his head as if annoyed but did as she asked. He felt stupid.

'Okay.'

'Okay, I want you to tell me a story about your mother. Whatever image or episode with her that you have the clearest in your mind, I want you to tell it to me.'

He thought hard. Images of her passed through and disappeared. Finally, he came to one that stayed.

'Okay.'

'Okay, tell it.'

'It was at McClaren. She had come to visit and we were out at the fence at the ballfield.'

'Why do you remember this story?'

'I don't know. Because she was there and that always made me feel good, even though we always ended up crying. You should have seen that place on visiting day. Everybody crying ... And I remember it, too, because it was near the end. It wasn't too long after that she was gone. Maybe a few months.'

'Do you remember what you talked about?'

'A lot of stuff. Baseball, she was a Dodgers fan. I remember one of the older kids had taken my new sneakers that she had given me for my birthday. She noticed I didn't have 'em on and she got pretty mad about it.'

'Why did the older boy take your sneakers?'

'She asked the same thing.'

'What did you tell her?'

'I told her the kid took my shoes because he could. You see, they could call that place whatever they wanted but basically it was a prison for kids and it had the same societies as a prison has. Your dominant cliques, your submissives, everything.'

'What were you?'

'I don't know. I pretty much kept to myself. But when some older, bigger kid took my shoes, I was a submissive. It was a way of surviving.'

'Your mother was unhappy about this?'

'Well, yeah, but she didn't know the score. She wanted to go complain or something. She didn't know that if she did that it would only make it worse for me there. Then she suddenly did realize what the deal was. She started crying.'

Bosch was silent, picturing the scene perfectly in his

mind. He remembered the dampness in the air and the smell of the orange blossoms from the nearby groves.

Hinojos cleared her throat before breaking into his memory.

'What did you do when she started crying?'

'I probably started crying, too. I usually did. I didn't want her to feel bad but there was a comfort in knowing she knew what was happening to me. Only mothers can do that, you know? Make you feel good when you're sad ...'

Bosch still had his eyes closed and was seeing only the memory.

'What did she tell you?'

'She ... she just told me she was going to get me out. She said that her lawyer was going to go to court soon to appeal the custody ruling and the unfit mother finding. She said there were other things she could do, too. The point was, she was getting me out.'

'That lawyer was your father?'

'Yes, but I didn't know it ... Anyway, what I'm saying is that the courts were wrong about her. That's the thing that bothers me. She was good to me and they didn't see that ... anyway, I remember she promised me that she would do what she had to do, but she would get me out.'

'But she never did.'

'No. Like I said, she ran out of time.'

'I'm sorry.'

Bosch opened his eyes and looked at her.

'So am I.'

Bosch had parked in a public lot off Hill Street. It cost him twelve dollars for his car. He then got onto the 101 and headed north toward the hills. As he drove, he occasionally looked over at the blue box on the seat next to him. But he didn't open it. He knew that he had to but he would wait for home.

He turned the radio on and listened as the DJ introduced a song by Abbey Lincoln. Bosch had never heard it before but he immediately liked the words and the woman's smoky voice.

> Bird alone, flying high
> Flying through a clouded sky
> Sending mournful, soulful sounds
> Soaring over troubled grounds

After he got to Woodrow Wilson and followed his usual routine of parking a half block away from his home, Bosch brought the box inside and placed it on the dining room table. He lit a cigarette and paced the room, looking down occasionally at the box. He knew what was in it. He had the evidence list from the murder book. But he couldn't overcome a feeling that by opening the box he was invading some secret privacy, committing a sin that he didn't understand.

Finally, he took his keys out. There was a small pen knife on the ring and he used it to slice through the red tape that sealed the box. He put the knife down and without thinking about it any further lifted the top off the box.

The victim's clothes and other belongings were wrapped individually in plastic bags, which Bosch took out of the box one by one and placed on the table. The clear plastic was yellowed but he could see through it. He did not remove anything from the bags but instead just held each piece of evidence up and studied it in its sterile covering.

He opened the murder book to the evidence list and made sure nothing was missing. It was all there. He held the small bag containing the gold earrings up to the light. They were like frozen tear drops. He put the bag back down and at the bottom of the box he saw the blouse, folded neatly in plastic, the spot of blood exactly where the evidence sheet said it was, on the left breast, about two inches from the center button.

Bosch ran his finger over the plastic where the spot was. It was then that he realized something. There was no other blood. He knew that it was the thing that had bothered him as he read the murder book but he had been unable to get ahold of the thought then. Now he had it. The blood. No blood on the undergarments, the skirt or the stockings, or pumps. Only on the blouse.

Bosch also knew the autopsy had described a body with no lacerations. Then where had the blood come from? He wanted to look at the crime scene and autopsy photos but knew that he couldn't. There was no way he would open that envelope.

Bosch pulled the bag containing the blouse from the box and read the evidence tag and other markings. Nowhere did it mention or give any reference code for any analysis ever being done on the blood.

This invigorated him. There was a good chance that the

blood spot came from the killer, not the victim. He had no idea whether blood that old could still be typed or even submitted for DNA analysis but he intended to find out. The problem, he knew, was comparison. It didn't matter if the blood could still be analyzed if there was nothing to compare it to. To get blood from Conklin or Mittel or anyone, for that matter, he would need a court order. And to get that, he needed evidence. Not just suspicions and hunches.

He had gathered the evidence bags together to replace in the box when he stopped to study one he had not considered closely before. It contained the belt that had been used to strangle the victim.

Bosch studied it a few moments as if it were a snake he was trying to identify before cautiously reaching into the box and picking it up. He could see the evidence tag tied through one of the belt holes. On the smooth silver sea shell buckle there was black powder. He could see that part of the ridge lines from a thumbprint were still there.

He held the belt up to the light. It pained him to look at it but he did. The belt was an inch in width, made of black leather. The sea shell buckle was the largest ornamentation but smaller silver shells were attached along its length. Looking at it brought back the memory. He hadn't really chosen it. Meredith Roman had taken him to the May Co. on Wilshire. She had seen the belt on a rack with many others and told him his mother would like it. She paid for it and allowed him to give it to his mother as a birthday present. Meredith had been right. His mother wore the belt often, including every time she visited him after the court took him away. And including the night she was murdered.

Bosch read the evidence tag but all it said was the case number and McKittrick's name. On the tongue he noticed that the second and fourth holes were imperfect circles, distended by the spoke of the buckle during wear. He guessed that maybe his mother wore it tighter at times, maybe to impress someone, or looser at times, over bulkier clothing. He now knew everything about the belt except who had used it last to kill her.

He realized then that whoever had held this belt, this weapon, before the police had been responsible for taking a life and indelibly changing his own. He carefully replaced it in the box and put the other clothing in on top of it. He then put the lid back on top.

Bosch couldn't stay in the house after that. He felt he had to get out. He didn't bother changing his clothes. He just got in the Mustang and started driving. It was dark now and he took Cahuenga down into Hollywood. He told himself he didn't know or care where he was going but that was a lie. He knew. When he got to Hollywood Boulevard he turned east.

The car took him to Vista, where he turned north and then cut into the first alley. The headlights sliced through the darkness and he saw a small homeless encampment. A man and woman huddled under a cardboard lean-to. Two other bodies, wrapped in blankets and newspapers, lay nearby. A small glow from dying flames came from the rim of a trash can. Bosch cruised by slowly, his eyes further down the alley, to the spot he knew from the crime scene drawing that was in the murder book.

The Hollywood souvenir store was now an adult book and video store. There was an alley entrance for shy customers and several cars were parked alongside the rear of the building. Bosch stopped near the door and killed the lights. He just sat in the car, feeling no need to get out. He had never been to the alley, to the spot, before. He just wanted to sit and watch and feel for a few moments.

He lit a cigarette and watched as a man carrying a bag

walked quickly out the door of the adult shop to a car parked at the end of the alley.

Bosch thought about a time when he was a small boy and still with his mother. They'd had a small apartment on Camrose then and during the summer they'd sit in the back courtyard on the nights she wasn't working or on Sunday afternoons and listen to the music coming over the hill from the Hollywood Bowl. The sound was bad, attacked by traffic and the white noise of the city before it got to them, but the high notes were clear. What he liked about it wasn't the music but that she was there. It was their time together. She always told him that she would take him one day to the bowl to hear 'Scheherazade.' It was her favorite. They never got the chance. The court took him away from her and she was dead before she could get him back.

Bosch finally heard the philharmonic perform 'Scheherazade' the year he spent with Sylvia. When she saw tears welling in the corners of his eyes, she thought it was because of the pure beauty of the music. He never got around to telling her it was something else.

A blur of motion caught his attention and someone banged a fist on the driver's side window. Bosch's left hand instinctively went under his jacket to his waist, but there was no gun there. He turned and looked into the face of an old woman whose years were etched like hash marks on her face. It looked like she was wearing three sets of clothes. When she was done knocking on the window, she opened her palm and held it out. Still startled, Bosch quickly reached into his pocket and pulled out a five. He started the car so he could put the window down and handed the money out to her. She said nothing. She just took it and walked away. Bosch watched her go and wondered how had she ended up in this alley. How had he?

Bosch drove out of the alley and back out to Hollywood Boulevard. He started cruising again. At first aimlessly but soon he found his purpose. He wasn't yet ready to confront Conklin or Mittel but he knew where they were and he wanted to see their homes, their lives, the places they had ended up.

He stayed on the Boulevard until Alvarado and then took that down to Third, where he started west. The drive took him from the Third World poverty of the area known as Little Salvador past the faded mansions of Hancock Park and then to Park La Brea, a huge complex of apartments, condominiums and attendant rest homes.

Bosch found Ogden Drive and cruised slowly down it until he saw the Park La Brea Lifecare Center. There's another irony, he thought. Lifecare. The only thing the place probably cared about was when you were going to die, so your space could be sold to the next one.

It was a nondescript twelve-story building of concrete and glass. Through the glass facade of the lobby Bosch could see a security guard at a post. In this town, even the elderly and infirm weren't safe. He glanced up the front of the building and saw most of the windows were dark. Only nine o'clock and the place was already dead. Someone honked at him from behind and he sped up and away, thinking about Conklin and what his life might be like. He wondered if the old man in his room up there ever gave a thought to Marjorie Lowe after so many years.

Bosch's next stop was Mount Olympus, the gaudy outcropping of modern Roman-style homes above Hollywood. The look was supposed to be neoclassical but he had heard it referred to more than once as neo*crassical*. The huge, expensive homes were jammed side by side as close as teeth. There were ornate columns and statues but the only thing that seemed classic about most of the place was the kitsch. Bosch took Mount Olympus Drive off Laurel

153

Canyon, turned on Electra and then went to Hercules. He was driving slowly, looking for addresses on curbs to match the one he had written in his notebook that morning.

When he found Mittel's house, he stopped on the street, stunned. It was a house that he knew. He had never been inside it, of course, but everyone knew it. It was a circular mansion that sat atop one of the most recognizable promontories in the Hollywood Hills. Bosch looked at the place with awe, imagining its interior size and its exterior ocean-to-mountain views. Its rounded walls lit from the outside with white lights, it looked like a spaceship that had alighted on a mountaintop and was poised to take to the air once again. Classic kitsch it wasn't. This was a home that bespoke its owner's power and influence.

An iron gate guarded a long driveway that went up a hill to the house. But tonight the gate was open and Bosch could see several cars and at least three limousines parked along one side of the drive. Other cars were parked in the circle at the top. It only dawned on Bosch that there was a party underway at the house when a red blur passed the car window and the door was suddenly sprung open. Bosch turned and looked into the face of a swarthy Latino man in a white shirt and red vest.

'Good evening, sir. We will take your car here. If you could walk up the drive on the left side, the greeters will find you.'

Bosch stared at the man unmoving, thinking.

'Sir?'

Bosch tentatively stepped out of the Mustang and the man in the vest gave him a slip of paper with a number on it. He then slipped into the car and drove away. Bosch stood there, aware that he was about to let events control him, something he knew he should avoid. He hesitated and looked back at the tail lights of the Mustang gliding away. He let the temptation take him.

Bosch fastened his top button and pulled his tie back into place as he walked up the driveway. He passed a small army of men in red vests and as he came all the way up past the limousines, a startling view of the lighted city came into view. He stopped and just looked for a moment. He could see from the moonlit Pacific in one direction to the towers of downtown in the other. The view alone was worth the price of the house, no matter how many millions that was.

The sound of soft music, laughter and conversation came from his left. He followed it down a stone path that curved along the form of the house. The drop-off to the houses down the hill was steep and deadly. He finally came to a flat yard that was lighted and full of people milling about beneath a tent as white as the moon. Bosch guessed there were at least a hundred and fifty well-dressed people sipping cocktails and taking small hors d'oeuvres off trays carried by young women wearing short black dresses, sheer stockings and white aprons. He wondered where the red vests were putting all the cars.

Bosch immediately felt underdressed and was sure he would be identified in seconds as a gate-crasher. But there was something so otherworldly about the scene that he held his ground.

A surfer in a suit approached him. He was about twenty-five, with short, sun-bleached hair and a dark tan. He wore a custom-fitted suit that looked as if it had cost more than every piece of clothing Bosch owned combined. It was light brown but the wearer probably described it as cocoa. He smiled the way enemies smile.

'Yes, sir, how are we doing tonight?'

'I'm doing fine. I don't know about you, yet.'

The surfer in a suit smiled a little more brightly at that.

'I'm Mr Johnson and I'm providing security for the benefit tonight. Might I inquire if you brought your invitation with you?'

Bosch hesitated for only a moment.

'Oh, I'm sorry. I didn't realize I needed to bring that along. I didn't think Gordon would need security at a benefit like this.'

He hoped dropping Mittel's first name would give the surfer pause before he did anything rash. The surfer frowned for only a moment.

'Then could I ask you just to sign in for me?'

'Of course.'

Bosch was led to a table to the side of the entrance area. Taped across the front of it was a red, white and blue banner that said ROBERT SHEPHERD NOW! It told Bosch all he needed to know about the affair.

There was a guest registry on the table and a woman sat behind it in a black crushed-velvet cocktail dress that did little to camouflage her breasts. Mr Johnson seemed more intent on these two items than on Bosch as he signed the name Harvey Pounds in the registry.

As he signed, Bosch noticed a stack of pledge cards and a champagne goblet filled with pencils on the table. He picked up an information sheet and started to read about the unannounced candidate. Johnson finally pulled his eyes away from the table hostess and checked the name Bosch had written.

'Thank you, Mr Pounds. Enjoy yourself.'

He disappeared into the crowd then, probably to check on whether a Harvey Pounds was on the list of invitees. Bosch decided he'd stay a few minutes, see if he could spot Mittel and then leave before the surfer came looking for him.

He stepped away from the entrance and out from beneath the tent. After crossing a short lawn to a retainer wall, he tried to act like he was just enjoying the view. And it was a view; the only higher one would have been from a jet coming in to LAX. But on the jet you wouldn't have the breadth of vision, the cool breeze, or the sounds from the city below.

Bosch turned around and looked back at the crowd under the tent. He studied the faces but could not spot Gordon Mittel. There was no sign of him. There was a large knot of people beneath the center of the tent and Bosch realized that it was a grouping of people trying to reach their hands toward the unannounced candidate, or at least the man Bosch assumed was Shepherd. Harry noticed that while the crowd seemed to exhibit solidarity in terms of wealth, it cut across all age lines. He guessed that many were there to see Mittel as much as Shepherd.

· One of the women in black-and-white came out from under the white canopy and toward him with a tray of champagne glasses. He took one, thanked her, and turned back to the view. He sipped at it and supposed that it was top quality, but he wouldn't be able to tell the difference. He decided he should gulp it and go when a voice from his left interrupted.

'Wonderful view, isn't it? Better than a movie. I could stand here for hours.'

Bosch turned his head to acknowledge the speaker but didn't look at him. He didn't want to get involved.

'Yeah, it's nice. But I'll take the mountains I have.'

'Really? Where is that?'

'The other side of the hill. On Woodrow Wilson.'

'Oh, yes. There are some very nice properties there.'

Not mine, Bosch thought. Unless you like neoearthquake classic.

'The San Gabriels are brilliant in the sun,' the conversationalist said. 'I looked there but then I bought here.'

Bosch turned. He was looking at Gordon Mittel. The host put out his hand.

'Gordon Mittel.'

Bosch hesitated but then figured Mittel was used to people losing a step or stuttering in his presence.

'Harvey Pounds,' Bosch said, taking his hand.

Mittel was wearing a black tuxedo. He was as over-dressed for the crowd as Bosch was underdressed. His gray hair was cropped short and he had a smooth machine tan. He was as trim and tight as a rubber band stretched around a stack of hundreds and looked at least five to ten years younger than he was.

'Glad to meet you, glad you could come,' he said. 'Did you meet Robert yet?'

'No, he's kind of in the middle of the pack there.'

'Yes, that's true. Well, he'll be happy to meet you when he gets the chance.'

'I guess he'll be happy to take my check as well.'

'That, too.' Mittel smiled. 'Seriously, though, I hope you can help us out. He's a good man and we need people like him in office.'

His smile seemed so phony that Harry wondered if Mittel had already pegged him as a crasher. Bosch smiled back and patted the right breast of his jacket.

'I've got the checkbook right here.'

Doing that, Bosch remembered what he really had in his pocket and got an idea. The champagne, though only a single glass, had emboldened him. He suddenly realized he wanted to spook Mittel and maybe get a look at his real colors.

'Tell me,' he said, 'is Shepherd the one?'

'I don't quite follow.'

'Is he going all the way to the White House someday? Is he the one that's going to take you?'

Mittel sloughed off a frown or maybe it was a glimmer of annoyance.

'I guess we shall see. We've got to get him into the Senate first. That's the important thing.'

Bosch nodded and made a show of scanning the crowd.

'Well, it looks like you have the right people here. But, you know, I don't see Arno Conklin. Are you still tight with him? He was your first, wasn't he?'

Mittel's forehead creased with a deep furrow.

'Well ...' Mittel seemed to be uncomfortable, but then it quickly passed. 'To tell the truth, we haven't spoken in a long time. He's retired now, an old man in a wheelchair. Do you know Arno?'

'Never spoken to him in my life.'

'Then tell me, what prompts a question about ancient history?'

Bosch hiked his shoulders.

'I guess I'm just a student of history, that's all.'

'What do you do for a living, Mr Pounds? Or are you a full-time student?'

'I'm in law.'

'We have something in common then.'

'I doubt it.'

'I'm a Stanford man. How about you?'

Bosch thought a moment.

'Vietnam.'

Mittel frowned again and Bosch saw the interest go out of his eyes like water down a drain.

'Well, I tell you, I ought to mingle a little more. Watch the champagne, and if you decide you don't want to drive, one of the boys on the driveway can get you home. Ask for Manuel.'

'The one in the red vest?'

'Uh, yes. One of them.'

Bosch held up his glass.

'Don't worry, this is only my third.'

Mittel nodded and disappeared back into the crowd. Bosch watched him cross beneath the tent, stop to shake a few hands, but eventually make it to the house. He entered through a wall of French doors into what looked like a living room or some sort of viewing area. Mittel walked to a couch and bent down to speak quietly to a man in a suit. This man looked to be about the same age as Mittel but with a harder appearance. He had a sharp face and, though sitting, clearly had a much heavier body. As a younger man he had probably used his strength, not his brain. Mittel straightened up and the other man just nodded. Mittel then disappeared into the further recesses of his house.

Bosch finished his glass of champagne and started moving through the crowd under the tent toward the house. As he got near the French doors, one of the black-and-white women asked if he needed help finding something. He said he was looking for the bathroom and she directed him to another door to the left. He went where he was told and found the door was locked. He waited for a few moments and the door finally opened, emitting a man and a woman. They giggled when they saw Bosch waiting and headed back to the tent.

Inside the bathroom Bosch opened his jacket and took a folded piece of paper from the inside pocket on the left. It was the photocopy of the Johnny Fox story that Keisha Russell had given him. He unfolded it and took out a pen. He circled the names Johnny Fox, Arno Conklin and Gordon Mittel, then, under the story, wrote, 'What prior work experience got Johnny the job?'

He refolded the page twice and ran his fingers tightly over the creases. Then, on the outside, he wrote, 'For Gordon Mittel Only!'

Back under the tent, Bosch found a black-and-white woman and gave her the folded paper.

'You have to find Mr Mittel right away,' he told her. 'Give him this note. He's waiting on it.'

He watched her go and then made his way back out through the crowd to the sign-in table at the entry area. He quickly bent over the guest registry and wrote his mother's name down. The table hostess protested that he had already signed in.

'This is for somebody else,' he said.

For an address, he wrote Hollywood and Vista. He left the line for a telephone number blank.

Bosch scanned the crowd again and saw neither Mittel nor the woman he had given the note to. Then he looked into the room beyond the French doors and Mittel appeared with the note in his hand. He walked slowly into the room, studying it. Bosch could tell by the direction of his eyes that he was studying the note scribbled on the bottom. Even with his phony tan, he seemed to Bosch to go pale.

Bosch took a step back into the entrance alcove and watched. He could feel his heart beating at a quicker pace. He felt like he was watching some secret play on a stage.

There was a look of perplexed anger on Mittel's face now. Bosch saw him hand the page to the rough man who still sat in the cushioned chair. Then Mittel turned to the glass panels and looked out at the people under the tent. He said something and Bosch thought he could read his lips.

'Son of a bitch.'

Then he started talking more quickly, barking orders. The man on the chair rose and Bosch knew instinctively that it was his cue to leave. He walked quickly back out to the driveway and trotted down to the group of men in red vests. He handed his valet ticket and a ten-dollar bill to one of them and said in Spanish that he was in a great hurry.

Still, it seemed to take forever. As he waited nervously, Bosch kept his eyes on the house, waiting for the rough man to appear. He had watched which direction the valet had gone for his car and he was ready to bolt that way if necessary. He began to wish he had his gun. Whether he really needed it or not did not matter. In this moment he knew it gave him a sense of security that he felt naked without.

The surfer in a suit appeared at the top of the driveway and strode down toward Bosch. At the same time, Bosch saw his Mustang approaching. He walked out into the street, ready to take it. The surfer got to him first.

'Hey, buddy, hold on a sec –'

Bosch turned from his approaching car and hit him in the jaw, sending him backward onto the driveway. He moaned and rolled onto his side, both hands clutching his jaw. Bosch was sure the jaw was dislocated if not broken. He shook away the pain in his hand as the Mustang screeched to a stop.

The man in the red vest was slow in getting out. Bosch pulled him away from the open door and jumped in. As he settled in behind the wheel he looked up the driveway and saw the rough man was now coming. When he saw the surfer on the ground, he started running but his steps were unsteady on the downgrade of the driveway. Bosch saw his heavy thighs pressing the fabric of his pants and suddenly he slipped and fell. Two of the red vests went to help him up but he angrily shoved them away.

Bosch gunned the car and sped away. He worked his way up to Mulholland and turned east toward home. He could feel adrenaline surging through him. Not only had he gotten away, but it was clear he had struck a nerve with a hammer. Let Mittel think about that for a while, he thought. Let him sweat. Then he yelled out loud in the car, though no one could hear except himself.

'Spooked ya, didn't I, you fuck!'

He banged his palm triumphantly on the steering wheel.

✥ ✥ ✥ ✥ ✥ ✥ ✥

He dreamed of the coyote again. The animal was on a mountain path where there were no homes, no cars, no people. It was moving very quickly through the dark as if it was trying to get away. But the path and place were his. He knew the land and knew he would escape. What it was he fled from was never clear, never seen. But it was there, behind him in the dark. And the coyote knew by instinct it must get away.

The phone woke Bosch, breaking into the dream like a knife stabbed through paper. Bosch pulled the pillow off his head, rolled to his right and his eyes were immediately assaulted by the light of dawn. He had forgotten to close the blinds. He reached for the phone on the floor.

'Hold on,' he said.

He put the phone down on the bed, sat up and rubbed a hand across his face. He squinted at the clock. It was ten minutes after seven. He coughed and cleared his throat, then picked the phone back up.

'Yeah.'

'Detective Bosch?'

'Yeah.'

'It's Brad Hirsch. I'm sorry to call so early.'

Bosch had to think a moment. Brad Hirsch? He had no idea who it was.

'Yeah, it's okay,' he said while he continued to search his mind for the name.

A silence followed.

'I'm the one ... In Latents? Remember, you –'

'Hirsch? Yeah, Hirsch. I remember. What's up?'

'I wanted to tell you I made the AFIS run you wanted. I came in early and ran it with another search I'm doing for Devonshire Homicide. I don't think anybody will know.'

Bosch kicked his legs over the side of the bed, opened a drawer in the bed table and took out a pad and a pencil. He noticed that he had taken the pad from the Surf and Sand Hotel in Laguna Beach. He remembered he had spent a few days with Sylvia there the year before.

'Yeah, you made the run? What'd you get?'

'Well, that's the thing. I'm sorry but I got nothing.'

Bosch threw the pad back into the open drawer and threw himself backward on the bed.

'No hits?'

'Well, the computer came up with two candidates. I then did a visual comparison and it was no good. No matches. I'm sorry. I know this case means ...'

He didn't finish.

'You took it through all the data bases?'

'Every one on our network.'

'Let me ask you something. All those data bases, do they include DA's employees and LAPD personnel?'

There was silence as Hirsch must have been mulling over what the question might mean.

'You there, Hirsch?'

'Yes. The answer is yes.'

'How far back? You know what I mean? These bases have prints going how far back?'

'Well, each data base is different. The LAPD's is extensive. I'd say we have prints on everybody who's worked here since World War II.'

Well, that clears Irving and the rest of the cops, Bosch

thought. But that didn't bother him much. His sights were definitely somewhere else.

'What about people working for the DA?'

'The DA's office would be different,' Hirsch said. 'I don't think they started printing employees until the middle sixties.'

Conklin had been there during that time, Bosch knew, but he would already have been elected DA. It would seem that he would not have submitted his own prints, especially if he knew there was a print card in a murder book somewhere that could possibly be matched to him.

He thought of Mittel. He would have been out of the DA's office by the time employees' prints were taken as a matter of course.

'What about the federal base?' he asked. 'What if some guy worked for a president and got the kind of clearance you need to go visit the White House, would those prints be in that base?'

'Yes, they'd be in twice. In the federal employees base and in the FBI's. They keep prints on record of everyone they do background investigations on, if that's what you mean. But remember, just because somebody visits the president, it doesn't mean they get printed.'

Well, Mittel isn't a scratch but it's close, Bosch thought.

'So what you're saying,' Bosch said, 'is that whether or not we have complete data files going back to 1961, whoever belongs to those prints I gave you hasn't been printed since then?'

'That's not one hundred percent but it's close. The person who left these prints probably hasn't been printed – at least by any contributor to the data banks. We can only reach so far with this. One way or another we can pull prints on one out of about every fifty or so people in the country. But I just didn't get anything this time. Sorry.'

'That's okay, Hirsch, you tried.'

'Well, I guess I'll be getting back to work now. What do you want me to do with the print card?'

Bosch thought a moment. He wondered if there was any other avenue to chase down.

'Tell you what, can you just hold on to it? I'll come by the lab and pick it up when I can. Probably be by later today.'

'Okay, I'll put it in an envelope for you in case I'm not here. Good-bye.'

'Hey, Hirsch?'

'Yeah?'

'It feels good, don't it?'

'What's that?'

'You did the right thing. You didn't get a match but you did the right thing.'

'Yeah, I guess.'

He was acting like he didn't understand because he was embarrassed, but he understood.

'Yeah, I'll see you Hirsch.'

After hanging up, Bosch sat on the side of the bed, lit a cigarette and thought about what he was going to do with the day. The news from Hirsch was not good but it wasn't daunting. It certainly didn't clear Arno Conklin. It might not even have cleared Gordon Mittel. Bosch wasn't sure whether Mittel's work for presidents and senators would have required a fingerprint check. He decided his investigation was still intact. He wasn't changing any plans.

He thought about the night before and the wild-ass chance he had taken confronting Mittel the way he had. He smiled at his own recklessness and thought about what Hinojos might make of it. He knew she'd say it was a symptom of his problem. She wouldn't see it as a tactful way of flushing the bird from the bush.

He got up and started the coffee and then showered, shaved and got ready for the day. He took his coffee and the box of cereal from the refrigerator out to the deck, leaving the sliding door open so he could hear the stereo. He had KFWB news on.

It was cool and crisp outside but he could tell it would get warmer later. Blue jays were swooping in and out of the arroyo below the deck and he could see black bees the size of quarters working in the yellow flowers of the primrose jasmine.

There was a story on the radio about a building contractor making a fourteen-million-dollar bonus for completing the rebuilding of the 10 freeway three months ahead of schedule. The officials who gathered to announce the engineering feat likened the fallen freeway to the city itself. Now that it was back upright, so, too, was the city. The city was on the move again. They had a lot to learn, Bosch thought.

Afterward, he went in and got out the yellow pages and started working the phone in the kitchen. He called the major airlines, shopped around and made arrangements to fly to Florida. But flying on one day's notice, the best deal he could get was still seven hundred dollars, a shocking amount to him. He put it on a credit card so that he could pay it off over time. He also reserved a rental car at Tampa International Airport.

When he had that finished he went back out to the deck and thought about the next project he had to tackle:

He needed a badge.

For a long time he sat on the deck chair and contemplated whether he needed it for his own sense of security or because it was a bona fide necessity to his mission. He knew how naked and vulnerable he had felt this week without the gun and the badge, extremities he had carried on his body for more than twenty years. But he had avoided the temptation to carry the backup gun that he knew was in the closet next to the front door. That he could do, he knew. But the badge was different. More so than the gun, the badge was the symbol of what he was. It opened doors better than any key, it gave him more authority than any words, than any weapon. He decided the badge was a necessity. If he was going to Florida and was going to scam McKittrick, he had to look legit. He had to have a badge.

He knew his badge was probably in a desk drawer in Assistant Chief Irvin S. Irving's office. There was no way he could get to it and not be discovered. But he knew where there was another one that would work just as well.

Bosch looked at his watch. Nine-fifteen. It was forty-five minutes until the daily command meeting at Holly-wood Station. He had plenty of time.

B osch pulled into the rear parking lot of the station at five minutes after ten. He was sure that Pounds, who was punctual about everything he did, would already have gone down the front hall to the captain's office with the overnight logs. The meeting was held every morning and included the station's CO, patrol captain, watch lieutenant and detective commander, who was Pounds. They were routine affairs and never lasted longer than twenty minutes. The members of the station's command staff simply drank coffee and went through the overnight reports and ongoing problems, complaints or investigations of particular note.

Bosch went in the back door by the drunk tank and then up the hallway to the detective bureau. It had been a busy morning. There were already four men handcuffed to benches in the hallway. One of them, a drug hype Bosch had seen in the station before and used as an unreliable informant on occasion, asked Bosch for a smoke. It was illegal to smoke in any city-owned building. Bosch lit a cigarette anyway and put it in the man's mouth because both his needle-scarred arms were cuffed behind his back.

'What is it this time, Harley?' Bosch asked.

'Shit, a guy leaves his g'rage open, he's asking me to come in. Isn't that right?'

'Tell that one to the judge.'

As Bosch walked away one of the other lockdowns yelled at him from down the hallway.

'What about me, man? I need a smoke.'

'I'm out,' Bosch said.

'Fuck you, man.'

'Yeah, that's what I thought.'

He came into the detective bureau through the rear door. The first thing he did was confirm that Pounds's glass office was empty. He was at the command meeting. Then he checked the coatrack up at the front and saw he was in business. As he walked down the aisle formed by the separation of the investigation tables, he exchanged nods with a few of the other detectives.

Edgar was at the homicide table sitting across from his new partner, who was in Bosch's old chair. Edgar heard one of the 'Hi, Harry' greetings and turned around.

'Harry, wassup?'

'Hey, man, just came in to get a couple things. Hang on a sec, it's hot outside.'

Bosch walked to the front of the bureau, where old Henry of the Nod Squad sat at the desk behind the counter. He was working on a crossword puzzle and Bosch could see several erasure marks had turned the grid gray.

'Henry, howzit hanging? You getting anywhere with that?'

'Detective Bosch.'

Bosch slipped his sport coat off and hung it on a hook on the rack next to a jacket with a gray cross-hatch pattern. It was on a hanger and Bosch knew it belonged to Pounds. As he put his coat on the hook with his back to Henry and the rest of the bureau, he snaked his left hand inside the other coat, felt for the interior pocket and then pulled out Pounds's badge wallet. He knew it would be there. Pounds was a creature of habit and Bosch had seen

171

the badge wallet in the suit coat once before. He put the wallet into his pants pocket and turned around as Henry continued talking. Bosch had only a momentary tinge of hesitation at the seriousness of what he was doing. Taking another cop's badge was a crime, but Bosch looked at Pounds as being the reason he did not have his own badge. In the inventory of his morality, what Pounds had done to him was equally wrong.

'If you want to see the lieutenant, he's down the hall at a meeting,' Henry said.

'No, I don't want to see the lieutenant, Henry. In fact, don't even tell him I was here. I don't want his blood pressure to go up, you know. I'm just going to get a few things and get out of here, okay?'

'That's a deal. I don't want him cranky, either.'

Bosch didn't have to worry about anyone else in the bureau telling Pounds he had been in. He gave Henry a friendly clasp on the shoulder as he walked behind him, sealing the agreement. He went back to the homicide table and as he approached, Burns began to rise from Bosch's old spot.

'You need to get in here, Harry?' he asked.

Bosch thought he could detect nervous energy in the other man's voice. He understood his predicament and wasn't going to make it a difficult time for him.

'Yeah, if you don't mind,' he said. 'I figured I'd get my personal stuff out of there so you can move in the right way.'

Bosch came around and opened the drawer at the table. There were two boxes of Junior Mints on top of old paperwork that had been shoved in long ago.

'Oh, those are mine, sorry,' Burns said.

He reached in for the two boxes of candy and stood next to the table, holding them like a big kid in a suit while Bosch went through the paperwork.

It was all a show. Bosch took some of the paperwork and dumped it in a manila file and then pointed with his hand, signaling to Burns he could put his candy back.

'Be careful, Bob.'

'It's Bill. Careful of what?'

'Ants.'

Bosch went to the bank of file cabinets that ran along the wall to the side of the table and opened one of the drawers with his business card taped to it. It was three up from the bottom, waist-high, and it was one he knew was almost empty. With his back to the table again, he pulled the badge wallet out of his pocket and put it in the drawer. Then, with his hands in the drawer and out of sight, he opened the wallet and took out the gold badge. He then put it in one pocket and the wallet back in the other. For good measure, he pulled a file out of the drawer and closed it.

He turned around and looked at Jerry Edgar.

'Okay, that's it. Just some personal stuff I might need. Anything going on?'

'Nah, quiet.'

Back at the coatrack, Bosch turned his back on the bureau again and used one hand to reach for his coat while using the other to take the badge wallet from his pocket and slip it back into Pounds's coat. He then put his coat on, said good-bye to Henry and went back to the homicide table.

'I'm outta here,' he said to Edgar and Burns while picking up the two files he had pulled. 'I don't want Ninety-eight to see me and throw a fit. Good luck, boys.'

On the way out, Bosch stopped and gave the hype another cigarette. The lockdown who had complained before was no longer on the bench or Bosch would have given him one, too.

Back in the Mustang, he dumped the files on the

173

backseat and took his empty badge wallet out of his briefcase. He slipped Pounds's badge into place next to his own ID card. It would work, he decided, as long as no one looked too closely at it. The badge said LIEUTENANT across it. Bosch's ID card identified him as a detective. It was a minor discrepancy and Bosch was happy with it. Best of all, he thought, there was a good chance Pounds would not notice that the badge was missing for some time. He rarely left the station to go to crime scenes and so rarely had to open the wallet or show his badge. There was a good chance its disappearance would go unnoticed. All he had to do was get it back into place when he was done with it.

Bosch ended up outside the door of Carmen Hinojos's office early for his afternoon session. He waited until exactly three-thirty and knocked. She smiled as he entered her office and he noticed that the late-afternoon sun came through the window and splashed light directly across her desk. He moved toward the chair he usually took but then stopped himself and sat on the chair to the left of the desk. She noticed this and frowned at him as if he were a schoolboy.

'If you think I care which chair you sit in, you are wrong.'

'Am I? Okay.'

He got up and moved to the other chair. He liked being near the window.

'I might not be here for Monday's session,' he said after settling in.

She frowned again, this time more seriously.

'Why not?'

'I'm going away. I'll try to be back.'

'Away? What happened to your investigation?'

'It's part of it. I'm going to Florida to track down one of the original investigators. One's dead, the other one's in Florida. So I've got to go to him.'

'Couldn't you just call?'

'I don't want to call. I don't want to give him the chance to put me off.'

She nodded.

'When do you leave?'

'Tonight. I'm taking a red-eye to Tampa.'

'Harry, look at you. You practically look like the walking dead. Can't you get some sleep and take a plane in the morning?'

'No, I've gotta get out there before the mail arrives.'

'What's that mean?'

'Nothing. It's a long story. Anyway, I wanted to ask you something. I need your help.'

She contemplated this for several seconds, apparently weighing how far she wanted to go into the pool without knowing how deep it was.

'What is it you want?'

'Do you ever do any forensic work for the department?'

She narrowed her eyes, not seeing where this was going.

'A little. From time to time somebody will bring me something, or maybe ask me to do a little profiling of a suspect. But mostly the department uses outside contractors. Forensic psychiatrists who have experience with this.'

'But you've been to crime scenes?'

'Actually, no. I've only looked at photos brought to me and worked from them.'

'Perfect.'

Bosch pulled his briefcase onto his lap and opened it. He took out the envelope of crime scene and autopsy photos that had been in the murder book and gently placed them on her desk.

'Those are from this case. I don't want to look at them. I can't look at them. But I need someone to do it and tell me what's there. There's probably nothing but I'd like another opinion. The investigation these two guys did on this case was ... well, it was almost like there was no investigation.'

'Oh, Harry.' She shook her head. 'I'm not sure this is wise. Why me?'

'Because you know what I'm doing. And because I trust you. I don't think I can trust anybody else.'

'Would you trust me if there was no ethical constraint on me telling others about what we've talked about here?'

Bosch studied her face.

'I don't know,' he finally said.

'I thought so.'

She slid the envelope to the side of the desk.

'Let's put these aside for now and go on with the session. I really have to think about this.'

'Okay, you can take them. But let me know, okay? I just want your feel for them. As a psychiatrist and as a woman.'

'We'll see.'

'What do you want to talk about?'

'What is happening with the investigation?'

'Is that a professional question, Dr Hinojos? Or are you just curious about the case?'

'No, I'm curious about you. And I'm worried about you. I'm still not convinced that what you are doing is safe – either psychologically or physically. You're mucking around in the lives of powerful people. And I'm caught in the middle. I know what you're doing but am almost powerless to make you stop. I'm afraid you tricked me.'

'Tricked you?'

'You pulled me into this. I bet you've wanted to show me these pictures since you told me what you're doing.'

'You're right, I have. But there was no trick. I thought this was a place where I could talk about anything. Isn't that what you said?'

'Okay, I wasn't tricked, just led down the path. I should've seen it coming. Let's move on. I want to talk more about the emotional aspect of what you are doing. I want to know more about why finding this killer is so important to you after so many years?'

'It should be obvious.'

'Make it more obvious for me.'

'I can't. I can't put it into words. All I know is that everything changed for me after she was gone. I don't know how things would have been if she hadn't been taken away but ... everything changed.'

'Do you understand what you're saying and what it means? You're looking at your life in two parts. The first part is with her, which you seem to have imbued with a happiness I'm sure was not always there. The second part is your life after, which you acknowledge has not met expectations or is in some way unsatisfactory. I think you've been unhappy for a long time, possibly all of that time. This recent relationship you had may have been a highlight but you were still and, I think, have always been, an unhappy man.'

She rested a moment but Bosch didn't speak. He knew she wasn't done.

'Now, maybe the traumas of the last few years – both personally for you and for your community at large – have made you take stock of yourself. And I fear that you believe, whether subconsciously or not, that by going back and bringing some form of justice to what happened to your mother, you will be righting your life. And there's the problem. Whatever happens with this private investigation of yours, it's not going to change things. It just can't be done.'

'You're saying that I can't blame what happened then for what I am now?'

'No, listen to me, Harry. All I'm saying is you are the sum of many parts, not the sum of one. It's like dominoes. Several different blocks must click together for you to arrive at the end, at the point you are at now. You don't jump from the first domino to the last.'

'So I should just give it up? Just let it go?'

'I'm not saying that. But I am finding it hard to see the emotional benefit or healing you will get from this. In fact, I think there is the possibility that you may do yourself more damage than repair. Does that make any sense?'

Bosch stood up and went to the window. He stared out but didn't compute what he saw. He felt the warmth of the sun on him. He didn't look at her as he spoke.

'I don't know what makes sense. All I know is that on every level it seems to make sense that I do this. In fact, I feel … I don't know what the word is, maybe ashamed. I feel ashamed that I haven't done this long before now. A lot of years have gone by and I just let them go. I feel like I let her down somehow … that I let myself down.'

'That's understa –'

'Remember what I told you the first day? Everybody counts or nobody counts. Well, for a long time she didn't count. Not with this department, this society, not even with me. I have to admit that, not even with me. Then I opened that file this week and I could see that her death was just put away. It was buried, just like I had buried it. Somebody put the fix in because she didn't count. They did it because they could. And then when I think about how long I've let it go … it makes me want to … I don't know, just hide my face or something.'

He stopped, unable to put into words what he wanted to say. He looked down and noticed there were no ducks in the butcher shop window.

'You know,' he said, 'she might've been what she was but sometimes I feel like I didn't even deserve that … I guess I got what I deserved in life.'

He stayed at the window, not looking at her. It was several moments before Hinojos spoke.

'I guess this is the point where I should tell you that you're being too hard on yourself, but I don't think that would help much.'

'No, it wouldn't.'

'Could you come back here and sit down? Please?'

Bosch did as he was asked. Finally, after he was seated, his eyes met hers. She spoke first.

'What I want to say is that you are mixing things up. Putting the cart before the horse. You can't take the blame because this case may have been covered up. First of all, you had nothing to do with that, and secondly, you didn't even realize that until you read through the file this week.'

'But don't you see? Why didn't I look at it before? I'm not new here. I've been a cop twenty years. I should've been there before this. I mean, so what that I didn't know the details. I knew she was killed and nothing was ever done about it. That was enough.'

'Look, Harry, think about this, okay? On the plane over tonight, just give it some thought. You've engaged yourself in a noble pursuit but you have to safeguard against damaging yourself further. The bottom line is that it is not worth that. It's not worth the toll you may have to pay.'

'Not worth it? There's a killer out there. He thinks he made it away free. For years, he has thought that. Decades. And I'm going to change that.'

'You're not understanding what I'm saying. I don't want any guilty person to get away, especially with murder. But what I am talking about here is you. You are my only concern here. There is a basic rule of nature. No living thing sacrifices itself or hurts itself needlessly. It's the will of survival and I fear the circumstances of your life may have blunted your own survival skills. You may be throwing it to the wind, not caring what happens to you emotionally, physically, in every way, in this pursuit. I don't want to see you hurt.'

She took a breather. He said nothing.

'I have to say,' she continued quietly, 'I'm very nervous about this. I've never had this situation come up before and I've counseled a lot of cops in nine years here.'

'Well, I got bad news for you.' He smiled. 'I went and crashed a party last night at Mittel's. I think I may have spooked him. At least, I spooked myself.'

'Shit!'

'Is that some new psychiatric term? I'm not familiar with it.'

'This isn't funny. Why'd you do that?'

Bosch thought a moment.

'I don't know. It was kind of a whim type of thing. I was just driving by his house and there was a party. It kind of … it just made me angry for some reason. Him having a party and my mother …'

'Did you speak to him about the case?'

'No. I didn't even tell him my name. We just kind've sparred around for a few minutes but then I left him something. Remember that newspaper clip I showed you Wednesday? I left that for him. I saw him read it. I think it struck a nerve.'

She exhaled loudly.

'Now, step outside yourself and look as an uninvolved observer at what you did. If you can. Was that a smart thing to do, going there like that?'

'I already have thought about it. No, it wasn't smart. It was a mistake. He'll probably warn Conklin. They'll both know somebody's out there, coming for them. They'll close ranks.'

'You see, you are proving my point for me. I want you to promise me you won't do anything foolish like that again.'

'I can't.'

'Well, then I have to tell you that a patient–doctor relationship can be broken if the therapist believes the patient is endangering himself or others. I told you I was almost powerless to stop you. Not completely.'

'You'd go to Irving?'

'I will if I believe you are being reckless.'

Bosch felt anger as he realized she had ultimate control over him and what he was doing. He swallowed the anger and held up his hands, surrendering.

'All right. I won't go crashing any parties again.'

'No. I want more than that. I want you to stay away from these men that you think may have been involved.'

'What I'll promise you is that I won't go to them until I have the whole thing in the bag.'

'I mean it.'

'So do I.'

'I hope so.'

They were silent for nearly a minute after that. It was a cooling-off period. She turned slightly in her chair, not looking at him, probably thinking what to say next.

'Let's move on,' she finally said. 'You understand that this whole thing, this pursuit of yours, has eclipsed what we're supposed to be doing here?'

'I know.'

'So we're prolonging my evaluation.'

'Well, that doesn't bother me as much anymore. I need the time off the job for this other thing.'

'Well, as long as you are happy,' she said sarcastically. 'Okay, then I want to go back to the incident that brought you to me. The other day you were very general and very short in your description of what happened. I understand why. I think we were both feeling each other out at that point. But we are far past that now. I'd like a fuller story.'

You said the other day that Lieutenant Pounds set things into motion?'

'That's right.'

'How?'

'First of all, he's a commander of detectives who has never been a detective himself. Oh, technically, he probably spent a few months on a table somewhere along the line so he'd have it on his résumé, but basically he's an administrator. He's what we call a Robocrat. A bureaucrat with a badge. He doesn't know the first thing about clearing cases. The only thing he knows about it is how to draw a line through the case on this little chart he keeps in his office. He doesn't know the first thing about the differences between an interview and an interrogation. And that's fine, the department is full of people like him. I say let them do their job and let me do mine. The problem is Pounds doesn't realize where he's good and where he's bad. It's led to problems before. Confrontations. It finally led to the incident, as you keep calling it.'

'What did he do?'

'He touched my suspect.'

'Explain what that means.'

'When you've got a case and you bring someone in, he's all yours. Nobody goes near him, understand? The wrong word, the wrong question and it could spoil a case. That's a cardinal rule; don't touch somebody else's suspect. It doesn't matter if you're a lieutenant or the damn chief, you stay clear until you check first with the guys with the collar.'

'So what happened?'

'Like I told you the other day, my partner Edgar and I brought in this suspect. A woman had been killed. One of these ones who puts ads in the sex tabs you can buy on the Boulevard. She gets called to one of those shithole motel rooms on Sunset, has sex with the guy and ends up stabbed to death. That's the short story. The stab wound's to the upper right chest. The john, he plays it cool, though. He calls the cops and says it was her knife and she tried to rob him with it. He says he turned her arm and put it into her. Self-defense. Okay, so that's when me and Edgar show up and right away we see some things don't fit with that story.'

'Like what?'

'First of all, she's a lot smaller than he is. I don't see her coming at him with a knife. Then there's the knife itself. It's a serrated steak knife, 'bout eight inches long, and she had one of those little purses without a strap.'

'A clutch.'

'Yeah, I guess. Anyway, that knife wouldn't've fit in it, so how'd she bring it in? As they say on the street, her clothes fit tighter than the rubbers in her purse, so she wasn't hiding it on her, either. And there was more. If her purpose was to rip the guy off, why have sex first? Why not pull the knife, take his shit and go? But that didn't happen. His story was that they did it first, then she came at him, which explained why she was still naked. Which, of course, raised another question. Why rob the guy when you're naked? Where you going to run like that?'

'The guy was lying.'

'Seemed obvious. Then we got something else. In her purse – the clutch – was a piece of paper on which she had written down the motel's name and the room number. It was consistent with a right-handed person. Like I said, the stab was to the upper right chest of the victim. So it doesn't add up. If she came at him, the chances are the knife would be in her right hand. If the john then turns it into her, it's likely the wound would be on the left side of the chest, not the right.'

Bosch made a motion of pulling his right hand toward

his chest, showing how awkward it would be for it to stab his right side.

'There was all kinds of stuff that wasn't right. It was a downward-grade wound, also inconsistent with it being in her hand. That would have been upward-grade.'

Hinojos nodded that she understood.

'The problem was, we had no physical evidence contradicting his story. Nothing. Just our feeling that she wouldn't have done it the way he said. The wound stuff wasn't enough. And then, in his favor, was the knife. It was on the bed, we could see it had fingerprints in the blood. I had no doubt they'd be hers. That's not hard to do once she's dead. So while it didn't impress me, that didn't matter. It's what the DA would think and then what a jury would think after that. Reasonable doubt is a big black hole that swallows cases like this. We needed more.'

'So what happened?'

'It's what we call a he-said-she-said. One person's word against the other, but only the other is dead in this case. Makes it even harder. We had nothing but his story. So what you do in a case like that is you sweat the guy. You turn him. And there's a lot of ways to do it. But, basically, you gotta break him down in the rooms. We –'

'The rooms?'

'The interrogation rooms. In the bureau. We took this guy into a room. As a witness. We didn't formally arrest him. We asked if he'd come down, said that we had to straighten a few things out about what she did, and he said sure. You know, Mr Cooperative. Still cool. We stuck him in a room and then Edgar and I went down to the watch office to get some of the good coffee. They've got good coffee there, one of those big urns that was donated by some restaurant that got wrecked in the quake. Everybody goes in there to get coffee. Anyway, we're takin' our time, talkin' about how we're going to go at this guy, which one of us wanted him first, and so on. Meantime, fuckin' Pounds – excuse me – sees the guy in the room through the little window and goes in and informs him. And –'

'What do you mean, informs him?'

'Reads him his rights. This is our goddamn witness and Pounds, who doesn't know what the hell he's doing, thinks he's gotta go in there and give the guy the spiel. He thinks like we forgot or something.'

Bosch looked at her with outrage on his face but immediately saw she didn't understand.

'Wasn't that the right thing to do?' she asked. 'Aren't you required by law to inform people of their rights?'

Bosch struggled to contain his anger, reminding himself that Hinojos might work for the department, but she was an outsider. Her perceptions of police work were likely based more on the media than on the actual reality.

'Let me give you a quick lesson on what's the law and what's real. We – the cops – have the deck stacked against us. What *Miranda* and all the other rules and regs amount to is that we have to take some guy we know is, or at least think is, guilty and basically say, 'Hey, look, we think you did it and the Supreme Court and every lawyer on the planet would advise you not to talk to us, but, how about it, will you talk to us?' It just doesn't work. You gotta get around that. You gotta use guile and some bluffing and you gotta be sneaky. The rules of the courts are like a tightrope that you're walking on. You have to be very careful but there is a chance you can walk on it to get to the other side. So when some asshole who doesn't know shit walks in on your guy and informs him, it can pretty much ruin your whole day, not to mention the case.'

He stopped and studied her. He still saw skepticism. He knew then that she was just another citizen who would be scared shitless if she ever got a dose of the way things really were on the street.

'When someone is informed, that's it,' he said. 'It's over. Me and Edgar came back in from coffee and the john sits there and says he thinks he wants his lawyer. I said, "What lawyer, who's talking about lawyers? You're a witness, not a suspect," and he tells us that the lieutenant just read him his rights. I don't know at that moment who I hated more, Pounds for blowing it or this guy for killing the girl.'

'Well, tell me this, what would have happened if Pounds had not done what he did?'

'We would've made friendly with the guy, asked him to tell his story in as much detail as possible and hoped there would be inconsistencies when compared to what he'd told the uniforms. Then we would have said, "The inconsistencies in your statements make you a suspect." *Then* we would have informed him and hopefully clubbed the shit out of him with the inconsistencies and the problems we found with the scene. We would have tried, and maybe succeeded, in finessing a confession. Most of what we do is just get people to talk. It's not like the stuff on TV. It's a hundred times harder and dirtier. But just like you, what we do is get people to talk … Anyway, that's my view. But we'll never know now what could've happened because of Pounds.'

'Well, what did happen after you found out he'd been informed?'

'I left the room and walked straight into where Pounds was in his office. He knew something was wrong because he stood up. I remember that. I asked him if he'd informed my guy and when he said yes, we got into it. Both of us, screaming … then I don't really remember how it happened. I'm not trying to deny anything. I just don't remember the details. I must've grabbed him and pushed him. And his face went through the glass.'

'What did you do when that happened?'

'Well, some of the guys came running in and pulled me out of there. The station commander sent me home. Pounds had to go to the hospital to fix his nose. IAD took a statement from him and I was suspended. And then Irving stepped in and changed it to ISL. Here I am.'

'What happened with the case?'

'The john never talked. He got his lawyer and waited it out. Edgar went with what we had to the DA last Friday and they kicked it. They said they weren't going into court with a no-witness case with a few minor inconsistencies ... Her prints were on the knife. Big surprise. What it came down to is that she didn't count. At least not enough for them to take the chance of losing.'

Neither of them spoke for a few moments. Bosch guessed that she was thinking about the corollaries between this case and his mother's.

'So what we've got,' he finally said, 'is a murderer out there on the street and the guy who allowed him to go free is back behind his desk, the broken glass already replaced, business as usual. That's our system. I got mad about it and look what it got me. Stress leave and maybe the end of my job.'

She cleared her throat before going into her appraisal of the story.

'As you have set down the circumstances of what happened, it is quite easy to see your rage. But not the ultimate action you took. Have you ever heard the phrase, "a mad minute?" '

Bosch shook his head.

'It's a way of describing a violent outburst that has its roots in several pressures on an individual. It builds up and is released in a quick moment – usually violently, often against a target not wholly responsible for the pressure.'

'If you need me to say Pounds was an innocent victim, I'm not going to say it.'

'I don't need that. I just need you to look at this situation and how it could happen.'

'I don't know. Shit just happens.'

'When you physically attack someone, don't you feel that you lower yourself to the same level as the man who was set free?'

'Not by a long shot, Doctor. Let me tell you something, you can look at all parts of my life, you can throw in earthquakes, fires, floods, riots and even Vietnam, but when it came down to just me and Pounds in that glass room, none of that mattered. You can call it a mad minute or whatever you want. Sometimes, the moment is all that matters and in that moment I was doing the right thing. And if these sessions are designed to make me see I did something wrong, forget it. Irving buttonholed me the other day in the lobby and asked me to think about an apology. Fuck that. I did the right thing.'

She nodded, adjusted herself in her seat and looked more uncomfortable than she had through his long diatribe. Finally, she looked at her watch and he looked at his. His time was up.

'So,' he said, 'I guess I've set the cause of psychotherapy back a century, huh?'

'No, not at all. The more you know of a person and the more you know of a story, the more you understand how things happen. It's why I enjoy my job.'

'Same here.'

'Have you spoken to Lieutenant Pounds since the incident?'

'I saw him when I dropped off the keys to my car. He had it taken away. I went into his office and he practically got hysterical. He's a very small man and I think he knows it.'

'They usually do.'

Bosch leaned forward, ready to get up and leave, when he noticed the envelope she had pushed to the side of her desk.

'What about the photos?'

'I knew you'd bring that up one more time.'

She looked at the envelope and frowned.

'I need to think about it. On several levels. Can I keep them while you go to Florida? Or will you need them?'

'You can keep 'em.'

At four-forty in the morning California time the air carrier landed at Tampa International Airport. Bosch leaned bleary-eyed against a window in the coach cabin, watching the sun rising in the Florida sky for the first time. As the plane taxied, he took off his watch and moved the hands ahead three hours. He was tempted to check into the nearest motel for some real sleep but knew he didn't have the time. From the AAA map he had brought with him, it looked like it was at least a two-hour drive down to Venice.

'It's nice to see a blue sky.'

It was the woman next to him in the aisle seat. She was leaning over toward him, looking out the window herself. She was in her mid-forties with prematurely gray hair. It was almost white. They had talked a bit in the early part of the flight and Bosch knew she was heading back to Florida rather than visiting as he was. She had given LA five years but had had enough. She was going home. Bosch didn't ask who or what she was coming home to, but had wondered if her hair was white when she had first landed in LA five years before.

'Yeah,' he replied. 'These night flights take forever.'

'No, I meant the smog. There is none.'

Bosch looked at her and then out the window, studying the sky.

'Not yet.'

But she was right. The sky had a quality of blue he rarely saw in LA It was the color of swimming pools, with billowing white cumulus clouds floating like dreams in the upper atmosphere.

The plane cleared out slowly. Bosch waited until the end, got up and rolled his back to relieve the tension. The joints of his backbone cracked like dominoes going down. He got his overnighter out of the compartment above and headed out.

As soon as he stepped off the plane into the jetway, the humidity surrounded him like a wet towel with an incubating warmth. He made it into the air-conditioned terminal and decided to scratch his plan to rent a convertible.

A half hour later he was on the 275 freeway crossing Tampa Bay in another rented Mustang. He had the windows up and the air conditioning on but he was sweating as his body still had not acclimated to the humidity.

What struck him most about Florida on this first drive was its flatness. For forty-five minutes not a hillrise came in sight until he reached the concrete-and-steel mountain called the Skyway Bridge. Bosch knew that the steeply graded bridge over the mouth of the bay was a replacement for one that had fallen but he drove across it fearlessly and above the speed limit. After all, he came from postquake Los Angeles, where the unofficial speed limit *under* bridges and overpasses was on the far right side of the speedometer.

After the skyway the freeway merged with the 75 and he reached Venice two hours after landing. Cruising along the Tamiami Trail, he found the small pastel-painted motels inviting as he struggled with fatigue, but he drove on and looked for a gift shop and a pay phone.

He found both in the Coral Reef Shopping Plaza. The

Tacky's Gifts and Cards store wasn't due to open until ten and Bosch had five minutes to waste. He went to a pay phone on the outside wall of the sand-colored plaza and looked up the post office in the book. There were two in town so Bosch took out his notebook and checked Jake McKittrick's zip code. He called one of the post offices listed in the book and learned that the other one catered to the zip code Bosch had. He thanked the clerk who had provided the information and hung up.

When the gift shop opened, Bosch went to the cards aisle and found a birthday card that came with a bright red envelope. He took it to the counter without even reading the inside or the outside of the card. He picked a local street map out of a display next to the cash register and put that on the counter as well.

'That's a nice card,' said the old woman who rang up the sale. 'I'm sure she'll just love it.'

She moved as if she were underwater and Bosch wanted to reach over the counter and punch in the numbers himself, just to get it going.

In the Mustang, Bosch put the card in the envelope without signing it, sealed it and wrote McKittrick's name and post office box number on the front. He then started the car and got back on the road.

It took him fifteen minutes working with the map to find the post office on West Venice Avenue. When he got inside, he found it largely deserted. An old man was standing at a table slowly writing an address on an envelope. Two elderly women were in line for counter service. Bosch stood behind them and realized that he was seeing a lot of senior citizens in Florida and he'd only been here a few hours. It was just like he had always heard.

Bosch looked around and saw the video camera on the wall behind the counter. He could tell by its positioning it was there more for recording customers and possible robbers than for surveilling the clerks, though their workstations were probably fully in view as well. He was undeterred. He took a ten-dollar bill out of his pocket, folded it cleanly and held it with the red envelope. He then checked his loose change and came up with the right amount. It seemed like an excruciatingly long time as the one clerk waited on the women.

'Next in line.'

It was Bosch. He walked up to the counter where the clerk waited. He was about sixty and had a perfect white beard. He was overweight and his skin seemed too red to Bosch. As if he was mad or something.

'I need a stamp for this.'

Bosch put down the change and the envelope. The ten-dollar bill was folded on top of it. The postman acted like he didn't see it.

'I was wondering, did they put the mail out yet in the boxes?'

'They're back there doin' it now.'

He handed Bosch a stamp and swiped the change off the counter. He didn't touch the ten or the red envelope.

'Oh, really?'

Bosch picked up the envelope, licked the stamp and put it on. He then put the envelope back down on top of the ten. He was sure the postman had observed this.

'Well, jeez, I really wanted to get this to my Uncle Jake. It's his birthday today. Any way somebody could run it back there? That way he'd get it when he came in today. I'd deliver it in person but I've got to get back to work.'

Bosch slid the envelope with the ten underneath it across the counter, closer to white beard.

'Well,' he said, 'I'll see what I can do.'

The postman shifted his body to the left and turned slightly, shielding the transaction from the video camera. In one fluid motion he took the envelope and the ten off the counter. He quickly transferred the ten to his other hand and it dove for cover in his pocket.

'Be right back,' he called to the people still in line.

Out in the lobby, Bosch found Box 313 and looked through the tiny pane of glass inside. The red envelope was there along with two white letters. One of the white envelopes was upside down and its return address was partially visible.

City of
Departm
P.O. Bo
Los Ang
90021–3

Bosch felt reasonably sure the envelope carried McKittrick's pension check. He had beaten the mail to him. He walked out of the post office, bought two cups of coffee and a box of doughnuts in the convenience store next door and then returned to the Mustang to wait in the day's growing heat. It wasn't even May yet. He couldn't imagine what a summer must be like here.

Bored with watching the post office door after an hour, Bosch turned on the radio and found it tuned to a channel featuring a southern evangelical ranter. It took several seconds before Harry realized that the speaker's subject was the Los Angeles earthquake. He decided not to change the station.

'And ah ask, is it a coincidence that this cata-clysmic calamity was centered in the very heart of the ind'stry that poe-loots this entarh nation with the smut of pone-ography? I think not! I believe the Lahd struck a mighty blow to the infidels engaged in this vile and mul-tie-billyon-dollah trade when he cracked the uth asundah. It is a sign, mah frens, a sign of things that ah to come. A sign that all is not right in –'

Bosch turned it off. A woman had just come out of the post office holding a red envelope among other pieces of mail. Bosch watched her cross the parking lot to a silver Lincoln Town Car. Bosch instinctively jotted the plate number down, though he had no law enforcement contact in this part of the state who would run it for him. The woman was in her mid-sixties, Bosch guessed. He had been waiting for a man, but her age made her fit. He started the Mustang and waited for her to pull out.

She drove north on the main highway toward Sarasota. Traffic moved slowly. After about fifteen minutes and maybe two miles, the Town Car took a left on Vamo Road and then almost immediately took a right on a private road camouflaged by tall trees and green growth. Bosch was only ten seconds behind her. As he came up to the drive, he slowed but didn't turn in. He saw a sign set back in the trees.

WELCOME TO

PELICAN COVE

Condominium Homes, Dockage

The Town Car passed by a guard shack with a red-and-white-striped gate arm coming down behind it.

'Shit!'

Bosch hadn't anticipated anything like a gated community. He assumed that such things were rare outside of Los Angeles. He looked at the sign again, then turned around and headed out to the main road. He remembered seeing another shopping plaza right before he had turned on to Vamo.

There were eight homes in Pelican Cove listed in the For Sale section of the *Sarasota Herald-Tribune*, but only three were for sale by owner. Bosch went to a pay phone in the plaza and called the first one. He got a tape. On the second call the woman who answered said her husband was golfing for the day and she felt uncomfortable showing the property without him. On the third call, the woman who answered invited Bosch to come over right away and even said she'd have fresh lemonade prepared when he got there.

Bosch felt a momentary pang of guilt about taking advantage of a stranger who was just trying to sell her home. But it passed quickly as he considered that the woman would never know she had been used in such a way, and he had no other alternative for getting to McKittrick.

After he was cleared at the gate and got directions to the lemonade lady's unit, Bosch drove through the densely wooded complex, looking for the silver Town Car. It didn't take him long to see that the complex was mostly a retirement community. He passed several elderly people in cars or on walks, almost all of them with white hair and skin browned by the sun. He quickly found the Town Car, checked his location against the map given to him at the guard shack and was about to make a cursory visit to the lemonade lady to avoid suspicion. But then he saw another silver Town Car. It was a popular car with the older set, he guessed. He took out his notebook and checked the plate number he had written down. Neither car had been the one he had followed earlier.

He drove on and finally found the right Town Car in a secluded spot in the far reaches of the complex. It was parked in front of a two-story building of dark wood siding surrounded by oak and paper trees. It looked to Bosch as if there were six units in the building. Easy enough, he thought. He consulted the map and got back on course to the lemonade lady. She was on the second floor of a building on the other side of the complex.

'You're young,' she said when she answered the door. Bosch wanted to say the same thing back to her but held his tongue. She looked like she was in her mid- to late thirties, which put her three decades behind anyone Bosch had seen around the complex so far. She had an attractive and evenly tanned face framed in brown shoulder-length hair. She wore blue jeans, a blue oxford shirt and a black vest with a colorful pattern in the front. She didn't bother with much makeup, which Bosch liked. She had serious green eyes, which he also didn't disagree with.

'I'm Jasmine. Are you Mr Bosch?'

'Yes. Harry. I just called.'

'That was quick.'

'I was nearby.'

She invited him in and started the rundown.

'It's three bedrooms, like the paper said. Master suite has a private bath. Second bath off the main hall. The view is what makes the place, though.'

She pointed Bosch toward a wall of sliding glass doors that looked out on a wide expanse of water dotted with mangrove islands. Hundreds of birds perched in the branches of these otherwise untouched islands. She was right, the view was beautiful.

'What is that?' Bosch asked. 'The water.'

'That's – you're not from around here, are you? That's Little Sarasota Bay.'

Bosch nodded while computing the mistake he had made by blurting out the question.

'No, I'm not from around here. I'm thinking of moving here though.'

'Where from?'

'Los Angeles.'

'Oh, yes, I've heard. A lot of people are bailing out. Because the ground won't stop shaking.'

'Something like that.'

She led him down a hallway to what must have been the master suite. Bosch was immediately struck by how the room didn't seem to fit this woman. It was all dark and old and heavy. A mahogany bureau that looked like it weighed a ton, matching bedside tables with ornate lamps and brocaded shades. The place smelled old. It couldn't be where she slept.

He turned and noticed on the wall next to the door an oil painting that was a portrait of the woman standing next to him. It was a younger likeness of her, the face much gaunter, more severe. Bosch was wondering what kind of person hangs a painting of herself in her bedroom when he noticed that the painting was signed. The artist's name was Jazz.

'Jazz. Is that you?'

'Yes. My father insisted on hanging that in here. I actually should have taken it down.'

She went to the wall and began to lift the painting off.

'Your father?'

He moved to the other side of the painting to help her.

'Yes. I gave this to him a long time ago. At the time I was thankful he didn't hang it out in the living room where his friends would see it but even here is a little too much.'

She turned the painting so the back faced outward and leaned it against the wall. Bosch put together what she had been saying.

'This is your father's place.'

'Oh, yes. I've just been staying here while the ad ran in the paper. You want to check out the master bath? It has a Jacuzzi tub. That wasn't mentioned in the ad.'

Bosch moved closely by her to the bathroom door. He looked down at her hands, a natural instinct, and saw no rings on any of her fingers. He could smell her as he passed and the scent he picked up was the same as her name: Jasmine. He was beginning to feel some kind of attraction to her but wasn't sure if it was the titillation of being there under false pretenses or an honest pull. He was exhausted, he knew, and decided that was it. His defenses were down. He gave the bathroom a quick once-over and stepped out.

'Nice. Did he live here alone?'

'My father? Yes, alone. My mother died when I was little. My father passed away over Christmas.'

'I'm sorry.'

'Thank you. What else can I tell you?'

'Nothing. I was just curious about who had been living here.'

'No. I mean, what else can I tell you about the condo?'

'Oh, I ... nothing. It's very nice. I'm still in the looking-around stage, I guess, not sure what I'm going to do. I –'

'What are you really doing?'

'Excuse me?'

'What are you doing here, Mr Bosch? You're not looking to buy a condo in here. You're not even looking at the place.'

There was no anger in her voice. It was a voice full of the confidence she had in reading people. Bosch felt himself turning red. He had been found out.

'I'm just ... I'm just here to look at places.'

It was a terribly weak comeback and he knew it. But it was all he could think of to say. She sensed his predicament and let him off the hook.

'Well, I'm sorry if I embarrassed you. Do you want to see the rest of the place?'

'Yes – uh, well, did you say it was three bedrooms? That's really too big for what I'm looking for.'

'Yes, three. But it said that in the newspaper ad, too.'

Luckily, Bosch knew he probably couldn't get any redder than he already was.

'Oh,' he said. 'I must've missed that. Uh, thanks for the tour, though. It's a very nice place.'

He moved quickly through the living room toward the

door. As he opened it he looked back at her. She spoke before he could say anything.

'Something tells me it's a good story.'

'What's that?'

'Whatever it is you're doing. If you ever feel like telling it, the number's in the paper. But you already know that.'

Bosch nodded. He was speechless. He stepped through the door and closed it behind him.

By the time he drove back to where he had seen the Town Car, his face had returned to its normal color but he still felt embarrassed about being cornered by the woman. He tried to dismiss it and concentrate on the task at hand. He parked and went to the first-floor door that was nearest the Town Car and knocked. Eventually, an old woman opened the door and stared at him with frightened eyes. One hand clasped the handle of a small two-wheeled cart that carried an oxygen bottle. Two clear plastic tubes snaked over her ears and across both cheeks to her nose.

'I'm sorry to disturb you,' he said quickly. 'I was looking for the McKittricks.'

She raised a frail hand, formed a fist with the thumb out and jerked it up toward the ceiling. Her eyes went up that way, too.

'Upstairs?'

She nodded. He thanked her and headed for the stairs.

The woman who had picked up the red envelope answered the next door he knocked on and Bosch exhaled as if he had spent a lifetime looking for her. It almost felt that way.

'Mrs McKittrick?'

'Yes?'

Bosch pulled out his badge case and flipped it open.

He held the wallet so that his first two fingers crossed most of the badge, obscuring the LIEUTENANT.

'My name's Harry Bosch. I'm a detective with the LAPD. I was wondering if your husband was here. I'd like to talk to him.'

An immediate concern clouded her face.

'LAPD? He hasn't been out there in twenty years.'

'It's about an old case. I was sent out to ask him about it.'

'Well, you could've called.'

'We didn't have a number. Is he here?'

'No, he's down with the boat. He's going fishing.'

'Where's that? Maybe I can catch him.'

'Well, he doesn't like surprises.'

'I guess it will be a surprise whether you tell him or I tell him. Doesn't make any difference to me. I just have to talk to him, Mrs McKittrick.'

Maybe she was used to the no-debate tone that cops can put into their voice. She gave in.

'You walk around the building here and go straight back past the next three buildings. Go left, you'll see the docks after that.'

'Where's his boat?'

'It's slip six. It says *Trophy* in big letters on the side. You can't miss it. He hasn't left yet because I'm supposed to bring his lunch down.'

'Thanks.'

He had started away from the door to the side of the building when she called after him.

'Detective Bosch? Are you going to be a while? Should I make you a sandwich, too?'

'I don't know how long I'll be but that would be nice of you.'

As he headed toward the docks, he realized that the

woman named Jasmine had never offered him the lemonade she had promised.

It took Bosch fifteen minutes to find the little inlet where the docks were. After that, McKittrick was easy enough to spot. There were maybe forty boats in slips but only one of them was occupied. A man with a deep tan set off by his white hair stood in the stern bending over the outboard engine. Bosch studied him as he got closer but saw nothing recognizable about the man. He did not fit with the image Bosch had in his mind's eye of the man who had pulled him from the pool so long ago.

The cover was off the boat engine and the man was doing something with a screwdriver. He wore khaki shorts and a white golf shirt that was too old and stained for golf but was fine for boating. The boat was about twenty feet long, Bosch guessed, and had a small cabin near the bow, where the helm was. There were fishing rods erected in holders along the sides of the boat, two rods per side.

Bosch stopped on the dock at the bow of the boat on purpose. He wanted to be at a distance from McKittrick when he showed the badge. He smiled.

'Never thought I'd see somebody from the Hollywood homicide table so far away from home,' he said.

McKittrick looked up but showed no surprise. He showed nothing.

'Nope, you're wrong. This is home. When I was over there, that's when I was far away.'

Bosch gave a that's-fair-enough nod and showed the

badge. He held it the same way as when he'd showed it to McKittrick's wife.

'I'm Harry Bosch, from Hollywood homicide.'

'Yeah, that's what I heard.'

Bosch was the one who showed surprise. He could not think of who in LA would have tipped McKittrick to his arrival. No one knew. He had only told Hinojos and he could not fathom that she would betray him.

McKittrick relieved him by gesturing to the portable phone on the dashboard of the boat.

'The wife called.'

'Oh.'

'So what's this all about, Detective Bosch? When I used to work there, we did things in pairs. It was safer that way. You folks that understaffed, you're going singleton?'

'Not really. My partner's chasing down another old case. These are such long shots, they're not wasting money sending two.'

'I assume you're going to explain that.'

'Yeah. As a matter of fact, I am. Mind if I come down there?'

'Suit yourself. I'm fixing to shove off as soon as the wife comes with the food.'

Bosch began walking along the finger dock to the side of McKittrick's boat. He then stepped down into the craft. It wobbled on the water with the added weight but then steadied. McKittrick lifted the engine cover and began snapping it back in place. Bosch felt grossly out of place. He wore street shoes with black jeans, an Army green T-shirt and a black light-weight sport jacket. And he was still hot. He took the jacket off and folded it over one of the two chairs in the cockpit.

'What are you going for?'

'Whatever's biting. What are you going for?'

He looked directly at Bosch when he asked this and Harry saw that his eyes were brown like beer-bottle glass.

'Well, you heard about the earthquake, didn't you?'

'Sure, who didn't? You know, I've been through quakes and 'canes and you can keep the quakes. At least with a hurricane, you see it coming. You take Andrew, he left a lot of devastation, but think how much it woulda been if nobody knew he was about to hit. That's what you get with your earthquakes.'

It took Bosch a few moments to place Andrew, the hurricane that had slammed the South Florida coast a couple of years earlier. It was hard to keep track of all the disasters in the world. There were enough just in LA. He looked out across the inlet. He saw a fish jump and its reentry create a stampede of jumping among the others in the school. He looked at McKittrick and was about to tell him when he realized it was probably something McKittrick saw every day of his life.

'When'd you leave LA?'

'Twenty-one years ago. I got my twenty in and *pffft*, I was gone. You can have LA, Bosch. Shit, I was out there for the Sylmar quake in seventy-one. Knocked down a hospital and a couple freeways. At the time we were living in Tujunga, a few miles from the epicenter. I'll always remember that one. It was like God and the devil meetin' in the room and you were there with 'em playin' referee. Goddamn ... So what's the quake got to do with you being here?'

'Well, it's kind of a strange phenomenon but the murder rate's fallen off. People are being more civil, I guess. We –'

'Maybe there's nothing left there worth killing for.'

'Maybe. Anyway, we're usually running seventy, eighty murders a year in the division, I don't know what it was like when you –'

'We'd do less than half that. Easy.'

'Well, we're running way below the average this year. It's given us time to go back through some of the old ones. Everybody on the table's taken a share. One of the ones I've got has your name on it. I guess you know your partner from back then passed away and –'

'Eno's dead? Goddamn, I didn't know that. I thought I would've heard about that. Not that it would've mattered a whole hell of a lot.'

'Yeah, he's dead. His wife gets the pension checks. Sorry, you hadn't heard.'

'That's okay. Eno and me ... well, we were partners. That's about it.'

'Anyway, I'm here because you're alive and he isn't.'

'What's the case?'

'Marjorie Lowe.' He waited a moment for a reaction from McKittrick's face and got none. 'You remember it? She was found in the trash in an alley off –'

'Vista. Behind Hollywood Boulevard between Vista and Gower. I remember them all, Bosch. Cleared or not, I remember every goddamn one of them.'

But you don't remember me, Bosch thought but didn't say.

'Yeah, that's the one. Between Vista and Gower.'

'What about it?'

'It was never cleared.'

'I know that,' McKittrick said, his voice rising. 'I worked sixty-three cases during seven years on the homicide table. I worked Hollywood, Wilshire, then RHD. Cleared fifty-six. I'll put that up against anybody. Today they're lucky if they clear half of 'em. I'll put it up against you blind.'

'And you'd win. That's a good record. This isn't about you, Jake. It's about the case.'

'Don't call me Jake. I don't know you. Never seen you before in my life. I – wait a minute.'

Bosch stared at him, astonished that he might actually remember the pool. But then he realized that McKittrick had stopped because of his wife's approach along the dock. She was carrying a plastic cooler. McKittrick waited silently for her to put it down on the dock near the boat and he hoisted it aboard.

'Oh, Detective Bosch, you'll be way too hot in that,' Mrs McKittrick said. 'Do you want to come back up and borrow a pair of Jake's shorts and a white T-shirt?'

Bosch looked at McKittrick, then up at her.

'No, thanks, ma'am, I'm fine.'

'You are going fishing, aren't you?'

'Well, I haven't exactly been invited and I –'

'Oh, Jake, invite him fishing. You're always looking for somebody to go out with you. Besides, you can catch up on all that blood-and-guts stuff you used to love in Hollywood.'

McKittrick looked up at her and Bosch could see the horses fighting against the restraints. He was able to get it under control.

'Mary, thanks for the sandwiches,' he said calmly. 'Now, could you go back up to the house and leave us be?'

She threw him a frown and shook her head as if he were a spoiled boy. She went back the way she had come without another word. The two of them left on the boat let some time go by before Bosch finally spoke and tried to recover the situation.

'Look, I'm not here for any reason other than to ask you a few questions about this case. I'm not trying to suggest there was anything wrong with the way it was handled. I'm just taking another look at it. That's all.'

'You left something out.'

'What's that?'

'That you're full of shit.'

Bosch could feel the horses rearing up in himself. He was angry at this man's questioning his motives, even though he was right to do so. He was on the verge of shedding the nice-guy skin and going at him. But he knew better. He knew that for McKittrick to act this way, there must be a reason. Something about the old case was like a pebble in his shoe. He had worked it over to the side where it didn't hurt when he walked. But it was still in there. Bosch had to make him want to take it out. He swallowed his own anger and tried to stay level.

'Why am I full of shit?' he said.

McKittrick's back was to him. The former cop was reaching down under the steering console. Bosch couldn't see what he was trying to do, except he guessed he was maybe looking for a hidden set of boat keys.

'Why are you full of shit?' McKittrick answered as he turned around. 'I'll tell you why. Because you come here flashing that bullshit badge around when we both know you don't have a badge.'

McKittrick was pointing a Beretta twenty-two at Bosch. It was small but it would do the job at this distance, and Bosch had to believe that McKittrick knew how to use it.

'Jesus, man, what's the problem with you?'

'I had no problem until you showed up.'

Bosch held his hands chest-high in a nonthreatening pose.

'Just take it easy.'

'You take it easy. Put your fucking hands down. I want to see that badge again. Take it out and toss it over here. Slowly.'

Bosch complied, all the while trying to look around the docks without turning his head more than a few inches. He didn't see anyone. He was alone. And unarmed. He threw the badge wallet down on the deck near McKittrick's feet.

'Now I want you to walk around the bridge to the bow up there. Stand against the bow rail where I can see you. I knew somebody would try to fuck with me someday. Well, you picked the wrong guy and the wrong day.'

Bosch did as instructed and went up to the bow. He grabbed the railing for support and turned around to face his captor. Without taking his eyes off Bosch, McKittrick bent and picked up the wallet. Then he moved into the cockpit and put the gun down on top of the console. Bosch knew if he tried for it McKittrick would get there first. McKittrick reached down and turned something and the engine kicked over.

'What are you doing, McKittrick?'

'Oh, now it's McKittrick. What happened to the friendly "Jake"? Well, what's doing is, we're going fishing. You wanted to fish, that's what we'll do. You try to jump and I'll shoot you in the water. I don't care.'

'I'm not going anywhere. Just take it easy.'

'Now, reach down to that cleat and unhook that line. Throw it up on the dock.'

When Bosch had finished completing the order, McKittrick picked up the gun and stepped back three paces into the stern. He untied the other line and pushed off from a pylon. He returned to the helm and gently put the boat in reverse. It glided out of the slip. McKittrick then put it in forward and they started moving through the inlet toward the mouth of the canal. Bosch could feel the warm salt breezes drying the sweat on his skin. He decided he would jump as soon as they got to some open water, or where there were other boats with people on them.

'Kind of surprised you're not carrying. What kind of guy says he's a cop, then doesn't carry a piece?'

'I am a cop, McKittrick. Let me explain.'

'You don't have to, boy, I already know. Know all about you.'

McKittrick flipped open the badge wallet and Bosch watched him study the ID card and the gold lieutenant's badge. He threw it on the console.

'What do you know about me, McKittrick?'

'Don't worry, I still have a few teeth left, Bosch, and I still have a few friends in the department. After the wife called, I made a call. One of my friends. He knew all about you. You're on leave, Bosch. Involuntary. So I don't know about this bullshit story about earthquakes you were spinning. Makes me think maybe you picked up a little freelance work while you're off the job.'

'You got it wrong.'

'Yeah, well, we'll see. Once we get out into some open water, you're gonna tell me who sent you or you're gonna be fish food. Makes no difference to me.'

'Nobody sent me. I sent myself.'

McKittrick slapped his palm against the red ball on the throttle lever and the boat surged forward. Its bow rose and Bosch grabbed the railing to hold on.

'Bullshit!' McKittrick yelled above the engine noise. 'You're a liar. You lied before, you're lying now.'

'Listen to me,' Bosch yelled. 'You said you remember every case.'

'I do, goddamnit! I can't forget them.'

'Cut it back!'

McKittrick pulled the throttle back and the boat evened off and the noise reduced.

'On the Marjorie Lowe case you pulled the dirty work. You remember that? Remember what we call the dirty work? You had to tell the next of kin. You had to tell her kid. Out at McClaren.'

'That was in the reports, Bosch. So –'

He stopped and stared at Bosch for a long moment.

212

Then he flipped open the badge case and read the name. He looked back at Bosch.

'I remember that name. The swimming pool. You're the kid.'

'I'm the kid.'

McKittrick let the boat drift in the shallows of Little Sarasota Bay while Bosch told the story. He asked no questions. He simply listened. At a moment where Bosch paused, he opened the cooler his wife had packed and took out two beers, handing one to Bosch. The can felt ice-cold in Bosch's hand.

Bosch didn't pull the tab on his beer until he finished the story. He had told everything he knew to McKittrick, even the nonessential part about his run-in with Pounds. He had a hunch, based on McKittrick's anger and bizarre behavior, that he had been wrong about the old cop. He had flown out to Florida believing he was coming to see either a corrupt or a stupid cop and he wasn't sure which he would dislike more. But now he believed that McKittrick was a man who was haunted by memories and the demons of choices made badly many years ago. Bosch thought that the pebble still had to come out of the shoe and that his own honesty was the best way to get to it.

'So that's my story,' he said at the end. 'I hope she packed more than two of these.'

He popped the beer and drank nearly a third of it. It tasted delicious going down his throat in the afternoon sun.

'Oh, there's plenty more where that came from,' McKittrick replied. 'You want a sandwich?'

'Not yet.'

'No, what you want is my story now.'

'That's what I came for.'

'Well, let's get out there to the fish.'

He restarted the engine and they followed a trail of channel markers south through the bay. Bosch finally remembered he had sunglasses in the pocket of his sport coat and put them on.

It seemed like the wind was cutting in on him from all directions and on occasion its warmth would be traded for a cool breeze that would come up off the surface of the water. It was a long time since Bosch had been on a boat or had even been fishing. For a man who had had a gun pointed at him twenty minutes earlier, he realized he felt pretty good.

As the bay tapered off into a canal, McKittrick pulled back on the throttle and cut their wake. He waved to a man on the bridge of a giant yacht tied up outside a waterside restaurant. Bosch couldn't tell if he knew the man or was just being neighborly.

'Take it on a line even with the lantern on the bridge,' McKittrick said.

'What?'

'Take it.'

McKittrick stepped away from the wheel and into the stern of the boat. Bosch quickly stepped behind the wheel, sighted the red lantern hanging at center point beneath the span of a drawbridge a half mile ahead and adjusted the wheel to bring the boat into line. He looked back and saw McKittrick pull a plastic bag of small dead fish out of a compartment in the deck.

'Let's see who we've got here today,' he said.

He went to the side of the boat and leaned well over the gunwale. Bosch saw him start slapping an open palm on the side of the boat. McKittrick then stood up, surveyed the water for about ten seconds and repeated the banging.

'What's going on?' Bosch asked.

Just as he said it, a dolphin crested the water off the port stern and reentered no more than five feet from where McKittrick was standing. It was a slippery gray blur and Bosch wasn't exactly sure at first what had happened. But the dolphin quickly resurfaced next to the boat, its snout out of the water and chattering. It sounded like it was laughing. McKittrick dropped two of the fish into its open mouth.

'That's Sergeant, see the scars?'

Bosch took a quick look back at the bridge to make sure they were still reasonably on line and then stepped back to the stern. The dolphin was still there. McKittrick pointed down into the water beneath its dorsal fin. Bosch could see three white stripes slashed across its smooth gray back.

'He got too close to a prop one time and it cut him up. The people up at Mote Marine took care of him. But he was left with those sergeant's stripes.'

Bosch nodded as McKittrick fed the dolphin again. Without looking up to see if they were off course, McKittrick said, 'You better get the wheel.'

Bosch turned and saw that they had drifted far off line. He went back to the wheel and corrected the course. He stayed there while McKittrick remained in the back, throwing fish to the dolphin, until they passed under the bridge. Bosch decided he could wait him out. Whether it was while they were going out or coming in didn't matter. He was going to get McKittrick's story. He was not going to leave without it.

Ten minutes after the bridge they came to a channel that took them out to the Gulf of Mexico. McKittrick dropped lures from two of the poles into the water and put out about a hundred yards of line on each one. He took the wheel back from Bosch then, yelling into the wind and engine noise.

'I want to take it out to the reefs. We'll troll until we're there and then we'll do some drift fishing in the shallows. We'll talk then.'

'Sounds like a plan,' Bosch yelled back.

Nothing hit either of the lures, and about two miles from the shore McKittrick killed the engines and told Bosch to bring in one line while he handled the other. It took Bosch, who was left handed, a few moments to get himself coordinated on the right-handed reel but then he started smiling.

'I don't think I've done this since I was a kid. At McClaren every now and then they'd put us on a bus and take us out to the Malibu Pier.'

'Jesus, that pier still there?'

'Yeah.'

'Must be like fishing in a cesspool by now.'

'I guess.'

McKittrick laughed and shook his head.

'Why do you stay there, Bosch? Doesn't sound like they particularly want you.'

Bosch thought a moment before answering. The comment was on point but he wondered if it was on point from McKittrick or whoever the source was he had called.

'Who'd you call back there about me?'

'I'm not telling you. That's why he talked to me, because he knew I wouldn't tell you.'

Bosch nodded, signaling he'd let it go.

'Well, you're right,' he said. 'I don't think they particularly want me back there. But I don't know. It's kind've like the more they push one way, the more I push the other. I feel like if they'd stop asking or trying to make me leave, then I'd probably want to do it.'

'I guess I know what you mean.'

McKittrick stowed the two rods they had used and set

217

to work outfitting the other two with hooks and buckshot weights.

'We're going to use mullet.'

Bosch nodded. He didn't know the first thing about it. But he watched McKittrick closely. He thought it might be a good time to start.

'So you punched out after your twenty in LA. What'd you do after that?'

'You're looking at it. I moved back here – I'm from Palmetto, up the coast, originally. I bought a boat and became a fishing guide. Did that another twenty, retired and now I fish for my own damned self.'

Bosch smiled.

'Palmetto? Isn't that the name of those big cockroaches?'

'No. Well, yeah, but it's also the name of a scrub palm. That's what the town's named for, not the bug.'

Bosch nodded and watched as McKittrick opened a bag of mullet strips and hooked pieces on each line. After opening fresh beers, they cast on separate sides of the boat and then sat on the gunwales, waiting.

'Then how'd you end up in LA?' Bosch asked.

'What was that somebody said about going west young man? Well, after Japan surrendered I passed through LA on my way back home and I saw those mountains going all the way up from the sea to the sky ... Damn, I ate dinner at the Derby my first night in town. I was going to blow my whole wallet and you know who saw me there in uniform and picked up the tab? Goddamn Clark Gable. I'm not kidding you. I fuckin' fell in love with that place and it took me almost thirty years to see the light ... Mary's from LA, you know. Born and raised. She likes it out here fine.'

He nodded to reassure himself. Bosch waited a few moments and McKittrick was still looking off at distant memories.

'He was a nice guy.'

'Who's that?'

'Clark Gable.'

Bosch crunched the empty beer can in his hand and got another.

'So tell me about the case,' he said after popping it. 'What happened?'

'You know what happened if you read the book. It was all in there. It got dumped. One day we had an investigation, the next we were writing 'No leads at this time.' It was a joke. That's why I remember the case so well. They shouldn't've done what they did.'

'Who's they?'

'You know, the big shots.'

'What did they do?'

'They took it away from us. And Eno let them. He cut some deal with them himself. Shit.'

He shook his head bitterly.

'Jake,' Bosch tried. He got no protest this time over using the first name. 'Why don't you start at the beginning. I need to know everything I can from you.'

McKittrick was quiet while he reeled in. His bait hadn't been touched. He recast it, put the rod in one of the gunwale pipes and got another beer. From beneath the console he grabbed a Tampa Bay Lightning cap and put it on. He leaned on the gunwale with his beer and looked at Bosch.

'Okay, kid, listen, I got nothin' against your mother. I'm just gonna tell you this the way it fell, okay?'

'That's all I want.'

'You want a hat? You're gonna get burned.'

'I'm fine.'

McKittrick nodded and finally started.

'Okay, so we got the call out from home. It was a Saturday morning. One of the footbeat guys had found her. She hadn't been killed in that alley. That much was clear. She'd been dropped off. By the time I got down there from Tujunga, the crime scene investigation was already underway. My partner was there, too. Eno. He was the senior man, he was there first. He took charge of it.'

Bosch put his rod in a pipe and went to his jacket.

'You mind if I take notes?'

'No, I don't mind. I guess I've been waiting for somebody to care about this one since I walked away from it.'

'Go ahead. Eno was in charge.'

'Yeah, he was the man. You've got to understand something. We'd been a team maybe three, four months at that time. We weren't tight. After this one, we'd never be tight. I switched off after about a year. I went in for the transfer. They moved me to Wilshire dicks, homicide table. Never had much to do with him after that. He never had much to do with me.'

'Okay, what happened with the investigation?'

'Well, it was like anything else that you'd expect. We were going through the routine. We had a list of her KAs – got it mostly from the vice guys – and were working our way through it.'

'The known associates, did they include clients? There was no list in the murder book.'

'I think there were a few clients. And the list didn't go into the book because Eno said so. Remember, he was the lead.'

'Okay. Johnny Fox was on the list?'

'Yeah, he was at the top of it. He was her ... uh, manager and –'

'Her pimp, you mean.'

McKittrick looked at him.

'Yeah. That's what he was. I wasn't sure what you, uh –'

'Forget it. Go on.'

'Yeah, Johnny Fox was on the list. We talked to about everybody who knew her and this guy was described by everybody as one mean guy. He had a history.'

Bosch thought of Meredith Roman's report that he had beaten her.

'We'd heard that she was trying to get away from him. I don't know, either to go out on her own or maybe go straight. Who knows? We heard –'

'She wanted to be a straight citizen,' Bosch interrupted. 'That way she could get me out of the hall.'

He felt foolish for saying it, knowing his saying it was not convincing.

'Yeah, whatever,' McKittrick said. 'Point is, Fox was none too happy about that. That put him at the top of our list.'

'But you couldn't find him. The chrono says you watched his place.'

'Yeah. He was our man. We had prints we had taken off the belt – the murder weapon – but we had no comparisons from him. Johnny had been pulled in a few times in the past but never booked. Never printed. So we really needed to bring him in.'

'What did it tell you, that he'd been picked up but never booked?'

McKittrick finished his beer, crunched it in his hand and walked the empty over to a large bucket in the corner of the deck and dropped it.

'To be honest, at the time it didn't hit me. Now, of course, it's obvious. He had an angel watching over him.'

'Who?'

'Well, on one of the days we were watching Fox's place, waiting for him to show up, we got a message on

221

the radio to call Arno Conklin. He wanted to talk about the case. ASAP. Now this was a holy shit kind of call. For two reasons. One, Arno was going great guns then. He was running the city's moral commandos at the time and had a lock on the DA's office, which was coming open in a year. The other reason was that we'd only had the case a few days and hadn't come near the DA's office with anything. So now all of a sudden the most powerful guy in the agency wants to see us. I'm thinking ... I don't really know what I was thinking. I just knew it – hey, you got one!'

Bosch looked at his pole and saw it bend from a violent jerk on the line. The reel started spinning as the fish pulled against the drag. Bosch grabbed the pole out of the pipe and jerked it back. The hook was set well. He started reeling but the fish had a lot of fight and was pulling out more line than he was reeling in. McKittrick came over and tightened the drag dial, which immediately put a more pronounced bend in the pole.

'Keep the pole up, keep the pole up,' McKittrick counseled.

Bosch did as he was told and spent five minutes battling the fish. His arms started to ache. He felt a strain on his lower back. McKittrick put on gloves and when the fish finally surrendered and Bosch had it alongside the boat, he bent over and hooked his fingers into the gills and brought it on board. Bosch saw a shiny blue-black fish that looked beautiful in the sunlight.

'Wahoo,' McKittrick said.

'What?'

McKittrick held the fish up horizontally.

'Wahoo. Over there in your fancy LA restaurants I think they call it Ono. Here, we just call it wahoo. Meat cooks up white as halibut, you wanna keep it?'

'No, put it back. It's beautiful.'

McKittrick roughly pulled the hook from the gulping mouth of the fish and then held the catch out to Bosch.

'You want to hold it? Must be twelve, thirteen pounds.'

'Nah, I don't need to hold it.'

Bosch stepped closer and ran his finger along the slick skin of the fish. He could almost see himself in the reflection of its scales. He nodded to McKittrick and the fish was thrown back into the water. For several seconds it remained motionless, about two feet below the surface. Post-traumatic stress syndrome, Bosch thought. Finally, the fish seemed to come out of it and darted down into the depths. Bosch put the hook through one of the eyelets on his pole and put the pole back in its pipe. He was done fishing. He got another beer out of the cooler.

'Hey, you want a sandwich, go ahead,' McKittrick said.

'No. I'm fine.'

Bosch wished the fish hadn't interrupted them.

'You were saying that you guys got the call from Conklin.'

'Yeah, Arno. Only I had it wrong. The request for a meeting was only for Claude. Not me. Eno went alone.'

'Why only Eno?'

'I never knew and he acted like he didn't know, either. I just assumed it was because he and Arno had a prior relationship of some kind.'

'But you don't know what.'

'No. Claude Eno was about ten years older than me. He'd been around.'

'So what happened?'

'Well, I can't tell you what happened. I can only tell you what my partner said happened. Understand?'

He was telling Bosch that he didn't trust his own partner. Bosch had known that feeling himself at times and nodded that he understood.

'Go ahead.'

'He came back from the meeting saying Conklin asked him to lay off Fox because Fox was clear on this case and Fox was working as an informant on one of the commando investigations. He said Fox was important to him and he didn't want him compromised or roughed up, especially over a crime he didn't commit.'

'How was Conklin so sure?'

'I don't know. But Eno told me that he told Conklin that assistant DAs, no matter who they are, didn't decide whether someone was clear or not for the police, and that we weren't backing off until we talked to Fox for ourselves. Faced with that, Conklin said he could deliver Fox to be interviewed and fingerprinted. But only if we did it on Conklin's turf.'

'Which was ... ?'

'His office in the old courthouse. That's gone now. They built that big square thing right before I left. Horrible-looking thing.'

'What happened in the office? Were you there for that?'

'Yeah, I was there but nothing happened. We interviewed him. Fox was there with Conklin, so was the Nazi.'

'The Nazi?'

'Conklin's enforcer, Gordon Mittel.'

'He was there?'

'Yup. I guess he was sort of watching out for Conklin while Conklin was watching out for Fox.'

Bosch showed no surprise.

'Okay, so what did Fox tell you?'

'Like I said, not much. At least, that's how I remember it. He gave us an alibi and the names of the people who could verify it. I took his prints.'

'What'd he say about the victim?'

'He said pretty much what we'd already heard from her girlfriend.'

'Meredith Roman?'

'Yeah, I think that's it. He said she went to a party, was hired as kind of a decoration to be on some guy's arm. He said it was in Hancock Park. He didn't have the address. He said he had nothing to do with setting it up. That didn't make sense to us. You know, a pimp not knowing where ... not knowing where one of his girls was. It was the one thing we had and when we started leaning on him about it, Conklin stepped in like a referee.'

'He didn't want you leaning on him.'

'Craziest thing I ever saw. Here was the next DA – everybody knew he was going to run. Here he was taking this bastard's side against us ... Sorry about that bastard comment.'

'Forget it.'

'Conklin was trying to make it seem like we were out of line, while all the time this big-piece-of-shit Fox was sitting there smiling with a toothpick in the side of his mouth. It's what, thirty-somethin' years ago and I can still remember that toothpick. Galled the Jesus out of me. So to make a long story short, we never did get to brace him on having set up the date she went on.'

The boat rocked on a high wake and Bosch looked around and didn't see any other boat. It was weird. He looked out across the water and for the first time realized how different it was from the Pacific. The Pacific was a cold and forbidding blue, the Gulf a warm green that invited you.

'We left,' McKittrick continued. 'I figured we'd have another shot at him. So we left and started to work on his alibi. It turned out to be good. And I don't mean it was good because his own witnesses said it was. We did the work. We found some independent people. People that didn't know him. As I remember it, it was rock solid.'

'You remember where he was?'

'Spent part of the night in a bar over there on Ivar, place a lot of the pimps hung around. Can't remember the name of it. Then later he drove out to Ventura, spent most of the rest of the night in a card room until he got a phone call, then he split. The other thing about this was that it didn't smack of an alibi set up for this particular night. This was his routine. He was well known in all of these places.'

'What was the phone call?'

'We never knew. We didn't know about it until we started checking his alibi and somebody mentioned it. We never got to ask Fox about it. But to be honest, we didn't care too much at that point. Like I said, his alibi was solid and he didn't get the call until later in the morning. Four, five o'clock. The vic – your mother had been dead a good long while by then. TOD was midnight. The call didn't matter.'

Bosch nodded but it was the kind of detail he would not have left open if it had been his investigation. It was too curious a detail. Who calls a poker room that early in the morning? What kind of call would make Fox up and leave the game?

'What about the prints?'

'I had 'em checked anyway and they didn't match those on the belt. He was clean. The dirtbag was clear.'

Bosch thought of something.

'You did check the prints on the belt against the victim's, right?'

'Hey, Bosch, I know you highfalutin' guys think you're the cat's ass now but we were known for having a brain or two back in those days.'

'Sorry.'

'There were a few prints on the buckle that were the victim's. That's it. The rest were definitely the killer's because of their location. We got good direct lifts and partials on two other spots where it was clear the belt had been grasped by the full hand. You don't hold a belt that way when you're putting it on. You hold it that way when you're putting it around someone's neck.'

They were both silent after that. Bosch couldn't figure out what McKittrick was telling him. He felt deflated. He had thought that if he got McKittrick to open up, the old cop would point the finger at Fox or Conklin or somebody. But he was doing none of that. He really wasn't giving Bosch anything.

'How come you remember so many details, Jake? It's been a long time.'

'I've had a long time to think about it. When you finish up, Bosch, you'll see, there'll always be one. One case that stays with you. This is the one that stayed with me.'

'So what was your final take on it?'

'My final take? Well, I never got over that meeting at Conklin's office. I guess you had to be there but it just … it just seemed that the one that was in charge of that meeting was Fox. It was like he was calling the shots.'

Bosch nodded. He could see that McKittrick was struggling for an explanation of his feelings.

'You ever interview a suspect with his lawyer there jumpin' in and out of the conversation?' McKittrick asked. 'You know, "Don't answer this, don't answer that." Shit like that.'

'All the time.'

'Well, it was like that. It was like Conklin, the next DA for Chrissake, was this shitheel's lawyer, objecting all the time to our questions. What it came down to was that if you didn't know who he was or where we were, you'd've sworn he was working for Fox. Both of them, Mittel, too. So, I felt pretty sure Fox had his hooks into Arno. Somehow he did. And I was right. It was all confirmed later.'

'You mean when Fox died?'

'Yeah. He got killed in a hit and run while working for the Conklin campaign. I remember the newspaper story on it didn't say nothin' about his background as a pimp, as a Hollywood Boulevard hoodlum. No, he was just this guy who got run down. Joe Innocent. I tell ya, that story must've cost Arno a few dollars and made a reporter a little richer.'

Bosch could tell there was more so he said nothing.

'I was in Wilshire dicks by then,' McKittrick continued. 'But I got curious when I heard about it. So I called over to Hollywood to see who was on it. It was Eno. Big surprise. And he never made a case on anybody. So that about confirmed what I was thinking about him, too.'

McKittrick stared off across the water to where the sun was getting low in the sky. He threw his empty beer can at the bucket. It missed and bounced over the side into the water.

'Fuck it,' he said. 'I guess we should head in.'

He started reeling in his line.

'What do you think Eno got out of all of this?'

'I don't know exactly. He might've just been trading favors, something like that. I'm not saying he got rich, but I think he got something out of the deal. He wouldn't do it for nothing. I just don't know what it was.'

McKittrick started taking the rods out of the pipes and stowing them on hooks along the sides of the stern.

'In 1972 you checked the murder book out of archives, how come?'

McKittrick looked at him curiously.

'I signed the same checkout slip a few days ago,' Bosch explained. 'Your name was still on it.'

McKittrick nodded.

'Yeah, that was right after I put in my papers. I was leaving, going through my files and stuff. I'd hung on to the prints we took off the belt. Kept the card. Also hung on to the belt.'

'Why?'

'You know why. I didn't think it would be safe in that file or in the evidence room. Not with Conklin as DA, not with Eno doing him favors. So I kept the stuff. Then a bunch of years went by and it was there when I was cleaning shit out and going to Florida. So right before I decided to punch out, I put the print card back in the murder book and went down and put the belt back in the evidence box. Eno was already in Vegas, retired. Conklin had crashed and burned, was out of politics. The case was long forgotten. I put the stuff back. I guess maybe I hoped someday somebody like you would take a look at it.'

'What about you? Did you look at the book when you put the card back?'

'Yeah, and I saw I had done the right thing. Somebody had gone through it, stripped it. They pulled the Fox interview out of it. Probably was Eno.'

'As the second man on the case you had to do the paper, right?'

'Right. The paperwork was mine. Most of it.'

'What did you put on the Fox interview summary that would have made Eno need to pull it?'

'I don't remember anything specific, just that I thought the guy was lying and that Conklin was out of line. Something like that.'

'Anything else you remember that was missing?'

'Nah, nothing important, just that. I think he just wanted to get Conklin's name out of it.'

'Yeah, well, he missed something. You'd noted his first call on the Chronological Record. That's how I knew.'

'Did I? Well, good for me. And here you are.'

'Yeah.'

'All right, we're heading in. Too bad they weren't really biting today.'

'I'm not complaining. I got my fish.'

McKittrick stepped behind the wheel and was about to start the engine when he thought of something.

'Oh, you know what?' He moved to the cooler and opened it. 'I don't want Mary to be disappointed.'

He pulled out the plastic bags that contained the sandwiches his wife had made.

'You hungry?'

'Not really.'

'Me neither.'

He opened the bags and dumped the sandwiches over the side. Bosch watched him.

'Jake, when you pulled out that gun, who'd you think I was?'

McKittrick didn't say anything as he neatly folded the plastic bags and put them back in the cooler. When he straightened up, he looked at Bosch.

'I didn't know. All I knew was that I thought I might have to take you out here and dump you like those sandwiches. Seems like I've been hiding out here all my life, waiting for them to send somebody.'

'You think they'd go that far over time and distance?'

'I don't have any idea. The more time that goes by, the more I doubt it. But old habits die hard. I always keep a gun nearby. Doesn't matter that most times I don't even remember why.'

They rode in from the Gulf with the engine roaring and the soft spray of the sea in their faces. They didn't talk. That was done with. Occasionally, Bosch glanced over at McKittrick. His old face fell under the shadow of his cap brim. But Bosch could see his eyes in there, looking at something that had happened a long time before and no longer could be changed.

After the boat trip Bosch felt the onset of a headache from the combination of too much beer and too much sun. He begged off an invitation to dinner from McKittrick, saying he was tired. Once in his car, he took a couple of Tylenol caplets out of his overnighter, downed them without any liquid chaser and hoped they would do the job. He took out his notebook and reviewed some of the things he had written about McKittrick's story.

He had come to like the old cop by the end of the fishing trip. Maybe he saw some of himself in the older man. McKittrick was haunted because he had let the case go. He had not done the right thing. And Bosch knew he was guilty of the same during all the years he had ignored the case that he knew was there waiting for him. He was making up for that now, and so was McKittrick by talking to him. But both of them knew it might be too little too late.

Bosch wasn't sure what he would do next when he got back to Los Angeles. It seemed to him that his only move was to confront Conklin. He was reluctant to do this because he knew he would go into such a confrontation soft, with only his suspicions and no hard evidence. Conklin would have the upper hand.

A wave of desperation came over him. He did not want the case to come to this. Conklin hadn't flinched in almost thirty-five years. He wouldn't with Bosch in his face now. Harry knew he needed something else. But he had nothing.

He started the car but left it in Park. He turned the air conditioner on high and added what McKittrick had told him into the stew of what he already knew. He began formulating a theory. For Bosch, this was one of the most important components of homicide investigation. Take the facts and shake them down into hypothesis. The key was not to become beholden to any one theory. Theories changed and you had to change with them.

It seemed clear from McKittrick's information that Fox had a hold on Conklin. What was it? Well, Bosch thought, Fox dealt in women. The theory that emerged was that Fox had gotten a hook into Conklin through a woman, or women. The news clips at the time reported Conklin was a bachelor. The morals of the time would have dictated then as now that as a public servant and soon-to-be candidate for top prosecutor, Conklin needed not necessarily to be celibate but, at least, not to have succumbed privately to the very vices he was publicly attacking. If he had done that and was exposed, he could kiss his political career good-bye, let alone his position as commander of the DA commandos. So, Bosch concluded, if this was Conklin's flaw and it was through Fox that such dalliances were arranged, then Fox would hold an almost unbeatable hand when it came to having juice with Conklin. It would explain the unusual circumstances of the interview McKittrick and Eno conducted with Fox.

The same theory, Bosch knew, would work to an even greater degree if Conklin had done more than succumb to the vice of sex but had gone further: if he had killed a woman Fox had sent to him, Marjorie Lowe. For one thing, it would explain how Conklin knew for sure that Fox was in the clear on the murder – because he was the killer himself. For another, it would explain how Fox got Conklin to run interference for him and why he was later hired as a Conklin campaign worker. The bottom line was, if Conklin was the killer, Fox's hook would be set even deeper and it would be set for good. Conklin would be like that wahoo at the end of the line, a pretty fish unable to get away.

Unless, Bosch knew, the man at the other end of the line and holding the rod were to go away somehow. He thought about Fox's death and saw how it fit. Conklin let some time separate one death from the other. He played like a hooked fish, even agreeing to Fox's demand for a straight job with the campaign, and then, when all seemed clear, Fox was run down in the street. Maybe a payoff to a reporter kept the victim's background quiet − if the reporter even knew it, and a few months later Conklin was crowned district attorney.

Bosch considered where Mittel would fit into the theory. He felt it was unlikely that all of this had transpired in a vacuum. It was Bosch's guess that Mittel, as Conklin's right-hand man and enforcer, would know what Conklin knew.

Bosch liked his theory but it angered him, largely because that was all it was, theory. He shook his head as he realized he was back to ground zero. All talk, no evidence of anything.

He grew weary thinking about it and decided to put the thoughts aside for a while. He turned the air down because it was too cool against his sunburned skin and put the car in gear. As he slowly cruised through Pelican Cove toward the gatehouse, his thoughts drifted to the woman who was trying to sell her dead father's condo. She had signed the name Jazz on the self-portrait. He liked that.

He turned the car around and drove toward her unit. It was still daylight and no lights shone from behind the building's windows when he got there. He couldn't tell if she was there or not. Bosch parked nearby and watched for a few minutes, debating what he should do, if anything at all.

Fifteen minutes later, when it seemed that indecisiveness had paralyzed him, she stepped out the front door. He was parked nearly twenty yards away, between two other cars. His paralytic affliction eased enough for him to slide down in his seat to avoid detection. She walked out into the parking lot and behind the row of cars which included Bosch's rental. He didn't move or turn to follow her movement. He listened. He waited for the sound of a car starting. Then what, he wondered. Follow her? What are you doing?

He jerked upright at the sound of sharp rapping on the window next to him. It was her. Bosch was flustered but managed to turn the key so he could lower the window.

'Yes?'

'Mr Bosch, what are you doing?'

'What do you mean?'

'You've been sitting out here. I saw you.'

'I ...'

He was too humiliated to finish.

'I don't know whether to call security or not.'

'No, don't do that. I, uh, I was just – I was going to go to your door. To apologize.'

'Apologize? Apologize for what?'

'For today. For earlier, when I was inside. I – you were right, I wasn't looking to buy anything.'

'Then what were you doing?'

Bosch opened the car door and stepped out. He felt disadvantaged with her looking down at him in the car.

'I'm a cop,' he said. 'I needed to get in here to see someone. I used you and I'm sorry. I am. I didn't know about your father and all of that.'

234

She smiled and shook her head.

'That's the dumbest story I've ever heard. What about LA, was that part of the story?'

'No. I'm from LA. I'm a cop there.'

'I don't know if I'd go around admitting that if I were you. You guys've got some bad PR problems.'

'Yeah, I know. So ...' He felt his courage rising. He told himself he was flying out in the morning and it didn't matter what happened because he'd never see her or this state again. 'You said something before about lemonade but I never got any. I was thinking, maybe I could tell you the story, apologize and have some lemonade or something.'

He looked over toward the door of the condo.

'You LA cops are pushy,' she said but she was smiling. 'One glass and the story better be good. After that, we both gotta go. I'm driving up to Tampa tonight.'

They started walking toward the door and Bosch realized he had a smile on his face.

'What's in Tampa?'

'It's where I live and I miss it. I've been down here more than up there since I put the condo on the market. I want to spend a Sunday at my own place and in my own studio.'

'That's right, a painter.'

'I try to be.'

She opened the door for him and allowed him in first.

'Well, that's okay by me. I have to get to Tampa sometime tonight. I fly out in the morning.'

While nursing a tall glass of lemonade, Bosch explained his scam of using her to get into the complex to see another resident and she didn't seem upset. In fact, he could tell she admired the ingenuity of it. Bosch didn't tell her how it had backfired anyway when McKittrick had pulled a gun on him. He gave her a vague outline of the case, never mentioning its personal connection to himself and she seemed intrigued by the whole idea of solving a murder that happened thirty-three years earlier.

The one glass of lemonade turned into four and the last two were spiked nicely with vodka. They took care of what was left of Bosch's headache and put a nice bloom on everything. Between the third and the fourth she asked if he would mind if she smoked and he lit cigarettes for both of them. And as the sky darkened over the mangroves outside, he finally turned the conversation toward her. Bosch had sensed a loneliness about her, a mystery of some sort. Behind the pretty face there were scars. The kind that couldn't be seen.

Her name was Jasmine Corian but she said that friends called her Jazz. She spoke of growing up in the Florida sun, of never wanting to leave it. She had married once but it was a long time ago. There was nobody in her life now and she was used to it. She said she concentrated most of her life on her art and, in a way, Bosch understood what she meant. His own art, though few would call it that, took most of his life as well.

'What do you paint?'

'Portraits mostly.'

'Who are they?'

'Just someone I know. Maybe I'll paint you, Bosch. Someday.'

He didn't know what to say to that so he made a clumsy transition to safer ground.

'Why don't you give this place to a realtor to sell? That way you could stay in Tampa and paint.'

'Because I wanted the diversion. I also didn't want to give a realtor the five percent. This is a nice complex. These units sell pretty well without realtors. A lot of Canadian investment. I think I'll sell it. This was only the first week I've run the ad.'

Bosch just nodded and wished he had kept the conversation on her painting instead of realtors. The clumsy change seemed to have clogged things up a bit.

'I was thinking, you want to have dinner?'

She looked at him solemnly, as if the request and her answer had far deeper implications. They probably did. At least, he thought they did.

'Where would we go?'

That was a stall but he played along.

'I don't know. It's not my town. Not my state. You could pick a place. Around here or on the way up to Tampa. I don't care. I'd like your company, though, Jazz. If you want to.'

'How long has it been since you were with a woman? I mean on a date.'

'On a date? I don't know. A few months, I guess. But, look, I'm not a hard-luck case. I'm just in town and alone and thought maybe you'd –'

'It's okay, Harry. Let's go.'

'To eat?'

'Yes, to eat. I know a place on the way up. It's above Longboat. You'll have to follow me.'

He smiled and nodded.

She drove a Volkswagen Beetle convertible that was powder blue with one red fender. He couldn't lose her in a hailstorm let alone the slow-moving Florida highways.

Bosch counted two drawbridges that they had to stop for before they got to Longboat Key. From there they headed north for the length of the island, crossed a bridge onto Anna Maria Island and finally stopped at a place called the Sandbar. They walked through the bar and sat on a deck overlooking the Gulf. It was cool and they ate crabs and oysters chased with Mexican beer. Bosch loved it.

They didn't talk much but didn't need to. It was always in the silences that Bosch felt most comfortable with the women who had moved through his life. He felt the vodka and beer working on him, warming him toward her, sanding off any sharp edges to the evening. He felt a desire for her growing and tugging at him. McKittrick and the case had somehow been pushed into the darkness at the back of his mind.

'This is good,' he said when he was finally nearing his capacity for food and drink. 'It's great.'

'Yeah, they do it right. Can I tell you something, Bosch?'

'Go ahead.'

'I was only kidding about what I was saying about LA cops before. But I have known some cops before ... and you seem different. I don't know what it is but it's like you've got too much of yourself left, you know?'

'I guess.' He nodded. 'Thanks. I think.'

They both laughed and then in a hesitant move, she leaned over and kissed him quickly on the lips. It was nice and he smiled. He could taste garlic.

'I'm glad you're already sunburned or you'd be turning red again.'

'No, I wouldn't. I mean, that was a nice thing to say.'

'You want to come home with me, Bosch?'

Now he hesitated. Not because there was any deliberation in his answer. But he wanted her to have the chance to withdraw it in case she had spoken too quickly. After a moment of silence from her he smiled and nodded.

'Yes, I would like that.'

They left then and cut inland to the freeway. Bosch wondered as he tailed the Volkswagen if she would change her mind as she drove alone. He got his answer at the Skyway bridge. As he pulled up to the tollbooth with his dollar already in hand, the tolltaker shook his head and waved off the money.

'Nope. That lady in the bug got ya covered.'

238

'Yeah?'
'Yeah. You know her?'
'Not yet.'
'I think you're goin' to. Good luck.'
'Thanks.'

Now Bosch couldn't lose her in a blizzard. As the drive grew longer, he found himself in a growing sense of an almost adolescent euphoria of anticipation. He was captured by the directness of this woman and he was wondering how and what that would translate to when they were making love.

She led him north to Tampa and then into an area called Hyde Park. Overlooking the bay, the neighborhood consisted of old Victorian and Craftsman-style houses with sweeping front porches. Her home was an apartment above the three-car garage set behind a gray Victorian with green trim.

As they got to the top of the steps and she was putting the key into the knob, Bosch thought of something and didn't know what to do. She opened the door and looked at him. She read him.

'What's wrong?'

'Nothing. But I was thinking, maybe I should go find a drugstore or something and then come back.'

'Don't worry, I've got what you'll need. But can you stand out here for a second? I just want to make a mad dash inside and clean up a few things.'

He looked at her.

'I don't care about that.'

'Please?'

'Okay. Take your time.'

He waited for about three minutes and then she opened the door and pulled him in. If she had cleaned up, she had done it in the dark. The only light came from what Bosch could see was the kitchen. She took his hand and led him away from the light to a darkened hallway that gave way to her bedroom. Here she turned on the light, revealing a sparely furnished room. A wrought-iron bed with a canopy was the centerpiece. There was a night table of unfinished wood next to it, a matching unfinished bureau and an antique Singer sewing machine table on which stood a blue vase with dead flowers in it. There was nothing hung on any of the walls, though Bosch saw a nail protruding from the plaster above the vase. Jasmine noticed the flowers and quickly took the vase off the table and headed out the door.

· 'I have to go dump this. I haven't been here in a week and forgot to change them.'

Moving the flowers raised a slightly acrid smell in the room. While she was gone Bosch looked at the nail again and thought he could see the delineation of a rectangle on the wall. Something had hung there, he decided. She hadn't come in to clean up. If she had, she would have gotten rid of the flowers. She'd come in to take down a painting.

When she came back into the room, she put the empty vase back on the table.

'Would you like another beer? I have some wine, too.'

Bosch moved toward her, intrigued even more by her mysteries.

'No, I'm fine.'

Without further word they embraced. He could taste beer and garlic and cigarette smoke as he kissed her but didn't care. He knew she was getting the same from him. He pressed his cheek against hers and with his nose he came across the spot on her neck where she had dabbed perfume. Night-blooming jasmine.

They moved onto the bed, each taking pieces of clothing off between hard kisses. Her body was beautiful, the tan lines distinct. He kissed her lovely small breasts and gently pushed her back on the bed. She told him to wait and she rolled to the side and from the drawer of the bed table extracted a strip of three condom packages and handed it to him.

'Is this wishful thinking?' he asked.

They both burst out laughing and it seemed to make things all the better.

'I don't know,' she said. 'We'll see.'

For Bosch, sexual encounters had always been a question of timing. The desires of two individuals rose and subsided on their own courses. There were emotional needs separate from physical needs. And sometimes all of those things clicked together in a person and then clicked in tandem with those of the other person. Bosch's encounter with Jasmine Corian was one of those times. The sex created a world without intrusion. One so vital that it could have lasted an hour or maybe only a few minutes and he wouldn't have known the difference. At the end, he was above her, looking into her open eyes, and she clutched his upper arms as if she were holding on for her life. Both of their bodies shuddered in unison and then he lay still on top of her, catching his breath from the hollow between her neck and shoulder. He felt so good he had the urge to laugh out loud but he didn't think she'd understand. He stifled it and made it sound like a muffled cough.

'Are you okay?' she asked softly.

'I've never felt better.'

Eventually, he moved off her, backing down over her body. He kissed both of her breasts, then sat up with her legs on either side of him. He removed the condom while using his body to shield her view of the process.

He got up and walked to the door he hoped was the bathroom and found it was a closet. The next door he tried was the bathroom and he flushed the condom down the toilet. He absentmindedly wondered if it would end up somewhere in Tampa Bay.

When he came back from the bathroom she was sitting up with the sheet bunched around her waist. He found his sport coat on the floor and got out his cigarettes. He gave her one and lit it. Then he bent over and kissed her breasts again. Her laugh was infectious and it made him smile.

'You know, I like it that you didn't come equipped.'

'Equipped? What are you talking about?'

'You know, that you offered to go to the drugstore. It shows what kind of man you are.'

'What do you mean?'

'If you had come over here from LA with a condom in your wallet, that would've been so ... I don't know, premeditated. Like some guy just on the make. The whole thing would have had no spontaneity. I'm glad you weren't like that, Harry Bosch, that's all.'

He nodded, trying to follow her line of thought. He wasn't sure he understood. And he wondered what he should think of the fact that she *was* equipped. He decided to drop it and lit his cigarette.

'How'd you hurt your hand like that?'

She had noticed the marks on his fingers. Bosch had taken the Band-Aids off while flying over. The burns had healed to the point that they looked like red welts on two of his fingers.

'Cigarette. I fell asleep.'

He felt he could tell her the truth about everything about himself.

'God, that's scary.'

'Yeah. I don't think it will happen again.'

'Do you want to stay with me tonight?'

He moved closer to her and kissed her on the neck.

'Yes,' he whispered.

She reached over and touched the zipper scar on his left shoulder. The women he was with in bed always seemed to do this. It was an ugly mark and he never understood why they were drawn to touch it.

'You got shot?'

'Yeah.'

'That's even scarier.'

He hiked his shoulders. It was history and he never really thought about it anymore.

'You know, what I was trying to say before is that you're not like most cops I've known. You've got too much of your humanity left. How'd that happen?'

He shook his shoulders again like he didn't know.

'Are you okay, Bosch?'

He stubbed out his cigarette.

'Yeah, I'm fine. Why?'

'I don't know. You know what that guy Marvin Gaye sang about, don't you? Before he got killed by his own dad? He sang about sexual healing. Said it's good for the soul. Something like that. Anyway, I believe it, do you?'

'I suppose.'

'I think you need healing in your life, Bosch. That's the vibe I'm getting.'

'You want to go to sleep now?'

She lay down again and pulled the sheet up. He walked around the room naked, turning out the lights. When he was under the sheet in the dark, she turned on her side so her back was to him and told him to put his arm around her. He moved up close behind her and did. He loved her smell.

'How come people call you Jazz?'

'I don't know. They just do. Because it goes with the name.'

After a few moments she asked him why he had asked that.

'Because. You smell like both your names. Like the flower and the music.'

'What does jazz smell like?'

'It smells dark and smoky.'

They were silent for a long while after that and eventually Bosch thought she was asleep. But he still could not make it down. He lay with his eyes open, looking at the shadows of the room. Then she spoke softly to him.

'Bosch, what's the worst thing you've ever done to yourself?'

'What do you mean?'

'You know what I mean. What's the worst thing? What's the thing that keeps you awake at night if you think about it too hard?'

He thought for a few moments before answering.

'I don't know.' He forced an uneasy and short laugh. 'I guess I've done a lot of bad things. I suppose a lot of them are to myself. At least I think about them a lot ...'

'What's one of them? You can tell me.'

And he knew that he could. He thought he could tell her almost anything and not be judged harshly.

'When I was a kid – I grew up mostly in a youth hall, like an orphanage. When I was new there, one of the older kids took my shoes, my sneakers. They didn't fit him or anything but he did it because he knew he could do it. He was one of the rulers of the roost and he took 'em. I didn't do anything about it and it hurt.'

'But you didn't do it. That's not what I –'

'No, I'm not done. I just told you that because you had to know that part. See, when I got older and I was one of the big shots in the place, I did the same thing. I took this

245

new kid's shoes. He was smaller, I couldn't even put 'em on. I just took them and I … I don't know, I threw them out or something. But I took them because I could. I did the same thing that was done to me … And sometimes, even now, I think about it and I feel bad.'

She squeezed his hand in a way he thought was meant to be comforting but said nothing.

'Is that the kind of story you wanted?'

She just squeezed his hand again. After a while he spoke.

'I think the one thing I did that I regret the most, though, was maybe letting a woman go.'

'You mean like a criminal?'

'No. I mean like we lived – we were lovers and when she wanted to go, I didn't really … do anything. I didn't put up a fight, you know. And when I think about it, sometimes I think that maybe if I had, I could've changed her mind … I don't know.'

'Did she say why she was leaving?'

'She just got to know me too well. I don't blame her for anything. I've got baggage. I guess maybe I can be hard to take. I've lived alone most of my life.'

Silence filled the room again and he waited. He sensed that there was something more she wanted to say or be asked. But when she spoke he wasn't sure if she was talking about him or herself.

'They say when a cat is ornery and scratches and hisses at everybody, even somebody who wants to comfort it and love it, it's because it wasn't held enough when it was a kitten.'

'I never heard that before.'

'I think it's true.'

He was quiet a moment and moved his hand up so that it was touching her breasts.

'Is that what your story is?' he asked. 'You weren't held enough.'

'Who knows.'

'What was the worst thing you ever did to yourself, Jasmine? I think you want to tell me.'

He knew she wanted him to ask it. It was true confessions time and he began to believe that the whole night had been directed by her to arrive at this one question.

'You didn't try to hold on to someone you should have,' she said. 'I held on to someone I shouldn't have. I held on too long. Thing is, I knew what it was leading to, deep down I knew. It was like standing on the tracks and seeing the train coming at you but being too mesmerized by the bright light to move, to save yourself.'

He had his eyes open in the dark still. He could barely see the outline of her shoulder and cheek. He pulled himself closer to her, kissed her neck and in her ear whispered, 'But you got out. That's what's important.'

'Yeah, I got out,' she said wistfully. 'I got out.'

She was silent for a while and then reached up under the covers and touched his hand. It was cupped over one of her breasts. She held her hand on top of it.

'Good night, Harry.'

He waited a while, until he heard the measured breathing of her sleep, and then he was finally able to drift off. There was no dream this time. Just warmth and darkness.

In the morning Bosch awoke first. He took a shower and borrowed Jasmine's toothbrush without asking. Then he dressed in the clothes he'd worn the day before and went out to his car to retrieve his overnight bag. Once he was dressed in fresh clothes he ventured into the kitchen to see about coffee. All he found was a box of tea bags.

Leaving the idea behind, he walked around the apartment, his steps creaking on the old pine floors. The living room was as spare as the bedroom. A sofa with an off-white blanket spread on it, a coffee table, an old stereo with a cassette but no CD player. No television. Again, nothing on the walls but the telltale indication that there had been. He found two nails in the plaster. They weren't rusted or painted over. They hadn't been there very long.

Through a set of French doors the living room opened up to a porch enclosed in windows. There was rattan furniture out here and several potted plants, including a dwarf orange tree with fruit on it. The entire porch was redolent with its smell. Bosch stepped close to the windows and by looking south down the alley behind the property, he could see the bay. The morning sun's reflection on it was pure white light.

He walked back across the living room to another door on the wall opposite the French doors. Immediately upon opening this door, he could smell the sharp tang of oils and turpentine. This was where she painted. He hesitated but only for a moment, then walked in.

The first thing he noticed was that the room had a window that gave a direct view of the bay across the backyards and garages of three or four houses down the alley. It was beautiful and he knew why she chose this room for her art. At center on a paint-dappled drop cloth was an easel but no stool. She painted standing. He saw no overhead lamp or artificial light source anywhere else in the room. She painted only by true light.

He walked around the easel and found the canvas on it had been untouched by the painter. Along one of the side walls was a high work counter with various tubes of paint scattered about. There were palette boards and coffee cans with brushes stacked in them. At the end of the counter was a large laundry sink for washing up.

Bosch noticed more canvases leaning against the wall under the counter. They were faced inward and appeared to be unused pieces like the one on the easel, waiting for the artist's hand. But Bosch suspected otherwise. Not with the exposed nails in the walls in the other rooms of the apartment. He reached under the counter and slid a few of the canvases out. As he did this he almost felt as if he was on some case, solving some mystery.

The three portraits he pulled out were painted in dark hues. None were signed though it was obvious all were the work of one hand. And that hand was Jasmine's. Bosch recognized the style from the painting he had seen at her father's house. Sharp lines, dark colors. The first one he looked at was of a nude woman with her face turned away from the painter and into the shadows. The sense Bosch felt was that the darkness was taking the woman, rather than her turning to the darkness. Her mouth was completely in shadow. It was as if she was mute. The woman, Bosch knew, was Jasmine.

The second painting seemed to be part of the same study as the first. It was the same nude in shadow, though she was now facing the viewer. Bosch noted that in the portrait Jasmine had given herself fuller breasts than in reality and he wondered if this was done on purpose and had some meaning, or was perhaps a subliminal improvement made by the painter. He noticed that beneath the veneer of gray shadow over the painting there were red highlights on the woman. Bosch knew little about the art, but he knew this was a dark portrait.

Bosch looked at the third painting he had pulled out and found this to be unattached to the first two, save for the fact that again it was a nude portrait of Jasmine. But this piece he clearly recognized as a reinterpretation of 'The Scream' by Edvard Munch, a painting that had always fascinated Bosch but that he had only seen in books. In the piece before him, the figure of the frightened person was Jasmine. The location had been transferred from Munch's horrific, swirling dreamscape, to the Skyway bridge. Bosch clearly recognized the bright yellow vertical piping of the bridge's support span.

'What are you doing?'

He jumped as if stabbed in the back. It was Jasmine, at the door of the studio. She wore a silk bathrobe she held closed with her arms. Her eyes were puffy. She had just woken up.

'I'm looking at your work, is that okay?'

'This door was locked.'

'No, it wasn't.'

She reached to the doorknob and turned it, as if that could disprove his claim.

'It wasn't locked, Jazz. I'm sorry. I didn't know you didn't want me in here.'

'Could you put those back under there, please?'

'Sure. But why'd you take them off the walls?'

'I didn't.'

'Was it because they're nudes, or is it because of what they mean?'

'Please don't ask me about this. Put them back.'

She left the doorway and he put the paintings back where he found them. He left the room and found her in the kitchen filling a tea kettle with water from the sink. Her back was to him and he walked in and lightly put a hand on her back. Even so, she started slightly at his touch.

'Jazz, look, I'm sorry. I'm a cop. I get curious.'

'It's okay.'

'Are you sure?'

'Yes, I'm sure. You want some tea?'

She had stopped filling the kettle but did not turn around or make a move to put it on the stove.

'No. I was thinking maybe I could take you out for breakfast.'

'When do you leave? I thought you said the plane's this morning.'

'That was the other thing I was thinking about. I could stay another day, leave tomorrow, if you want me to. I mean, if you'll have me. I'd like to stay.'

She turned around and looked at him.

'I want you to stay, too.'

They embraced and kissed but she quickly pulled back.

'It's not fair, you brushed your teeth. I have monster breath.'

'Yeah, but I used your toothbrush, so it evens out.'

'Gross. Now I have to get a new one.'

'That's right.'

They smiled and she gave him a tight hug around the neck, his trespass in her studio seemingly forgotten.

'You call the airline and I'll get ready. I know where we can go.'

When she pulled away he held her in front of him. He wanted to bring it up again. He couldn't help it.

'I want to ask you something.'

'What?'

'How come those paintings aren't signed?'

'They're not ready to be signed.'

'The one at your father's was signed.'

'That was for him, so I signed it. Those others are for me.'

'The one on the bridge. Is she going to jump?'

She looked at him a long time before answering.

'I don't know. Sometimes when I look at it, I think she is. I think the thought is there, but you never know.'

'It can't happen, Jazz.'

'Why not?'

'Because it can't.'

'I'll get ready.'

She broke away from him then and left the kitchen.

He went to the wall phone next to the refrigerator and dialed the airline. While making the arrangements to fly out Monday morning, he decided on a whim to ask the airline agent if it was possible to route his new flight back to Los Angeles through Las Vegas. She said not without a three-hour-and-fourteen-minute layover. He said he'd take it. He had to pay fifty dollars on top of the seven hundred they already had from him in order to make the needed changes. He put it on his credit card.

He thought about Vegas as he hung up. Claude Eno might be dead but his wife was still cashing his checks. She might be worth the fifty-dollar layover.

'Ready?'

It was Jasmine calling from the living room. Bosch stepped out of the kitchen and she was waiting for him in cut-off jeans and a tank top beneath a white shirt she left open and tied above her waist. She already had on sunglasses.

She took him to a place where they poured honey on top of the biscuits and served the eggs with grits and butter. Bosch hadn't had grits since basic training at Benning. The meal was delicious. Neither of them spoke much. The paintings and the conversation they had before falling asleep the night before were not mentioned. It seemed that what they had said was better left for the dark shadows of night, and maybe her paintings, too.

When they were done with their coffee, she insisted on picking up the check. He got the tip. They spent the afternoon cruising in her Volkswagen with the top down. She took him all over the place, from Ybor City to St Petersburg Beach, burning up a tank of gas and two packs of cigarettes. By late in the afternoon they were at a place called Indian Rocks Beach to look at the sunset over the Gulf.

· 'I've been a lot of places,' Jasmine told him. 'I like the light here the best.'

'Ever been out to California?'

'No, not yet.'

'Sometimes the sunset looks like lava pouring down on the city.'

'That must be beautiful.'

'It makes you forgive a lot, forget a lot … That's the thing about Los Angeles. It's got a lot of broken pieces to it. But the ones that still work, really do work.'

'I think I know what you mean.'

'I'm curious about something.'

'Here we go again. What?'

'If you don't show your paintings to anybody, how do you make a living?'

It was from out of left field but he had been thinking about it all day.

'I have money from my father. Even before he died. It's not a lot but I don't need a lot. It's enough. If I don't feel the need to sell my work when it is finished, then as I am doing it, it won't be compromised. It will be pure.'

It sounded to Bosch like a convenient way of explaining away the fear of exposing oneself. But he let it go. She didn't.

'Are you always a cop? Always asking questions?'

'No. Only when I care about someone.'

She kissed him quickly and walked back to the car.

After stopping by her place to change, they had dinner in a Tampa steak house where the wine list was actually a book so thick it came on its own pedestal. The restaurant itself seemed to be the work of a slightly delusional Italian decorator, a dark blend of gilded rococo, garish red velvet and classical statues and paintings. It was the kind of place he would expect her to suggest. She mentioned that this meateater's palace was actually owned by a vegetarian.

'Sounds like somebody from California.'

She smiled and was quiet for a while after that. Bosch's mind wandered to the case. He had spent the entire day without giving it a thought. Now a pang of guilt thrummed in his mind. It was almost as if he felt he was shunting his mother aside to pursue the selfish pleasure of Jasmine's company. Jasmine seemed to read him and to know he was privately debating something.

'Can you stay another day, Harry?'

He smiled but shook his head.

'I can't. I gotta go. But I'll be back. As soon as I can.'

Bosch paid for dinner with a credit card he guessed was reaching its limit and they headed back to her apartment. Knowing their time together was drawing to a close, they went right to the bed and made love.

The feel of her body, its taste and its scent seemed perfect to Bosch. He didn't want the moment to end. He'd had immediate attractions to women before in his life and had even acted on them. But never one that felt so fully engaging and complete. He guessed that it was because of all he did not know about her. That was the hook. She was a mystery. Physically, he could not get any closer than he was to her during these moments, yet there was so much of her hidden, unexplored. They made love in gentle rhythm and held each other in a deep, long kiss at the end.

Later, he lay on his side, next to her, his arm across the flatness of her belly. One of her hands traced circles in his hair. The true confessions began.

'Harry, you know, I haven't been with a lot of men in my life.'

He didn't respond because he didn't know what the proper response could be. He was well past caring about a woman's sexual history for anything other than health reasons.

'What about you?' she asked.

He couldn't resist.

'I haven't been with a lot of men, either. In fact, none, as far as I know.'

She punched him on the shoulder.

'You know what I mean.'

'The answer is no. I haven't been with a lot of women in my life. Not enough, at least.'

'I don't know, the men that I've been with, most of them, it's like they wanted something from me I didn't have. I don't know what it was but I just didn't have it to give. Then I either left too soon or stayed too long.'

He propped himself up on one elbow and looked at her.

'Sometimes I think that I know strangers better than I know anybody else, even myself. I learn so much about people in my job. Sometimes I think I don't even have a life. I only have their life … I don't know what I'm talking about.'

'I think you do. I understand. Maybe everybody's like this.'

'I don't know. I don't think so.'

They were quiet for a while after that. Bosch leaned down and kissed her breasts, holding a nipple between his lips for a long moment. She brought her hands up and held his head to her chest. He could smell the jasmine.

'Harry, have you ever had to use your gun?'

He pulled his head up. The question seemed out of place. But through the darkness he could see her eyes on him, watching and waiting for an answer.

'Yes.'

'You killed someone.'

It wasn't a question.

'Yes.'

She said nothing else.

'What is it, Jazz?'

'Nothing. I was just wondering how that would be. How you would go on.'

'Well, all I can tell you is that it hurts. Even when there was no choice and they had to go down, it hurts. You just have to go on.'

She was silent. Whatever she had needed to hear from him he hoped she had gotten. Bosch was confused. He didn't know why she had asked such questions and wondered if she was testing him in some way. He lay back on his pillow and waited for sleep but confusion kept it away from him. After a while she turned on the bed and put her arm over him.

'I think you are a good man,' she whispered close to his ear.

'Am I?' he whispered back.

'And you will come back, won't you?'

'Yes. I'll come back.'

Bosch went to every rental counter in McCarran International Airport in Las Vegas but none had a car left. He silently chastised himself for not making a reservation and walked outside the terminal into the dry crisp air to catch a cab. The driver was a woman and when Bosch gave the address, on Lone Mountain Drive, he could clearly see her disappointment in the rearview mirror. The destination wasn't a hotel, so she wouldn't be picking up a return fare.

'Don't worry,' Bosch said, understanding her problem. 'If you wait for me, you can take me back to the airport.'

'How long you gonna be? I mean, Lone Mountain, that's way out there in the sand pits.'

'I might be five minutes, I might be less. Maybe a half hour. I'd say no longer than a half hour.'

'You waiting on the meter?'

'On the meter or you. Whatever you want to do.'

She thought about it a moment and put the car in drive.

'Where are all the rental cars, anyway?'

'Big convention in town. Electronics or something.'

It was a thirty-minute ride out into the desert northwest of the strip. The neon-and-glass buildings retreated and the cab passed through residential neighborhoods until these, too, became sparse. The land was a ragged brown out here and dotted unevenly with scrub brush. Bosch knew the roots of every bush spread wide and sucked up what little moisture was in the earth. It made for a terrain that seemed dying and desolate.

The houses, too, were few and far between, each one an outpost in a no-man's-land. The streets had been gridded and paved long ago but the boomtown of Las Vegas hadn't quite caught up yet. It was coming, though. The city was spreading like a patch of weeds.

The road began to rise toward a mountain the color of cocoa mix. The cab shook as a procession of eighteen-wheel dump trucks thundered by with loads of sand from the excavation pits the driver had mentioned. And soon the paved roadway gave way to gravel and the cab sent up a tail of dust in its wake. Bosch was beginning to think the address the smarmy supervising clerk at City Hall had given him was a phony. But then they were there.

The address to which Claude Eno's pension checks were mailed each month was a sprawling ranch-style house of pink stucco and dusty white tile roof. Looking past it, Bosch could see where even the gravel road ended just past it. It was the end of the line. Nobody had lived farther away than Claude Eno.

'I don't know about this,' the driver said. 'You want me to wait? This is like the goddamn moon out here.'

She had pulled into the driveway behind a late 1970s-model Olds Cutlass. There was a carport where another car was parked hidden beneath a tarp that was blue in the further recesses of the carport but bleached nearly white along the surfaces sacrificed to the sun.

Bosch took out his fold of money and paid the driver thirty-five dollars for the ride out. Then he took two twenties, ripped them in half and handed one side of each over the seat to her.

'You wait, you get the other half of those.'

'Plus the fare back to the airport.'

'Plus that.'

Bosch got out, realizing it would probably be the quickest forty bucks ever lost in Las Vegas if nobody answered the door. But he was in luck. A woman who looked to be in her late sixties opened the door before he could knock. And why not, he thought. In this house, you could see visitors coming for a mile.

Bosch felt the blast of air conditioning escaping through the open door.

'Mrs Eno?'

'No.'

Bosch pulled out his notebook and checked the address against the black numbers tacked on the front wall next to the door. They matched.

'Olive Eno doesn't live here?'

'You didn't ask that. I'm not Mrs Eno.'

'Can I please speak with Mrs Eno then?' Annoyed with the woman's preciseness, Bosch showed the badge he had gotten back from McKittrick after the boat ride. 'It's police business.'

'Well, you can try. She hasn't spoken to anybody, at least anybody outside her imagination, in three years.'

She motioned Bosch in and he stepped into the cool house.

'I'm her sister. I take care of her. She's in the kitchen. We were in the middle of lunch when I saw the dust come up on the road and heard you arrive.'

Bosch followed her down a tiled hallway toward the kitchen. The house smelled like old age, like dust and mold and urine. In the kitchen a gnome-like woman with white hair sat in a wheelchair, barely taking up half of the space it gave for an occupant. There was a slide-on tray in front of it and the woman's gnarled pearl-white hands were folded together on top of it. There were milky blue cataracts on both eyes and they seemed dead to the world outside the body. Bosch noticed a bowl of applesauce on the nearby table. It only took him a few seconds to size up the situation.

'She'll be ninety in August,' said the sister. 'If she makes it.'

'How long has she been like this?'

'Long time. I've been taking care of her for three years now.' She then bent into the gnome's face and loudly added, 'Isn't that right, Olive?'

The loudness of the question seemed to kick a switch and Olive Eno's jaw started working but no sound that was intelligible issued. She stopped the effort after a while and the sister straightened up.

'Don't worry about it, Olive. I know you love me.'

She wasn't as loud with that sentence. Maybe she feared Olive might actually muster a denial.

'What's your name?' Bosch asked.

'Elizabeth Shivone. What's this about? I saw that badge of yours says Los Angeles, not Las Vegas. Aren't you off the beat here a bit?'

'Not really. It's about her husband. One of his old cases.'

'Claude's been dead going on five years now.'

'How did he die?'

'Just died. His pump went out. Died right there on the floor, about where you're standing.'

They both looked down at the floor as if maybe his body was still there.

'I came to look through his things,' Bosch said.

'What things?'

'I don't know. I was thinking maybe he kept files from his time with the police.'

'You better tell me what you're doing here. This doesn't sound right to me.'

'I'm investigating a case he worked back in 1961. It's still open. Parts of the file are missing. I thought maybe he'd taken it. I thought maybe there might be something important that he kept. I don't know what. Anything. I just thought it was worth a try.'

He could see that her mind was working and her eyes suddenly froze for a second when her memory snagged on something.

'There is something, isn't there?' he said.

'No. I think you should go.'

'It's a big house. Did he have a home office?'

'Claude left the police thirty years ago. He built this house in the middle of nowhere just to be away from all of that.'

'What did he do when he moved out here?'

'He worked casino security. A few years at the Sands, then twenty at the Flamingo. He was getting two pensions and took good care of Olive.'

'Speaking of which, who's signing those pension checks these days?'

Bosch looked at Olive Eno to make his point. The other woman was silent a long moment, then went on the offense.

'Look, I could get power of attorney. Look at her. It wouldn't be a problem. I take care of her, mister.'

'Yeah, you feed her applesauce.'

'I have nothing to hide.'

'You want somebody to make sure or do you want to let it end right here? I don't really care what you're doing, lady. I don't really care if you're even her sister or not. If I was betting, I'd say you're not. But I don't really care right now. I'm busy. I just want to look through Eno's things.'

He stopped there and let her think about it. He looked at his watch.

'No warrant then, right?'

'I don't have a warrant. I've got a cab waiting. You make me get a warrant and I'm going to stop being such a nice guy.'

Her eyes went up and down his body as if to measure how nice and how not nice he could be.

'The office is this way.'

She said the words as if they were bites out of wood planks. She swiftly led him down the hall again and then off to the left into a study. There was an old steel desk as the room's centerpiece, a couple of four-drawer file cabinets, an extra chair and not much else.

'After he died, Olive and I moved everything into those file cabinets and haven't looked at it since.'

'They're all full?'

'All eight. Have at it.'

Bosch reached his hand into his pocket and took out another twenty-dollar bill. He tore it in half and gave one side to Shivone.

'Take that out to the cab driver. Tell her I'm going to be a little longer than I thought.'

She exhaled loudly, snatched the half and left the room. After she was gone Bosch went to the desk and opened each of the drawers. The first two he tried were empty. The next contained stationery and office supplies. The fourth drawer contained a checkbook that he quickly leafed through and saw it was an account covering household expenses. There was also a file containing recent receipts and other records. The last drawer in the desk was locked.

He started with the bottom file drawers and worked his way up. Nothing in the first few seemed even remotely connected with what Bosch was working on. There were files labeled with the names of different casinos and gaming organizations. The files in another drawer were labeled by people's names. Bosch looked through a few of these and determined they were files on known casino cheats. Eno had built a library of home intelligence files. By this time, Shivone had come back from her errand and had taken the seat opposite the desk. She was watching Bosch and he threw a few idle questions at her while he looked.

'So what did Claude do for the casinos?'

'He was a bird dog.'

'What's that?'

'Kind've an undercover thing. He mingled in the casinos, gambled with house chips, watched people. He was good at picking out the cheats and how they did it.'

'Guess it takes one to know one, right?'

'What's that crack supposed to mean? He did a good job.'

'I'm sure he did. Is that how he met you?'

'I'm not answering any of your questions.'

'Okay by me.'

He had only the two top drawers left. He opened one and found it contained no files at all. Just an old, dust-covered Rolodex and other items that had probably sat on the top of the desk at one point. There was an ashtray, a clock and a pen holder made of carved wood that had Eno's name carved on it. Bosch took the Rolodex out and put it on top of the cabinet. He blew the dust off it and then began turning it until he came to the Cs. He looked through the cards but found no listing for Arno Conklin. He met with similar failure when he tried to find a listing for Gordon Mittel.

'You're not going to look through that whole thing, are you?' Shivone asked in exasperation.

'No, I'm just going to take it with me.'

'Oh, no you don't. You can't just come in here and –'

'I'm taking it. If you want to make a complaint about it, be my guest. Then I'll make a complaint about you.'

She went quiet after that. Bosch went on to the next drawer and found it contained about twelve files on old LAPD cases from the 1950s and early 1960s. Again, he didn't have the time to study them, but he checked all the labels and none was marked Marjorie Lowe. By randomly pulling out a few of the files it became clear to him that Eno had made copies of files on some of his cases to take with him when he left the department. Of the random selections, all were murders, including two of prostitutes. Only one of the cases was closed.

'Go get me a box or a bag or something for these files,' Bosch said over his shoulder. When he sensed the woman in the room had not moved, he barked, 'Do it!'

She got up and left. Bosch stood gazing at the files and thinking. He had no idea if these were important or not. He had no idea what they meant. He only knew he should take them in case they turned out to be important. But what bothered him more than what the files that were in the drawer could mean was the feeling that something was certainly missing. This was based on his belief in McKittrick. The retired detective was sure his former partner, Eno, had some kind of hold on Conklin, or at the very least, some kind of deal with him. But there was nothing here about that. And it seemed to Bosch that if Eno was holding something on Conklin, it would still be here. If he kept old LAPD files, then he kept whatever he had on Conklin. In fact, he would have kept it in a safe place. Where?

The woman came back and dropped a cardboard box on the floor. It was the kind a case of beer had come in. Bosch put a foot-thick stack of files in it along with the Rolodex.

'You want a receipt?' he asked.

'No, I don't want anything from you.'

'Well, there is still something I need from you.'

'This doesn't end, does it?'

'I hope it does.'

'What do you want?'

'When Eno died, did you help the old lady – uh, your

264

sister, that is – did you help her clear out his safe deposit box?'

'How'd –'

She stopped herself but not soon enough.

'How'd I know? Because it's obvious. What I'm looking for, he would have kept in a safe place. What did you do with it?'

'We threw everything away. It was meaningless. Just some old files and bank statements. He didn't know what he was doing. He was old himself.'

Bosch looked at his watch. He was running out of time if he was going to make his plane.

'Get me the key for this desk drawer.'

She didn't move.

'Hurry up, I don't have a lot of time. You open it or I'll open it. But if I do it, that drawer isn't going to be much use to you anymore.'

She reached into the pocket of her house dress and pulled out the house keys. She reached down and unlocked the desk drawer, pulled it open and then stepped away.

'We didn't know what any of it was, or what it meant.'

'That's fine.'

Bosch moved to the drawer and looked in. There were two thin manila files and two packs of envelopes with rubber bands holding them together. The first file he looked through contained Eno's birth certificate, passport, marriage license and other personal records. He put it back in the drawer. The next file contained LAPD forms and Bosch quickly recognized them as the pages and reports that had been removed from the Marjorie Lowe murder book. He knew he had no time to read them at the moment and put the file in the beer box with the other files.

The rubber band on the first package of envelopes

snapped when he tried to remove it and he was reminded of the band that had been around the blue binder that contained the case files. Everything about this case was old and ready to snap, he thought.

The envelopes were all from a Wells Fargo Bank branch in Sherman Oaks and each one contained a statement for a savings account in the name of McCage Inc. The address of the corporation was a post office box, also in Sherman Oaks. Bosch randomly took envelopes from different spots in the pack and studied three of them. Though separated by years in the late 1960s, each statement was basically the same. A deposit of one thousand dollars was made in the account on the tenth of each month and on the fifteenth a transfer of an equal amount was made to an account with a Nevada Savings and Loan branch in Las Vegas.

Without looking further, Bosch concluded that the bank statements might be the records of some kind of payoff account Eno kept. He quickly looked through the envelopes at the postmarks looking for the most recent one. He found none more recent than the late 1980s.

'What about these envelopes? When did he stop getting them?'

'What you see is what you get. I have no idea what they mean and Olive didn't know either back when they drilled his box.'

'Drilled his box?'

'Yeah, after he died. Olive wasn't on the safe deposit box. Only him. We couldn't find his key. So we had to have it drilled.'

'There was money, too, wasn't there?'

She waited a moment, probably wondering if he was going to demand that, too.

'Some. But you're too late, it's already spent.'

'I'm not worried about that. How much was there?'

266

She pinched her lips and acted like she was trying to remember. It was a bad act.

'C'mon. I'm not here for the money and I'm not from the IRS.'

'It was about eighteen thousand.'

Bosch heard a horn honk from outside. The cabdriver was getting restless. Bosch looked at his watch. He had to go. He tossed the envelope packs into the beer box.

'What about his account at Nevada Savings and Loan? How much was in it?'

It was a scam question based on his guess that the account that the money from Sherman Oaks was transferred to was Eno's. Shivone hesitated again. A delay punctuated by another horn blast.

'It was about fifty. But most of that's gone, too. Taking care of Olive, you know?'

'Yeah, I bet. Between that and the pensions, it's gotta be rough,' Bosch said with all the sarcasm he could put into it. 'I bet your accounts aren't too thin, though.'

'Look, mister, I don't know who you think you are but I'm the only one in the world that she has and who cares about her. That's worth something.'

'Too bad she doesn't get to decide what it's worth instead of you. Answer one question for me and then I'm out of here and you can go back to taking whatever you can off her … Who are you? You're not her sister. Who are you?'

'It's none of your business.'

'That's right. But I could make it my business.'

She put on a look that showed Bosch what an affront he was to her delicate sensibilities but then seemed to gain a measure of self-esteem. Whoever she was, she was proud of it.

'You want to know who I am? I was the best woman he ever had. I was with him for a long time. She had his wedding band but I had his heart. Near the end, when they were both old and it didn't matter, we dropped the pretension and he brought me in here. To live with them. Take care of them. So don't you dare tell me I don't deserve something out of it.'

Bosch just nodded. Somehow, as sordid as the story seemed, he found a measure of respect for her for just having told the truth. And he felt sure it was.

'When did you meet?'

'You said one question.'

'When did you meet?'

'When he was at the Flamingo. We both were. I was a dealer. Like I said, he was a bird dog.'

'He ever talk about LA, about any cases, any people from back there?'

'No, never. He always said that was a closed chapter.'

Bosch pointed to the envelope stacks in the box.

'Does the name McCage mean anything?'

'Not to me.'

'What about these account statements?'

'I never saw any of those things until the day we opened that box. Didn't know he even had an account over at Nevada Savings. Claude had secrets. He even kept secrets from me.'

At the airport Bosch paid off the cabdriver and struggled into the main terminal with his overnighter and the beer box full of files and other things. In one of the stores along the main terminal mall he bought a cheap canvas satchel and transferred the items he had taken from Eno's office into it. It was small enough so he didn't have to check it. Printed on the side of the bag was LAS VEGAS — LAND OF SUN AND FUN! There was a logo depicting the sun setting behind a pair of dice.

At his gate he had a half hour before they loaded the plane, so he found a section of open seats as far away as possible from the cacophony of the rows of slot machines set in the center of the circular terminal.

He began going through the files in the satchel. The one he was most interested in was the one containing records stolen from the Marjorie Lowe murder book. He looked through the documents and found nothing unusual or unexpected.

The summary of the McKittrick-Eno interview of Johnny Fox with Arno Conklin and Gordon Mittel present was here and Bosch could sense the contained outrage at the situation in McKittrick's writing. In the last paragraph it was no longer contained.

> Interview with suspect was regarded by the undersigned as fruitless because of the intrusive behavior of A. Conklin and G. Mittel. Both 'prosecutors' refused

to allow 'their' witness to answer questions fully or in the undersign's opinion with the whole truth. J. Fox remains suspect at this time until verification of his alibi and fingerprint analysis.

Nothing else in the documents was of note and Bosch realized that they were probably removed from the file by Eno solely because they mentioned Conklin's involvement in the case. Eno was covering up for Conklin. When Bosch asked himself why Eno was doing this, he immediately thought of the bank statements that had been in the safe deposit box with the stolen documents. They were records of the deal.

Bosch took out the envelopes and, going by the postmarks, began putting them in chronological order. The earliest one he could find was mailed to the McCage Inc. postal drop in November 1962. That was one year after the death of Marjorie Lowe and two months after the death of Johnny Fox. Eno had been on the Lowe case and then, according to McKittrick, he had investigated the Fox killing.

Bosch felt in his gut that he was right. Eno had squeezed Conklin. And maybe Mittel. He somehow knew what McKittrick didn't, that Conklin had been involved with Marjorie Lowe. Maybe he even knew Conklin had killed her. He had enough to put Conklin on the line for a thousand bucks a month for life. It wasn't a lot. Eno wasn't greedy, though a thousand a month in the early sixties probably more than matched what he was making on the job. But the amount didn't matter to Bosch. The payment did. It was an admission. If it could be traced to Conklin, it was hard evidence. Bosch felt himself getting excited. The records hoarded by a corrupt cop dead five years now might be all he needed to go head to head with Conklin.

He thought of something and looked around for the usual bank of phones. He checked his watch and looked over at the gate. People were milling about, ready to board and getting anxious. Bosch put the file and envelopes back into the satchel and carried his things to the phone.

Using his AT&T card, he dialed information in Sacramento and then dialed the state offices and asked for the corporate records unit. In three minutes he knew that McCage Inc. was not a California corporation and never was, at least in records going back to 1971. He hung up and went through the same process again, this time calling the Nevada state offices in Carson City.

The phone clerk told him the incorporation of McCage Inc. was defunct and asked if he was still interested in what information the state had. He excitedly said yes and was told by the clerk that she had to switch to microfiche and it would take a few minutes. While he waited, Bosch got out a notebook and got ready to take notes. He saw the gate door had been opened and people were just starting to board the plane. He didn't care, he'd miss it if he had to. He was too juiced to do anything but hang on to the phone.

Bosch studied the rows of slot machines in the center of the terminal. They were crowded with people trying their last chance at luck before leaving or their first chance after stepping off planes from all over the country and the world. Gambling against the machines had never appealed much to Bosch. He didn't understand it.

As he watched those milling about, it was easy to pick who was winning and who wasn't. It didn't take a detective to study the faces and know. He saw one woman with a stuffed teddy bear clamped under her arm. She was working two machines at once and Bosch could see that all she was doing was doubling her losses. To her left was a man in a black cowboy hat who was filling the machine with coins and pulling the arm back as quickly as he could. Bosch could see he was playing a dollar machine and was

271

going to the five-dollar max on every roll. Bosch figured that, in the few minutes he watched, the man had spent sixty dollars with no return. At least he wasn't carrying a stuffed animal.

Bosch turned back to check the gate. The line of boarders had thinned to a few stragglers. Bosch knew he was going to miss it. But that was okay. He hung on and stayed calm.

Suddenly there was a shout and Bosch looked over and saw the man with the cowboy hat waving it as his machine was paying off a jackpot. The woman with the stuffed animal stepped back from her machines and solemnly watched the payoff. Each metallic *ching* of the dollars dropping in the tray must have been like a hammer pounding in her skull. A steady reminder that she was losing.

'Take a look at me now, baby!' the cowboy whooped.

It didn't appear that the exclamation was directed at anyone in particular. He stooped down and started scooping the coins into his hat. The woman with the teddy bear went back to work on her machines.

Just as the gate door was being closed, the clerk came back on the phone. She told Bosch the immediately available records showed McCage was incorporated in November 1962 and was dissolved by the state twenty-eight years later when a year went by without renewal fees or taxes being paid to keep the incorporation current. Bosch knew this had occurred because Eno had died.

'Do you want the officers?' the clerk asked.

'Yes, I do.'

'Okay, president and chief executive officer is Claude Eno. That's E-N-O. Vice president is Gordon Mittel with two Ts. And the treasurer is listed as Arno Conklin. That first name's spelled —'.

'I got it. Thanks.'

Bosch hung up the phone, grabbed his overnighter and the satchel and ran to the gate.

'Just in time,' the attendant said with a tone of annoyance. 'Couldn't leave those one-armed bandits alone, huh?'

'Yeah,' Bosch said, not caring.

She opened the door and he went down the hallway and onto the plane. It was only half filled. He ignored his seat assignment and found an empty row. While he was pushing his luggage into the overhead storage bin, he thought of something. Once in his seat he took out his notebook and opened it to the page where he had just written the notes of his conversation with the incorporation clerk. He looked at the abbreviated notations.

Prez., CEO – C.E.
VP – G.M.
Treas. – A.C.

He then wrote only the initials in a line.

CE GM AC

He looked at the line for a moment and then smiled. He saw the anagram and wrote it on the next line.

MC CAGE

Bosch felt the blood jangling through his body. It was the feeling of knowing he was close. He was on a roll those people out there at the slot machines and all the casinos in the desert could never understand. It was a high they would never feel, no matter how many sevens came up on the dice or how many black jacks they were dealt. Bosch was getting close to a killer and that made him as juiced as any jackpot winner on the planet.

Driving the Mustang out of LAX an hour later, Bosch rolled the windows down and bathed his face in the cool, dry air. The sound of the breeze through the grove of eucalyptus trees at the airport gateway was always there like a welcome home. Somehow, he always found it reassuring when he came back from his trips. It was one of the things he loved about the city and he was glad it always greeted him.

He caught the light at Sepulveda and used the time to change the time on his watch. It was five minutes after two. He decided that he would have just enough time to get home, change into fresh clothes and grab something to eat before heading to Parker Center and his appointment with Carmen Hinojos.

He drove quickly under the 405 overpass and then took the curving on-ramp up onto the crowded freeway. As he turned the wheel to negotiate the turn, he realized that his upper arms ached deep in the biceps and he wasn't sure if it was from his fight with the fish on Saturday or from the way Jasmine had gripped his arms while they made love. He thought about her for a few more minutes and decided he would call her at the house before heading downtown. Their parting that morning already seemed long ago to him. They had made promises to meet again as soon as possible and Bosch hoped the promises would be kept. She was a mystery to him, one in which he knew he had not yet even begun to scratch the surface.

The 10 wasn't set to reopen until the following day, so Bosch bypassed the exit and stayed on the 405 until it rose over the Santa Monica Mountains and dropped into the Valley. He took the long way because he bet it would be faster, and because he had a mail drop in Studio City that he had been using since the post office refused to deliver mail to a red-tagged structure.

He transferred onto the 101 and promptly hit a wall of traffic inching its way along the six lanes. He stayed with it until impatience got the better of him. He exited Coldwater Canyon Boulevard and started taking surface streets. On Moorpark Road he passed several apartment buildings that still hadn't been demolished or repaired, the red tags and yellow tape bleached near-white by the months in the sun. Many of the condemned buildings still had signs like $500 MOVES YOU IN! and NEWLY REMODELED. On one red-tagged structure with the telltale crisscross stress fractures running along its entire length, someone had spray-painted a slogan that many took as the epitaph of the city in the months since the earthquake.

THE FAT LADY HAS SUNG

Somedays it was hard not to believe it. But Bosch tried to keep the faith. Somebody had to. The newspaper said more people were leaving than coming. But no matter, Bosch thought, I'm staying.

He cut over to Ventura and stopped at the private mailbox office. There was nothing but bills and junk mail in his box. He stopped at a deli next door and ordered the special, turkey on wholewheat with avocado and bean sprouts, to go. After that, he stayed on Ventura until it became Cahuenga and then took the turn off to Woodrow

Wilson Drive and the climb up the hill to home. On the first curve he had to slow on the narrow road to squeeze by an LAPD squad car. He waved but he knew they wouldn't know him. They would be out of North Hollywood Division. They didn't wave back.

He followed his usual practice of parking a half block away from his house and then walking back. He decided to leave the satchel in the trunk because he might need the files downtown. He headed down the street to his house with his overnighter in one hand and the sandwich bag in the other.

As he got to the carport, he noticed a patrol car coming up the road. He watched it and noticed it was the same two patrolmen he had just passed. They had turned around for some reason. He waited at the curb to see if they would stop to ask him for directions or maybe an explanation of his wave, and because he didn't want them to see him enter the condemned house. But the car drove by with neither of the patrolmen even looking at him. The driver had his eyes on the road and the passenger was talking into the radio microphone. It must be a call, Bosch thought. He waited until the car had gone around the next curve and then headed into the carport.

After opening the kitchen door, Bosch stepped in and immediately felt that something was amiss. He took two steps in before placing it. There was a foreign odor in the house, or at least the kitchen. It was the scent of perfume, he realized. No, he corrected, it was cologne. A man wearing cologne had either recently been in the house or was still there.

Bosch quietly placed his overnighter and the sandwich bag on the kitchen floor and reached to his waist. Old habits died hard. He still had no gun and he knew his backup was on the shelf in the closet near the front door. For a moment he thought about running out to the street in hopes of catching the patrol car but he knew it was long gone.

Instead, he opened a drawer and quietly withdrew a small paring knife. There were longer blades in there but the small knife would be easier to handle. He stepped toward the archway that led from the kitchen to the house's front entry. At the threshold, still hidden from whoever might be out there, he stopped, tilted his head forward and listened. He could hear the low hiss of the freeway down the hill behind the house, but nothing from within. Nearly a minute of silence passed. He was about to step out of the kitchen when he heard a sound. It was the slight whisper of cloth moving. Maybe the crossing or uncrossing of legs. He knew someone was in the living room. And he knew by now that they would know that he knew.

'Detective Bosch,' a voice said from the silence of the house. 'It is safe for you. You can come out.'

Bosch knew the voice but was operating at such an acute level of intensity, he couldn't immediately compute it and place it. All he knew was that he had heard it before.

'It's Assistant Chief Irving, Detective Bosch,' the voice said. 'Could you please step out? That way you don't get hurt and we don't get hurt.'

Yes, that was the voice. Bosch relaxed, put the knife down on the counter, the sandwich bag in the refrigerator and stepped out of the kitchen. Irving was there, sitting in the living room chair. Two men in suits whom Bosch didn't recognize sat on the couch. Looking around, Bosch could see his box of letters and cards from the closet sitting on the coffee table. He saw the murder book that he had left on the dining room table was sitting on the lap of one of the strangers. They had been searching his house, going through his things.

Bosch suddenly realized what had happened outside.

277

'I saw your lookout. Anybody want to tell me what's going on?'

'Where've you been, Bosch?' one of the suits asked.

Bosch looked at him. Not a single glimmer of recognition hit him.

'Who the fuck are you?'

He bent down and picked the box of cards and letters up off the coffee table, where it had been in front of the man.

'Detective,' Irving said, 'This is Lieutenant Angel Brockman and this is Earl Sizemore.'

Bosch nodded. He recognized one of the names.

'I've heard of you,' he said, looking at Brockman. 'You're the one who sent Bill Connors to the closet. That must've been good for IAD man of the month. Quite an honor.'

The sarcasm in Bosch's voice was unmistakable, as he intended it to be. The closet was where most cops kept their guns while off duty; going to the closet was department slang for a cop killing himself. Connors was an old beat cop in Hollywood Division who had killed himself the year before while he was under IAD investigation for trading dime bags of heroin to runaway girls for sex. After he was dead, the runaways had admitted making up the complaints because Connors was always hassling them to move off his beat. He had been a good man but saw everything stacked against him and decided to go to the closet.

'That was his choice, Bosch. And now you've got yours. You want to tell us where you've been the last twenty-four?'

'You want to tell me what this is about?'

He heard a clunking sound coming from the bedroom.

'What the hell?' He walked to the door and saw another suit in his bedroom, standing over the open drawer of the

278

night table. 'Hey, fuckhead, get out of there. Get out now!'

Bosch stepped in and kicked the drawer closed. The man stepped back, raised his hands like a prisoner and walked out to the living room.

'And this is Jerry Toliver,' Irving added. 'He's with Lieutenant Brockman, IAD. Detective Sizemore has joined us here from RHD.'

'Fantastic,' Bosch said. 'So everybody knows everybody. What's going on?'

He looked at Irving as he said this, believing if he was going to get a straight answer from anyone here, it would be him. Irving was generally a straight shooter when it came to his dealings with Bosch.

'De – Harry, we have got to ask you some questions,' Irving said. 'It would be best if we explain things later.'

Bosch could tell this one was serious.

'You got a warrant to be in here?'

'We'll show it to you later,' Brockman said. 'Let's go.'

'Where are we going?'

'Downtown.'

Bosch had had enough run-ins with the Internal Affairs Division to know things were being handled differently here. Just the fact that Irving, the second-highest-ranking officer in the department, was with them was an indication of the gravity of the situation. He guessed it was more than their simply finding out about his private investigation. If it was just that, Irving wouldn't have been here. There was something terribly wrong.

'All right,' Bosch said, 'who's dead?'

All four looked at him with faces of stone, confirming that in fact someone was dead. Bosch felt his chest tighten and for the first time he began to be scared. The names and faces of people he had involved flashed through his mind. Meredith Roman, Jake McKittrick, Keisha Russell, the

279

two women in Las Vegas. Who else? Jazz? Could he have possibly put her in some kind of danger? Then it hit him. Keisha Russell. The reporter had probably done what he told her not to. She had gone to Conklin or Mittel and asked questions about the old clip she had pulled for Bosch. She had walked in blindly and was now dead because of her mistake.

'Keisha Russell?' he asked.

He got no reply. Irving stood up and the others followed. Sizemore kept the murder book in his hand. He was going to take it. Brockman went into the kitchen, picked up the overnighter and carried it to the door.

'Harry, why don't you ride with Earl and I?' Irving said.

'How 'bout I meet you guys down there.'

'You ride with me.'

It was said sternly. It invited no further debate. Bosch raised his hands, acknowledging he had no choice, and moved toward the door.

Bosch sat in the back of Sizemore's LTD, directly behind Irving. He looked out the window as they went down the hill. He kept thinking of the young reporter's face. Her eagerness had killed her but Bosch couldn't help but share the blame. He had planted the seed of mystery in her mind and it had grown until she couldn't resist it.

'Where'd they find her?' he asked.

He was met only with silence. He couldn't understand why they said nothing, especially Irving. The assistant chief had led him to believe in the past that they had an understanding, if not a liking, between each other.

'I told her not to do anything,' he said. 'I told her to sit on it a few days.'

Irving turned his body so that he could partially see Bosch behind him.

'Detective, I don't know who or what you're talking about.'

'Keisha Russell.'

'Don't know her.'

He turned back around. Bosch was puzzled. The names and faces went through his mind again. He added Jasmine but then subtracted her. She knew nothing about the case.

'McKittrick?'

'Detective,' Irving said and again struggled to turn around to look at Bosch. 'We are involved in the investigation of the homicide of Lieutenant Harvey Pounds. These other names are not involved. If you think they are people that should be contacted, please let me know.'

Bosch was too stunned to answer. Harvey Pounds? That made no sense. He had nothing to do with the case, didn't even know about it. Pounds never left the office, how could he have gotten into danger? Then it came to him, washing over him like a wave of water that brought with it a chill. He understood. It made sense. And in the moment that he saw that it did, he also saw his own responsibility as well as his own predicament.

'Am I ... ?'

He couldn't finish.

'Yes,' Irving said. 'You are currently considered a suspect. Now maybe you will be quiet until we can set up a formal interview.'

Bosch leaned his head against the window glass and closed his eyes.

'Ah, Jesus ...'

And in that moment he realized he was no better than Brockman was for having sent a man to the closet. For Bosch knew in the dark part of his heart that he was responsible. He didn't know how or when it had happened but he knew.

He had killed Harvey Pounds. And he carried Pounds's badge in his pocket.

osch was numb to most of what was going on around him. After they reached Parker Center he was escorted up to Irving's office on the sixth floor and then placed in a chair in the adjoining conference room. He was in there alone for a half hour before Brockman and Toliver came in. Brockman sat directly across from Bosch, Toliver to Harry's right. It was obvious to Bosch by their being in Irving's conference room instead of an IAD interview room that Irving wanted to keep a tight control on this one. If it turned out to be a cop-killed-cop case, he'd need all the control he could muster to contain it. It could be a publicity debacle to rival those of the Rodney King days.

Through his daze and the jarring images of Pounds being dead, a pressing thought finally got Bosch's attention: he was in serious trouble himself. He told himself he couldn't retreat into a shell. He must be alert. The man sitting across from him would like nothing better than to hang a killing on Bosch and he was willing to go to any extreme to do it. It wasn't good enough that Bosch knew in his own mind that he had not, at least physically, killed Pounds. He had to defend himself. And so he resolved that he would show Brockman nothing. He would be just as tough as anybody in the room. He cleared his throat and began before Brockman got the chance.

'When did it happen?'

'I'm asking the questions.'

'I can save you time, Brockman. Tell me when it happened and I'll tell you where I was. We'll get this over with. I understand why I'm a suspect. I won't hold it against you but you're wasting your time.'

'Bosch, don't you feel anything at all? A man is dead. You worked with him.'

Bosch stared at him a long moment before answering in an even voice.

'What I feel doesn't matter. Nobody deserves to be killed, but I'm not going to miss him and I certainly won't miss working for him.'

'Jesus.' Brockman shook his head. 'The man had a wife, a kid in college.'

'Maybe they won't miss him, either. You never know. The guy was a prick at work. No reason to expect him to be anything else at home. What's your wife think about you, Brockman?'

'Save it, Bosch. I'm not falling for any of your –'

'Do you believe in God, Brickman?'

Bosch used Brockman's nickname in the department, awarded to him for his methodical way of building cases against other cops, like the late Bill Connors.

'This isn't about me or what I believe in, Bosch. We're talking about you.'

'That's right, we're talking about me. So, I'll tell you what I think. I'm not sure what I believe. My life's more than half over and I still haven't figured it out. But the theory I'm leaning toward is that everybody on this planet has some kind of energy that makes them what they are. It's all about energy. And when you die, it just goes somewhere else. And Pounds? He was bad energy and now it's gone somewhere else. So I don't feel too bad about him dying, to answer your question. But I'd like to know where that bad energy went. Hope you didn't get any, Brickman. You already have a lot.'

He winked at Brockman and saw the momentary confusion in the IAD detective's face as he tried to interpret what the jibe had meant. He seemed to shake it off and go on.

'Enough of the bullshit. Why did you confront Lieutenant Pounds in his office on Thursday? You know that was off limits while you are on leave.'

'Well, it was kind've like one of those Catch-22 situations. I think that's what they call 'em. It was off limits to go there but then Pounds, my commanding officer, called me up and told me I had to turn in my car. See, it was that bad energy working. I was already on involuntary leave but he couldn't leave well enough alone. He had to take my car, too. So I brought him in the keys. He was my supervisor and it was an order. So going there broke one of the rules but not going would have broken one, too.'

'Why'd you threaten him?'

'I didn't.'

'He filed an addendum to the assault complaint of two weeks earlier.'

'I don't care what he filed. There was no threat. The guy was a coward. He probably felt threatened. But there was no threat. There is a difference.'

Bosch looked over at the other suit. Toliver. It looked as if he was going to be silent the whole time. That was his role. He just stared at Bosch as if he were a TV screen.

Bosch looked around the rest of the room and for the first time noticed the phone on the banquette to the left of the table. The green light signaled a conference call was on. The interview was being piped out of the room. Probably to a tape recorder. Probably to Irving in his office next door.

'There is a witness,' Brockman said.

'To what?'

'The threat.'

'I'll tell you what, Lieutenant, why don't you tell me exactly what the threat was so I know what we're talking about. After all, if you believe I made it, what's wrong with me knowing what it was I said?'

Brockman gave it some thought before answering.

'Very simple, as most are, you told him if he ever, quote, fucked with you again, you'd kill him. Not too original.'

'But damning as hell, right? Well, fuck you, Brockman, I never said that. I don't doubt that that asshole wrote up an addendum, that was just his style, but whoever this wit is you got, they're full of shit.'

'You know Henry Korchmar?'

'Henry Korchmar?'

Bosch had no idea whom he was talking about. Then he realized Brockman meant old Henry of the Nod Squad. Bosch had never known his last name and so hearing it in this context had confused him.

'The old guy? He wasn't in the room. He's no witness. I told him to get out and he did. Whatever he told you, he probably backed Pounds because he was scared. But he wasn't there. You go ahead with it, Brockman. I'll be able to pull twelve people out of that squadroom who watched the whole thing through the glass. And they'll say Henry wasn't in there, they'll say Pounds was a liar and everybody knew it, and then where's your threat?'

Brockman said nothing into the silence so Bosch continued.

'See, you didn't do your work. My guess is that you know everybody who works in that squadroom thinks people like you are the bottom feeders of this department. They've got more respect for the people they put in jail.

285

And you know that, Brickman, so you were too intimidated to go to them. Instead, you rely on some old man's word and he probably didn't even know Pounds was dead when you talked to him.'

Bosch could tell by the way Brockman's eyes darted away that he had nailed him. Empowered with the victory, he stood up and headed toward the door.

'Where are you going?'

'To get some water.'

'Jerry, go with him.'

Bosch paused at the door and looked back.

'What, do you think I'm going to run, Brockman? You think that and you don't know the first thing about me. You think that and you haven't prepared for this interview. Why don't you come over to Hollywood one day and I'll teach you how to interview murder suspects. Free of charge.'

Bosch walked out, Toliver following. At the water fountain down the hall, he took a long drink of water and then wiped his mouth with his hand. He felt nervous, frayed. He didn't know how long it would be before Brockman could see through the front he was putting up.

As he walked back to the conference room, Toliver stayed a silent three paces behind him.

'You're still young,' Bosch said over his shoulder. 'There might be a chance for you, Toliver.'

Bosch stepped back into the conference room just as Brockman stepped through a door from the other side of the room. Bosch knew it was a direct entrance to Irving's office. He had once worked an investigation of a serial killer out of this room and under Irving's thumb.

Both men sat down across from each other again.

'Now, then,' Brockman started. 'I'm going to read you your rights, Detective Bosch.'

He took a small card from his wallet and proceeded to

read to Bosch the Miranda warning. Bosch knew for sure the phone line was going to a tape recorder. This was something they would want on tape.

'Now,' Brockman said when he was finished. 'Do you agree to waive those rights and talk to us about this situation?'

'It's a situation now, huh? I thought it was a murder. Yeah, I'll waive.'

'Jerry, go get a waiver, I don't have one here.'

Jerry got up and left through the hallway door. Bosch could hear his feet moving quickly on the linoleum, then a door open. He was taking the stairs down to IAD on the fifth.

'Uh, let's start by –'

'Don't you want to wait until you have your witness back? Or is this being secretly recorded without my knowledge?'

This immediately flustered Brockman.

'Yes, Bosch it's being sec – it's being recorded. But not secretly. We told you before we started that we'd be taping.'

'Good cover-up, Lieutenant. That last line, that was a good one. I'll have to remember that one.'

'Now, let's start with –'

The door opened and Toliver came in with a sheet of paper. He handed it to Brockman, who studied it a moment, made sure it was the correct form and slid it across the table to Bosch. Harry grabbed it and quickly scribbled a signature on the appropriate line. He was familiar with the form. He slid it back and Brockman put it off to the side of the table without looking at it. So he didn't notice the signature Bosch had written was 'Fuck You.'

'All right, let's get this going. Bosch, give us your whereabouts over the last seventy-two hours.'

287

'You don't want to search me first, do you? How 'bout you, Jerry?'

Bosch stood up, opening his jacket so they could see he was not armed. He thought by taunting them like this they would do the exact opposite and not search him. Carrying Pounds's badge was a piece of evidence that would probably put him in the ground if they discovered it.

'Siddown, Bosch!' Brockman barked. 'We're not going to search you. We're trying to give you every benefit of the doubt but you make it damn hard.'

Bosch sat back down, relieved for the time being.

'Now, just give us your whereabouts. We don't have all day.'

Bosch thought about this. He was surprised by the window of time they wanted. Seventy-two hours. He wondered what had happened to Pounds and why they hadn't narrowed time of death to a shorter span.

'Seventy-two hours ago. Well, about seventy-two hours ago it was Friday afternoon and I was in Chinatown at the Fifty-One-Fifty building. Which reminds me, I'm due over there in ten minutes. So, boys, if you'll excuse me …'

He stood up.

'Siddown, Bosch. That's been taken care of. Sit down.'

Bosch sat down and said nothing. He realized, though, that he actually felt disappointed he would miss the session with Carmen Hinojos.

'Come on, Bosch, let's hear it. What happened after that?'

'I don't remember all the details. But I ate over at the Red Wind that night, also stopped at the Epicentre for a few drinks. Then I got to the airport about ten. I took a red-eye to Florida, to Tampa, spent the weekend there and got back about an hour and a half before I found you people illegally inside my home.'

'It's not illegal. We had a warrant.'

'I've been shown no warrant.'

'Never mind that, what do you mean you were in Florida?'

'I guess I mean I was in Florida. What do you think it means?'

'You can prove this?'

Bosch reached into his pocket, took out his airline folder with the ticket receipt and slid it across the table.

'For starters there's the ticket receipt. I think there's one in there for a rental car, too.'

Brockman quickly opened the ticket folder and started reading.

'What were you doing there?' he asked without looking up.

'Dr Hinojos, that's the company shrink, said I should try to get away. And I thought, how 'bout Florida? I'd never been there and all my life I've liked orange juice. I thought, what the hell? Florida.'

Brockman was flustered again. He wasn't expecting something like this. Bosch could tell. Most cops never realized how important the initial interview with a suspect or witness was to an investigation. It informed all other interviews and even court testimony that followed. You had to be prepared. Like lawyers, you had to know most of the answers before you asked the questions. The IAD relied so much on its presence as an intimidating factor that most of the detectives assigned to the division never really had to prepare for interviews. And when they hit a wall like this, they didn't know what to do.

'Okay, Bosch, uh, what did you do in Florida?'

'You ever heard that song Marvin Gaye sang? Before he got killed? It's called –'

'What are you talking about?'

'– "Sexual Healing." It says it's good for the soul.'

'I've heard it,' Toliver said.

Both Brockman and Bosch looked at him.

'Sorry,' he offered.

'Again, Bosch,' Brockman said. 'What are you talking about?'

'I'm talking about that I spent most of the time with a woman I know there. Most of the other time I spent with a fishing guide on a boat in the Gulf of Mexico. What I'm talking about, asshole, is that I was with people almost every minute. And the times I wasn't weren't long enough for me to fly back here and kill Pounds. I don't even know when he was killed but I'll tell you right now you don't have a case, Brockman, because there is no case. You're looking in the wrong direction.'

Bosch had chosen his words carefully. He was unsure what, if anything, they knew about his private investigation and he wasn't going to give them anything if he could help it. They had the murder book and the evidence box but he thought that he might be able to explain all of that away. They also had his notebook because he had stuffed it into his overnighter at the airport. In it were the names, numbers and addresses of Jasmine and McKittrick, the address of the Eno house in Vegas, and other notes about the case. But they might not be able to put together what it all meant. Not if he was lucky.

Brockman pulled a notebook and pen from the inside pocket of his jacket.

'Okay, Bosch, give me the name of the woman and this fishing guide. I need their numbers, everything.'

'I don't think so.'

Brockman's eyes widened.

'I don't care what you think, give me the names.'

Bosch said nothing, just stared down at the table in front of him.

'Bosch, you've told us your whereabouts, now we need to confirm them.'

'I know where I was at, that's all I need.'

'If you're in the clear, as you claim, let us check it out, clear you and move on to other things, other possibilities.'

'You've got the airlines and the car rental right there. Start with that. I'm not dragging people into this who don't need to be. They're good people and unlike you, they like me. I'm not going to let you spoil that by having you come in with your concrete block feet and step all over the relationships.'

'You don't have a choice, Bosch.'

'Oh, yes, I do. Right now, I do. You want to try to make a case against me, do it. If it gets to that point, I'll bring these people out and they'll blow your shit away, Brockman. You think at the moment you've got PR problems in the department over sending Bill Connors to the closet? You'll end this case with worse PR than Nixon had. I'm not giving you the names. If you want to write something down there in your notebook, just write that I said "Fuck you." That ought to cover it.'

Brockman's face got kind of blotchy with pinks and whites. He was quiet a moment before speaking.

'Know what I think? I still think you did it. I think you hired somebody to do it and you went waltzing off to Florida so you'd be nowhere near here. A fishing guide. If that doesn't sound like a conjured-up piece of shit I don't know what does. And the woman? Who was she, some hooker you picked up in a bar? What was she, a fifty-dollar alibi? Or did you go a hundred?'

In one explosive move, Bosch shoved the table toward Brockman, catching him completely by surprise. It slid under his arms and crashed into his chest. His chair tipped back against the wall behind him. Bosch kept the pressure on his end and pinned Brockman against the wall. Bosch pushed back on his own chair until it was against the wall behind him. He raised his left leg and put his foot against the table to keep the pressure on it. He saw the blotches of color on Brockman's face become more pronounced as he went without air. His eyes bugged. But he had no leverage and couldn't move the table off himself.

Toliver was slow to react. Stunned, he seemed to look at Brockman for a long moment as if awaiting orders before jumping up and moving toward Bosch. Bosch was able to fend off his first effort, shoving the younger man back into a potted palm tree that was in the corner of the room. While Bosch did this, he saw in his peripheral vision a figure enter the room through the other door. Then his chair was abruptly knocked over and he was on the ground with a heavy weight on top of him. By turning his head slightly he could see it was Irving.

'Don't move, Bosch!' Irving yelled in his ear. 'Settle down right now!'

Bosch went limp to signify his compliance and Irving got off him. Bosch stayed still for a few moments and then put a hand up on the table to pull himself up. As he got up, he saw Brockman hacking and trying to get air into his lungs while holding both hands against his chest. Irving held one hand out to Bosch's chest as a calming gesture and a means of stopping him from taking another run at Brockman. With his other hand, he pointed at Toliver, who was trying to right the potted palm. It had become uprooted and wouldn't stand up. He finally just leaned it against the wall.

'You,' Irving snapped at him. 'Out.'

'But, sir, the –'

'Get out!'

Toliver quickly left through the hallway door as Brockman was finally finding his voice.

'Buh ... Bosch, you sonova bitch, you ... you're going to jail. You –'

'Nobody's going to jail,' Irving said sternly. 'Nobody's going to jail.'

Irving stopped to gulp down some air. Bosch noticed that the assistant chief seemed just as winded as anybody in the room.

'There will be no charges on this,' Irving finally continued. 'Lieutenant, you baited him and got what you got.'

Irving's tone invited no debate. Brockman, his chest still heaving, put his elbows on the table and began running his fingers through his hair, trying to look as if he still had some composure but all he had was defeat. Irving turned to Bosch, anger bunching the muscles of his jaw into hard surfaces.

'And you. Bosch, I don't know how to help you. You're always the loose cannon. You knew what he was doing, you've done it yourself. But you couldn't sit there and take it. What kind of man are you?'

Bosch didn't say anything and he doubted Irving wanted a spoken answer. Brockman started coughing and Irving looked back at him.

'Are you all right?'

'I think.'

'Go across the street, have one of the paramedics check you out.'

'No, I'm all right.'

'Good, then go down to your office, take a break. I have someone else I want to have talk to Bosch.'

'I want to continue the inter –'

'The interview is over, Lieutenant. You blew it.' Then, looking at Bosch, he added, 'You both did.'

I rving left Bosch alone in the conference room and in a
few moments Carmen Hinojos walked in. She took the
same seat that Brockman had sat in. She looked at
Bosch with eyes that seemed filled with equal parts anger
and disappointment. But Bosch didn't flinch under her
gaze.

'Harry, I can't believe –'

He held a finger up to his mouth, silencing her.

'What is it?'

'Are our sessions still supposed to be private?'

'Of course.'

'Even in here?'

'Yes. What is it?'

Bosch got up and walked to the phone on the counter.
He pushed the button that disconnected the conference
call. He returned to his seat.

'I hope that was left on unintentionally. I'm going to
speak to Chief Irving about that.'

'You're probably speaking to him right now. The
phone was too obvious. He's probably got the room
wired.'

'C'mon, Harry, this isn't the CIA.'

'No, it's not. Sometimes it's even worse. All I'm saying
is Irving, the IAD, they still might be listening somehow.
Be careful what you say.'

Carmen Hinojos looked exasperated.

'I'm not paranoid, Doctor. I've been through this before.'

'All right, never mind. I really don't care who's listening or not. I can't believe what you just did. It makes me very sad and disappointed. What have our meetings been about? Nothing? I'm sitting in there hearing you resort to the same type of violence that brought you to me in the first place. Harry, this isn't some joke. This is real life. And I have to make a decision that could very well decide your future. This makes it all the more difficult to do.'

He waited until he was sure she was done.

'You were in there with Irving the whole time?'

'Yes, he called and explained the situation and asked me to come over and sit in. I have to say –'

'Wait a minute. Before we go any further. Did you talk to him? Did you tell him about our sessions?'

'No, of course not.'

'Okay, for the record, I just want to reiterate that I do not give up any of my protections under the patient-doctor relationship. We okay on that?'

For the first time she looked away from him. He could see her face turning dark with anger.

'Do you know what an insult that is for you to tell me that? What, do you think I'd tell him about our sessions just because he may have ordered me to?'

'Did he?'

'You don't trust me at all, do you?'

'Did he?'

'No, he didn't.'

'That's good.'

'It's not just me. You don't trust anyone.'

Bosch realized that he had been out of line. He could see, though, that there was more hurt than anger in her face.

'I'm sorry, you're right, I shouldn't have said that. I'm

just … I don't know, I've got my back to the corner here, Doctor. When that happens, sometimes you forget who's on your side and who isn't.'

'Yes, and as a matter of course you respond with violence against those who you perceive are not on your side. This is not good to see. It's very, very disappointing.'

He looked away from her and over to the potted palm in the corner. Before leaving the room, Irving had replanted it, getting his hands dirty with black soil. Bosch noticed it was still slightly tilted to the left.

'So what are you doing up here?' he asked. 'What does Irving want?'

'He wanted me to sit in his office and listen to your interview on the conference line. He said he was interested in my evaluation of your answers as to whether I believed you could have been responsible for the death of Lieutenant Pounds. Thanks to you and your attack on your interviewer, he didn't need any evaluation from me. It's clear at this point you are prone to and quite capable of violence against fellow police officers.'

'That's bullshit and you know it. Damn it, what I did in here to that guy masquerading as a cop was a lot different than what they think I did. You're talking about things that are worlds apart and if you don't see that, you're making your living in the wrong business.'

'I'm not so sure.'

'Have you ever killed anyone, Doctor?'

Saying the question reminded him of his true confessions conversation with Jasmine.

'Of course not.'

'Well, I have. And believe me it's a lot different than roughing up some pompous ass in a suit with a shine on its ass. A lot different. If you or they think that doing one means you can do the other, you all have a lot to learn.'

296

They were both quiet for a long while, letting their anger ebb away.

'All right,' he finally said. 'So what happens now?'

'I don't know. Chief Irving just asked me to sit in with you, to calm you. I guess he's figuring out what to do next. I guess I'm not doing a very good job of calming you.'

'What did he say when he first asked you to come up here and listen?'

'He just called me and explained what happened and said he wanted my take on the interview. You have to understand something, despite your problems with authority, he is one person who I think is in your court on this. I don't think he honestly believes you're involved in the death of your lieutenant – at least directly. But he realizes that you are a viable suspect who needs to be questioned. I think if you had held your temper during the interview this all might've been over for you soon. They would've checked your story in Florida and that would have been the end of it. I even told them that you told me you were going to Florida.'

'I don't want them checking my story. I don't want them involved.'

'Well, it's too late. He knows you're up to something.'

'How?'

'When he called to ask me to come over he mentioned the file on your mother's case. The murder book. He said it was found at your house. He also said they found the stored evidence from the case there ...'

'And?'

'And he asked if I knew what you were doing with all of it.'

'So he did ask you to reveal what we've talked about in our sessions.'

'In an indirect way.'

'Sounds pretty direct to me. Did he say specifically that it was my mother's case?'

'Yes, he did.'

'What did you tell him?'

'I told him that I was not at liberty to discuss anything that was talked about in our sessions. It didn't satisfy him.'

'I'm not surprised.'

Another wave of silence washed between them. Her eyes wandered the room. His stayed on hers.

'Listen, what do you know about what happened to Pounds?'

'Very little.'

'Irving must have told you something. You must've asked.'

'He said Pounds was found in the trunk of his car Sunday evening. I guess he had been there a while. A day maybe. The chief said he ... the body showed signs of torture. Particularly sadistic mutilation, he said. He didn't go into detail. It had happened before Pounds was dead. They do know that. He said that he'd been in a lot of pain. He wanted to know if you were the type of man who could've done that.'

Bosch said nothing. He was imagining the crime scene in his mind. His guilt came crushing back down on him and for a moment he thought he might even get nauseous.

'For what it's worth, I said no.'

'What?'

'I told him you weren't the type of man who could've done that.'

Bosch nodded. But his thoughts were already a great distance away again. What had happened to Pounds was becoming clear and Bosch carried the guilt of having set things in motion. Though legally innocent, he knew he was morally culpable. Pounds was a man he despised, had less respect for than some of the murderers he had known.

But the weight of the guilt was bearing down on him. He ran his hands hard over his face and through his hair. He felt a shudder move through his body.

'Are you all right?' Hinojos asked.

'I'm fine.'

Bosch took out his cigarettes and started to light one with his Bic.

'Harry, you better not. This isn't my office.'

'I don't care. Where was he found?'

'What?'

'Pounds! Where was he found?'

'I don't know. You mean where was the car? I don't know. I didn't ask.'

She studied him and he noticed the hand that held his cigarette was shaking.

'All right, Harry, that's it. What's the matter? What is going on?'

Bosch looked at her for a long moment and nodded.

'Okay, you want to know? I did it. I killed him.'

Her face immediately reacted as if perhaps she had seen the killing firsthand, so close that she had been spattered with blood. It was a horrible face. Repulsed. And she moved back in her chair as if even a few more inches of separation from him were needed.

'You ... you mean this story about Florida was –'

'No. I don't mean I killed him. Not with my hands. I mean what I've done, what I've been doing. It got him killed. I got him killed.'

'How do you know? You can't know for sure that –'

'I know. Believe me, I know.'

He looked away from her to a painting on the wall over the banquette. It was a generic depiction of a beach scene. He looked back at Hinojos.

'It's funny ... ,' he said but didn't finish. He just shook his head.

'What is?'

He got up and reached to the potted palm and stubbed the cigarette out in the dark soil.

'What is funny, Harry?'

He sat back down and looked at her.

'The civilized people in the world, the ones who hide behind culture and art and politics ... and even the law, they're the ones to watch out for. They've got that perfect disguise goin' for them, you know? But they're the most vicious. They're the most dangerous people on earth.'

It seemed to Bosch that the day would never end, that he would never get out of the conference room. After Hinojos left, it was Irving's turn. He came in silently, took the Brockman seat and folded his hands on the table and said nothing. He looked irritated. Bosch thought maybe he smelled the smoke. Bosch didn't care about that but he found the silence discomforting.

'What about Brockman?'

'He's gone. You heard me tell him, he blew it. So did you.'

'How's that?'

'You could've talked your way out of it. Could've let him check your story and be done with it. But you had to make another enemy. You had to be Harry Bosch.'

'That's where you and I differ, Chief. You oughta get out of the office and come out on the street again sometime. I didn't make Brockman an enemy. He was my enemy before I even met him. They all are. And, you know, I'm really getting tired of everybody analyzing me and sticking their noses up my ass. It's getting real old.'

'Somebody's got to do it. You don't.'

'You don't know a thing about it.'

Irving waved Bosch's pale defense away like cigarette smoke.

'So what now?' Bosch continued. 'Why are you here?

You going to try to break my alibi now? Is that it? Brockman's out and you're in?'

'I don't need to break your alibi. It's been checked and it looks like it holds. Brockman and his people have already been instructed to follow other avenues of investigation.'

'What do you mean, it's been checked?'

'Give us some credit here, Bosch. The names were in your notebook.'

He reached into his coat and pulled out the notebook. He tossed it across the table to Bosch.

'This woman that you spent some time with over there, she told me enough to the point that I believed it. You might want to call her yourself, though. She certainly seemed confused by my call. I was rather circumspect in my explanation.'

'I appreciate that. So, then, I guess I'm free to split?' Bosch stood up.

'In a technical sense.'

'And the other senses?'

'Sit down for a minute, Detective.'

Bosch held his hands up. He'd gone this far. He decided he might as well go all the way and hear it all. He sat back down in his chair with a meager protest.

'My butt's getting sore from all this sitting.'

'I knew Jake McKittrick,' Irving said. 'Knew him well. We worked Hollywood together many years ago. But you know that already. As nice as it is to touch base with an old colleague, I can't say I enjoyed anything about the conversation I had with my old friend Jake.'

'You called him, too.'

'While you were in here with the doctor.'

'So then what do you want from me? You got the story from him, what's left?'

Irving drummed his fingers on the tabletop.

302

'What do I want? What I want is for you to tell me that what you are doing, what you have been doing, is in no way connected to what has happened to Lieutenant Pounds.'

'I can't, Chief. I don't know what happened to him, other than that he's dead.'

Irving studied Bosch for a long moment, contemplating something, deciding whether to treat him as an equal and tell him the story.

'I guess I expected an immediate denial. Your answer already suggests that you think there might be a correlation. I can't tell you how much that bothers me.'

'Anything is possible, Chief. Let me ask you this. You said Brockman and his crew were out chasing other leads – I guess avenues is what you said. Are any of these avenues viable? I mean, did Pounds have a secret life or are they just out there chasing their tails?'

'There's nothing that stands out. I'm afraid you were the best lead. Brockman still thinks so. He wants to pursue the theory that you hired a hitman of some sort and then flew to Florida to establish an alibi.'

'Yeah, that's a good one.'

'I think it stretches credibility some. I told him to drop it. For the moment. And I'm telling you to drop what you are doing. This woman in Florida sounds like the kind of person you could spend some time with. I want you to get on a plane and go back to her. Stay a couple weeks. When you come back, we'll talk about going back on the homicide table at Hollywood.'

Bosch was unsure whether there was a threat in all that Irving had just said. If not a threat, then maybe a bribe.

'And if I don't?'

'If you don't, then you are stupid. And you deserve whatever happens to you.'

'What is it that you think I'm doing, Chief?'

'I don't *think*, I *know* what you're doing. It's easy. You pulled the book on your mother's homicide. Why at this particular point in time you've done this, I don't know. But you're out running a freelance investigation and that's a problem for us. You have to stop it, Harry, or I'll stop you. I'll shut you down. Permanently.'

'Who are you protecting?'

Bosch saw the anger move into Irving's face as his skin turned from pink to an intense red. His eyes seemed to grow smaller and darker with fury.

'Don't you ever suggest such a thing. I've dedicated my life to this depart –'

'It's yourself, isn't it? You knew her. You found her. You're afraid of being dragged into this if I put something together on it. I bet you already knew everything McKittrick told you on the phone.'

'That's ridiculous, I –'

'Is it? Is it? I don't think so. I've already talked to one witness who remembers you from those days on the Boulevard beat.'

'What witness?'

'She said she knew you. She knows my mother knew you, too.'

'The only person I am protecting is you, Bosch. Can't you see that? I'm *ordering* you to stop this investigation.'

'You can't. I don't work for you anymore. I'm on leave, remember? Involuntary leave. That makes me a citizen now, and I can do whatever I goddamn want to do as long as it's legal.'

'I could charge you with possession of stolen documents – the murder book.'

'It wasn't stolen. Besides, what if you bullshit a case, what's that, a misdemeanor? They'll laugh you out of the city attorney's office on your ass with that.'

'But you'd lose your job. That would be it.'

'You're a little late with that one, Chief. A week ago that would've been a valid threat. I'd have to consider it. But it doesn't matter anymore. I'm free of all of that bullshit now and this is all that matters to me and I don't care what I have to do, I'm doing it.'

Irving was silent and Bosch guessed that the assistant chief was realizing that Bosch had moved beyond his reach. Irving's hold over Bosch's job and future had been his leverage before. But Bosch had finally broken free. Bosch began again in a low, calm voice.

'If you were me, Chief, could you just walk away? What does doing what I do for the department matter if I can't do this for her … and for me?'

He stood up and put the notebook into his jacket pocket.

'I'm going. Where's the rest of my stuff?'

'No.'

Bosch hesitated. Irving looked up at him and Bosch saw the anger was gone now.

'I did nothing wrong,' Irving said quietly.

'Sure you did,' Bosch said just as quietly. He leaned over the table until he was only a few feet away. 'We all did, Chief. We let it go. That was our crime. But not anymore. At least, not with me. If you want to help, you know how to reach me.'

He headed toward the door.

'What do you want?'

Bosch looked back at him.

'Tell me about Pounds. I need to know what happened. It's the only way I'll know if it's connected.'

'Then sit down.'

Bosch took the chair by the door and sat down. They both took some time to calm down before Irving finally spoke.

'We started looking for him Saturday night. We found

his car Sunday noon in Griffith Park. One of the tunnels closed after the quake. It was like they knew we'd be looking from the air, so they put the car in a tunnel.'

'Why'd you start looking before you knew he was dead?'

'The wife. She started calling Saturday morning. She said he'd gotten a call Friday night at home, she didn't know who. But whoever it was managed to convince Pounds to leave the house and meet him. Pounds didn't tell his wife what it was about. He said he'd be back in an hour or two. He left and never came back. In the morning she called us.'

'Pounds is unlisted, I assume.'

'Yes. That gives rise to the probability it was someone in the department.'

Bosch thought about this.

'Not necessarily. It just had to be someone with connections to people in the city. People that could get his number with a phone call. You ought to put out the word. Grant amnesty to anyone who comes forward and says they gave up the number. Say you'll go light in exchange for the name of the person they gave it to. That's who you want. Chances are whoever gave out the number didn't know what was going to happen.'

Irving nodded.

'That's an idea. Within the department there are hundreds who could get his number. There may be no other way to go.'

'Tell me more about Pounds.'

'We went to work right there in the tunnel. By Sunday the media had wind that we were looking for him, so the tunnel worked to our advantage. No helicopters flying over, bothering us. We just set up lights in the tunnel.'

'He was in the car?'

Bosch was acting like he knew nothing. He knew that if

he expected Hinojos to respect his confidences, he must in turn respect hers.

'Yes, he was in the trunk. And, my God, was it bad. He ... He'd been stripped of his clothes. He'd been beaten. Then – then there was the evidence of torture ...'

Bosch waited but Irving had stopped.

'What? What did they do to him?'

'They burned him. The genitals, nipples, fingers ... My God.'

Irving ran his hand over his shaven scalp and closed his eyes while he did it. Bosch could see that he could not get the images out of his mind. Bosch was having trouble with it, too. His guilt was like a palpable object in his chest.

'It was like they wanted something from him,' Irving said. 'But he couldn't give it. He didn't have it and ... and they kept at him.'

Suddenly, Bosch felt the slight tremor of an earthquake and reached for the table to steady himself. He looked at Irving for confirmation and realized there was no tremor. It was himself, shaking again.

'Wait a minute.'

The room tilted slightly then righted itself.

'What is it?'

'Wait a minute.'

Without another word Bosch stood up and went out the door. He quickly went down the hall to the men's room by the water fountain. There was someone in front of one of the sinks shaving but Bosch didn't take the time to look at him. He pushed through one of the stall doors and vomited into the toilet, barely making it in time.

He flushed the toilet but the spasm came again and then again until he was empty, until he had nothing left inside but the image of Pounds naked and dead, tortured.

'You okay in there, buddy?' a voice said from outside the stall.

'Just leave me alone.'

'Sorry, just asking.'

Bosch stayed in the stall a few more minutes, leaning against the wall. Eventually, he wiped his mouth with toilet paper and then flushed it down. He stepped out of the stall unsteadily and went to the sink. The other man was still there. Now he was putting on a tie. Bosch glanced at him in the mirror but didn't recognize him. He bent over the sink and rinsed his face and mouth out with cold water. He then used paper towels to dry off. He never looked at himself once in the mirror.

'Thanks for asking,' he said as he left.

Irving looked as if he hadn't moved while Bosch was gone.

'Are you all right?'

Bosch sat down and took out his cigarettes.

'Sorry, but I'm gonna smoke.'

'You already have been.'

Bosch lit up and took a deep drag. He stood up and walked to the trash can in the corner. There was an old coffee cup in it and he took it to use as an ashtray.

'Just one,' he said. 'Then you can open the door and air the place out.'

'It's a bad habit.'

'In this town so is breathing. How did he die? What was the fatal injury?'

'The autopsy was this morning. Heart failure. The strain on him was too much, his heart gave way.'

Bosch paused a moment. He felt the beginning of his strength coming back.

'Why don't you tell me the rest of it?'

'There is no rest of it. That's it. There was nothing there. No evidence on the body. No evidence in the car. It had been wiped clean. There was nothing to go on.'

'What about his clothes?'

'They were there in the trunk. No help. The killer kept one thing, though.'

'What?'

'His shield. The bastard took his badge.'

Bosch just nodded and averted his eyes. They were both silent for a long time. Bosch couldn't get the images out of his mind and he guessed Irving was having the same problem.

'So,' Bosch finally said, 'looking at what had been done to him, the torture and everything, you immediately thought of me. That's a real vote of confidence.'

'Look, Detective, you had put the man's face through a window two weeks earlier. We had gotten an added report from him that you had threatened him. What –'

'There was no threat. He –'

'I don't care if there was or wasn't. He made the report. That's the point. True or false, he made the report, therefore, he felt threatened by you. What were we supposed to do, ignore it? Just say, "Harry Bosch? Oh, no, there's no way our own Harry Bosch could do this," and go on? Don't be ridiculous.'

'All right, you're right. Forget it. He didn't say anything at all to his wife before leaving?'

'Only that someone called and he had to go out for an hour to a meeting with a very important person. No name was mentioned. The call came in about nine Friday night.'

'Is that exactly how she said he said it?'

'I believe so. Why?'

'Because if he said it in that way, then it sounds like two people may be involved.'

'How so?'

'It just sounds as though one person called him to set up a meeting with a second person, this very important person. If that person had made the call, then he would have told the wife that so and so, the big important guy, just called and I have to go meet him. See what I mean?'

'I do. But whoever called could have also used the name of an important person as bait to draw Pounds out. That actual person may not have been involved at all.'

'That's also true. But I think that whatever was said, it would have to have been convincing to get Pounds out at night, by himself.'

'Maybe it was someone he already knew.'

'Maybe. But then he probably would have told his wife the name.'

'True.'

'Did he take anything with him? A briefcase, files, anything?'

'Not that we know of. The wife was in the TV room. She didn't see him actually go out the door. We've been over all of this with her, we've been all over the house. There's nothing. His briefcase was in his office at the station. He didn't even take it home with him. There's nothing to go on. To be honest, you were the best candidate and you're clear now. It brings me back to my question. Could what you've been doing have had anything to do with this?'

Bosch could not bring himself to tell Irving what he thought, what he knew in his gut had happened to Pounds. It wasn't the guilt that stopped him, though. It was the desire to keep his mission to himself. In that moment he realized that vengeance was a singular thing, a solo mission, something never to be spoken of out loud.

'I don't know the answer,' he said. 'I told Pounds nothing. But he wanted me to go down. You know that. The guy's dead but he was an asshole and he wanted me to go down. So he'd have had his ear to the ground for anything about me. A couple people have seen me around in the last week. Word could've gotten back to him and he could've blundered into something. He wasn't much of an investigator. He could've made a mistake. I don't know.'

Irving looked at him through dead eyes. Bosch knew he was trying to determine how much was true and how much was bullshit. Bosch spoke first.

'He said he was going to meet someone important.'

'Yes.'

'Look, Chief, I don't know what McKittrick told you about the conversation I had out there with him, but you know there were important people involved back ... you know, with my mother. You were there.'

'Yes, I was there, but I wasn't part of the investigation, not after the first day.'

'Did McKittrick tell you about Arno Conklin?'

'Not today. But back then. I remember once when I asked him what was happening with the case, he told me to ask Arno. He said Arno was running interference for someone on it.'

'Well, Arno Conklin was an important person.'

'But now? He's an old man if he's even still alive.'

'He's alive, Chief. And you have to remember something. Important men surround themselves with important men. They're never alone. Conklin may be old but there could be someone else who isn't.'

'What are you telling me, Bosch?'

'I'm telling you to leave me alone. I have to do this. I'm the only one who can. I'm telling you to keep Brockman and everybody else away from me.'

Irving stared at him a long moment and Bosch could tell he didn't know which way to go with this. Bosch stood up.

'I'll keep in touch.'

'You're not telling me everything.'

'It's better that way.'

He stepped through the door into the hallway, remembered something and then stepped back into the room with Irving.

'How am I going to get home? You brought me here.'

Irving reached over to the phone.

B osch went through the fifth-floor door to the
Internal Affairs Division and found no one behind
the counter. He waited a few moments for Toliver
to show up since Irving had just ordered him to drive
Bosch home, but the young IAD detective never showed.
Bosch figured it was just one more mind game they were
trying to play with him. He didn't want to walk around
the counter and have to find Toliver so he just yelled his
name out. Behind the counter was a door that was slightly
ajar and he was reasonably sure Toliver heard the call.

But the person who stepped through the door was
Brockman. He stared at Bosch for a long moment without
saying anything.

'Look, Brockman, Toliver is supposed to run me
home,' Bosch said to him. 'I don't want anything else to
do with you.'

'Yeah, well, that's too bad.'

'Just get Toliver.'

'You better watch out for me, Bosch.'

'Yeah, I know. I'll be watching.'

'Yeah, and you won't see me coming.'

Bosch nodded and looked past him to the door where
he expected Toliver to step out any moment. He just
wanted to diffuse the situation and get his ride home. He
considered walking out and catching a cab, but he knew in
rush hour it would probably cost him fifty bucks. He

didn't have it on him. Plus, he liked the idea of having an IAD shine chauffeur him home.

'Hey, killer?'

Bosch looked back at Brockman. He was getting tired of this.

'What's it like to fuck another killer? Must really be something, to go all the way to Florida for it.'

Bosch tried to stay cool but he felt his face betray himself. For he suddenly knew who and what Brockman was talking about.

'What are you talking about?'

Brockman's face lit up with a bully's delight as he read Bosch's surprised look.

'Oooh, baby! She didn't even bother telling you, did she?'

'Tell me what?'

Bosch wanted to reach over the counter and drag Brockman across it but at least outwardly he maintained his cool.

'Tell you what? I'll tell you what. I think your whole story stinks and I'm going to bust it open. Then Mr Clean upstairs isn't going to be able to protect you.'

'He said you were told to leave me alone, that I was clear.'

'Fuck him and fuck you. When I come in with your alibi in a bag, he's not going to have a choice but to cut you loose.'

Toliver stepped through the doorway behind the counter. He was holding a set of car keys in his hands. He stood silently behind Brockman with his eyes down.

'First thing I did was run her on the computer,' Brockman said. 'She's got a record, Bosch. You didn't know that? She's a killer, just like you. Takes one to know one, I guess. Nice couple.'

Bosch wanted to ask a thousand questions but he

wouldn't ask any of this man. He felt a deep void opening inside as he began jettisoning his feelings for Jazz. He realized that she had left all the signs out for him but he hadn't read them. Even so, the feeling that descended on him with the strongest grip was one of betrayal.

Bosch pointedly ignored Brockman and looked at Toliver.

'Hey, kid, you going to give me a ride or what?'

Toliver moved around the counter without answering.

'Bosch, I already got you on an association beef,' Brockman said. 'But I'm not satisfied.'

Bosch went to the hallway door and opened it. It was against LAPD regulations to associate with known criminals. Whether Brockman could make a charge like that stick was the least of Bosch's worries. He headed out the door with Toliver following. Before it closed Brockman yelled after them.

'Give her a kiss for me, killer.'

At first, Bosch sat silently next to Jerry Toliver on the ride back to his house. He had a waterfall of thoughts dropping through his mind and decided to simply ignore the young IAD detective. Toliver left the police scanner on and the sporadic chatter was the only thing resembling conversation in the car. They had caught the crest of the evening commute out of downtown and were moving at an excruciatingly slow pace toward the Cahuenga pass.

Bosch's guts ached from the wracking convulsions of nausea of an hour earlier and he kept his arms crossed in front of him as if he were cradling a baby. He knew he had to compartmentalize his thoughts. As much as he was confused and curious about what Brockman had alluded to in regard to Jasmine, he knew he had to put it aside. At the moment, Pounds and what had happened to him were more important.

He tried to piece together the chain of events and the conclusion he drew was obvious. His stumbling into the party at Mittel's and delivery of the photocopy of the *Times* clip had set off a reaction that ended with the murder of Harvey Pounds, the man whose name he had used. Though he had given Mittel only the name at the party, it was somehow traced back to the real Pounds, who was then tortured and killed.

Bosch guessed that it was the DMV calls that had

doomed Pounds. Fresh from receiving the threatening news clip at the fund-raiser from a man who had introduced himself as Harvey Pounds, Mittel likely would have put his lengthy arm out to find out who this man was and what his purpose was. Mittel had connections from LA to Sacramento to Washington, DC. He could have quickly found out that Harvey Pounds was a cop. Mittel's campaign financing work had put a good number of legislators in seats in Sacramento. He would certainly have the connections in the capital city to find out if anyone was running traces on his name. And if he had that done, then he would have learned that Harvey Pounds, an LAPD lieùtenant, had inquired not only about him but about four other men who would be of vital interest to him as well. Arno Conklin, Johnny Fox, Jake McKittrick and Claude Eno.

True, all the names were involved in a case and conspiracy almost thirty-five years old. But Mittel was at the center of that conspiracy and the snooping around by Pounds would be more than enough, Bosch believed, for someone of his position to take some kind of action to find out what Pounds was doing.

Because of the approach the man he thought was Pounds had made at the party, Mittel had probably concluded he was being set upon by a chiseler, an extortionist. And he knew how to eliminate the problem. Like Johnny Fox had been eliminated.

That was the reason Pounds had been tortured, Bosch knew. For Mittel to make sure the problem went no further than Pounds, he had to know who else knew what Pounds knew. The problem was that Pounds didn't know anything himself. He had nothing to give. He was tormented until his heart could take it no longer.

A question that remained unanswered in Bosch's mind was what Arno Conklin knew of all this. He had not yet been contacted by Bosch. Did he know of the man who approached Mittel? Did he order the hit on Pounds or was it solely Mittel's reaction?

Then Bosch saw a bump in his theory that needed refining. Mittel had come face to face with him posing as Harvey Pounds at the fund-raiser. The fact that Pounds was tortured before he died indicated that Mittel was not present at the time, or he would have seen that they were brutalizing the wrong man. Bosch wondered now if they understood that they had, in fact, killed the wrong man, and if they would be looking for the right one.

He mulled over the point that Mittel could not have been there and decided that it fit. Mittel was not the type to get involved in the blood work. He'd have no problem calling the shots, he just wouldn't want to see them fired. Bosch realized the surfer in a suit had also seen him at the party and, therefore, could not have been directly involved in the killing of Harvey Pounds, either. That left the man Bosch had seen through the French doors at the house. The man with the wide body and thick neck whom he had seen Mittel show the newspaper clip to. The man who had slipped and fallen while coming down the driveway for Bosch.

Bosch realized that he didn't know how close he had come to being where Pounds was now. He reached into his jacket pocket for his cigarettes and started to light one.

'Do you mind not smoking?' Toliver asked, his first words of the thirty-minute journey.

'Yeah, I do mind.'

Bosch finished lighting the smoke and put his Bic away. He lowered the window.

'There. You happy? The exhaust fumes are worse than the smoke.'

'It's a nonsmoking vehicle.'

Toliver tapped his finger on a plastic magnet that was on

the dashboard ashtray cover. It was one of the little doodads that were distributed when the city passed a widespread antismoking law that forbade the practice in all city buildings and allowed for half of the department's fleet to be declared nonsmoking vehicles. The magnet showed a cigarette in the middle of a red circle with a slash through it. Beneath the circle it said THANK YOU FOR NOT SMOKING. Bosch reached over, peeled the magnet off and threw it out the open window. He saw it bounce once on the pavement and stick on the door of a car one lane over.

'Now it's not. Now it's a smoking car.'

'Bosch, you're really fucked, you know that?'

'Write me up, kid. Add it to the association beef your boss is working on. I don't care.'

They were silent for a few moments and the car crept further away from Hollywood.

'He's bluffing you, Bosch. I thought you knew that.'

'How so?'

He was surprised that Toliver was turning.

'He's just bluffing, that's all. He's still hot about what you did with that table. But he knows it won't stick. It's an old case. Voluntary manslaughter. A domestic violence case. She walked on five years probation. All you have to do is say you didn't know and it gets shitcanned.'

Bosch could almost guess what the case was about. She had practically told him during true confessions. She stayed too long with someone. That was what she had said. He thought of the painting he had seen in her studio. The gray portrait with the highlights red like blood. He tried to pull his mind away from it.

'Why're you telling me this, Toliver? Why are you going against your own?'

'Because they're not my own. Because I want to know what you meant by what you said to me in the hallway.'

Bosch couldn't even remember what he said.

'You told me it wasn't too late. Too late for what?'

'Too late to get out,' Bosch said, recalling the words he had thrown as a taunt. 'You're still a young guy. You better get yourself out of IAD before it's too late. You stay too long and you'll never get out. Is that what you want, spend your career busting cops for trading hookers dime bags?'

'Look, I want to work out of Parker and I don't want to wait ten years like everybody else. It's the easiest and fastest way for a white guy to get in there.'

'It's not worth it, is what I'm telling you. Anybody stays in IAD more than two, three years, they're there for life because nobody else wants 'em, nobody else trusts 'em. They're lepers. You better think about it. Parker Center isn't the only place in the world to work.'

A few moments of silence passed as Toliver tried to muster a defense.

'Somebody's got to police the police. A lot of people don't seem to understand that.'

'That's right. But in this department nobody polices the police who police the police. Think about that.'

The conversation was interrupted by the sharp tone he recognized as his mobile phone. On the back seat of the car were the items the searchers had taken from his apartment. Irving had ordered it all returned. Among them was his briefcase and inside it he heard his phone. He reached back, flipped the briefcase open and grabbed the phone.

'Yeah. It's Bosch.'

'Bosch, it's Russell.'

'Hey, I got nothing to tell you yet, Keisha. I'm still working on it.'

'No, I have something to tell you. Where are you?'

'I'm in the soup. The 101 coming up to Barham, my exit.'

'Well, I have to talk to you, Bosch. I'm writing a story for tomorrow. You will want to comment, I think, if only in your defense.'

'My defense?'

A dull thud went through him and he felt like saying, What now? But he held himself in check.

'What are you talking about?'

'Did you read my story today?'

'No, I haven't had the time. What –'

'It's about the death of Harvey Pounds. Today I have a follow ... It concerns you, Bosch.'

Jesus, he thought. But he tried to keep calm. He knew that if she detected any panic in his voice she would gain confidence in whatever it was she was about to write. He had to convince her she had bad information. He had to undermine that confidence. Then he realized Toliver was sitting next to him and would hear everything he said.

'I have a problem talking now. When is your deadline?'

'Now. We have to talk now.'

Bosch looked at his watch. It was twenty-five minutes until six.

'You can go to six, right?'

He'd worked with reporters before and knew that was the deadline for the *Times*'s first edition.

'No, I can't go to six. If you want to say something, say it now.'

'I can't. Give me fifteen minutes and then call back. I can't talk now.'

There was a pause and then she said, 'Bosch, I can't push it far past then. You better be able to talk then.'

They were at the Barham exit now and they'd be up to his house in ten minutes.

'Don't worry about it. In the meantime, you go warn your editor that you might be pulling the story.'

'I will not.'

'Look, Keisha, I know what you're going to ask me about. It's a plant and it's wrong. You have to trust me. I'll explain in fifteen minutes.'

'How do you know it's a plant?'

'I know. It came from Angel Brockman.'

He flipped the phone closed and looked over at Toliver.

'See, Toliver? Is that what you want to do with your job? With your life?'

Toliver said nothing.

'When you get back, you can tell your boss that he can shove tomorrow's *Times* up his ass. There isn't going to be any story. See, even the reporters don't trust IAD guys. All I had to do was mention Brockman. She'll start backpedaling when I tell her I know what's going on. Nobody trusts you guys, Jerry. Get out of it.'

'Oh, and like *everybody* trusts you, Bosch.'

'Not everybody. But I can sleep at night and I've been on the job twenty years. Think you'll be able to? What have you got in, five, six years? I'll give you ten, Jerry. That's all for you. Ten and out. But you'll look like one of these guys who puts in thirty.'

His prediction was met with a stony silence from Toliver. Bosch didn't know why he even cared. Toliver was part of the team trying to put him in the dirt. But something about the young cop's fresh face gave him the benefit of the doubt.

They made the last curve on Woodrow Wilson and Bosch could see his house. He could also see a white car with a yellow plate parked in front of it and a man wearing a yellow construction helmet standing in front holding a toolbox. It was the city building inspector. Gowdy.

'Shit,' Bosch said. 'This one of IAD's tricks, too?'

'I don't – if it is, I don't know anything about it.'

'Yeah, sure.'

Without a further word Toliver stopped in front of the

house and Bosch got out with his returned property. Gowdy recognized him and immediately came over as Toliver pulled away from the curb.

'Listen, you're not living in this place, are ya?' Gowdy asked. 'It's been red-tagged. We gotta call said somebody bootlegged the electric.'

'I gotta call, too. See anybody? I was just going to check it out.'

'Don't bullshit me, Mr Bosch. I can see you've made some repairs. You gotta know something, you can't repair this place, you can't even go in. You gotta demolition order and it's overdue. I'm gonna put in a work order and have a city contractor do it. You'll get the bill. No use waitin' any longer. Now, you might as well get out of here because I'm going to pull the electric and padlock it.'

He bent down to put the toolbox on the ground and proceeded to open it up and retrieve a set of stainless steel hinges and hasp locks he would apply to the doors.

'Look, I've got a lawyer,' Bosch said. 'He's trying to work it out with you people.'

'There's nothing to work out. I'm sorry. Now if you go in there again, you're subject to arrest. If I find these locks have been tampered with, you're also subject to arrest. I'll call North Hollywood Division. I'm not fooling with you anymore.'

For the first time it occurred to Bosch that it might be a show, that the man might want money. He probably didn't even know Bosch was a cop. Most cops couldn't afford to live up here and wouldn't want to if they could. The only reason Bosch could afford it was he had bought the property with a chunk of money he had made years earlier on a TV movie deal based on a case he had solved.

'Look, Gowdy,' he said, 'just spell it out, okay? I'm slow about these things. Tell me what you want and you've got it. I want to save the house. That's all I care about.'

Gowdy looked at him for a long moment and Bosch realized he had been wrong. He could see the indignation in Gowdy's eyes.

'You keep talking like that and you could go to jail, son. I'll tell you what I'm going to do. I'm going to forget what you just said. I —'

'Look, I'm sorry …' Bosch looked back at the house. 'It's just like, I don't know, the house is the only thing I've got.'

'You've got more than that. You just haven't thought about it. Now, I'm going to cut you a break here. I'll give you five minutes to go inside and get what you need. After that, I'm putting the locks on it. I'm sorry. But that's the way it is. If that house goes down the hill on the next one, maybe you'll thank me.'

Bosch nodded.

'Go on. Five minutes.'

Bosch went inside and grabbed a suitcase from the top shelf of the hallway closet. First he put his second gun in it, then he dumped in as much of the clothing from the bedroom closet as he could. He walked the overstuffed suitcase out to the carport, then came back inside for another load. He opened the drawers of his bureau and dumped them on the bed, then wrapped everything in the bedclothes and carried that out as well.

He went past the five-minute mark but Gowdy didn't come in after him. Bosch could hear him working with a hammer on the front door.

After ten minutes he had a large stack of belongings gathered in the carport. Included there was the box in which he kept his keepsakes and photos, a fireproof box containing his financial and personal records, a stack of unopened mail and unpaid bills, the stereo and two boxes containing his collection of jazz and blues LPs and CDs. Looking at the pile of belongings, he felt forlorn. It was a lot to fit into a Mustang, but he knew it wasn't much to show for almost forty-five years on the planet.

'That it?'

Bosch turned around. It was Gowdy. He was holding a hammer in one hand and a steel latch in the other. Bosch saw a keyed lock was hooked through one of the belt loops on his pants.

'Yeah,' Bosch said. 'Do it.'

He stepped back and let the inspector go to work. The hammering had just begun when his phone rang. He had forgotten about Keisha Russell.

He had the phone in his jacket pocket instead of his briefcase now. He took it out and flipped it open.

'Yeah, it's Bosch.'

'Detective, it's Dr Hinojos.'

'Oh ... Hi.'

'Something wrong?'

'No, uh, yeah, I was expecting somebody else. I've got to keep this line open for a few minutes. I've got a call coming in. Can I call you back?'

Bosch looked at his watch. It was five minutes until six.

'Yes,' Hinojos said. 'I'll be at the office until six-thirty. I want to talk to you about something, and to see how you fared on the sixth floor after I left.'

'I'm fine, but I'll call you back.'

As soon as he flipped the phone closed, it rang again in his hand.

'Bosch.'

'Bosch, I'm up against it and don't have time for bullshit.' It was Russell. She also didn't have time to identify herself. 'The story is that the investigation into the killing of Harvey Pounds has turned inward and detectives spent several hours with you today. They searched your home and they believe you are the prime suspect.'

'Prime suspect? We don't even use those words, Keisha.

325

Now I *know* you're talking to one of those squints in IAD. They wouldn't know how to run a homicide investigation if the doer came up and bit them on their shiny ass.'

'Don't try to deflect what we're talking about here. It's really simple. Do you or don't you have a comment on the story for tomorrow's paper? If you want to say something, I have just enough time to get it in the first run.'

'On the record, I have no comment.'

'And off?'

'Off the record, not for attribution or any use at all, I can tell you that you're full of shit, Keisha. Your story is wrong. Flat-out wrong. If you run it as you have just summarized it for me, you will have to write another one tomorrow correcting it. It will say I am not a suspect at all. Then, after that, you'll have to find another beat to cover.'

'And why is that?' she asked haughtily.

'Because this is a smear orchestrated by Internal Affairs. It's a plant. And when it is read tomorrow by everybody else in the department they'll know it is and they'll know you fell for it. They won't trust you. They'll think you're just a front for people like Brockman. No one that it is important for you to have a source relationship with will want to have that relationship with you. Including me. You'll be left covering the police commission and rewriting the press releases out of media relations. And then, of course, whenever Brockman wants to cream somebody else, he'll pick up the phone and call.'

There was silence on the line. Bosch looked up at the sky and saw it turning pink with the start of sunset. He looked at his watch. It was one minute until her deadline.

'You there, Keisha?'

'Bosch, you're scaring me.'

'You should be scared. You got about a minute to make a big decision.'

'Let me ask you this. Did you attack Pounds two weeks ago and throw him through a window?'

'On or off the record?'

'It doesn't matter. I just need an answer. Quick!'

'Off the record, that's more or less accurate.'

'Well, that would seem to make you a suspect in his death. I don't see –'

'Keisha, I've been out of the state for three days. I got back today. Brockman brought me in and talked to me for less than an hour. My story checked and I was kicked free. I'm not a suspect. I'm talking to you from the front of my house. You hear that hammering? That's my house. I've got a carpenter here. Are prime suspects allowed to go home at night?'

'How can I confirm all of this?'

'Today? You can't. You've got to pick. Brockman or me. Tomorrow, you can call Assistant Chief Irving and he'll confirm – if he is willing to talk to you.'

'Shit! Bosch, I can't believe this. If I go to my editor at deadline and tell him a story that they had budgeted for the front page since the three o'clock meeting is not a story … I might be looking for a new beat and a new paper to cover it for.'

'There's other news in the world, Keisha. They can find something for the front page. This will pay off for you in the long run, anyway. I'll spread the word about you.'

There was a brief silence while she made her decision.

'I can't talk. I have to get in there and grab him. Good-bye, Bosch. I hope I'm still working here the next time we talk.'

She was gone before he could say good-bye.

He walked up the street to the Mustang and drove it down to the house. Gowdy had finished with the latches and both doors now had locks on them. The inspector was out at his car using the front hood as a desk. He was writing on a clipboard and Bosch guessed he was moving slowly so as to make sure Bosch left the property. Bosch started loading his pile of belongings into the Mustang. He didn't know where he was going to take himself.

He put the thought of his homelessness aside and began thinking about Keisha Russell. He wondered if she would be able to stop the story so late in the game. It had probably taken on a life of its own. Like a monster in the newspaper's computer. And she, its Dr Frankenstein, would likely have little power over stopping it.

When he had everything in the Mustang, he waved a salute to Gowdy, got in and drove down the hill. Down at Cahuenga he didn't know which way to turn because he still didn't know where he should go. To the right was Hollywood. To the left was the Valley. Then he remembered the Mark Twain. In Hollywood, only a few blocks from the station on Wilcox, the Mark Twain was an old residence hotel with efficiencies that were generally clean and neat – a lot more so than the surrounding neighborhood. Bosch knew this because he had stashed witnesses there on occasion. He also knew that there were a couple of units that were two-room efficiencies with private baths. He decided he would go for one of them and turned right. The phone rang almost as soon as he had made the decision. It was Keisha Russell.

'You owe me big time, Bosch. I killed it.'

He felt relief and annoyance at the same time. It was typical thinking for a reporter.

'What are you talking about?' he countered. 'You owe me big time for saving your ass.'

'Well, we'll see about that. I'm still going to check this out tomorrow. If it falls the way you said, I'm going to Irving to complain about Brockman. I'll burn him.'

'You just did.'

328

Realizing she had just confirmed Brockman as the source, she laughed uneasily.

'What did your editor say?'

'He thinks I'm an idiot. But I told him there's other news in the world.'

'Good line.'

'Yeah, I'm going to keep that one in my computer. So what's going on? And what's happening with those clips I got you?'

'The clips are still percolating. I can't really talk about anything yet.'

'Figures. I don't know why I keep helping you, Bosch, but here goes. Remember you asked about Monte Kim, the guy who wrote that first clip I gave you?'

'Yeah. Monte Kim.'

'I asked about him around here and one of the old rewrite guys told me he's still alive. Turns out that after he left the *Times* he worked for the DA's office for a while. I don't know what he's doing now but I got his number and his address. He's in the Valley.'

'Can you give it to me?'

'I guess so, since it was in the phonebook.'

'Damn, I never thought of that.'

'You might be a good detective, Bosch, but you wouldn't make much of a reporter.'

She gave him the number and address, said she'd be in touch and hung up. Bosch put the phone down on the seat and thought about this latest piece of information as he drove into Hollywood. Monte Kim had worked for the district attorney. Bosch had a pretty good idea which one that would be.

The man behind the front desk at the Mark Twain didn't seem to recognize Bosch, though Harry was reasonably sure he was the same man he had dealt with before while renting rooms for witnesses. The counterman was tall and thin and had the hunched-over shoulders of someone carrying a heavy burden. He looked like he'd been behind the desk since Eisenhower.

'You remember me? From down the street?'

'Yeah, I remember. I didn't say anything 'cause I didn't know if this was an undercover job or not.'

'No. No undercover. I wanted to know if you have one of the big rooms in the back open. One with a phone.'

'You want one?'

'That's why I'm asking.'

'Who you going to put in there this time? I don't want no gangbangers again. Last time, they –'

'No, no gangbangers. Only me. I want the room.'

'You want the room?'

'That's right. And I won't paint on the walls. How much?'

The desk man seemed nonplussed by the fact that Bosch wanted to stay there himself. He finally recovered and told Bosch he had his choice: thirty dollars a day, two hundred a week or five hundred a month. All in advance. Bosch paid for a week with his credit card and waited anxiously while the man checked to make sure the charge would clear.

'Now, how much for the parking space in the loading zone out front?'

'You can't rent that.'

'I want to park out front, make it harder for one of your other tenants to rip my car off.'

Bosch took out his money and slid fifty dollars across the counter.

'If parking enforcement comes by, tell them it's cool.'

'Yeah.'

'You the manager?'

'And owner. Twenty-seven years.'

'Sorry.'

Bosch went out to get his things. It took him three trips to bring everything up to room 214. The room was in the back and its two windows looked across an alley to the back of a one-story building that housed two bars and an adult film and novelties store. But Bosch had known all along it would be no garden spot. It wasn't the kind of place where he would find a terry cloth robe in the closet and mints on the pillow at night. It was just a couple of notches up from the places where you slid your money to the clerk through a slot in the bulletproof glass.

One room had a bureau and a bed, which had only two cigarette burns in the bedspread, and a television mounted in a steel frame that was bolted to the wall. There was no cable, no remote and no courtesy *TV Guide*. The other room had a worn green couch, a small table for two and a kitchenette that had a half refrigerator, a bolted-down microwave and a two-coil electric range. The bathroom was off the hallway that connected the two rooms and came complete with white tile that had yellowed like old men's teeth.

Despite the drab circumstances and his hopes that his

stay would be temporary, Bosch tried his best to transform the hotel room into a home. He hung some clothes in the closet, put his toothbrush and shaving kit in the bathroom and set the answering machine up on the phone, though nobody knew his number. He decided that in the morning he'd call the telephone company and have a forwarding tape put on his old line.

Next he set up the stereo on the bureau. For the time being he just placed the speakers on the floor on either side of the bureau. He then rummaged through his box of CDs and came across a Tom Waits recording called 'Blue Valentine.' He hadn't listened to it in years so he put it on.

He sat down on the bed near the phone and listened and thought for a few minutes about calling Jazz in Florida. But he wasn't sure what he could say or ask. He decided it might be better to just let it go for now. He lit a cigarette and went to the window. There was nothing happening in the alley. Across the tops of the buildings he could see the ornate tower of the nearby Hollywood Athletic Club. It was a beautiful building. One of the last in Hollywood.

He closed the musty curtains, turned around and studied his new home. After a while he yanked the spread off the bed along with the other covers and then remade it with his own sheets and blanket. He knew it was a small gesture of continuity but it made him feel less lonely. It also made him feel a little bit as though he knew what he was doing with his life at that point and it made him forget for a few more moments about Harvey Pounds.

Bosch sat on the newly made bed and leaned back on the pillows propped against the headboard. He lit another cigarette. He studied the wounds on his two fingers and saw that the scabs had been replaced with hard pink skin. They were healing nicely. He hoped the rest of him would, too. But he doubted it. He knew he was responsible. And he knew he had to pay. Somehow.

332

He absentmindedly pulled the phone off the bed table and placed it on his chest. It was an old one with a rotary dial. Bosch lifted the receiver and looked at the dial. Who was he going to call? What was he going to say? He replaced the receiver and sat up. He decided he had to get out.

❖ ❖ ❖ ❖ ❖ ❖ ❖

Monte Kim lived on Willis Avenue in Sherman Oaks in the midst of a ghost town of apartment buildings red-tagged after the quake. Kim's apartment building was a gray-and-white Cape Cod affair that sat between two empties. At least they were supposed to be empty. As Bosch pulled up he saw lights go out in one of the buildings. Squatters, he guessed. Like Bosch had been, always on alert for the building inspector.

Kim's building looked as though it had been either completely spared by the quake or already completely repaired. Bosch doubted it was the latter. He believed the building was more a testament to the serendipitous violence of nature, and maybe a builder who didn't cut corners. The Cape Cod had stood up while the buildings around it cracked and slid.

It was a common, rectangular building with apartment entrances running down each side of it. But to get to one of the doors, you had to be buzzed through a six-foot-tall electronic gate. The cops called them 'feel good' gates because they made the dwellers inside feel safer, but they were worthless. All they did was put up a barrier for legitimate visitors to the building. Others could simply climb over, and they did, all over the city. Feel good gates were everywhere.

He said only that it was the police when Kim's voice sounded on the intercom and he was buzzed in. He took the badge wallet out of his pocket as he walked down to apartment eight. When Kim opened up, Bosch shoved the open badge wallet through the door and about six inches from his face. He held it so his finger was across the badge and obscured the marking that said LIEUTENANT. He then pulled the wallet back quickly and put it away.

'I'm sorry, I didn't catch the name on there,' Kim said, still blocking the way.

'Hieronymus Bosch. But people call me Harry.'

'You're named for the painter.'

'Sometimes I feel old enough that I think he was named for me. Tonight's one of those nights. Can I come in? This shouldn't take long.'

Kim led him into the living room with a confused look on his face. It was a decent-sized and neat room with a couch and two chairs and a gas fireplace next to the TV. Kim took one of the chairs and Bosch sat on the end of the couch. He noticed a white poodle sleeping on the carpet next to Kim's chair. Kim was an overweight man with a wide, florid face. He wore glasses that pinched his temples and what was left of his hair was dyed brown. He wore a red cardigan sweater over a white shirt and old khakis. Bosch guessed Kim wasn't quite sixty. He had been expecting an older man.

'I guess this is where I ask, "What's this all about?" '

'Yeah, and I guess this is where I tell you. Problem is I'm not sure how to begin. I'm investigating a couple of homicides. You can probably help. But I wonder if you'd indulge me and let me ask you some questions going a while back? Then, when we're done, I'll explain why.'

'Seems unusual but ...'

Kim raised his hands and waved off any problems. He made a movement in his chair as if to get more comfortable. He checked the dog and then squinted his eyes as if that might better help him understand and answer the questions. Bosch could see a film of sweat developing in the defoliated landscape that had once been his scalp.

'You were a reporter for the *Times*. How long did that last?'

'Oh, boy, that was just a few years in the early sixties. How do you know that?'

'Mr Kim, let me ask these questions first. What kind of reporting did you do?'

'Back then they called us cub reporters. I was on the crime beat.'

'What do you do now?'

'Currently, I work out of my home. I'm in public relations. I have an office upstairs in the second bedroom. I had an office in Reseda but the building was condemned. You could see daylight through the cracks.'

He was like most people in LA. He didn't have to preface his remarks by saying he was talking about earthquake damage. It was understood.

'I have several small accounts,' he continued. 'I was a local spokesman for the GM plant in Van Nuys until they closed it down. Then I went out on my own.'

'What made you quit the *Times* back in the sixties?'

'I got – Am I a suspect in something?'

'Not at all, Mr Kim. I'm just trying to get to know you. Indulge me. I'll get to the point. You were saying why you quit the *Times*.'

'Yes, well, I got a better job. I was offered the position of press spokesman for the district attorney at the time, Arno Conklin. I took it. Better pay, more interesting than the cop beat and a brighter future.'

'What do you mean, brighter future?'

'Well, actually I was wrong about that. When I took the job I thought the sky would be the limit with Arno. He was a good man. I figured I'd eventually – you know, if I stayed with him – ride with him to the governor's mansion, maybe the Senate in Washington. But things didn't turn out. I ended up with an office in Reseda with a crack in the wall I could feel the wind come through. I don't see why the police would be interested in all –'

'What happened with Conklin? Why didn't things turn out?'

'Well, I'm not the expert on this. All I know is that in sixty-eight he was planning on running for attorney general and the office was practically his for the taking. Then he just ... dropped out. He quit politics and went back to practice law. And it wasn't to harvest the big corporate bucks that sit out there when these guys go into private practice. He opened a one-man law firm. I admired him. As far as I heard, sixty percent or better of his practice was pro bono. He was working for free most of the time.'

'Like he was serving a penance or something?'

'I don't know. I guess.'

'Why'd he drop out?'

'I don't know.'

'Weren't you part of the inner circle?'

'No. He didn't have a circle. He had one man.'

'Gordon Mittel.'

'Right. You want to know why he didn't run, ask Gordon.' Then it clicked in Kim's brain that Bosch had introduced the name Gordon Mittel to the conversation. 'Is this about Gordon Mittel?'

'Let me ask the questions first. Why do you think Conklin didn't run? You must have some idea.'

'He wasn't officially in the race in the first place, so he didn't have to make any public statement about dropping out. He just didn't run. There were a lot of rumors, though.'

'Like what?'

'Oh, lots of stuff. Like he was gay. There were others.

337

Financial trouble. Supposedly there was a threat from the mob that if he won, they'd kill him. Just stuff like that. None of it was ever more than backroom talk amongst the town politicos.'

'He was never married?'

'Not as far as I know. But as far as him being gay, I never saw anything like that.'

Bosch noted that the top of Kim's head was slick now with sweat. It was already warm in the room but he kept the cardigan on. Bosch made a quick change of tracks.

'Okay, tell me about the death of Johnny Fox.'

Bosch saw the quick glimmer of recognition pass behind the glasses but then it disappeared. But it was enough.

'Johnny Fox, who's that?'

'C'mon, Monte, it's old news. Nobody cares what you did. I just need to know the story behind the story. That's why I'm here.'

'You're talking about when I was a reporter? I wrote a lot of stories. That was thirty-five years ago. I was a kid. I can't remember everything.'

'But you remember Johnny Fox. He was your ticket to that brighter future. The one that didn't happen.'

'Look, what are you doing here? You're not a cop. Did Gordon send you? After all these years, you people think I ...'

He stopped.

'I am a cop, Monte. And you're lucky I got here before Gordon did. Something's coming undone. The ghosts are coming back. You read in the paper today about that cop found in his trunk in Griffith Park?'

'I saw it on the news. He was a lieutenant.'

'Yeah. He was my lieutenant. He was looking into a couple old cases. Johnny Fox was one of them. Then he ended up in his trunk. So you'll have to excuse me if I'm a little nervous and pushy, but I need to know about Johnny

Fox. And you wrote the story. You wrote the story after he got killed that made him out to be an angel. Then you end up on Conklin's team. I don't care what you did, I just want to know what you did.'

'Am I in danger?'

Bosch hiked his shoulders in his best who-knows-and-who-cares gesture.

'If you are, then we can protect you. You don't help us, we can't help you. You know how it goes.'

'Oh my God! I knew this – What other cases?'

'One of Johnny's girls who got killed about a year before him. Her name was Marjorie Lowe.'

Kim shook his head. He didn't recognize the name. He ran his hand over his scalp, using it like a squeegee to move the sweat into the thicker hair. Bosch could tell he had perfectly primed the fat man to answer the questions.

'So what about Fox?' Bosch asked. 'I don't have all night.'

'Look, I don't know anything. All I did was a favor for a favor.'

'Tell me about it.'

He composed himself for a long moment before speaking.

'Look, you know who Jack Ruby was?'

'In Dallas?'

'Yeah, the guy who killed Oswald. Well, Johnny Fox was the Jack Ruby of LA, okay? Same era, same kind of guy. Fox ran women, was a gambler, knew which cops could be greased and greased them when he needed to. It kept him out of jail. He was a classic Hollywood bottom feeder. When he ended up dead on the Hollywood Division blotter, I saw it but was going to pass. He was trash and we didn't write about trash. Then a source I had in the cop shop told me Johnny had been on Conklin's payroll.'

'That made it a story.'

'Yeah. So I called up Mittel, Conklin's campaign manager, and ran it by him. I wanted a response. I don't know how much you know about that time, but Conklin had this squeaky-clean image. He was the guy attacking every vice in the city and here he had a vice hoodlum on the payroll. It was a great story. Though Fox didn't have a record, I don't think, there were intel files on him and I had access to them. The story was going to do damage and Mittel knew it.'

He stopped there at the edge of the story. He knew the rest but to speak of it out loud he had to be pushed over the edge.

'Mittel knew it,' Bosch said. 'So he offered you a deal. He'd make you Conklin's flak if you cleaned up the story.'

'Not exactly.'

'Then what? What was the deal?'

'I'm sure any kind of statute has passed ...'

'Don't worry about it. Just tell me and only me, you and your dog will ever know it.'

Kim took a deep breath and continued.

'This was mid-campaign so Conklin already had a spokesman. Mittel offered me a job as deputy spokesman after the election. I'd work out of the office in the Van Nuys Courthouse, handle the Valley stuff.'

'If Conklin won.'

'Yeah, but that was a given. Unless this Fox story caused a problem. But I held out, used some leverage. I told Mittel I wanted to be the main spokesman after Arno's election or forget it. He got back to me later and agreed.'

'After he talked to Conklin.'

'I guess. Anyway, I wrote a story that left out the details of Fox's past.'

'I read it.'

'That's all I did. I got the job. It was never mentioned again.'

Bosch sized Kim up for a moment. He was weak. He didn't see that being a reporter was a calling just the same as being a cop. You took an oath to yourself. Kim had seemingly had no difficulty breaking it. Bosch could not imagine someone like Keisha Russell acting the same way under the same circumstances. He tried to cover his distaste and move on.

'Think back now. This is important. When you first called up Mittel and told him about Fox's background, did you get the impression that he already knew the background?'

'Yes, he knew. I don't know if the cops had told him that day or he had known all along. But he knew Fox was dead and he knew who he was. I think he was a little surprised that I knew and he became eager to make a deal to keep it out of the paper ... It was the first time I ever did anything like that. I wish I hadn't done it.'

Kim looked down at the dog and then to the beige rug and Bosch knew it was a screen on which he saw how his life diverged sharply the moment he took the deal. It went from where it was going to where it eventually was.

'Your story didn't name any cops,' Bosch said. 'Do you remember who handled it?'

'Not really. It was so long ago. It would have been a couple guys from the Hollywood homicide table. Back then, they handled fatal accidents. Now there's a division for that.'

'Claude Eno?'

'Eno? I remember him. It might've been. I think I remember that it ... Yes, it was. Now I remember. He was on it alone. His partner had transferred or retired or something and he was working alone, waiting for his next partner to transfer in. So they gave him the traffic cases.

They were usually pretty light, as far as any investigation went.'

'How do you remember so much of this?'

Kim pursed his lips and struggled for an answer.

'I guess … Like I said, I wish I never did what I did. So, I guess, I think about it a lot. I remember it.'

Bosch nodded. He had no more questions and was already thinking of the implications of how Kim's information fit with his own. Eno had worked both cases, Lowe and Fox, and later retired, leaving behind a mail-drop corporation with Conklin's and Mittel's name on it that collected a thousand dollars a month for twenty-five years. He realized that compared to Eno, Kim had settled for too little. He was about to get up when he thought of something.

'You said that Mittel never mentioned the deal you made or Fox again.'

'That's right.'

'Did Conklin ever say anything about either one?'

'No, he never mentioned a thing, either.'

'What was your relationship like? Didn't he treat you as a chiseler?'

'No, because I wasn't a chiseler,' Kim protested but the indignation in his voice was hollow. 'I did a job for him and I did it well. He was always very nice to me.'

'He was in your story on Fox. I don't have it here but in it he said he had never met Fox.'

'Yeah, that was a lie. I made that up.'

Bosch was confused.

'What do you mean? You mean, you made up the lie?'

'In case they went back on the deal. I put Conklin in the story saying he didn't know the guy because I had evidence he did. They knew I had it. That way, if after the election they reneged on the deal, I could dredge up the story again and show Conklin said he didn't know Fox but

342

he did. I could then make the inference that he also knew Fox's background when he hired him. It wouldn't have done much good because he'd have already been elected, but it would do some PR damage. It was my little insurance policy. Understand?'

Bosch nodded.

'What was the evidence you had that Conklin knew Fox?'

'I had photos.'

'What photos?'

'They were taken by the society photographer for the *Times* at the Hollywood Masonic Lodge's St Patrick's Day dance a couple of years before the election. There's two of them. Conklin and Fox are at a table. They were scratches but one day I was –'

'What do you mean, scratches?'

'Photos never published. Outtakes. But, see, I used to look at the society stuff in the photo lab, so I could learn who the big shots in the city were and who they were out with and so on. It was useful information. One day I saw these photos of Conklin and some guy that I recognized but wasn't sure from where. It was because of the social background. This wasn't Fox's turf so at the time I didn't recognize him. Then, when Fox got killed and I was told he worked for Conklin, I remembered the photos and who the other man was. Fox. I went back to the scratch files and pulled them out.'

'They were just sitting there together at this dance?'

'In the photos? Yeah. And they were smiling. You could tell they knew each other. These weren't posed shots. In fact, that's why each was a scratch. They weren't good photos, not for the society page.'

'Anybody else with them?'

'A couple women, that was it.'

'Go get the photos.'

'Oh, I don't have them anymore. I tossed them after I didn't need them anymore.'

'Kim, don't bullshit me, okay? There was never a time you didn't need them. Those photos are probably why you are alive today. Now go get them or I'll take you downtown for withholding evidence, then I'll come back with a warrant and tear this place apart.'

'All right! Jesus! Wait here. I have one of them.'

He got up and went up the stairs. Bosch just stared at the dog. It was wearing a sweater that matched Kim's. He heard a closet door being moved on rollers, then a heavy thud. He guessed a box had been taken off the shelf and dropped to the floor. In a few more moments, Kim's heavy steps were coming down the stairs. As he passed the couch, he handed Bosch a black-and-white eight-by-ten that was yellowed around the edges. Bosch stared at it for a long time.

'I have the other in a safe deposit box,' Kim said. 'It's a clearer shot of the two of them. You can tell it's Fox.'

Bosch didn't say anything. He was still looking at the photo. It was a flashbulb shot. Everybody's face was lit up white as snow. Conklin sat across a table from the man Bosch assumed was Fox. There were a half dozen drink glasses on the table. Conklin was smiling and heavy-lidded – that was probably why the photo was a scratch – and Fox was turned slightly away from the camera, his features indistinguishable. Bosch guessed you would have had to know him to recognize him. Neither of them seemed aware of the photographer's presence. Flashbulbs were probably going off all over the place.

But more so than the men, Bosch studied the two women in the photo. Standing next to Fox and bending over to whisper in his ear was a woman in a dark one-piece dress that was tight around the middle. Her hair was swirled on top of her head. It was Meredith Roman. And sitting across the table and next to Conklin, mostly obscured by him, was Marjorie Lowe. Bosch guessed that if you didn't already know her, she wouldn't have been recognizable. Conklin was smoking and had his hand up to his face. His arm blocked off half of Bosch's mother's face. It almost looked as if she was peeking around a corner at the camera.

Bosch turned the photo over and there was a stamp on the back that said TIMES PHOTO BY BORIS LUGAVERE. It was dated March 17, 1961, seven months before his mother's death.

'Did you ever show this to Conklin or Mittel?' Bosch finally asked.

'Yeah. When I made my case for head spokesman. I gave Gordon a copy. He saw that it was proof the candidate knew Fox.'

Mittel must also have seen that it was proof that the candidate knew a murder victim, Bosch realized. Kim didn't know what he had. But no wonder he got the head spokesman's job. You're lucky you're alive, he thought but didn't say.

'Did Mittel know it was only a copy?'

'Oh yeah, I made that clear. I wasn't stupid.'

'Did Conklin ever mention it to you?'

'Not to me. But I assume Mittel told him about it. Remember, I said he had to get back to me about the job I wanted. Who would he have to clear it with, he was campaign manager? So he must've talked to Conklin.'

'I'm going to keep this.'

Bosch held up the photo.

'I've got the other.'

'Have you stayed in touch with Arno Conklin over the years?'

'No. I haven't spoken to him in, I don't know, twenty years.'

'I want you to call him now and I –'

'I don't even know where he is.'

'I do. I want you to call him and tell him you want to see him tonight. Tell him it has to be tonight. Tell him it's about Johnny Fox and Marjorie Lowe. Tell him not to tell anyone you are coming.'

'I can't do that.'

'Sure you can. Where's your phone? I'll help you.'

'No, I mean, I can't go see him tonight. You can't make –'

'You're not going to see him tonight, Monte. I'm going to be you. Now where's your phone?'

❖ ❖ ❖ ❖ ❖ ❖ ❖

At Park La Brea Lifecare, Bosch parked in a visitor's space in the front lot and got out of the Mustang. The place looked dark; few windows in the upper stories had lights on behind them. He checked his watch – it was only nine-fifty – and moved toward the glass doors of the lobby.

He felt a slight pull in his throat as he made the walk. Deep down he had known as soon as he finished reading the murder book that his sights were set on Conklin and that it would come to this. He was about to confront the man he believed had killed his mother and then used his position and the people he surrounded himself with to walk away from it. To Bosch, Conklin was the symbol of all that he never had in his life. Power, home, contentment. It didn't matter how many people had told him on the trail that Conklin was a good man. Bosch knew the secret behind the good man. His rage grew with each step he took.

Inside the door a uniformed guard sat behind a desk working on a crossword puzzle torn from the *Times Sunday Magazine*. Maybe he had been working on it since then. He looked up at Bosch as if he was expecting him.

'Monte Kim,' Bosch said. 'One of the residents is expecting me. Arno Conklin.'

'Yeah, he called down.' The guard consulted a clipboard, then turned it around and handed the pen to Bosch.

'Been a long time since he's had any visitors. Sign here, please. He's up in nine-oh-seven.'

Bosch signed and dropped the pen on the clipboard.

'It's kind of late,' the guard said. 'Visitation is usually over by nine.'

'What's that mean? You want me to leave? Fine.' He held his briefcase up. 'Mr Conklin can just roll his wheelchair down to my office tomorrow to pick this stuff up. I'm the one making a special trip here, buddy. For him. Let me up or not, I don't care. He cares.'

'Whoah, whoah, whoah, hold on there, partner. I was just saying it was late and you didn't let me finish. I'm going to let you go up. No problem. Mr Conklin specifically requested it and this ain't no prison. I'm just saying all the visitors are gone, okay? People are sleeping. Just keep it down, is all. No reason to blow a gasket.'

'Nine-oh-seven, you said?'

'That's right. I'll call him and tell him you're on your way up.'

'Thanks.'

Bosch moved past the guard toward the elevators without apology. He was forgotten as soon as he was out of Bosch's sight. Only one thing, one person, occupied his mind now.

The elevator moved about as quickly as the building's inhabitants. When he finally got to the ninth floor, Bosch walked past a nurses' station but it was empty, the night nurse apparently tending to a resident's needs. Bosch headed the wrong way down the hall, then corrected himself and headed back the other way. The paint and linoleum in the hallway were fresh but even top-dollar places like this couldn't completely eliminate the lingering smell of urine, disinfectant and the sense of closed lives behind the closed doors. He found the door to nine-oh-seven and knocked once. He heard a faint voice telling him to enter. It was more like a whimper than a whisper.

Bosch was unprepared for what he saw when he opened the door. There was a single light on in the room, a small reading lamp to the side of the bed. It left most of the room in shadow. An old man sat on the bed propped against three pillows, a book in his frail hands, bifocals on the bridge of his nose. What Bosch found so eerie about the tableau before him was that the bedcovers were bunched around the old man's waist but were flat on the remainder of the bed. The bed was flat. There were no legs. Compounding this shock was the wheelchair to the right of the bed. A plaid blanket had been thrown over the seat. But two legs in black pants and loafers extended from beneath it and down to the chair's footrests. It looked as if half the man was in his bed but he had left his other half in the chair. Bosch's face must have shown his confusion.

'Prosthesis,' said the raspy voice from the bed. 'Lost my legs ... diabetes. Almost nothing of me left. Except an old man's vanity. I had the legs made for public appearances.'

Bosch stepped closer to the light. The man's skin was like the back of peeled wallpaper. Yellowish, pale. His eyes were deep in the shadows of his skeletal face, his hair just a whisper around his ears. His thin hands were ribbed with blue veins the size of earthworms under his spotted skin. He was death, Bosch knew. Death certainly had a better grip on him than life did.

Conklin put the book on the table near the lamp. It seemed to be a labor for him to make the reach. Bosch saw the title. *The Neon Rain.*

'A mystery,' Conklin said, a small cackle following. 'I indulge myself with mysteries. I've learned to appreciate the writing. I never did before. Never took the time. Come in, Monte, no need to be afraid of me. I'm a harmless old man.'

Bosch stepped closer until the light was on his face. He saw Conklin's watery eyes study him and conclude that he was not Monte Kim. It had been a long time but Conklin seemed to be able to tell.

'I came in Monte's place,' he whispered.

Conklin turned his head slightly and Bosch saw his eyes fall on the emergency call button on the bed table. He must have figured he had no chance and no strength for another reach. He turned back to Bosch.

'Who are you, then?'

'I'm working on a mystery, too.'

'A detective?'

'Yes. My name's Harry Bosch and I want to ask you about ...'

He stopped. There was a change in Conklin's face. Bosch could not tell if it was fear or maybe recognition but something had changed. Conklin brought his eyes up to Bosch's and Bosch realized the old man was smiling.

'Hieronymus Bosch,' he whispered. 'Like the painter.'

Bosch nodded slowly. He now realized he was as shocked as the old man.

'How do you know that?'

'Because I know of you.'

'How?'

'Through your mother. She told me about you and your special name. I loved your mother.'

It was like getting hit in the chest with a sandbag. Bosch felt the air go out of him and he put a hand down on the bed to hold himself steady.

'Sit. Please. Sit.'

Conklin held out a shaky hand, motioning Bosch onto the bed. He nodded when Bosch did as he had been told.

'No!' Bosch said loudly as he rose off the bed almost as soon as he had sat down on it. 'You used her and you killed her. Then you paid off people to bury it with her.

That's why I'm here. I came for the truth. I want to hear you tell it and I don't want to hear any bullshit about loving her. You're a liar.'

Conklin had a pleading look in his eyes, then he turned them away, toward the dark side of the room.

'I don't know the truth,' he said, his voice like dried leaves blown along the sidewalk. 'I take responsibility and therefore, yes, it could be said I killed her. The only truth I know is that I loved her. You can call me a liar but that is the truth. You could make an old man whole again if you believed that.'

Bosch couldn't fathom what was happening, what was being said.

'She was with you that night. In Hancock Park.'

'Yes.'

'What happened? What did you do?'

'I killed her ... with my words, my actions. It took me many years to realize that.'

Bosch moved closer until he was hovering over the old man. He wanted to grab him and shake some sense out of him. But Arno Conklin was so frail that he might shatter.

'What are you talking about? Look at me. What are you talking about?'

Conklin turned his head on a neck no wider than a glass of milk. He looked at Bosch and nodded solemnly.

'You see, we made plans that night. Marjorie and I. I had fallen for her against all better judgment and advice. My own and others. We were going to get married. We'd decided. We were going to get you out of that youth hall. We had many plans. That was the night we made them. We were both so happy that we cried. The next day was Saturday. I wanted to go to Las Vegas. Take the car and drive through the night before we could change our minds or have them changed for us. She agreed and went home to pick up her things ... She never came back.'

'That's your story? You expect me —'

'You see, after she had left, I made one call. But that was enough. I called my best friend to tell him the good news and to ask him to stand with me as my best man. I wanted him to go with us to Las Vegas. Do you know what he said? He declined the honor of being my best man. He said that if I married that ... that woman, I'd be finished. He said he wouldn't let me do that. He said he had great plans for me.'

'Gordon Mittel.'

Conklin nodded sadly.

'So what are you saying, Mittel killed her? You didn't know?'

'I didn't know.'

He looked down at his feeble hands and balled them into tiny fists on the blanket. They looked completely powerless. Bosch only watched.

'I did not realize it for many years. It was beyond the pale to consider that he had done it. And then, of course, I must admit I was thinking of myself at the time. I was a coward, thinking only of my escape.'

Bosch was not tracking what he was saying. But it didn't seem that Conklin was talking to him, anyway. The old man was really telling himself the story. He suddenly looked up from his reverie at Bosch.

'You know, I knew someday you would come.'

'How?'

'Because I knew you would care. Maybe no one else. But I knew you would. You had to care. You were her son.'

'Tell me about what happened that night. Everything.'

'I need you to get me some water. For my throat. There's a glass there on the bureau, a fountain in the hallway. Don't let it run too long. It gets too cold and hurts my teeth.'

352

Bosch looked at the glass on the bureau and then back at Conklin. He was seized with a fear that if he left the room for even a minute the old man might die and take the story with him. Bosch would never hear it.

'Go. I'll be fine. I certainly can't go anywhere.'

Bosch glanced at the call button. Again, Conklin knew his thoughts.

'I am closer to hell than heaven for what I've done. For my silence. I need to tell my story. I think you'd be a better confessor than any priest could be.'

As Bosch stepped into the hallway with the glass, he saw a figure of a man turn the corner at the end of the hall and disappear. He thought the man was wearing a suit. It wasn't the guard. He saw the fountain and filled the glass. Conklin smiled weakly as he took the glass and murmured a thanks before drinking. Bosch then took the glass back and put it on the night table.

'Okay,' Bosch said. 'You said she left that night and never came back. How did you find out what happened?'

'By the next day, I was afraid something had happened. I finally called my office and made a routine check to see what had come in on the overnight reports. Among the things they told me was that there had been a homicide in Hollywood. They had the victim's name. It was her. It was the most horrible day of my life.'

'What happened next?'

Conklin rubbed a hand on his forehead and continued.

'I learned that she had been found that morning. She – I was in shock. I couldn't believe this could have happened. I had Mittel make some inquiries but there was nothing useful coming out. Then the man who had ... introduced me to Marjorie called.'

'Johnny Fox.'

'Yes. He called and he said he had heard the police were looking for him. He said he was innocent. He threatened me. He said if I did not protect him, he would reveal to the police that Marjorie was with me that last night. It would be the end of my career.'

'So you protected him.'

'I turned it over to Gordon. He investigated Fox's claim and confirmed his alibi. I cannot remember it now but it was confirmed. He had been in a card game or somewhere where there had been many witnesses. Since I was confident that Fox was not involved, I called the detectives assigned to the case and arranged for him to be interviewed. In order to protect Fox and thereby protect myself, Gordon and I concocted a story in which we told the detectives that Fox was a key witness in a grand jury investigation. The plan was successful. The detectives turned their attention elsewhere. At one point I spoke to one of them and he told me he believed that Marjorie was the victim of some sort of a sex killer. You see, they were quite rare back then. The detective said the outlook on the case was not good. I'm afraid that I never suspected ... Gordon. Such a horrible thing to do to an innocent person. It was right there in front of my face but I didn't see it for so long. I was a fool. A puppet.'

'You're saying that it wasn't you and that it wasn't Fox. You're saying that Mittel killed her to eliminate a threat to your political career. But that he didn't tell you. It was all his idea and he just went out and did it.'

'Yes, I say that. I told him, I told him that night when I called, I said that she meant more to me than all of the plans he had for me, that I had for myself. He said it would mean the end of my career and I accepted it. I accepted it as long as I started the next part of my life with her. I believe those minutes were the most peaceful of my life. I was in love and I had made a stand.'

He softly pounded a fist onto the bed, an impotent gesture.

'I told Mittel I didn't care what he thought the damage to my career would be. I told him we were going to move away. I didn't know where. La Jolla, San Diego, I threw a few places out. I didn't know where we were going to go but I was defiant. I was mad at him for not sharing the joy of our decision. And in doing so I provoked him, I know now, and I hastened your mother's death.'

Bosch studied him a long moment. His agony seemed sincere. Conklin's eyes looked as haunted as the portholes on a sunken ship. There was only blackness behind them.

'Did Mittel ever admit this to you?'

'No, but I knew. I guess it was a subconscious knowledge but then something he said years later brought it out. It confirmed it in my mind. And that was the end of our relationship.'

'What did he say? When?'

'Many years later. It was at the time I was preparing for a run for attorney general. Do you believe such a charade occurred? Me the liar, the coward, the conspirator being groomed for the office of the state's top law enforcement officer. Mittel came to me one day and said that I needed to take a wife before the election year. He was that blunt about it. He said there were rumors about me that could cost me votes. I said that was preposterous and that I wouldn't take a wife just to assuage some rednecks out in Palmdale or the desert somewhere. Then he made a comment, just a flippant, offhand comment as he was leaving my office.'

He broke off to reach for the glass of water. Bosch helped him and he slowly drank. Bosch noticed the medicinal smell about him. It was horrible. It reminded him of dead people and the morgue. Bosch took the glass when Conklin was done and put it back.

'What was the comment?'

'As he was leaving my office, he said, and I remember it

word for word, he said, "Sometimes I wish I hadn't saved you from that whore scandal. Maybe if I hadn't, we wouldn't have this problem now. People would know you aren't queer." Those were his words.'

Bosch just stared at him for a moment.

'It might've been just a figure of speech. He could have just meant that he had saved you from the scandal of knowing her by taking the steps to keep you out of it. It's not evidence that he killed her or had her killed. You were a prosecutor, you know that's not enough. It wasn't direct evidence of anything. Didn't you ever directly confront him?'

'No. Never. I was too intimidated by him. Gordon was becoming a powerful man. More powerful than I. So I said nothing to him. I simply dismantled my campaign and folded my tent. I left the public life and haven't spoken to Gordon Mittel since that time. More than twenty-five years.'

'You went into private practice.'

'Yes. I took up pro bono work as my self-imposed penance for what I was responsible for. I wish I could say it helped suture the wounds of my soul but it did not. I'm a helpless man, Hieronymus. So tell me, did you come here to kill me? Don't let my story dissuade you from believing I deserve it.'

The question at first startled Bosch into silence. Finally, he shook his head and spoke.

'What about Johnny Fox? He had his hooks into you after that night.'

'Yes, he did. He was very capable as extortionists go.'

'What happened with him?'

'I was forced to hire him as a campaign employee, paying him five hundred dollars a week for practically nothing. You see what a farce my life had become? He was killed in a hit and run before picking up his first paycheck.'

'Mittel?'

'I would assume that he was responsible, though I must admit he's a rather convenient scapegoat for all the bad deeds I've been involved in.'

'You didn't think that it was just a little too coincidental that he got killed?'

'Things are so much clearer in hindsight.' He shook his head sadly. 'At the time I remember being thrilled with my luck. The one thorn in my side had been removed by serendipity. You have to remember, at the time I had no inkling that Marjorie's death was in any way connected to me. I simply saw Fox as being a man on the make. When he was removed through the luck of an automobile mishap, I was pleased. A deal was made with a reporter to keep Fox's background on the QT and everything was fine … But, of course, it wasn't. It never was. Gordon, genius that he was, didn't plan on me not being able to get over Marjorie. And I'm still not.'

'What about McCage?'

'Who?'

'McCage Incorporated. Your payoffs to the cop. Claude Eno.'

Conklin was quiet a moment while he composed an answer.

'Of course, I knew Claude Eno. I didn't care for him. And I never paid him a dime.'

'McCage was incorporated in Nevada. It was Eno's company. You and Mittel are both listed as corporate officers. It was a payoff scam. Eno was getting a grand a month from somewhere. You and Mittel.'

'No!' Conklin said as forcefully as he could. The word came out as little more than a cough. 'I don't know about McCage. Gordon could have set it up, even signed for me

357

or made me sign unwittingly. As district attorney he took care of things for me. I signed when he told me to sign.'

He said it while looking directly at Bosch and Harry believed him. Conklin had admitted to far worse deeds. Why would he lie about paying off Eno?

'What did Mittel do when you folded your tent, when you told him you were through?'

'By then he was already quite powerful. Politically. His law firm represented the city's upper tier and his political work was branching out, growing. Still, I was the centerpiece. The plan was to take the attorney general's office and then the governor's mansion. Who knows what after that. So Gordon … he was unhappy. I refused to see him but we talked on the phone. When he could not convince me to change my mind, he threatened me.'

'How?'

'He told me that if I ever attempted to assault his reputation, he would see to it that I was indicted for Marjorie's death. And I had no doubt that he could have done it.'

'From best man to greatest enemy. How'd you ever get hooked up with him?'

'I guess he slipped in the door while I wasn't looking. I never saw the real face until it was too late … I don't think in my life I've come across anyone as cunningly focused as Gordon. He was – is – a dangerous man. I'm sorry I ever brought your mother into his path.'

Bosch nodded. He had no more questions and didn't know what else to say. After a few moments during which Conklin seemed to be lost in thought, the old man spoke up.

'I think, young man, that you only run into a person that is a perfect fit once in your life. When you find the one that you think fits, then grab on for dear life. And it's no matter what she's done in the past. None of that matters. Only the holding on matters.'

Bosch nodded again. It was all he could think of to do.

'Where did you meet her?'

'Oh ... I met her at a dance. She was introduced and, of course, she was younger than me so I didn't think there would be any interest from her. But I was wrong ... We danced. We dated. And I fell in love.'

'You didn't know about her past?'

'At the time, no. But she told me eventually. By then I didn't care.'

'What about Fox?'

'Yes, he was the liaison. He introduced us. I didn't know who he was, either. He said he was a business man. You see, for him, it was a business move. Introduce the girl to the prosecutor, sit back and see what happens. I never paid her and she never asked me for money. All the while we fell in love, Fox must have been weighing his options.'

Bosch wondered if he should take the photo from Monte Kim out of his case and show it to Conklin, but he decided not to tempt the old man's memory with the reality of a photo. Conklin spoke while Bosch was still thinking about it.

'I'm very tired now and you never answered my question.'

'What question?'

'Did you come here to kill me?'

Bosch looked at his face and his useless hands and realized he felt the stirring of sympathy.

'I didn't know what I was going to do. I just knew I was coming.'

'You want to know about her?'

'My mother?'

'Yes.'

Bosch thought about the question. His own memories of his mother were dim and fading farther all the time. And he had few recollections about her that came from others.

'What was she like?' he said.

Conklin thought for a moment.

'She is hard for me to describe. I felt a great attraction to her ... that crooked smile ... I knew she had secrets. I suppose all people do. But hers ran deep. And despite all of that, she was full of life. And, you see, I didn't think I was at the time we met. That's what she gave to me.'

He drank from the glass of water again, emptying it. Bosch offered to get more but Conklin waved off the offer.

'I had been with other women and they wanted to show me off like a trophy,' he said. 'Your mother wasn't like that. She'd rather stay at home or take a picnic basket to Griffith Park than go to the clubs on the Sunset Strip.'

'How did you find out about ... what she did?'

'She told me. The night she told me about you. She said she needed to tell me the truth because she needed my help. I have to admit ... the shock was ... I initially thought of myself. You know, protecting myself. But I admired her courage in telling me and I was in love by then. I couldn't turn away.'

'How did Mittel know?'

'I told him. I regret it to this day.'

'If she ... If she was as you described her, why did she do what she did? I've never ... understood.'

'I haven't, either. As I told you, she had her secrets. She didn't tell me them all.'

Bosch looked away from him and out the window. The view was to the north. He could see the lights of the Hollywood Hills glimmering in the mist from the canyons.

'She used to tell me that you were a tough little egg,'

Conklin said from behind him. His voice was almost hoarse now. It was probably more talking than he had done in months. 'She once told me that she knew it didn't matter what happened to her because you were tough enough to make it through.'

Bosch said nothing. He just looked through the window.

'Was she right?' the old man asked.

Bosch's eyes followed the crestline of the hills directly north. Somewhere up there the lights glowed from Mittel's spaceship. He was up there somewhere waiting for Bosch. He looked back at Conklin, who was still waiting for an answer.

'I think maybe the jury's still out.'

Bosch leaned against the stainless steel wall of the elevator as it descended. He realized how different his feelings were from those that he held while the elevator had been carrying him up. He had ridden up with hatred pounding in his chest like a cat in a burlap bag. He didn't even know the man he carried it for. Now he looked upon that man as a pitiful character, a half of a man who lay with his frail hands folded on the blanket, waiting, maybe hoping, for death to come and end his private misery.

Bosch believed Conklin. There was something about his story and his pain that seemed too genuine to be dismissed as an act. Conklin was far beyond posing. He was facing his grave. He had called himself a coward and a puppet and Bosch could think of nothing much harsher that a man could put on his own tombstone.

In realizing that Conklin spoke the truth, Bosch knew that he had already met the real enemy face to face. Gordon Mittel. The strategist. The fixer. The killer. The man who held the strings to the puppet. Now they would meet again. But this time, Bosch planned to make it on his terms.

He pushed the L button again as if that might coax the elevator to descend faster. He knew it was a useless gesture but he did it again.

When the elevator finally opened, the lobby seemed

empty and sterile. The guard was there, behind his desk, working on his word puzzle. There wasn't even the sound of a far-off TV. Only the silence of old people's lives. He asked the guard if he needed him to sign out and he was waved off.

'Look, sorry I was an asshole before,' Bosch offered.

'Don't worry about it, partner,' the guard replied. 'It gets to the best of us.'

Bosch wondered what the 'it' was he was talking about but said nothing. He nodded solemnly, as if he got most of his life lessons from security guards. He pushed through the glass doors and headed down the steps into the parking lot. It was getting cool and he turned up the collar of his jacket. He saw the sky was clear and the moon as sharp as a sickle. As he approached the Mustang he noticed the trunk of the car next to it was open and a man was bent over, attaching a jack to the rear bumper. Bosch picked up his pace and hoped he wouldn't be asked to help out. It was too cold and he was tired of talking to strangers.

He passed the crouched man and then, not used to the rental car keys, he fumbled as he tried to get the proper key into the Mustang's door lock. Just as he got the key in the slot, he heard a shoe scuff along the pavement behind him and a voice said, 'Excuse me, fella.'

Bosch turned, trying to quickly think of an excuse for why he couldn't help the man. But all he saw was the blur of the other man's arm coming down. Then he saw an explosion of red the color of blood.

Then all he saw was black.

B osch followed the coyote again. But this time the animal did not take him on the path through the mountain brush. The coyote was out of his element. He led Bosch up a steep incline of pavement. Bosch looked around and realized he was on a tall bridge over a wide expanse of water that his eyes followed to the horizon. Bosch became panicked as the coyote got too far ahead of him. He chased the animal but it crested the rise of the bridge and disappeared. The bridge was now empty, except for Bosch. He struggled to the top and looked around. The sky was blood red and seemed to be pulsing with the sound of a heartbeat.

Bosch looked in all directions but the coyote was gone. He was alone.

But suddenly he wasn't alone. The hands of someone unseen grabbed him from behind and pushed him toward the railing. Bosch struggled. He swung his elbows wildly and dug his heels in and tried to stop his movement to the edge. He tried to speak, to yell for help, but nothing came from his throat. He saw the water shimmering like the scales of a fish below him.

Then, as quickly as they had taken hold of him, the hands were gone and he was alone. He spun around and no one was there. From behind he heard a door close sharply. He turned again and there was no one. And there was no door.

Bosch woke up in darkness and pain to the sound of muffled shouting. He was lying on a hard surface and at first it was a struggle just to move. Eventually, he slid his hand across the ground and determined it was carpet. He knew he was inside somewhere, lying on a floor. Across the expanse of darkness he saw a small line of dim light. He stared at it for some time, using it as a focal point, before realizing that it was the crack of light emitted at the bottom edge of a door.

He pulled himself up into a sitting position and the movement made his interior world slide and melt like a Dalí painting. A feeling of nausea came over him and he closed his eyes and waited for several seconds until equilibrium returned. He raised his hand to the side of his head where the pain came from and found the hair matted with a stickiness he knew by smell was blood. His fingers carefully traced the matted hair to a two-inch-long gash in his scalp. He touched it gingerly and determined that the blood had clotted for now. The wound was no longer bleeding.

He didn't think he could stand so he crawled toward the light. The dream of the coyote broke into his mind and then disappeared in a flash of red pain.

He found the door knob was locked. That didn't surprise him. But the effort exhausted him. He leaned back against the wall and closed his eyes. Inside, his instinct to seek a means of escape and his desire to lay up and mend fought for his attention. The battle was interrupted only by the start of the voices again. Bosch could tell they did not come from the room on the other side of the door. They were farther away, yet near enough to be understood.

'Stupid fuck!'

'Look, I tol' you, you didn't say anything about any briefcase. You –'

'There had to have been one. Use your common sense.'

'You said bring the man. I brang the man. You want, I go back to the car and look for a briefcase. But you dint say nothin' about –'

'You can't go back, you fool! The place will be crawling with cops. They probably have his car and the briefcase already.'

'I didn't see any briefcase. Maybe he didn't have one.'

'And maybe I should have depended on someone else.'

Bosch realized that they were talking about him. He also recognized the angry voice as belonging to Gordon Mittel. It had the crisp delivery and haughtiness of the man Bosch had met at the fund-raiser. The other voice Bosch didn't recognize, though he had a good idea who it was. Though defensive and submissive, it was a gruff voice full of the timbre of violence. Bosch guessed it was the man who had hit him. And he imagined that to be the man he had seen Mittel with inside the house during the fund-raiser.

It took Bosch several minutes to consider the content of what they were arguing about. A briefcase. His briefcase. It wasn't in the car, he knew. Then he realized he must have forgotten it, left it in Conklin's room. He had brought it up with him so he could take out the photo Monte Kim had given him and the bank statements from Eno's safe deposit box and confront the old man with his lies. But the old man hadn't lied. He hadn't denied Bosch's mother.

And so the photo and statements weren't necessary. The briefcase lay at the foot of the bed, forgotten.

He thought about the last exchange he had heard. Mittel told the other man he could not go back, that the police would be there. This made no sense to him. Unless someone had witnessed the attack on him. Maybe the security guard. It gave him hope, then he dashed it himself when he thought of another possibility. Mittel was taking care of all the loose ends and Conklin had to be one of them. Bosch slumped against the wall. He knew he was now the last loose end. He sat there in silence until he heard Mittel's voice once more.

'Go get him. Bring him outside.'

As quickly as he could, not yet formulating a plan, Bosch crawled back toward the spot where he thought he had been when he woke up. He rammed into something heavy, put his hands on it and determined it was a pool table. He quickly found the corner and reached into the pocket. His hand closed on a billiard ball. He pulled it out, quickly trying to think of a way to conceal it. Finally, he shoved it inside his sport coat so that it rolled down the inside of the left sleeve to the crook in his elbow. There was more than enough room. Bosch liked large jackets because they gave him room to grab his gun. That made the sleeves baggy. He believed that by cocking his arm he could conceal the heavy ball in the folds of the sleeve.

As he heard a key hit the door knob, he moved to his right and sprawled on the carpet, closed his eyes and waited. He hoped he was in or close to the spot on the carpet where he had been dropped by his captors. In moments, he heard the door open and then light burned through his eyelids. There was nothing after that. No sound or movement. He waited.

'Forget it, Bosch,' the voice said. 'That only works in movies.'

Bosch didn't move.

'Look, your blood is all over the carpet. It's on the door knob here.'

Bosch realized he must have left a trail to the door and back. His half-hatched plan to surprise his captor and overtake him had no chance now. He opened his eyes. There was a light on the ceiling directly overhead.

'All right,' he said. 'What do you want?'

'Get up. Let's go.'

Bosch slowly got up. It was an actual struggle but he added to it, ad libbing a bit. And when he was all the way up, he saw blood on the green felt bumper of the pool table. He quickly stumbled and grabbed the spot for support. He hoped the man in the room had not seen the blood was already there.

'Get away from there, goddamnit. That's a five-thousand-dollar table. Look at the blood … shit.'

'Sorry. I'll pay for it.'

'Not where you're going. Let's go.'

Bosch recognized him. It was the man he guessed it would be. Mittel's man from the party. And his face matched his voice. Gruff, strong, he had broken a few boards with it. He had a ruddy complexion set off by two small brown eyes that never seemed to blink.

He wore no suit this time. At least that Bosch could see. He was dressed in a bulky blue jumpsuit that looked brand-new. It was a splatter suit. Bosch knew that professional killers often used them. It was easier to clean up after a job and you didn't mess up your suit. Just zip off the splatter suit, dump it, and you're on your way.

Bosch stood on his own and took a step but immediately bent over and folded his arms across his stomach. He thought this was the best way to conceal the weapon he had.

'You really hit me, man. My balance is shot. I think I might get sick or something.'

'You get sick and I'll make you clean it up with your tongue. Like a fuckin' cat.'

'I guess I won't get sick then.'

'You're a funny guy. Let's go.'

The man backed away from the door and into the room. He then signaled Bosch out. For the first time Bosch saw that he carried a gun. It looked like a Beretta twenty-two and was held down low at his side.

'I know what you're thinking,' he said. 'Only a twenty-two. You think you could take maybe two, three shots and still get to me. Wrong. I got hollow points in here. I'll put you down with one shot. Tear a hole the size of a soup bowl outta your back. Remember that. Walk ahead a'me.'

He was playing it smart, Bosch noticed, not coming closer than five or six feet even though he had the gun. Once Bosch was through the door, the man issued directions. They walked down a hallway, through what looked like a living room and then through another room that Bosch thought would also qualify as a living room. This one Bosch recognized by the French doors and windows. It was the room off the party lawn at Mittel's mansion on Mount Olympus.

'Go out the door. He's waiting for you out there.'

'What did you hit me with, man?'

'Tire iron. Hope it put a splinter in your skull, but it don't matter if it did or didn't.'

'Well, I think it did anyway. Congratulations.'

Bosch stopped at one of the French doors as if he expected it to be opened for him. Outside the party tent was gone. And out near the edge of the overhang he saw Mittel standing with his back turned to the house. He was silhouetted by the lights of the city extending out into infinity from below.

369

'Open it.'

'Sorry, I thought … never mind.'

'Yeah, never mind. Just get out there. We don't have all night.'

Out on the lawn, Mittel turned around. Bosch could see he was holding the badge wallet with his ID in one hand and the lieutenant's badge in the other. The gunman stopped Bosch with a hand on his shoulder, then moved back to his six-foot distance.

'So, then, Bosch is the real name?'

Bosch looked at Mittel. The former prosecutor turned political backdoor man smiled.

'Yes. That's the real name.'

'Well, then, how do you do, Mr Bosch?'

'It's Detective, actually.'

'Detective, actually. You know, I was wondering about that. Because that's what this ID card says but then this badge says something completely different. It says lieutenant. And that's curious. Wasn't that a lieutenant I read about in the papers? The one who was found dead and without his badge? Yes, I'm sure it was. And wasn't his name, Harvey Pounds, the same name that you used when you were parading around here the other night? Again, I think so, but correct me if I am wrong, Detective Bosch.'

'It's a long story, Mittel, but I am a cop. LAPD. If you want to save yourself a few years in prison, you'll get this old fuck with the gun away from me and call me an ambulance. I've got a concussion, at least. It might be worse.'

Before speaking, Mittel put the badge in one of the pockets of his jacket and the ID wallet in the other.

'No, I don't think we'll be making any calls on your behalf. I think things have gone a little too far for humanitarian gestures like that. Speaking of the human existence, it's a shame that your play here the other night cost an innocent man his life.'

'No. It's a fucking crime *you* killed an innocent man.'

'Well, I was thinking more along the lines that it was you who killed him. I mean, of course, you are ultimately responsible.'

'Just like a lawyer, passing the buck. Should've stayed out of politics, Gordie. Stuck to the law. You'd probably have your own TV commercials by now.'

Mittel smiled.

'And what? Given up all of this?'

He spread his arms to take in the house and the magnificent view. Bosch followed the arc of his arm to look at the house but he was really trying to get a bead on the other man, the one with the gun. He spotted him standing five feet directly behind him, the gun at his side. He was still too far away for Bosch to risk making a move. Especially in his condition. He moved his arm slightly and felt the billiard ball nesting in the crook of his elbow. It was reassuring to him. It was all he had.

'The law is for fools, Detective Bosch. But I must correct you. I don't really consider myself to be in politics. I consider myself to be just a fixer. A solver of problems of any kind for anyone. Political problems just happen to be my forte. But now, you see, I have to fix a problem that is neither political nor someone else's. This one is my own.'

He raised his eyebrows as though he could hardly believe it himself.

'And that's why I have invited you here. Why I asked Jonathan to bring you along. You see, I had an idea that if we watched Arno Conklin, our mystery party crasher of the other night would eventually show up. And I wasn't disappointed.'

'You're a clever man, Mittel.'

Bosch turned his head slightly so that he could see

Jonathan in his peripheral vision. He was still out of reach. Bosch knew he had to draw him closer.

'Hold your ground, Jonathan,' Mittel said. 'Mr Bosch is not one to get excited about. Just a minor inconvenience.'

Bosch looked back at Mittel.

'Just like Marjorie Lowe, right? She was just a minor inconvenience. Just a nobody who didn't count.'

'Now, that's an interesting name to bring up. Is that what this is about, Detective Bosch?'

Bosch stared at him, too angry to speak.

'Well, the only thing I can admit to is that I did use her death to my advantage. I saw it as an opportunity, you could say.'

'I know all about it, Mittel. You used her to get control of Conklin. But eventually even he saw through your lies. It's over now. It doesn't matter what you do to me here, my people will be coming. You can count on it.'

'The old give-up-the-place-is-surrounded ploy. I don't think so. This badge business ... something tells me that you've exceeded your bounds on this one. I think maybe this is what they call an unofficial investigation and the fact that you used a false name before and were carrying a dead man's badge tends to bear me out ... I don't think anyone is coming. Are they?'

Bosch's mind raced but he drew a blank and remained silent.

'I think you're just a small-time extortionist who stumbled onto something somehow and wants a payoff to go away. Well, we're going to give you a payoff, Detective Bosch.'

'There are people who know what I know, Mittel,' Bosch blurted. 'What are you going to do, go out and kill them all?'

'I'll take that suggestion under advisement.'

'What about Conklin? He knows the whole story.

Anything happens to me, I guarantee he'll go right to the cops.'

'As a matter of fact, you could say Arno Conklin is with the police right now. But I don't think he's saying much.'

Bosch dropped his head and slumped a little. He had guessed that Conklin was dead but had hoped he was wrong. He felt the billiard ball move in his sleeve and he folded his arms again to cover up.

'Yes. Apparently, the former district attorney threw himself from his window after your visit.'

Mittel stepped aside and pointed out into the lights below. Far off Bosch could see the cluster of lighted buildings that were Park La Brea. And he could see blue and red lights flashing at the base of one of the buildings. It was Conklin's building.

'Must have been a truly traumatic moment,' Mittel continued. 'He chose death rather than give in to extortion. A principled man to the end.'

'He was an old man!' Bosch yelled angrily. 'Goddamnit, why?'

'Detective Bosch, keep your voice down or Jonathan will have to lower it for you.'

'You're not getting away this time,' Bosch said in a lower, tighter, controlled voice.

'As far as Conklin goes, I assume the final declaration will be suicide. He was very sick, you know.'

'Right, a guy with no legs walks over to the window and decides to throw himself out.'

'Well, if the authorities don't believe that, then maybe they will come up with an alternate scenario when they find your fingerprints in the room. I'm sure you obliged us by leaving a few.'

'Along with my briefcase.'

That hit Mittel like a slap across the face.

'That's right. I left it there. And there's enough in it to

bring them up this mountain to see you, Mittel. They'll
come for you!'

Bosch yelled the last line at him as a test.

'Jon!' Mittel barked.

Almost before the word was out of Mittel's mouth,
Bosch was clubbed from behind. The impact came on the
right side of the neck and he went down to his knees,
careful to keep his arm bent and the heavy ball in place.
He slowly, more slowly than was needed, got up. Since
the impact had been on the right, he assumed that
Jonathan had hit him with his gun hand.

'By providing me with the location of the briefcase, you
have answered the most important question I had,' Mittel
said. 'The other, of course, was what was in the briefcase
and how it would concern me. Now, the problem I have
is that without the briefcase or the ability to get it I have
no way of checking the veracity of what you tell me here.'

'So I guess you're fucked.'

'No, Detective, I think that would more accurately
describe your situation. However, I have one other
question before you go off. Why, Detective Bosch? Why
were you bothering with something so old and so
meaningless?'

Bosch looked at him for a long time before answering.

'Because everybody counts, Mittel. Everybody.'

Bosch saw Mittel nod in the direction of Jonathan. The
meeting was over. He had to make his play.

'*Help!*'

Bosch yelled it as loudly as he could. And he knew the
gunman would make his move toward him immediately.
Anticipating the same swing of the gun to the right side of
the neck, Bosch spun to his right. As he moved he
straightened his left arm and used the centrifugal force of
the move to let the billiard ball roll down his sleeve into
his hand. In continuing the move, he swung his arm up

and out. And as he turned his face he saw Jonathan inches behind him, swinging his own hand down, the fingers laced around the Beretta. He also saw the surprise on Jonathan's face as he realized his swing would surely miss and that his momentum prevented him from correcting the course.

After Jonathan's arm went by harmlessly and he was vulnerable, Bosch's arm arced downward. Jonathan made a last-second lunge to his left but the billiard ball in Bosch's fist still caught him with a glancing blow to the right side of his head. It made a sound like a lightbulb popping and Jonathan's body followed the momentum of his falling arm. He fell face first on the grass, his body on top of the gun.

Almost immediately, the man tried to get up and Bosch delivered a vicious kick to his ribs. Jonathan rolled off the gun and Bosch came down on his body with his knees, swinging his fist into the back of his head and neck two more times before realizing that he still gripped the billiard ball and that he had hurt the man enough.

Breathing as if he had just come up for air, Bosch glanced around and saw the gun. He quickly grabbed it up and looked for Mittel. But he was gone.

The slight sound of running on grass caught his attention and he looked to the far northern line of the lawn. He caught a glimpse of Mittel then, just as he disappeared into the darkness at the spot where the flat, manicured grass gave way to the rugged brush of the hilltop.

'Mittel!'

Bosch jumped up and followed. At the point where he had last seen Mittel, he found a path worn into the brush. He realized it was an old coyote trail that had been widened over time by human feet. He raced down it, the yawning drop-off to the city below no more than two feet on his right.

He saw no sign of Mittel and followed the trail along the edge of the drop-off until the house was no longer in sight behind him. Finally he stopped after coming across nothing that indicated Mittel was even near or had taken this path.

Breathing heavily, his head pounding where he was wounded, Bosch came upon a steep bluff rising off the side of the trail and saw that it was ringed with old beer bottles and other debris. The bluff was a popular lookout spot. He put the gun in his waistband and then used his hands for balance and purchase as he climbed ten feet to its top. He did a slow three-sixty-degree turn while on top of the bluff but saw nothing. He listened but the hiss of the city's traffic precluded any chance of his hearing Mittel moving in the brush. He decided to give it up, to get back to the house and call out an air unit before Mittel could get away. They'd find him with a spotlight if the chopper could get out here quickly enough.

As he gingerly slid back down the bluff, Mittel suddenly came at him from the darkness to the right. He had been hiding behind a thick growth of brush and Spanish sword plants. He dove into Bosch's midsection, knocking him down onto the trail, his weight on top of him. Bosch felt the man's hands going for the gun still in his waistband. But Bosch was younger and stronger. The surprise attack was Mittel's last card. Bosch closed his arms around him and rolled to his left. Suddenly, the weight was off and Mittel was gone.

Bosch sat up and looked about, then pulled himself over to the edge. He pulled the gun out of his waistband and then leaned over and looked down. There was only darkness when he looked directly down the side of the rugged hill. He could see the rectangular roofs of houses about a hundred and fifty yards down. He knew they were built along the twisting roads that fed off Hollywood Boulevard and Fairfax Avenue. He did another complete turn and then looked down again. He didn't see Mittel anywhere.

Bosch surveyed the scene beneath him in its entirety until his eyes caught the backyard lights flicking on behind one of the houses directly below. He watched as a man came out of the house carrying what looked like a rifle. The man slowly approached a round backyard spa platform, the rifle pointed ahead of him. The man stopped at the edge of the spa and reached to what must have been the outdoor electrical box.

The tub light came on, silhouetting the body of a man floating in a circle of blue. Even from on top of the hill Bosch could see the swirls of blood seeping from Mittel's body. Then the voice of the man with the rifle came up the hillside intact.

'Linda, don't come out! Just call the police. Tell them we got a body in our hot tub.'

Then the man looked up the hillside and Bosch moved back away from the edge. Immediately, he wondered why he'd had the instinctive reaction to hide.

He got up and slowly made his way back to Mittel's house along the path. As he walked, he looked out across the city at the lights shimmering in the night and thought it was beautiful. He thought about Conklin and Pounds and then pushed the guilt out of his mind with thoughts about Mittel, about how his death finally closed the circle begun so long ago. He thought of the image of his mother in Monte Kim's photo. Her looking timidly around the edge of Conklin's arm. He waited for the feeling of satisfaction and triumph that he knew was supposed to come with vengeance accomplished. But none of it ever came to him. He only felt hollow and tired.

When he got back to the perfect lawn behind the perfect mansion, the man called Jonathan was gone.

Assistant Chief Irvin S. Irving stood in the open doorway of the examination suite. Bosch was sitting on the side of the padded table holding an ice pack to his head. The doctor had given it to him after putting in the stitches. He noticed Irving when he adjusted the bag in his hand.

'How do you feel?'

'I'll live, I guess. That's what they tell me, at least.'

'Well, that's better than you can say for Mittel. He took the high dive.'

'Yeah. What about the other one?'

'Nothing on him. We got his name, though. You told the uniforms Mittel called him Jonathan. So that means he's probably Jonathan Vaughn. He's worked for Mittel for a long time. They're working on it, checking the hospitals. Sounds like you might've hurt him enough that he'd come in.'

'Vaughn.'

'We're trying to do a background on him. So far, not much. He's got no record.'

'How long was he with Mittel?'

'That we're not sure of. We've talked to Mittel's people at the law firm. Not what you'd call cooperative. But they say Vaughn has been around forever. He was described by most people as Mittel's personal valet.'

Bosch nodded and put the information away.

'There's also a driver. We picked him up but he isn't saying much. A little surfer punk. He couldn't talk if he wanted to anyway.'

'What do you mean?'

'His jaw is broken. Wired shut. He won't talk about that, either.'

Bosch just nodded again and looked at him. There didn't seem to be anything hidden in what he had said.

'The doctor said you have a severe concussion but the skull is not fractured. Minor laceration.'

'Could've fooled me. My head feels like the Goodyear blimp with a hole in it.'

'How many stitches?'

'I think he said eighteen.'

'He said you'll probably have headaches and keep the knot up there and the eye hemorrhages for a few days. It'll look worse than it is.'

'Well, nice to know he's telling somebody what's going on. I haven't heard anything from him. Just the nurses.'

'He'll be in in a minute. He was probably waiting for you to come out of it a little more.'

'Come out of what?'

'You were a little dazed when we got up there to you, Harry. You sure you want to talk about this now? It can wait. You're hurt and need to take it –'

'I'm okay. I want to talk. You been by the scene at Park La Brea?'

'Yes, I was there. I was there when we got the call from Mount Olympus. I've got your briefcase in the car, by the way. You left it there, didn't you? With Conklin?'

He started to nod but stopped because it made things swirl.

'Good,' he said. 'There's something there I want to keep.'

'The photo?'

'You looked through it?'

'Bosch! You must be groggy. It was found at the scene of a crime.'

'Yeah, I know, sorry.'

He waved off his objection. He was tired of fighting.

'So, the crew working the scene up on the hill already told me what happened. At least, the early version based on the physicals. What I'm not clear about is what got you up there. You know, how all of this figures. You want to run it down for me or wait until maybe tomorrow?'

Bosch nodded once and waited a moment for his mind to clear. He hadn't tried to collect the story into one cohesive thought yet. He thought about it some more and finally gave it a shot.

'I'm ready.'

'Okay, I want to read you your rights first.'

'What, again?'

'It's just a procedure so it doesn't look like we're cutting any slack to one of our own. You've got to remember, you were at two places tonight and at both somebody took a big fall. It doesn't look good.'

'I didn't kill Conklin.'

'I know that and we have the security guard's statement. He says you left before Conklin took the dive. So you're gonna be okay. You're clear but I have to follow procedure. Now, you still want to talk?'

'I waive my rights.'

Irving read them to him from a card anyway and Bosch waived them again.

'Okay, then, I don't have a waive form. You'll have to sign that later.'

'You want me to tell the story?'

'Yes, I want you to tell the story.'

'Okay, here we go.'

But then he stopped as he tried to put it into words.

'Harry?'

'Okay, here it is. In 1961 Arno Conklin met Marjorie Lowe. He was introduced by local scumbucket Johnny Fox, who made his living off making such introductions and arrangements. Usually for money. This initial meeting between Arno and Marjorie was at the St Pat's party at the Masonic Lodge on Cahuenga.'

'That's the photo in the briefcase, right?'

'Right. Now, at that first meeting, according to Arno's story, which I believe, he didn't know that Marjorie was a pro and Fox was a pimp. Fox arranged the introduction because he probably saw the opportunity and had one eye on the future. See, if Conklin knew it was a pay-to-play sort of thing, he would have walked away. He was the top county vice commando. He would have walked away.'

'So he didn't know who Fox was either?' Irving asked.

'That's what he said. He just said he was innocent. If you find that hard to take, the alternative is harder; that this prosecutor would openly consort with these types of people. So, I'm going with Arno's story. He didn't know.'

'Okay, he didn't know he was being compromised. So what was in it for Fox and … your mother?'

'Fox is easy. Once Conklin went with her, Fox had a nice hook into him and he could reel him in whenever he wanted. Marjorie is something else and I've been thinking about it but it still isn't clear. But you can say this, most women in that situation are looking for a way out. She could have played along with Fox's plan because she had her own plan. She was looking for a way out of the life.'

Irving nodded and added to the hypothesis.

'She had a boy in the youth hall and wanted to get him out. Being with Arno could only help.'

'That's right. The thing of it was, Arno and Marjorie did something none of the three of them expected. They fell

382

in love. Or at least Conklin did. And he believed she did, too.'

Irving took a chair in the corner, crossed his legs and stared thoughtfully at Bosch. He said nothing. Nothing about his demeanor indicated he was anything else but totally interested and believing in Bosch's story. Bosch's arm was getting tired of holding the ice pack up and he wished he could lie down. But there was only the table in the examination suite. He continued the story.

'So they fall in love and their relationship continues and somewhere along the line she tells him. Or maybe Mittel did some checking and told him. It doesn't matter. What matters is that at some point Conklin knew the score. And again, he surprises everybody.'

'How?'

'On October twenty-seven, nineteen sixty-one, he proposes marriage to Marj –'

'He told you this? Arno told you this?'

'He told me tonight. He wanted to marry her. She wanted to marry him. On that night back then, he finally decided to chuck it all, to risk losing everything he had to gain the one thing he wanted most.'

Bosch reached into his jacket on the table and took out his cigarettes. Irving spoke up.

'I don't think this is a – nothing, never mind.'

Bosch lit a smoke with his lighter.

'It was the bravest act of his life. You realize that? That took balls to be willing to risk everything like that … But he made a mistake.'

'What?'

'He called his friend Gordon Mittel to ask him to go with them to Vegas to be best man. Mittel refused. He knew it would be the end of a promising political career for Conklin, maybe even his own career, and he wanted no part of it. But then he went further than just refusing to be best man. See, he saw Conklin as the white horse on which he would be able to ride into the castle. He had big plans for himself and Conklin and he wasn't going to sit back and let some ... some Hollywood whore ruin it. He knew from Conklin's call that she had gone home to pack. So Mittel went there and intercepted her somehow. Maybe told her that Conklin had sent him. I don't know.'

'He killed her.'

Bosch nodded and this time he didn't go dizzy.

'I don't know where, maybe in his car. He made it look like a sex crime by tying the belt around her neck and tearing up her clothes. The semen ... it was already there because she had been with Conklin ... After she was dead, Mittel took the body to the alley near the Boulevard and put her in the trash. The whole thing stayed a secret for a lot of years after that.'

'Until you came along.'

Bosch didn't answer. He was savoring his cigarette and the relief of the end of the case.

'What about Fox?' Irving asked.

'Like I said, Fox knew about Marjorie and Arno. And he knew they were together the night before Marjorie was found dead in that alley. That knowledge gave Fox a powerful piece of leverage over an important man, even if the man was innocent. Fox used it. In who knows how many ways. Within a year he was on Arno's campaign payroll. He was hooked on him like a bloodsucking leech. So Mittel, the fixer, finally stepped in. Fox died in a hit and run while supposedly handing out Conklin campaign fliers. Would've been easy to set up, make it look like it was an accident and the driver just fled. But that's no surprise. The same guy who worked the Marjorie Lowe case worked the hit and run. Same result. Nobody ever arrested.'

'McKittrick?'

'No. Claude Eno. He's dead now. Took his secrets with him. But Mittel was paying him off for twenty-five years.'

'The bank statements?'

'Yeah, in the briefcase. You look, you'll probably find records somewhere linking Mittel to the payments. Conklin said he didn't know about them and I believe him ... You know, somebody ought to check all the elections Mittel worked on over the years. They'll probably find out he was a rat fucker that could've held his own in the Nixon White House.'

Bosch ground his cigarette out on the side of a trash can next to the table and dropped the butt in. He started to feel very cold and put his jacket back on. It was smudged with dirt and dried blood.

'You look like a mess in that, Harry,' Irving said. 'Why don't you –'

'I'm cold.'

'Okay.'

'You know, he didn't even scream.'

'What?'

'Mittel. He didn't even scream when he went down that hill. I can't figure that out.'

'You don't have to. It's just one of those –'

'And I didn't push him. He jumped me in the brush and when we rolled, he went over. He didn't even scream.'

'I understand. No one is saying –'

'All I did was start to ask questions about her and people started dying.'

Bosch was staring at an eye chart on the far wall of the room. He could not figure out why they would have such a thing in an emergency room examination suite.

'Christ ... Pounds ... I –'

'Yes, I know what happened,' Irving interrupted.

Bosch looked over at him.

'You do?'

'We interviewed everyone in the squad. Edgar told me that he made a computer run for you on Fox. My only conclusion is that Pounds either overheard or somehow got wind of it. I think he was monitoring what your close associates were doing after you went on ISL. Then he must've taken it a step further and stumbled into Mittel and Vaughn. He ran DMV traces on the parties involved. I think it got back to Mittel. He had the connections that would have warned him.'

Bosch was silent. He wondered if Irving really believed that scenario or if he was signaling to Bosch that he knew what had really happened and was letting it go by. It didn't matter. Whether or not Irving blamed him or took departmental action against him, Bosch's own conscience would be the hardest thing to live with.

'Christ,' he said again. 'He got killed instead of me.'

His body started shuddering then. As if saying the words out loud had started some kind of exorcism. He threw the ice pack into the trash can and wrapped his arms around himself. But the shuddering wouldn't stop. It seemed to him that he would never be warm again, that his shaking was not a temporary affliction but a permanent part of him now. He had the warm salty taste of tears in his mouth and he realized then that he was crying. He turned his face away from Irving and tried to tell him to leave but he couldn't say anything. His jaw was locked as tight as a fist.

'Harry?' he heard Irving say. 'Harry, you okay?'

Bosch managed to nod, not understanding how Irving could not see his body shaking. He moved his hands into the pockets of his jacket and pulled it closed around him. He felt something in his left pocket and started absent-mindedly pulling it out.

'Look,' Irving was saying, 'the doctor said you could get emotional. This knock on the head ... they do weird things to you. Don't wor – Harry, are you sure you're okay? You're turning blue, son. I'm gonna – I'll go get the doctor. I'll –'

He stopped as Bosch managed to remove the object from his jacket. He held his palm upright. Clasped in his shaking hand was a black eight ball. Much of it was smeared with blood. Irving took it from him, having to practically pry his fingers off it.

'I'll go get somebody,' was all he said.

Then Bosch was alone in the room, waiting for someone to come and the demon to leave.

❖ ❖ ❖ ❖ ❖ ❖ ❖

Because of the concussion, Bosch's pupils were dilated unevenly and purple hemorrhages bulged below them. He had a hell of a headache and a one-hundred-degree temperature. As a precaution, the emergency room physician ordered that he be admitted and monitored, not allowed to sleep until four in the morning. He tried to pass the time by reading the newspaper and watching the talk shows but they only seemed to worsen the pain. Finally, he just stared at the walls until a nurse came in, checked on him and told him he could sleep. After that, nurses kept coming into his room and waking him at two-hour intervals. They checked his eyes and temperature and asked if he was okay. They never gave him anything for the headache. They told him to go back to sleep. If he dreamed of the coyote during the short sleep cycles, or anything else, he didn't remember it.

Finally, at noon, he got up for good. He was unsteady on his feet at first but equilibrium quickly came back to him. He made his way into the bathroom and studied his image in the mirror. He burst out laughing at what he saw, though it was not that funny. It was just that he seemed to be about to laugh or cry or do both at any given moment.

He had a small shaved spot on his skull where there was an L-shaped seam of stitches. It hurt when he touched the wound but he laughed about that, too. He managed to comb hair over it with his hand, fairly well camouflaging the injury.

The eyes were another matter. Still dilated unevenly and now cracked with red veins, they looked like the bad end of a two-week bender. Below them, deep purple triangles pointed to the corners of the eyes. A double shiner. Bosch didn't think he'd ever had one before.

Stepping back into the room he saw that his briefcase had been left by Irving next to the bed table. He bent to pick it up and almost lost his balance, grabbing on to the table at the last moment. He got back into bed with the briefcase and began examining its contents. He had no purpose in mind, he just wanted to be doing something.

He leafed through his notebook, finding it hard to concentrate on the words. He then reread the five-year-old Christmas card from Meredith Roman, now Katherine Register. He realized he needed to call her, that he wanted to tell her what happened before she read about it in the paper or heard it on the news. He found her number in his notebook and dialed on the room's phone. He got her answering machine and left a message.

'Meredith, uh, Katherine … this is Harry Bosch. I need to talk to you today when you get a minute. Some things have happened and I think you'll, uh, feel better about things when you hear from me. So, give me a call.'

Bosch left a variety of numbers on the tape, including his mobile, the Mark Twain and the hospital room and then hung up.

He opened the accordion pocket in the lid of the briefcase and slipped out the photo Monte Kim had given him. He studied his mother's face for a long time. The thought that eventually poked through was a question. Bosch had no doubt from what Conklin had said that he had loved her. But he wondered if she really loved Conklin back. Bosch remembered a time when she had visited him at McClaren. She had promised to get him out. At the time, the legal effort was going slowly and he knew that she had no faith in courts. When she made the promise, he knew she wasn't thinking about the law, only ways to get around it, to manipulate it. And he believed she would have found a way to do it if her time hadn't been taken away.

He realized, looking at the photo, that Conklin might simply have been part of the promise, part of the manipulation. Their marriage plan was her way of getting Harry out. From unwed mother with an arrest record to wife of an important man. Conklin would be able to get Harry out, to win back Marjorie Lowe's custody of her son. Bosch considered that love may have had nothing to do with it on her part, that it was only opportunity. In all the visits to McClaren, she had never spoken of Conklin or any man in particular. If she had truly been in love, wouldn't she have told him?

And in considering that question, Bosch realized that his mother's effort to save him was what might ultimately have led to her death.

'Mr Bosch, are you okay?'

The nurse moved quickly into the room and put the food tray down on the table with a rattle. Bosch didn't answer her. He barely noticed her. She took the napkin off the tray and used it to wipe the tears off his cheeks.

'It's okay,' she soothed. 'It's okay.'

'Is it?'

'It's the injury. Nothing to be embarrassed about. Head injuries jumble the emotions. One minute you're crying, the next you're laughing. Let me open these curtains. Maybe that will cheer you up.'

'I think I just want to be left alone.'

She ignored him and opened the curtains and Bosch had a view of another building twenty yards away. It did cheer him up, though. The view was so bad it made him laugh. It also reminded him he was in Cedars. He recognized the other medical tower.

The nurse then closed his briefcase so she could roll the table over the bed. On the tray was a plate containing Salisbury steak, carrots and potatoes. There was a roll that looked as hard as the eight ball he had found in his pocket the night before and some kind of red dessert wrapped in plastic. The tray and its smell made him feel the onset of nausea.

'I'm not going to eat this. Is there any Frosted Flakes?'

'You have to eat a full meal.'

'I just woke up. You people kept me up all night. I can't eat this. It's making me sick.'

She quickly picked up the tray and headed to the door.

'I'll see what I can do. About the Frosted Flakes.'

She looked back at him and smiled before heading out the door.

'Cheer up.'

'Yeah, that's the prescription.'

Bosch didn't know what to do with himself but wait for time to pass. He started thinking about his encounter with Mittel, about what was said and what was meant. There was something about it that bothered him.

He was interrupted by a beeping sound coming from the side panel of the bed. He looked down and found it was the phone.

'Hello?'

'Harry?'

'Yes.'

'It's Jazz. Are you okay?'

There was a long silence. Bosch didn't know if he was ready for this yet, but now it was unavoidable.

'Harry?'

'I'm fine. How'd you find me?'

'The man who called me yesterday. Irving something. He –'

'Chief Irving.'

'Yes. He called and told me you were hurt. He gave me the number.'

That annoyed Bosch but he tried not to show it.

'Well, I'm fine, but I can't really talk.'

'Well, what happened?'

'It's just a long story. I don't want to go through it now.'

Now she was quiet. It was one of those moments when both people try to read the silence, pick up each other's meanings in what they weren't saying.

'You know, don't you?'

'Why didn't you tell me, Jasmine?'

'I …'

More silence.

'Do you want me to tell you now?'

'I don't know …'

'What did he tell you?'

'Who?'

'Irving.'

'It wasn't from him. He doesn't know. It was somebody else. Somebody trying to hurt me.'

'It was a long time ago, Harry. I want to tell you what happened … but not on the phone.'

He closed his eyes and thought for a minute. Just hearing her voice had renewed his sense of connection to her. But he had to question whether he wanted to get into this.

'I don't know, Jazz. I've got to think about –'

'Look, what was I supposed to do? Wear a sign or something to warn you away from the start? You tell me, when was a good time for me to tell you? Was it right after that first lemonade? Should I have said, "Oh, by the way, six years ago I killed the man I was living with when he tried to rape me for the second time in the same night?" Would that have been proper?'

'Jazz, don't ...'

'Don't what? Look, the cops didn't believe my story here, what should I expect from you?'

He could tell she was crying now, not so that he was supposed to hear. But he could tell it in her voice, full of loneliness and pain.

'You said things to me,' she said. 'I thought ...'

'Jazz, we spent a weekend together. You're putting too much –'

'Don't you dare! Don't you tell me it didn't mean anything.'

'You're right. I'm sorry ... Look, this isn't the right time. I've got too much going on. I gotta call you back ...'

She didn't say anything.

'Okay?'

'Okay, Harry, you call me.'

'Okay, good-bye, Jazz.'

He hung up and kept his eyes closed for a while. He felt the numbness of disappointment that comes from broken hopes and wondered if he would ever talk to her again. In analyzing his thoughts he realized how much they seemed to be the same. And so his fear was not of what she had done, whatever the details were. His fear was that he would indeed call her and that he would become entwined with someone with more baggage than himself.

He opened his eyes and tried to put the thoughts aside. But he came back to her. He found himself marveling at the randomness of their meeting. A newspaper want ad. It might as well have said Single White Killer Seeks Same. He laughed out loud but it wasn't funny.

He turned the television on as a distraction. There was a talk show on and the host was interviewing women who

393

stole their best friends' men. The best friends were also on and every question devolved into a verbal cat fight. Bosch turned the sound down and watched for ten minutes in silence, studying the contortions of the women's angry faces.

After a while he turned it off and rang the nurses' station on the intercom to inquire about his cereal. The nurse he spoke to knew nothing about his request for breakfast at lunch time. He tried Meredith Roman's number again but hung up when he got the tape.

Just as Bosch was getting hungry enough to be tempted to call for the return of the Salisbury steak, a nurse finally came back in with another food tray. This one contained a banana, a small glass of orange juice, a plastic bowl with a little box of Frosted Flakes in it and a pint-size carton of milk. He thanked her and began eating the cereal out of the box. The other stuff he didn't want.

He picked up the phone and dialed the main number at Parker Center and asked for Assistant Chief Irving's office. The secretary who eventually answered said Irving was in conference with the police chief and could not be disturbed. Bosch left his number.

Next he dialed Keisha Russell's number at the paper.

'It's Bosch.'

'Bosch, where have you been? You turn your phone off?'

Bosch reached into his briefcase and took the phone out. He checked the battery.

'Sorry, it's dead.'

'Great. That doesn't help me any, does it? The two biggest names in that clip I gave you end up dead last night and you don't even call. Some deal we made.'

'Hey, this is me on the phone, right?'

'So what've you got for me?'

'What've you got already? What are they saying about it?'

'They're not saying jack. I've been waiting on you, man.'

'But what are they really saying?'

'I mean it, nothing. They're saying both deaths are being investigated and that there is no clear connection. They're trying to pass it off as a big coincidence.'

'What about the other man? Did they find Vaughn?'

'Who's Vaughn?'

Bosch couldn't figure out what was happening, why there was a cover-up. He knew he should wait to hear from Irving but the anger was growing in his throat.

'Bosch? You there? What other man?'

'What are they saying about me?'

'You? They're not saying anything.'

'The other man's name is Jonathan Vaughn. He was there, too. Up at Mittel's last night.'

'How do you know?'

'I was there, too.'

'Bosch, you were there?'

Bosch closed his eyes but his mind couldn't penetrate the shroud being thrown over the case by the department. He didn't get it.

'Harry, we had a deal. Tell me the story.'

He noted that it was the only time she had ever used his first name. He continued to say nothing while he tried to figure out what was happening and weighed the consequences of talking to her.

'Bosch?'

Back to normal.

'All right. You got your pencil? I'm going to give you enough to get started. You'll have to go to Irving to get the rest.'

'I've been calling him. He won't even take my calls.'

'He will when he knows you have the story. He'll have to.'

By the time he was done telling her the story he was fatigued and his head was hurting again. He was ready to go to sleep, if it would have him. He wanted to forget everything and just sleep.

'That's an incredible story, Bosch,' she said when he was done. 'I'm sorry, you know, about your mother.'

'Thanks.'

'What about Pounds?'

'What about him?'

'Is it connected? Irving was honchoing that investigation. Now he's doing this one.'

'You'll have to ask him.'

'If I can get him on the line.'

'When you call over there, tell the adjutant to tell Irving you're calling on behalf of Marjorie Lowe. He'll call you back when he gets the message. I guarantee it.'

'Okay, Bosch, last thing. We didn't talk about this at the start like we should have. Can I use your name as a source?'

Bosch thought about it but only for a few moments.

'Yeah, you can use it. I don't know what my name's worth anymore but you can use it.'

'Thanks. I'll see you. You're a pal.'

'Yeah, I'm a pal.'

He hung up and closed his eyes. He dozed off but wasn't sure for how long. He was interrupted by the phone. It was Irving and he was angry.

'What did you do?'

'What do you mean?'

'I just got a message from a reporter. She says she's calling because of Marjorie Lowe. Have you talked to reporters about this?'

'I talked to one.'

'What did you tell her?'

'I told her enough so that you won't be able to let this one blow away.'

'Bosch ...'

He didn't finish. There was a long silence and then Bosch spoke first.

'You were going to cover it all up, weren't you? Shove it in the trash with her. You see, after everything that's happened, she still doesn't count, does she?'

'You don't know what you're talking about.'

Bosch sat up. Now he was angry. Immediately, he was hit with vertigo. He closed his eyes until it passed.

'Well, then why don't you tell me what I don't know? Okay, Chief? You're the one who doesn't know what you're talking about. I heard what you people put out. That there may be no connection between Conklin and Mittel. What kind of – you think I'm going to sit here for that? And Vaughn. Not even a mention of him. A fucking mechanic in a splatter suit, he throws Conklin out the window and is ready to put me in the dirt. He's the one who did Pounds and he doesn't even rate a mention by you people. So, Chief, why don't you tell me what the fuck I don't know, okay?'

'Bosch, listen to me. *Listen* to me. Who did Mittel work for?'

'I don't know and I don't care.'

'He was employed by very powerful people. Some of the most powerful in this state, some of the most powerful in the country. And –'

'I don't give a shit!'

'– a majority of the city council.'

'So? What are you telling me? The council and the governor and the senators and all of those people, what, are they all involved now, too? You covering their asses, too?'

'Bosch, would you calm down and make sense? Listen to yourself. Of course, I'm not saying that. What I am trying to explain to you is that if you taint Mittel with this, then you taint many very powerful people who associated with him or who used his services. That could come back to haunt this department as well as you and me in immeasurable ways.'

That was it, Bosch saw. Irving the pragmatist had made a choice, probably along with the police chief, to put the department and themselves ahead of the truth. The whole deal stunk like rotting garbage. Bosch felt exhaustion roll over him like a wave. He was drowning in it. He'd had enough of this.

'And by covering it up, you are helping them in immeasurable ways, right? And I'm sure you and the chief have been on the phone all morning letting each of those powerful people know just that. They'll all owe you, they'll all owe the department a big one. That's great, Chief. That's a great deal. I guess it doesn't matter that the truth is nowhere to be found in it.'

'Bosch, I want you to call her back. Call that reporter and tell her that you took this knock on the head and you –'

'No! I'm not calling anybody back. It's too late. I told the story.'

'But not the whole story. The whole story is just as damaging to you, isn't it?'

There it was. Irving knew. He either outright knew or had made a pretty good guess that Bosch had used Pounds's name and was ultimately responsible for his death. That knowledge was now his weapon against Bosch.

'If I can't contain this,' Irving added, 'I may have to take action against you.'

'I don't care,' Bosch said quietly. 'You can do whatever

you want to me, but the story is coming out, Chief. The truth.'

'But is it the truth? The whole truth? I doubt it and deep in inside I know you doubt it, too. We'll never know the whole truth.'

A silence followed. Bosch waited for him to say more and when there was only more silence, he hung up. He then disconnected the phone and finally went to sleep.

❖ ❖ ❖ ❖ ❖ ❖ ❖

Bosch awoke at six the next morning with dim memories of his sleep having been interrupted by a horrible dinner and the visits of nurses through the night. His head felt thick. He gently touched the wound and found it not as tender as the day before. He got up and walked around the room a bit. His balance seemed back to normal. In the bathroom mirror his eyes were still a colorful mess but the dilation of the pupils had evened out. It was time to go, he knew. He got dressed and left the room, briefcase in hand and carrying his ruined jacket over his arm.

At the nurses' station he pushed the elevator button and waited. He noticed one of the nurses behind the counter eyeing him. She apparently didn't readily recognize him, especially with his street clothes on.

'Excuse me, can I help you?'

'No, I'm fine.'

'Are you a patient?'

'I was. I'm leaving. Room four-nineteen. Bosch.'

'Wait a moment, sir. What are you doing?'

'I'm leaving. Going home.'

'What?'

'Just send me the bill.'

The elevator doors opened and he stepped in.

'You can't do that,' the nurse called. 'Let me get the doctor.'

Bosch raised his hand and waved good-bye.

'Wait!'

The doors closed.

He bought a newspaper in the lobby and caught a cab outside. He told the driver to take him to Park La Brea. Along the way, he read Keisha Russell's story. It was on the front page and it was pretty much an abbreviated account of what he had told her the day before. Everything was qualified with the caveat that it was still under investigation, but it was a good read.

Bosch was mentioned throughout by name as a source and main player in the story. Irving was also a named source. Bosch figured the assistant chief must have decided in the end to throw in with the truth, or a close approximation of it, once Bosch had already let it out. It was the pragmatic thing to do. This way it seemed like he had a handle on things. He was the voice of conservative reason in the story. Bosch's statements were usually followed by those from Irving cautioning that the investigation was still in its infancy and no final conclusions had been made.

The part Bosch liked best about the story were the statements from several statesmen, including most of the city council, expressing shock both at the deaths of Mittel and Conklin and at their involvement in and/or cover-up of murders. The story also mentioned that Mittel's employee, Jonathan Vaughn, was being sought by police as a murder suspect.

The story was most tenuous in regard to Pounds. It contained no mention that Bosch was suspected or known to have used the lieutenant's name or that his using it had led to Pounds's death. The story simply quoted Irving as saying the connection between Pounds and the case was still under investigation but that it appeared that Pounds might have stumbled onto the same trail Bosch had been following.

Irving had held back when he talked to Russell even after threatening Bosch. Harry could only believe it was the assistant chief's desire not to see the department's dirty laundry in print. The truth would hurt Bosch but could damage the department as well. If Irving was going to make a move against him, Bosch knew it would be inside the department. It would remain private.

Bosch's rented Mustang was still in the La Brea Lifecare parking lot. He had been lucky; the keys were in the door lock where he had left them a moment before being attacked by Vaughn. He paid the driver and went to the Mustang.

Bosch decided to take a cruise up Mount Olympus before going to the Mark Twain. He plugged his phone into the cigarette lighter so it would recharge and headed up Laurel Canyon Boulevard.

On Hercules Drive, he slowed outside the gate in front of Mittel's grounded spaceship. The gate was closed and there was yellow police-line tape still hanging from it. Bosch saw no cars in the driveway. It was quiet and peaceful. And soon he knew that a FOR SALE sign would be erected and the next genius would move in and think he was master of all he surveyed.

Bosch drove on. Mittel's place wasn't what he really wanted to see, anyway.

Fifteen minutes later Bosch came around the familiar turn on Woodrow Wilson but immediately found things unfamiliar. His house was gone, its disappearance as glaring in the landscape as a tooth missing from a smile.

At the curb in front of his address were two huge construction waste bins filled with splintered wood, mangled metal and shattered glass, the debris of his home. A mobile storage container had also been placed at the curb and Bosch assumed – hoped – it contained the salvageable property removed before the house was razed.

He parked and walked over to the flagstone path that formerly had led to his front door. He looked down and all that was left were the six pylons that poked out of the hillside like tombstones. He could rebuild upon these. If he wanted.

Movement in the acacia trees near the footings of the pylons caught his eye. He saw a flash of brown and then the head of a coyote moving slowly through the brush. It never heard Bosch or looked up. Soon it was gone. Harry lost sight of it in the brush.

He spent another ten minutes there, smoking a cigarette and waiting, but he saw nothing else. He then said a silent good-bye to the place. He had the feeling he wouldn't be back.

When Bosch got to the Mark Twain, the city's morning was just starting. From his room he heard a garbage truck making its way down the alley, taking away another week's debris. It made him think of his house again, fitted nicely into two dumpsters.

Thankfully, the sound of a siren distracted him. He could identify it as a squad car as opposed to a fire engine. He knew he'd get a lot of that with the police station just down the street. He moved about his two rooms and felt restless and out of it, as if life was passing by while he was stuck here. He made coffee with the machine he had brought from home and it only served to make him more jittery.

He tried the paper again but there was nothing of real interest to him except the story he had already read on the front page. He paged through the thin Metro section anyway and saw a report that the county commission chambers were being outfitted with bulletproof desk blotters that the commissioners could hold up in front of them in the event a maniac came in spraying bullets. He threw the section aside and picked up the front section again.

Bosch reread the story about his investigation and couldn't escape a growing feeling that something was wrong, that something was left out or incomplete. Keisha Russell's reporting had been fine. That wasn't the problem. The problem was in seeing the story in words, in print. It didn't seem as convincing to him as it had been when he recounted it for her or for Irving or even for himself.

He put the newspaper aside, leaned back on the bed and closed his eyes. He went over the sequence of events once more and in doing so finally realized the problem that gnawed at him was not in the paper but in what Mittel had said to him. Bosch tried to recall the words exchanged between them on the manicured lawn behind the rich man's house. What had really been said there? What had Mittel admitted to?

Bosch knew that at that moment on the lawn, Mittel was in a position of seeming invulnerability. He had Bosch captured, wounded and doomed before him. His attack dog, Vaughn, stood ready with a gun to Bosch's back. In that situation, Bosch believed there would be no reason for a man of Mittel's ego to hold back. And, in fact, he had not held back. He had boasted of his scheme to control Conklin and others. He had freely, though indirectly, admitted that he had caused the deaths of Conklin and Pounds. But despite those admissions, he had not done the same when it came to the killing of Marjorie Lowe.

Through the fragmented images of that night, Bosch tried to recall the exact words said and couldn't quite get to them. His visual recollection was good. He had Mittel standing in front of the blanket of lights. But the words weren't there. Mittel's mouth moved but Bosch couldn't get the words. Then, finally, after working at it for a while, it came to him. He had it. Opportunity. Mittel had called her death an opportunity. Was that an acknowledgement of culpability? Was he saying he killed her or had her killed? Or was he simply admitting that her death presented an opportunity for him to take advantage of?

Bosch didn't know and not knowing felt like a heavy

weight in his chest. He tried to put it out of his mind and eventually started drifting off toward sleep. The sounds of the city outside, even the sirens, were comforting. He was at the threshold of unconsciousness, almost there, when he suddenly opened his eyes.

'The prints,' he said out loud.

Thirty minutes later he was shaved, showered and in fresh clothes heading downtown. He had his sunglasses on and he checked himself in the mirror. His battered eyes were hidden. He licked his fingers and pressed his curly hair down to better cover the shaved spot and the stitches in his scalp.

At County-USC Medical Center, he drove through the back lot to the parking slots nearest the rear garage bays of the Los Angeles County medical examiner's office. He walked in through one of the open garage doors and waved to the security guard, who knew him by sight and nodded back. Investigators weren't supposed to go in the back way but Bosch had been doing it for years. He wasn't going to stop until someone made a federal case out of it. The minimum-wage guard was an unlikely candidate to do that.

He went up to the investigators' lounge on the second floor, hoping not only that there would be someone there he knew but, more important, someone Bosch hadn't alienated over the years.

He swung the door open and immediately was hit with the smell of fresh coffee. But the room was bad news. Only Larry Sakai was in the room, sitting at a table with newspapers spread across it. He was a coroner's investigator Bosch had never really liked and the feeling was mutual.

'Harry Bosch,' Sakai said after looking up from the newspaper he held in his hands. 'Speak of the devil, I'm reading about you here. Says here you're in the hospital.'

'Nah, I'm here, Sakai. See me? Where's Hounchell and Lynch? Either of them around?'

Hounchell and Lynch were two investigators who Bosch knew would do him a favor without having to think about it too long. They were good people.

'Nah, they're out baggin' and taggin'. Busy morning. Guess things are picking up again.'

Bosch had heard a rumor through the grapevine that while removing victims from one of the collapsed apartment buildings after the earthquake, Sakai had gone in with his own camera and taken photos of people dead in their beds – the ceilings crushed down on top of them. He then sold the prints to the tabloid newspapers under a false name. That was the kind of guy he was.

'Anybody else around?'

'No, Bosch, jus' me. Whaddaya want?'

'Nothing.'

Bosch turned back to the door, then hesitated. He needed to make the print comparison and didn't want to wait. He looked back at Sakai.

'Look, Sakai, I need a favor. You want to help me out? I'll owe you one.'

Sakai leaned forward in his chair. Bosch could see just the point of a toothpick poking out between his lips.

'I don't know, Bosch, having you owe me one is like having the old whore with AIDS say she'll give me a free one if I pay for the first.'

Sakai laughed at the comparison he had created.

'Okay, fine.'

Bosch turned and pushed through the door, keeping his anger in check. He was two steps down the hall when he heard Sakai call him back. Just as he had hoped. He took a deep breath and went back into the lounge.

'Bosch, c'mon, I didn't say I wouldn't help you out.

407

Look, I read your story here and I feel for what you're going through, okay?'

Yeah, right, Bosch thought but didn't say.

'Okay,' he said.

'What do you need?'

'I need to get a set of prints off one of the customers in the cooler.'

'Which one?'

'Mittel.'

Sakai nodded toward the paper, which he had thrown back onto the table.

'That Mittel, huh?'

'Only one I know of.'

Sakai was quiet while he considered the request.

'You know, we make prints available to investigating officers assigned to homicides.'

'Cut the crap, Sakai. You know I know that and you know, if you read the paper, that I'm not the IO. But I still need the prints. You going to get them for me or am I just wasting my time here?'

Sakai stood up. Bosch knew that Sakai knew that if he backed down now after making the overture, then Bosch would gain a superior position in the netherworld of male interaction and in all their dealings that would follow. If Sakai followed through and got the prints, then the advantage would obviously go to him.

'Cool your jets, Bosch. I'm gonna get the prints. Why don't you get yourself a cup of coffee and sit down? Just put a quarter in the box.'

Bosch hated the idea of being beholden to Sakai for anything but he knew this was worth it. The prints were the one way he knew to end the case. Or tear it open again.

Bosch had a cup of coffee and in fifteen minutes the coroner's investigator was back. He was still waving the card so the ink would dry. He handed it to Bosch and went to the counter to get another cup of coffee.

'This is from Gordon Mittel, right?'

'Right. That's what it said on the toe tag. And, man, he got busted up pretty good in that fall.'

'Glad to hear it.'

'You know, it sounds to me like that story in the newspaper ain't as solid as you LAPD guys claim if you're sneaking around here gettin' the guy's prints.'

'It's solid, Sakai, don't worry about it. And I better not get any calls from any reporters about me picking up prints. Or I'll be back.'

'Don't give yourself a hernia, Bosch. Just take the prints and leave. Never met anybody who tried so hard to make the person doin' him a favor feel bad.'

Bosch dumped his coffee cup in a trash can and started out. At the door he stopped.

'Thanks.'

It burned him to say it. The guy was an asshole.

'Just remember, Bosch, you owe me.'

Bosch looked back at him. He was stirring cream into his cup. Bosch walked back, sticking his hand in his pocket. When he got to the counter he pulled out a quarter and dropped it into the slotted tin box that was the coffee fund.

'There, that's for you,' Bosch said. 'Now we're even.'

He walked out and in the hallway he heard Sakai call him an asshole. To Bosch that was a sign that all might be right in the world. His world, at least.

When Bosch got to Parker Center fifteen minutes later, he realized he had a problem. Irving had not returned his ID tag because it was part of the evidence recovered from Mittel's jacket in the hot tub. So Bosch loitered around the front of the building until he saw a group of detectives and administrative types walking toward the building from the

City Hall annex. When the group moved inside and around the entry counter, Bosch stepped up behind them and got by the duty officer without notice.

Bosch found Hirsch at his computer in the Latent Fingerprint Unit and asked him if he still had the Lifescan from the prints off the belt buckle.

'Yeah, I've been waiting for you to pick them up.'

'Well, I got a set I want you to check against them first.'

Hirsch looked at him but hesitated only a second.

'Let's see 'em.'

Bosch got the print card Sakai had made out of his briefcase and handed it over. Hirsch looked at it a moment, turning the card so it reflected the overhead light better.

'These are pretty clean. You don't need the machine, right? You just want to compare these to the prints you brought in before.'

'That's right.'

'Okay, I can eyeball it right now if you want to wait.'

'I want to wait.'

Hirsch got the Lifescan card out of his desk and took it and the coroner's card to the work counter, where he looked at them through a magnifying lamp. Bosch watched his eyes going back and forth between the prints as if he were watching a tennis ball go back and forth across a net.

Bosch realized as he watched Hirsch work that more than anything else in the world he wanted the print man to look up at him and say that the prints from the two cards in front of him matched. Bosch wanted this to be over. He wanted to put it away.

After five minutes of silence, the tennis match was over and Hirsch looked up at him and gave him the score.

✦ ✦ ✦ ✦ ✦ ✦ ✦

When Carmen Hinojos opened her waiting room door she seemed pleasantly surprised to see Bosch sitting on the couch.

'Harry! Are you all right? I didn't expect to see you here today.'

'Why not? It's my time, isn't it?'

'Yes, but I read in the paper you were at Cedars.'

'I checked out.'

'Are you sure you should have done that? You look …'

'Awful?'

'I didn't want to say that. Come in.'

She ushered him in and they took their usual places.

'I actually look better than I feel right now.'

'Why? What is it?'

'Because it was all for nothing.'

His statement put a confused look on her face.

'What do you mean? I read the story today. You solved the murders, including your mother's. I thought you'd be quite different than this.'

'Well, don't believe everything you read, Doctor. Let me clarify things for you. What I did on my so-called mission was cause two men to be murdered and another to die by my own hands. I solved, let's see, I solved one, two, three murders, so that's good. But I didn't solve the murder I set out to solve. In other words, I've been running around in circles causing people to die. So, how did you expect me to be during our session?'

'Have you been drinking?'

'I had a couple beers with lunch but it was a long lunch and I think that a minimum of two beers is required considering what I just told you. But I am not drunk, if that is what you want to know. And I'm not working, so what's the difference?'

'I thought we agreed to cut back on –'

'Oh, fuck that. This is the real world here. Isn't that what you called it? The real world? Between now and the last time we talked, I've killed someone, Doc. And you want to talk about cutting back on booze. Like it means anything anymore.'

Bosch took out his cigarettes and lit one. He kept the pack and the Bic on the arm of the chair. Carmen Hinojos watched him for a long time before speaking again.

'You're right. I'm sorry. Let's go to what I think is the heart of the problem. You said you didn't solve the murder you set out to solve. That, of course, is your mother's death. I am only going by what I read, but today's *Times* attributes her killing to Gordon Mittel. Are you telling me that you now know that to be incontrovertibly wrong?'

'Yes. I now know that to be incontrovertibly wrong.'

'How?'

'Simple. Fingerprints. I went down to the morgue, got Mittel's prints and had them compared to those on the murder weapon, the belt. No match. He didn't do it. Wasn't there. Now, I don't want you to get the wrong idea. I'm not sitting here with a guilty conscience over Mittel. He was a man who decided to kill people and then had them killed. Just like that. At least two times I'm sure of, then he was going to have me killed, too. So I say fuck him. He got what he had coming. But I'll carry Pounds and Conklin around with me for a long time. Maybe forever. And one way or another, I'll pay for it. It's just that it would make that weight easier to carry if there had been a reason. Any good reason. Know what I mean? But there isn't a reason. Not anymore.'

'I understand. I don't – I'm not sure how to proceed with this. Do you want to talk some about your feelings in regard to Pounds and Conklin?'

'Not really. I've thought about it enough already. Neither man was innocent. They did things. But they didn't have to die like they did. Especially Pounds. Jesus. I can't talk about it. I can't even think about it.'

'Then how will you go on?'

'I don't know. Like I said, I have to pay.'

'What is the department going to do, any idea?'

'I don't know. I don't care. It's bigger than the department to decide. I have to decide my penance.'

'Harry, what does that mean? That concerns me.'

'Don't worry, I'm not going to the closet. I'm not that type.'

'The closet?'

'I'm not going to stick a gun in my mouth.'

'Through what you've said here today, it is already clear you have accepted responsibility for what happened to these two men. You're facing it. In effect, you are denying denial. That is a foundation you can build on. I am concerned about this talk about penance. You have to go on, Harry. No matter what you do to yourself, it doesn't bring them back. So the best you can do is go on.'

He didn't say anything. He suddenly grew tired of all the advice, of her intervention in his life. He was feeling resentful and frustrated.

'Do you mind if we cut the session short today?' he asked. 'I'm not feeling so hot.'

'I understand. It's no problem. But I want you to

promise me something. Promise me we will talk again before you make any decisions.'

'You mean about my penance?'

'Yes, Harry.'

'Okay, we'll talk.'

He stood up and attempted a smile but it came out more like a frown. Then he remembered something.

'By the way, I apologize for not getting back to you the other night when you called. I was waiting on a call and couldn't talk and then I just kind of forgot. I hope you were just checking on me and it wasn't too important.'

'Don't worry about it. I forgot myself. I was just calling to see how you made it through the rest of the afternoon with Chief Irving. I also wanted to see if you wanted to talk about the photos. It doesn't matter now.'

'You looked at them?'

'Yes. I had a couple of comments but –'

'Let's hear them.'

Bosch sat back down. She looked at him, weighing his suggestion, and decided to go ahead.

'I have them here.'

She bent down to get the envelope out of one of the lower drawers of the desk. She almost disappeared from Bosch's view. Then she was up and placed the envelope on the desk.

'I guess you should take these back.'

'Irving took the murder book and the evidence box. He's got it all now except for those.'

'You sound like you're unhappy about that, or that you don't trust him with it. That's a change.'

'Aren't you the one who said I don't trust anyone?'

'Why don't you trust him?'

'I don't know. I just lost my suspect. Gordon Mittel's clear and I'm starting from ground zero. I was just thinking about the percentages ...'

'And?'

'Well, I don't know the numbers but a significant number of homicides are reported by the actual doer. You know, the husband who calls up crying, saying his wife is missing. More often than not, he's just a bad actor. He killed her and thinks calling the cops helps convince everybody he's clean. Look at the Menendez brothers. One of 'em calls up boohooing about mom and dad being dead. Turns out he and the brother were the ones who shotgunned them. There was a case up in the hills a few years back. This little girl was missing. It was Laurel Canyon. It made the papers, TV. So the people up there organized search parties and all of that and a few days later one of the searchers, a teen-aged boy who was one of the girl's neighbors, found her body under a log near Lookout Mountain. It turned out he was the killer. I got him to confess in fifteen minutes. The whole time of the search I was just waiting for the one who would find the body. It was percentages. He was a suspect before I even knew who it was.'

'Irving found your mother's body.'

'Yes. And he knew her before that. He told me once.'

'It seems like a stretch to me.'

'Yeah. Most people probably thought that about Mittel, too. Right up until they fished him out of the hot tub.'

'Isn't there an alternative scenario? Isn't it possible that maybe the original detectives were correct in their assumption back then that there was a sex killer out there and that tracking him was hopeless?'

'There's always alternative scenarios.'

'But you always seem drawn toward finding someone of power, a person of the establishment, to blame. Maybe that's not the case here. Maybe it's a symptom of your larger desire to blame society for what happened to your mother … and to you.'

Bosch shook his head. He didn't want to hear this.

'You know, all this psychobabble … I don't … Can we just talk about the photos?'

'I'm sorry.'

She looked down at the envelope as if she was seeing right through it to the photos inside it.

'Well, it was very difficult for me to look at them. As far as their forensic value goes, there wasn't a lot there. The photos show what I would call a statement homicide. The fact that the ligature, the belt, was still wrapped around her neck seems to indicate that the killer wanted police to know exactly what he did, that he had been deliberate, that he had had control over this victim. I also think the choice of placement is significant as well. The trash bin had no top. It was open. That suggests that placing the body there may not have been an effort to hide it. It was also a –'

'He was saying she was trash.'

'Right. Again, a statement. If he was just getting rid of a body, he could've put it anywhere in that alley, but he chose the open dumpster. Subconsciously or not, he was making a statement about her. So to make a statement such as that about a person, he would have to have known her to some degree. Known about her. Known she was a prostitute. Known enough to judge her.'

Irving came to Bosch's mind again but he said nothing.

'Well,' he said instead, 'couldn't it have been a statement about all women? Could it be some sick fuck who – excuse me – some nut who hated all women and thought all women were trash? That way he wouldn't have to have known her. Maybe somebody who simply wanted to kill a prostitute, any prostitute, to make a statement about them.'

'Yes, that's a possibility, but like you I'm going with the percentages. The kind of sick fuck you are talking about –

which, incidentally, in psychobabble we call a sociopath – is much rarer than the one who keys on specific targets, specific women.'

Bosch shook his head dismissively and looked out the window.

'What is it?'

'It's just frustrating, that's all. There wasn't much in the murder book about them taking a hard look at anybody in her circle, any of the neighbors, nothing like that. To do it now is impossible. It makes me feel like it's hopeless.'

He thought of Meredith Roman. He could go to her to ask about his mother's acquaintances and customers, but he didn't know if he had the right to reawaken that part of her life.

'You have to remember,' Hinojos said, 'in 1961 a case like this would probably have seemed impossible to solve. They wouldn't even have known how to start. It just didn't happen as often as today.'

'They're almost impossible to solve today, too.'

They sat in silence for a few moments. Bosch thought about the possibility that the killer was some hit-and-run nut. A serial killer who was long gone into the darkness of time. If that was the case, then his private investigation was over. It was a failure.

'Do you have anything else on the photos?'

'That's really all I had – no, wait. There was one thing. And you may already have this.'

She picked the envelope up and opened it. She reached in and began sliding out a photo.

'I don't want to look at that,' Bosch said quickly.

'It's not a photo of her. Actually, it's her clothing, laid out on a table. Is that okay to look at?'

She paused, her hand holding the photo half in and half out of the envelope. Bosch waved his hand, telling her to go ahead.

'I've already seen the clothes.'

'Then you've probably already considered this.'

She slid the photo to the edge of the desk and Bosch leaned forward to study it. It was a color photo that had yellowed with age, even inside the envelope. The same items of clothing he had found in the evidence box were spread out on a table in a formation that outlined a body, in the way a woman might put them out on a bed before dressing. It reminded Bosch of cutouts for paper dolls. Even the belt with the sea shell buckle was there, but it was between the blouse and the black skirt, not at the imaginary neck.

'Okay,' she said. 'What I found odd here was the belt.'

'The murder weapon.'

'Yes. Look, it has the large silver shell as the buckle and there are smaller silver shells as ornamentation. It's rather showy.'

'Right.'

'But the buttons on the blouse are gold. Also, the photos of the body, they show she was wearing gold teardrop earrings and a gold neck chain. Also a bracelet.'

'Right, I know that. They were in the evidence box, too.'

Bosch didn't understand what she was getting at.

'Harry, this is not a universal rule or anything, that's why I hesitate to bring it up. But usually people – women – don't mix and match gold and silver. And it appears to me your mother was well dressed on this evening. That she had jewelry on that matched the buttons of her blouse. She was coordinated and she had style. What I am saying is that I don't think she would have worn this belt with those other items. It was silver and it was showy.'

Bosch said nothing. Something was poking its way into his mind and its point was sharp.

'And lastly, this skirt buttons on the hip. It's a style that is still around and I even have something similar to it myself. What's so functional about it is that because of the wide waistband it can be worn with or without a belt. There are no loops.'

Bosch stared at the photo.

'No loops.'

'Right.'

'So what you're saying is ...'

'This might not have been her belt. It might have –'

'But it was. I remember it. The sea shell belt. I gave it to her for her birthday. I identified it for the cops, for McKittrick the day he came to tell me.'

'Well ... then that shoots down everything I was going to say. I guess maybe when she came into the apartment the killer was already waiting with it.'

'No, it didn't happen in her apartment. They never found the crime scene. Listen, never mind whether it was her belt or not, what were you going to say?'

'Oh, I don't know, just a theory about it possibly being the property of another woman who may have been the motivating factor behind the killer's action. It's called aggression transference. It doesn't make sense now with this evidence but there are examples of what I was going to suggest. A man takes his ex-girlfriend's stockings and strangles another woman with them. In his mind, he's strangling the girlfriend. Something like that. I was going to suggest it could have happened in this case with the belt.'

But Bosch was no longer listening. He turned and looked out the window but wasn't seeing anything either. In his mind, he was seeing the pieces falling together. The silver and gold, the belt with two of the punch holes worn, two friends as close as sisters. One for both and both for one.

But then one was leaving the life. She'd found a white knight.

And one was staying behind.

'Harry, are you okay?'

He looked over at Hinojos.

'You just did it. I think.'

'Did what?'

He reached for his briefcase and from it withdrew the photo taken at the St Patrick's Day dance more than three decades before. He knew it was a long shot but he needed to check. This time he didn't look at his mother. He looked at Meredith Roman, standing behind the sitting Johnny Fox. And for the first time he saw that she wore the belt with the silver sea shell buckle. She had borrowed it.

It dawned on him then. She had helped Harry pick the belt out for his mother. She had coached him and she chose it not because his mother would like it but because she liked it and knew she would get to use it. Two friends who shared everything.

Bosch shoved the photo back into the briefcase and shut it. He stood up.

'I gotta go.'

✦ ✦ ✦ ✦ ✦ ✦ ✦

Bosch used the same ruse he had earlier to get back into Parker Center. Coming out of the elevator on the fourth floor, he practically ran into Hirsch, who was waiting to go down. He grabbed hold of the young print tech's arm and held him in the hallway as the elevator doors closed.

'You going home?'

'I was trying to.'

'I need one more favor. I'll buy you lunch, I'll buy you dinner, I'll buy you whatever you want if you do it for me. It's important and it won't take long.'

Hirsch looked at him. Bosch could see he was beginning to wish he'd never gotten involved.

'What's that saying, Hirsch? "In for a penny, in for a pound." Whaddaya say?'

'I've never heard it.'

'Well, I have.'

'I'm having dinner with my girlfriend tonight and I –'

'That's great. This won't take that long. You'll make it to your dinner.'

'All right. What is it you need?'

'Hirsch, you're my goddamn hero, you know that?'

Bosch doubted he even had a girlfriend. They went back to the lab. It was deserted, since it was almost five on a slow day. Bosch put his briefcase on one of the abandoned desks and opened it. He found the Christmas card and took it out by holding a corner between two fingernails. He held it up for Hirsch to see.

'This came in the mail five years ago. You think you can pull a print off it? A print from the sender? My prints are going to be on there, too, I'm sure.'

Hirsch furrowed his brow and studied the card. His lower lip jutted outward as he contemplated the challenge.

'All I can do is try. Prints on paper are usually pretty stable. The oils last long and sometimes leave ridge patterns in the paper even when they evaporate. Has it been in its envelope?'

'Yeah, for five years, until last week.'

'That helps.'

Hirsch carefully took the card from Bosch and walked over to the work counter, where he opened the card and clipped it to a board.

'I'm going to try the inside. It's always better. Less chance of you having touched it inside. And the writer always touches the inside. Is it all right if this gets kind of ruined?'

'Do what you have to do.'

Hirsch studied the card with a magnifying glass, then lightly blew over the surface. He reached to a rack of spray bottles over the work table and took down one marked NINHYDRIN. He sprayed a light mist over the surface of the card and in a few minutes it began to turn purple around the edges. Then light shapes began to bloom like flowers on the card. Fingerprints.

'I've got to bring this out some,' Hirsch said, more to himself than Bosch.

Hirsch looked up at the rack and his eyes followed the row of chemical reagents until he found what he was looking for. A spray bottle marked ZINC CHLORIDE. He sprayed it on the card.

'This should bring the storm clouds in.'

422

The prints turned the deep purple shade of heavy rain clouds. Hirsch then took down a bottle labeled PD, which Bosch knew meant physical developer. After the card was misted with PD, the prints turned a grayish black and were more defined. Hirsch looked them over with his magnifying lamp.

'I think this is good enough. We won't need the laser. Now, look at these here, Detective.'

Hirsch pointed to a print that appeared to have been left by a thumb on the left side of Meredith Roman's signature and two smaller finger marks above it.

'These look like marks left by someone trying to hold the card steady while it was being written on. Any chance that you might've touched it this way?'

Hirsch held his fingers in place an inch over the card in the same position that the hand that left the prints would have been in. Bosch shook his head.

'All I ever did was open it and read it. I think those are the prints we want.'

'Okay. Now what?'

Bosch went to his briefcase and pulled out the print cards Hirsch had returned to him earlier in the day. He found the card containing the lifts from the belt with the sea shell buckle.

'Here,' he said. 'Compare this to what you got on the Christmas card.'

'You got it.'

Hirsch pulled the magnifying glass with the ringed light attachment in front of him and once again began his tennis match eye movement as he compared the prints.

Bosch tried to envision what had happened. Marjorie Lowe was going to Las Vegas to get married to Arno Conklin. The very thought of it must have been absurdly wonderful to her. She had to go home and pack. The plan was to drive through the night. If Arno was planning to bring along a best man, perhaps Marjorie was to bring a maid of honor. Maybe she would have gone upstairs to ask Meredith to come. Or maybe she would have gone to to her to borrow back the belt that her son had given her. Maybe she would have gone to say good-bye.

But something happened when she got there. And on her happiest night Meredith killed her.

Bosch thought about the interview reports that had been in the murder book. Meredith told Eno and McKittrick that Marjorie's date on the night she died had been arranged by Johnny Fox. But she didn't go to the party herself because she said Fox had beaten her the night before and she was not presentable. The detectives noted in the report that she had a bruise on her face and a split lip.

Why didn't they see it then, Bosch wondered. Meredith had sustained those injuries while killing Marjorie. The drop of blood on Marjorie's blouse had come from Meredith.

But Bosch knew why they hadn't seen it. He knew the investigators dismissed any thought in that direction, if they ever even had any, because she was a woman. And because Fox backed her story. He admitted he beat her.

Bosch now saw what he believed was the truth. Meredith killed Marjorie and then hours later called Fox at his card game to give him the news. She asked him to help her get rid of the body and hide her involvement.

Fox must have readily agreed, even to the point of his willingness to say he beat her, because he saw the larger picture. He lost a source of income when Marjorie was killed but that would have been tempered by the increased leverage the murder would give him over Conklin and Mittel. Keeping it unsolved would make it even better. He'd always be a threat to them. He could walk into the police station at any time to tell what he knew and lay it on Conklin.

What Fox didn't realize was that Mittel could be as cunning and vicious as he was. He learned that a year later on La Brea Boulevard.

Fox's motivation was clear. Bosch still wasn't sure about Meredith's. Could she have done it for the reasons Bosch had set out in his mind? Would the abandonment of a friend have led to the rage of murder? He began to believe there was still something left out. He still didn't know it all. The last secret was with Meredith Roman and he would have to go get it.

An odd thought pushed through these questions to Bosch. The time of death of Marjorie Lowe was about midnight. Fox didn't get his call and leave his card game until roughly four hours later. Bosch now assumed that the murder scene was Meredith's apartment. Now he wondered, what did she do in that place for four hours with the body of her best friend lying there?

'Detective?'

Bosch looked away from his thoughts to Hirsch, who was sitting at the desk nodding his head.

'You got something?'

'Bingo.'

Bosch just nodded.

It was confirmation of more than just the match of fingerprints. He knew it was a confirmation that all the things he had accepted as the truths of his life could be as false as Meredith Roman.

The sky was the color of a ninhydrin bloom on white paper. It was cloudless and growing dark purple with the aging of dusk. Bosch thought of the sunsets he had told Jazz about and realized that even that was a lie. Everything was a lie.

He stopped the Mustang at the curb in front of Katherine Register's home. There was another lie. The woman who lived here was Meredith Roman. Changing her name didn't change what she had done, didn't change her from guilty to innocent.

There were no lights on that he could see from the street, no sign of life. He was prepared to wait but didn't want to deal with the thoughts that would intrude as he sat alone in the car. He got out, crossed the lawn to the front porch and knocked on the door.

While he waited, he got out a cigarette and was lighting it when he suddenly stopped. He realized that what he was doing was his reflex of smoking at death scenes where the bodies were old. His instincts had reacted before he had consciously registered the odor from the house. Outside the door it was barely noticeable, but it was there. He looked back out to the street and saw no one. He looked back at the door and tried the knob. It turned. As he opened it, he felt a rush of cool air and the odor came out to meet him.

The house was still, the only sound the hum of the air

426

conditioner in the window of her bedroom. That was where he found her. He could tell right away that Meredith Roman had been dead for several days. Her body was in the bed, the covers pulled up to her head on the pillow. Only her face, what was left of it, was visible. Bosch's eyes did not linger on the image. The deterioration had been extensive and he guessed that maybe she had been dead since the day he had visited.

On the table next to the bed were two empty glasses, a half-gone fifth of vodka and an empty bottle of prescription pills. Bosch bent down to read the label and saw the prescription was for Katherine Register, one each night before bed. Sleeping pills.

Meredith had faced her past and administered her own penance. She had taken the blue canoe. Suicide. Bosch knew it wasn't for him to decide but it looked that way. He turned to the bureau because he remembered the Kleenex box and he wanted to use a tissue to cover his tracks. But there on the top, near the photos in gilded frames, was an envelope that had his name on it.

He picked it up, took some tissues and left the room. In the living room, a bit farther away from the source of the horrible odor but not far enough, he turned the envelope over to open it and noticed the flap was torn. The envelope had been opened already. He guessed maybe Meredith had reopened it to read again what she had written. Maybe she'd had second thoughts about what she was doing. He dismissed the question and took the note out. It was dated a week earlier. Wednesday. She had written it the day after his visit.

Dear Harry,
If you are reading this then my fears that you would learn the truth were well founded. If you are reading this then the decision I have made tonight was the correct one and I have no regrets as I make it. You

see, I would rather face the judgment of afterlife than have you look at me while knowing the truth.

I know what I have taken from you. I have known all my life. It does no good to say I am sorry or to try to explain. But it still amazes me how one's life can change forever in a few moments of uncontrolled rage. I was angry at Marjorie when she came to me that night so full of hope and happiness. She was leaving me. For a life with you. With him. For a life we had only dreamed was possible.

What is jealousy but a reflection of your own failures? I was jealous and angry and I struck at her. I then made a feeble effort to cover what I had done. I am sorry, Harry, but I took her from you and with that took any chance you ever had. I've carried the guilt every day since then and I take it with me now. I should have paid for my sin a long time ago but someone convinced me otherwise and helped me get away. There is no one left to convince me now.

I don't ask for your forgiveness, Harry. That would be an insult. I guess all I want is for you to know my regrets and to know that sometimes people who get away don't really get away. I didn't. Not then, not now. Good-bye.

Meredith

Bosch reread the note and then stood there thinking about it for a long time. Finally, he folded it and put it back in its envelope. He walked over to the fireplace, lit the envelope on fire with his Bic and then tossed it onto the grate. He watched the paper bend and burn until it bloomed like a black rose and went out.

He went to the kitchen and lifted the receiver off the phone after wrapping his hand in tissue. He put it on the counter and dialed nine-one-one. As he walked toward the front door, he could hear the tiny voice of the Santa

Monica police operator asking who was there and what the problem was.

He left the door unlocked and wiped the exterior knob with the tissue after stepping out onto the porch. He heard a voice from behind him.

'She writes a good letter, don't she?'

Bosch turned around. Vaughn was sitting on the rattan love seat on the porch. He was holding a new twenty-two in his hand. It looked like another Beretta. He looked none the worse for wear. He didn't have the black eyes that Bosch had, or the stitches.

'Vaughn.'

Bosch couldn't think of anything else to say. He couldn't imagine how he had been found by him. Could Vaughn have been daring enough to hang around Parker Center and follow Bosch from there? Bosch looked out into the street and wondered how long it would take the police operator to dispatch a car to the address the computer gave her for the 911 call. Even though Bosch had said nothing on the line, he knew they would eventually send a car to check it out. He had wanted them to find Meredith. If they took their time about it, they would probably find him as well. He had to stall Vaughn for as long as possible.

'Yeah, nice note,' the man with the gun said. 'But she left something out, don't you think?'

'What's left out?'

Vaughn seemed not to have heard him.

'It's funny,' he said. 'I knew your mother had a kid. But I never met you, never even saw you. She kept you away from me. I wasn't good enough, I guess.'

Bosch continued to stare as things began to fall together.

'Johnny Fox.'

'In the flesh.'

'I don't understand. Mittel ...'

'Mittel had me killed? No, not really. I killed myself, I guess you could say. I read that story you people put in the paper today. But you had it wrong. Most of it, at least.'

Bosch nodded. He knew now.

'Meredith killed your mother, kid. Sorry about that. I just helped her take care of it after the fact.'

'And then you used her death to get to Conklin.'

Bosch didn't need any confirmation from Fox. He was just trying to chew up time.

'Yeah, that was the plan, to get to Conklin. Worked pretty good, too. Got me out of the sewer. Only I found out pretty fast that the real power was Mittel. I could tell. Between the two of them, Mittel could go the distance. So I threw in with him, you could say. He wanted a better hold on the golden boy. He wanted an ace up his own sleeve. So I helped.'

'By killing yourself? I don't get it.'

'Mittel told me that supreme power over someone is the power they don't know you have until you need to use it. You see, Bosch, Mittel always suspected that Conklin was really the one who did your mother.'

Bosch nodded. He saw where the story was going.

'And you never told Mittel that Conklin wasn't the killer.'

'That's right. I never told him about Meredith. So knowing that, look at it from his side. Mittel figured that if Conklin was the doer and he believed I was dead, then he'd think he was home free. See, I was the only loose end, the one who could tie him in. Mittel wanted him to think he was clear. He wanted it because he wanted Conklin at ease. He didn't want him to lose his drive, his ambition. Conklin was going places and Mittel didn't want him to even hesitate. But he also wanted to keep an ace up his sleeve, something that he could always pull out if Conklin tried to step out of line. That was me. I was the ace. So we arranged that little hit and run, me and Mittel. Thing is, Mittel never had to play the ace with Conklin. Conklin gave Mittel a lot of good years after that. By the time he backed out on that attorney general thing, Mittel was well diversified. By then he had a congressman, a senator, a quarter of the local pols on his client list. You could say by then he had already climbed on Conklin's shoulders to the higher ground. He didn't need Arno anymore.'

Bosch nodded again and thought a moment about the scenario. All those years. Conklin believed it had been Mittel who killed her and Mittel believed it had been Conklin. It was neither.

'So who was the one you ran over?'

'Oh, just somebody. It doesn't matter. He was just a volunteer, you could say. I picked him up on Mission Street. He thought he was handing out Conklin fliers. I planted my ID in the bottom of the satchel I gave him. He never knew what hit him or why.'

'How'd you get away with it?' Bosch asked, though he thought he already knew the answer to that as well.

'Mittel had Eno on the line. We set it up so that it happened when he was next up on call. He took care of everything and Mittel took care of him.'

Bosch could see that the setup also gave Fox a share of power over Mittel. And he'd ridden along with him ever since. A little plastic surgery, a nicer set of clothes, and he was Jonathan Vaughn, aid to the wunderkind political strategist and rainmaker.

'So how'd you know I'd show up here?'

'I'd kept tabs on her over the years. I knew she was here. Alone. After our little run-in on the hill the other night, I came here to hide, to sleep. You gave me a headache – what the hell you hit me with?'

'The eight ball.'

'I guess I should have thought of that when I put you in there. Anyway, I found her like that in the bed. I read the note and knew who you were. I figured you'd be back. Especially after you left that message on the phone yesterday.'

'You've been here all this time with ...'

'You get used to it. I put the air on high, closed the door. You get used to it.'

Bosch tried to imagine it. Sometimes he believed that he was used to the smell, but he knew he wasn't.

'What did she leave out of the note, Fox?'

'That was the part about her wanting Conklin for herself. See, I tried her with Conklin first. But it didn't take. Then I set him up with Marjorie and got the fireworks. Nobody expected that he'd want to end up marrying her, though. Least of all Meredith. There was only room on the horse with the white knight for one rider. That was Marjorie. Meredith couldn't handle that. Must've been a hell of a cat fight.'

Bosch said nothing. But the truth stung his face like a sunburn. That's what it had all come down to, a cat fight between whores.

'Let's go to your car now,' Fox said.

'Why?'

'We need to go to your place now.'

'For what?'

Fox never answered. A Santa Monica squad car stopped in front of the house just as Bosch asked his question. Two officers started getting out.

'Be cool, Bosch,' Fox said quietly. 'Be cool if you want to live a little longer.'

Bosch saw Fox turn the aim of his gun toward the approaching officers. They could not see it because of the thick bougainvillea running along the front of the porch. One of them started to speak.

'Did someone here call nine –'

Bosch took two steps and launched himself over the railing to the lawn. As he did it, he yelled a warning.

'He's got a gun! He's got a gun!'

On the ground, Bosch heard Fox start running on the wood decking of the porch. He guessed he was going for the door. Then came the first shot. He was sure it came from behind him, from Fox. Then the two cops opened up like the Fourth of July. Bosch couldn't count all the shots. He stayed on the grass with his arms spread wide and his hands up, just hoping they wouldn't send one his way.

It was over in no more than eight seconds. When the echoes died and silence returned, Bosch yelled again.

'I'm unarmed! I'm a police officer! I am no threat to you! I am an unarmed police officer!'

He felt the end of a hot gun barrel pressed against his neck.

'Where's the ID?'

'Right inside coat pocket.'

Then he remembered he still didn't have it. The cop's hands grasped him by the shoulders.

'I'm going to roll you over.'

'Wait a minute. I don't have it.'

'What is this? Roll over.'

Bosch complied.

'I don't have it with me. I've got other ID though. Left inside pocket.'

The cop started going through his jacket. Bosch was scared.

'I'm not going to do anything wrong here.'

'Just be quiet.'

The cop got Bosch's wallet out and looked at the driver's license that was behind a clear plastic window.

'Whaddaya got, Jimmy?' the other cop yelled. Bosch couldn't see him. 'He legit?'

433

'Says he's a cop, got no badge. Got a DL here.'

Then he hunched back down over Bosch and patted the rest of his body in a search for weapons.

'I'm clean.'

'All right, turn back over.'

Bosch did so and his hands were cuffed behind his back. He then heard the man above him call in for backup and an ambulance on his radio.

'All right, get up.'

Bosch did as he was told. For the first time he could see the porch. The other cop stood with his handgun pointing down at Fox's crumpled body at the front door. Bosch was led up the steps to the porch. He could see Fox was still alive. His chest was heaving, he had wounds in both legs and the stomach and it looked like one slug had gone through both cheeks. His jaw hung open. But his eyes seemed even wider as he stared at death coming for him.

'I knew you'd fire, you fuck,' Bosch said to him. 'Just die now.'

'Shut up,' the one called Jimmy ordered. 'Right now.'

The other cop pulled him away from the front door. Out in the street, Bosch could see neighbors joining together in little knots or watching from their own porches. Nothing like gunshots in suburbia for getting people together, he thought. The smell of spent gunpowder in the air does it better than a barbecue any day.

The young cop got right up in Bosch's face. Harry could see that his name plate identified him as D. Sparks.

'Okay, what the fuck's going on here? If you're a cop, tell us what's going on.'

'You two are a couple of heroes, that's what's going on.'

'Tell the story, man. I don't have time for bullshit.'

Bosch could hear approaching sirens now.

'My name's Bosch. I'm with LAPD. This man you shot is the suspect in the killing of Arno Conklin, the former

434

district attorney of this county, and LAPD Lieutenant Harvey Pounds. I'm sure you've heard about these cases.'

'Jim, you hear that?' He turned back to Bosch. 'Where's your badge?'

'Stolen. I can give you a number to call. Assistant Chief Irvin Irving. He'll tell you about me.'

'Never mind that. What's he doing here?'

He pointed to Fox.

'He told me he was hiding out. Earlier today I got a call to come to this address and he was here waiting to ambush me. See, I could identify him. He had to take me out.'

The cop looked down at Fox wondering if he should believe such an incredible story.

'You got here right in time,' Bosch said. 'He was going to kill me.'

D. Sparks nodded. He was beginning to like the sound of this story. Then concern creased his brow.

'Who called 911?' he asked.

'I did,' Bosch said. 'I came here, found the door open and went in. I was calling 911 when he got the jump on me. I just dropped the phone because I knew you people would come.'

'Why call 911 if he hadn't grabbed you yet?'

'Because of what's in the back bedroom.'

'What?'

'There's a woman in the bed. She looks like she's been dead about a week.'

'Who is she?'

Bosch looked at the young cop's face.

'I don't know.'

❖ ❖ ❖ ❖ ❖ ❖ ❖

'W hy didn't you reveal that you knew she was your mother's killer? Why did you lie?'

'I don't know. I haven't figured it out. It's just that there was something about what she wrote and what she did at the end that ... I don't know, I just felt like that was enough. I just wanted to let it go.'

Carmen Hinojos nodded her head as if she understood but Bosch wasn't sure he did himself.

'I think that's a good decision, Harry.'

'You do? I don't think anybody else would think it was a good decision.'

'I'm not talking about on a procedural or criminal justice level. I'm just talking about on a human level. I think you did the right thing. For yourself.'

'I guess ...'

'Do you feel good about it?'

'Not really ... You were right, you know.'

'I was? About what?'

'About what you said about me finding out who did it. You warned me. Said it might do me more harm than good. Well, that was an understatement ... Some mission I gave myself, right?'

'I'm sorry if I was right. But as I said in the last session, the deaths of those men can't be –'

'I'm not talking about them anymore. I'm talking about something else. You see, I know now that my mother was

436

trying to save me from that place I was at. Like she had promised me that day out by the fence that I told you about. I think that whether she loved Conklin or not, she was thinking of me. She had to get me out and he was the way to do it. So, ultimately, you see, it was because of me that she died.'

'Oh, please, don't tell yourself that, Harry. That's ridiculous.'

Bosch knew that the anger in her voice was real.

'If you are going to take that form of logic,' she continued, 'you can come up with any reason why she was killed, you can argue that your own birth set circumstances in motion that led to her death. You see how silly that is?'

'Not really.'

'It's the same argument you made the other day about people not taking responsibility. Well, the inverse of that is people who take too much responsibility. And you are becoming one of them. Let that go, Harry. Let it go. Let someone else take some responsibility for some things. Even if that someone else is dead. Being dead does not absolve them of everything.'

He was cowed by the forcefulness of her admonition. He just looked at her for a long moment. He could tell her outburst would signal a natural break in the session. The discussion of his guilt was done. She had ended it and he had his instructions.

'I'm sorry to have raised my voice.'

'No problem.'

'Harry, what do you hear from the department?'

'Nothing. I'm waiting on Irving.'

'What do you mean?'

'He kept my ... culpability out of the paper. Now it's his move. He's either going to come at me with IAD – if he can make a case against me impersonating Pounds – or he's going to let it go. I'm betting he's going to let it go.'

437

'Why?'

'The one thing about the LAPD is that it is not into self-flagellation. Know what I mean? This case is very public and if they do something to me, they know there's always the danger it will get out and it will be one more black eye for the department. Irving sees himself as the protector of the department's image. He'll put that ahead of taking me down. Besides, he'll have leverage on me now. I mean, he thinks he will.'

'You seem to know Irving and the department well.'

'Why?'

'Chief Irving called me this morning and asked me to forward a positive RTD evaluation to his office as soon as possible.'

'He said that? He wants a positive return-to-duty report?'

'Yes, those were his words. Do you think you are ready for that?'

He thought a few moments but didn't answer the question.

'Has he done that before? Told you how to evaluate somebody?'

'No. It's a first time and I'm very concerned about it. It undermines my position here if I simply accede to his wishes. It's quite a dilemma because I don't want you caught in the middle.'

'What if he didn't tell you which way to go, what would your evaluation be? Positive or negative?'

She played with a pencil on the desktop for a few moments while considering the question.

'It's very close, Harry, but I think you need more time.'

'Then don't do it. Don't give in to him.'

'That's quite a change. Only a week ago all you could talk about was getting back to the job.'

'That was a week ago.'

There was a palpable sadness in his voice.

'Stop beating yourself to death with it,' she said. 'The past is like a club and you can only hit yourself in the head with it so many times before there is serious and permanent damage. I think you're at your limit. For what it's worth, I think you are a good and clean and ultimately kind man. Don't do this to yourself. Don't ruin what you have, what you are, with this kind of thinking.'

He nodded as if he understood but he had dismissed her words as soon as he heard them.

'I've been doing a lot of thinking the last couple of days.'

'About what?'

'Everything.'

'Any decisions on anything?'

'Almost. I think I'm going to pull the pin, leave the department.'

She leaned forward and folded her arms on the desk. A serious look creased her brow.

'Harry, what are you talking about? This is not like you. Your job and your life are the same. I think it's good to have some distance but not total separation. I –' She stopped when she seemed to come upon an idea. 'Is this your idea of penance, of making up for what happened?'

'I don't know … I just … For what I did, something has to be paid. That's all. Irving's not going to do anything. I will.'

'Harry, you made a mistake. A serious mistake, yes. But for that you are giving up your career, the one thing that even you readily admit you do well? You're going to throw it all away?'

He nodded.

'Did you pull the papers yet?'

'Not yet.'

'Don't do it.'

'Why not? I can't do this anymore. It's like I'm walking around handcuffed to a chain of ghosts.'

He shook his head. They were having the same debate that he had been having in his mind for the last two days, since the night at Meredith Roman's house.

'Give it some time,' Hinojos said. 'All I'm saying is, think about it. You're on paid leave now. Use it. Use the time. I'll tell Irving he's not getting an RTD from me yet. Meantime, you just give it some time and think hard on it. Go away somewhere, sit on the beach. But think about it before you turn in your papers.'

Bosch raised his hands in surrender.

'Please, Harry. I want to hear you say it.'

'All right. I'll do some more thinking.'

'Thank you.'

She let some silence underline his agreement.

'Remember what you said about seeing the coyote on the street last week?' she asked quietly. 'About it being the last coyote?'

'I remember.'

'I think I know how you felt. I'd hate to think that I was seeing the coyote for the last time, too.'

From the airport Bosch took the freeway to the Armenia exit and then south to Swann. He found that he didn't even need the rent-a-car map. He went east on Swann into Hyde Park and then down South Boulevard to her place. He could see the bay shimmering in the sun at the end of the street.

At the top of the stairs the door was open but the screen door was closed. Bosch knocked.

'Come in. It's open.'

It was her. Bosch pushed through the screen into the living room. She wasn't there but the first thing he noticed was a painting on the wall where before there had been only the nail. It was a portrait of a man in shadows. He was sitting at a table alone. The figure's elbow was on the table and the hand was up against his cheek, obscuring the face and making the deep set of the eyes the focal point of the painting. Bosch stared at it a moment until she called again.

'Hello? I'm in here.'

He saw the door to her studio was open a half foot. He stepped over and pushed it open. She was there, standing in front of the easel, dark earth-tone oils on the palette in her hand. There was a single errant slash of ocher on her right cheek. She immediately smiled.

'Harry.'

'Hello, Jasmine.'

He moved in closer to her and stepped around the side

441

of the easel. The portrait had only just been started. But she had begun with the eyes. The same eyes in the portrait that hung on the wall in the other room. The same eyes he saw in the mirror.

She hesitantly came closer to him. There was not a glimmer of embarrassment or unease in her face.

'I thought that if I painted you, you would come back.'

She dropped her brush into an old coffee can bolted to the easel and came even closer. She embraced him and they kissed silently. At first it was a gentle reunion, then he put his hand against her back and pulled her tightly against his chest as if she were a bandage that could stop his bleeding. After a while she pulled back, brought her arms up and held his face in her hands.

'Let me see if I got the eyes right.'

She reached up and took off his sunglasses. He smiled. He knew the purple below his eyes was almost gone but they were still red-rimmed and shot with swollen capillaries.

'Jesus, you took the red-eye.'

'It's a long story. I'll tell you later.'

'God, put these back on.'

She hooked the glasses back on and laughed.

'It's not that funny. It hurt.'

'Not that. I got paint on your face.'

'Well, then I'm not alone.'

He traced the slash on her face. They embraced again. Bosch knew they could talk later. For now he just held her and smelled her and looked over her shoulder to the brilliant blue of the bay. He thought of something the old man in the bed had told him. When you find the one that you think fits, then grab on for dear life. Bosch didn't know if she was the one, but for the moment he held on with everything he had left.

If you have enjoyed *The Last Coyote*
here is a taste of another Michael Connelly
bestseller

CITY OF BONES

Published in Allen&Unwin Paperback
ISBN: 1 7414 942 8

1

The old lady had changed her mind about dying but by then it was too late. She had dug her fingers into the paint and plaster of the nearby wall until most of her fingernails had broken off. Then she had gone for the neck, scrabbling to push the bloodied fingertips up and under the cord. She broke four toes kicking at the walls. She had tried so hard, shown such a desperate will to live, that it made Harry Bosch wonder what had happened before. Where was that determination and will and why had it deserted her until after she had put the extension cord noose around her neck and kicked over the chair? Why had it hidden from her?

These were not official questions that would be raised in his death report. But they were the things Bosch couldn't avoid thinking about as he sat in his car outside the Splendid Age Retirement Home on Sunset Boulevard east of the Hollywood Freeway. It was 4:20 P.M. on the first day of the year. Bosch had drawn holiday call-out duty.

The day more than half over and that duty consisted of two suicide runs — one a gunshot, the other the hanging. Both victims were women. In both cases there was evidence of depression and desperation. Isolation. New Year's Day was always a big day for suicides. While most people greeted the day with a sense of hope and renewal, there were those who saw it as a good day to die, some — like the old lady — not realizing their mistake until it was too late.

Bosch looked up through the windshield and watched as the latest victim's body, on a wheeled stretcher and covered in a green blanket, was loaded into the coroner's blue van. He saw there was one other occupied stretcher in the van and knew it was from the first suicide — a thirty-four-year-old actress who had shot herself while parked at a Hollywood overlook on Mulholland Drive. Bosch and the body crew had followed one case to the other.

Bosch's cell phone chirped and he welcomed the intrusion into his thoughts on small deaths. It was Mankiewicz, the watch sergeant at the Hollywood Division of the Los Angeles Police Department.

"You finished with that yet?"

"I'm about to clear."

"Anything?"

"A changed-my-mind suicide. You got something else?"

"Yeah. And I didn't think I should go out on the radio with it. Must be a slow day for the media — getting more what's-happening calls from reporters than I am getting service calls from citizens. They all want to do something on the first one, the actress on Mulholland. You know, a death-of-a-Hollywood-dream story. And they'd probably jump all over this latest call, too."

"Yeah, what is it?"

"A citizen up in Laurel Canyon. On Wonderland. He just called up and said his dog came back from a run in the woods with a bone in its mouth. The guy says it's human — an arm bone from a kid."

Bosch almost groaned. There were four or five call outs like this a year. Hysteria always followed by simple explanation: animal bones. Through the windshield he saluted the two body movers from the coroner's office as they headed to the front doors of the van.

"I know what you're thinking, Harry. Not another bone run. You've done it a hundred times and it's always the same thing. Coyote, deer, whatever. But listen, this guy with the dog, he's an MD. And he says there's no doubt. It's a humerus. That's the upper arm bone. He says it's a child, Harry. And then, get this. He said . . ."

There was silence while Mankiewicz apparently looked for his notes. Bosch watched the coroner's blue van pull off into traffic. When Mankiewicz came back he was obviously reading.

"The bone's got a fracture clearly visible just above the medial epicondyle, whatever that is."

Bosch's jaw tightened. He felt a slight tickle of electric current go down the back of his neck.

"That's off my notes, I don't know if I am saying it right. The point is, this doctor says it was just a kid, Harry. So could you humor us and go check out this humerus?"

Bosch didn't respond.

"Sorry, had to get that in."

"Yeah, that was funny, Mank. What's the address?"

Mankiewicz gave it to him and told him he had already dispatched a patrol team.

"You were right to keep it off the air. Let's try to keep it that way."

Mankiewicz said he would. Bosch closed his phone and started the car. He glanced over at the entrance to the retirement home before pulling away from the curb. There was nothing about it that looked splendid to him. The woman who had hung herself in the closet of her tiny bedroom had no next of kin, according to the operators of

3

the home. In death, she would be treated the way she had been in life, left alone and forgotten.

Bosch pulled away from the curb and headed toward Laurel Canyon.

2

Bosch listened to the Lakers game on the car radio while he made his way into the canyon and then up Lookout Mountain to Wonderland Avenue. He wasn't a religious follower of professional basketball but wanted to get a sense of the situation in case he needed his partner, Jerry Edgar. Bosch was working alone because Edgar had lucked into a pair of choice seats to the game. Bosch had agreed to handle the call outs and to not bother Edgar unless a homicide or something Bosch couldn't handle alone came up. Bosch was alone also because the third member of his team, Kizmin Rider, had been promoted nearly a year earlier to Robbery-Homicide Division and still had not been replaced.

It was early third quarter, and the game with the Trail Blazers was tied. While Bosch wasn't a hardcore fan he knew enough from Edgar's constant talking about the game and begging to be left free of call-out duty that it was an important matchup with one of the Los Angeles team's top rivals. He decided not to page Edgar until he had gotten to the scene and assessed the situation. He turned the radio off when he started losing the AM station in the canyon.

The drive up was steep. Laurel Canyon was a cut in the Santa Monica Mountains. The tributary roads ranged up toward the crest of the mountains. Wonderland Avenue dead-ended in a remote spot where the half-million-dollar homes were surrounded by heavily wooded and steep terrain. Bosch instinctively knew that searching for bones in the area would be a logistical nightmare. He pulled to a stop behind a patrol car already at the address Mankiewicz had provided and checked his watch. It was 4:38, and he wrote it down on a fresh page of his legal pad. He figured he had less than an hour of daylight left.

A patrol officer he didn't recognize answered his knock. Her nameplate said Brasher. She led him back through the house to a home office where her partner, a cop whom Bosch recognized and knew was named Edgewood, was talking to a white-haired man who sat behind a cluttered desk. There was a shoe box with the top off on the desk.

Bosch stepped forward and introduced himself. The white-haired man said he was Dr. Paul Guyot, a general practitioner. Leaning forward Bosch could see that the shoe box contained the bone that had drawn them all together. It was dark brown and looked like a gnarled piece of driftwood.

He could also see a dog lying on the floor next to the doctor's desk chair. It was a large dog with a yellow coat.

"So this is it," Bosch said, looking back down into the box.

"Yes, Detective, that's your bone," Guyot said. "And as you can see . . ."

He reached to a shelf behind the desk and pulled down a heavy copy of *Gray's Anatomy*. He opened it to a previously marked spot. Bosch noticed he was wearing latex gloves.

The page showed an illustration of a bone, anterior and posterior views. In the corner of the page was a small sketch of a skeleton with the humerus bone of both arms highlighted.

6

"The humerus," Guyot said, tapping the page. "And then we have the recovered specimen."

He reached into the shoe box and gently lifted the bone. Holding it above the book's illustration he went through a point-by-point comparison.

"Medial epicondyle, trochlea, greater and lesser tubercle," he said. "It's all there. And I was just telling these two officers, I know my bones even without the book. This bone is human, Detective. There's no doubt."

Bosch looked at Guyot's face. There was a slight quiver, perhaps the first showing of the tremors of Parkinson's.

"Are you retired, Doctor?"

"Yes, but it doesn't mean I don't know a bone when I see —"

"I'm not challenging you, Dr. Guyot." Bosch tried to smile. "You say it is human, I believe it. Okay? I'm just trying to get the lay of the land here. You can put that back into the box now if you want."

Guyot replaced the bone in the shoe box.

"What's your dog's name?"

"Calamity."

Bosch looked down at the dog. It appeared to be sleeping.

"When she was a pup she was a lot of trouble."

Bosch nodded.

"So, if you don't mind telling it again, tell me what happened today."

Guyot reached down and ruffled the dog's collar. The dog looked up at him for a moment and then put its head back down and closed its eyes.

"I took Calamity out for her afternoon walk. Usually when I get up to the circle I take her off the leash and let her run up into the woods. She likes it."

"What kind of dog is she?" Bosch asked.

"Yellow Lab," Brasher answered quickly from behind him.

Bosch turned and looked at her. She realized she had made a mistake by intruding and nodded and stepped back toward the door of the room where her partner was.

"You guys can clear if you have other calls," Bosch said. "I can take it from here."

Edgewood nodded and signaled his partner out.

"Thank you, Doctor," he said as he went.

"Don't mention it."

Bosch thought of something.

"Hey, guys?"

Edgewood and Brasher turned back.

"Let's keep this off the air, okay?"

"You got it," said Brasher, her eyes holding on Bosch's until he looked away.

After the officers left, Bosch looked back at the doctor and noticed that the facial tremor was slightly more pronounced now.

"They didn't believe me at first either," he said.

"It's just that we get a lot of calls like this. But I believe you, Doctor, so why don't you continue with the story?"

Guyot nodded.

"Well, I was up on the circle and I took off the leash. She went up into the woods like she likes to do. She's well trained. When I whistle she comes back. Trouble is, I can't whistle very loud anymore. So if she goes where she can't hear me, then I have to wait, you see."

"What happened today when she found the bone?"

"I whistled and she didn't come back."

"So she was pretty far up there."

"Yes, exactly. I waited. I whistled a few more times, and

8

then finally she came down out of the woods next to Mr. Ulrich's house. She had the bone. In her mouth. At first I thought it was a stick, you see, and that she wanted to play fetch with it. But as she came to me I recognized the shape. I took it from her — had a fight over that — and then I called you people after I examined it here and was sure."

You people, Bosch thought. It was always said like that, as if the police were another species. The blue species which carried armor that the horrors of the world could not pierce.

"When you called you told the sergeant that the bone had a fracture."

"Absolutely."

Guyot picked up the bone again, handling it gently. He turned it and ran his finger along a vertical striation along the bone's surface.

"That's a break line, Detective. It's a healed fracture."

"Okay."

Bosch pointed to the box, and the doctor returned the bone.

"Doctor, do you mind putting your dog on a leash and taking a walk up to the circle with me?"

"Not at all. I just need to change my shoes."

"I need to change, too. How about if I meet you out front?"

"Right away."

"I'm going to take this now."

Bosch put the top back on the shoe box and then carried it with two hands, making sure not to turn the box or jostle its contents in any way.

Outside, Bosch noticed the patrol car was still in front of the house. The two officers sat inside it, apparently writing out reports. He went to his car and placed the shoe box on the front passenger seat.

Since he had been on call out he had not dressed in a suit. He had on a sport coat with blue jeans and a white oxford shirt. He stripped off his coat, folded it inside out and put it on the backseat. He noticed that the trigger from the weapon he kept holstered on his hip had worn a hole in the lining and the jacket wasn't even a year old. Soon it would work its way into the pocket and then all the way through. More often than not he wore out his coats from the inside.

He took his shirt off next, revealing a white T-shirt beneath. He then opened the trunk to get out the pair of work boots from his crime scene equipment box. As he leaned against the rear bumper and changed his shoes he saw Brasher get out of the patrol car and come back toward him.

"So it looks legit, huh?"

"Think so. Somebody at the ME's office will have to confirm, though."

"You going to go up and look?"

"I'm going to try to. Not much light left, though. Probably be back out here tomorrow."

"By the way, I'm Julia Brasher. I'm new in the division."

"Harry Bosch."

"I know. I've heard of you."

"I deny everything."

She smiled at the line and put her hand out but Bosch was right in the middle of tying one of the boots. He stopped and shook her hand.

"Sorry," she said. "My timing is off today."

"Don't worry about it."

He finished tying the boot and stood up off the bumper.

"When I blurted out the answer in there, about the dog,

I immediately realized you were trying to establish a rapport with the doctor. That was wrong. I'm sorry."

Bosch studied her for a moment. She was mid-thirties with dark hair in a tight braid that left a short tail going over the back of her collar. Her eyes were dark brown. He guessed she liked the outdoors. Her skin had an even tan.

"Like I said, don't worry about it."

"You're alone?"

Bosch hesitated.

"My partner's working on something else while I check this out."

He saw the doctor coming out the front door of the house with the dog on a leash. He decided not to get out his crime scene jumpsuit and put it on. He glanced over at Julia Brasher, who was now watching the approaching dog.

"You guys don't have calls?"

"No, it's slow."

Bosch looked down at the MagLite in his equipment box. He looked at her and then reached into the trunk and grabbed an oil rag, which he threw over the flashlight. He took out a roll of yellow crime scene tape and the Polaroid camera, then closed the trunk and turned to Brasher.

"Then do you mind if I borrow your Mag? I, uh, forgot mine."

"No problem."

She slid the flashlight out of the ring on her equipment belt and handed it to him.

The doctor and his dog came up then.

"Ready."

"Okay, Doctor, I want you to take us up to the spot where you let the dog go and we'll see where she goes."

"I'm not sure you'll be able to stay with her."

"I'll worry about that, Doctor."

"This way then."

They walked up the incline toward the small turn-around circle where Wonderland reached a dead end. Brasher made a hand signal to her partner in the car and walked along with them.

"You know, we had a little excitement up this way a few years ago," Guyot said. "A man was followed home from the Hollywood Bowl and then killed in a robbery."

"I remember," Bosch said.

He knew the investigation was still open but didn't mention it. It wasn't his case.

Dr. Guyot walked with a strong step that belied his age and apparent condition. He let the dog set the pace and soon moved several paces ahead of Bosch and Brasher.

"So where were you before?" Bosch asked Brasher.

"What do you mean?"

"You said you were new in Hollywood Division. What about before?"

"Oh. The academy."

He was surprised. He looked over at her, thinking he might need to reassess his age estimate.

She nodded and said, "I know, I'm old."

Bosch got embarrassed.

"No, I wasn't saying that. I just thought that you had been somewhere else. You don't seem like a rookie."

"I didn't go in until I was thirty-four."

"Really? Wow."

"Yeah. Got the bug a little late."

"What were you doing before?"

"Oh, a bunch of different things. Travel mostly. Took me a while to figure out what I wanted to do. And you want to know what I want to do the most?"

Bosch looked at her.

"What?"

"What you do. Homicide."

He didn't know what to say, whether to encourage her or dissuade her.

"Well, good luck," he said.

"I mean, don't you just find it to be the most fulfilling job ever? Look at what you do, you take the most evil people out of the mix."

"The mix?"

"Society."

"Yeah, I guess so. When we get lucky."

They caught up to Dr. Guyot, who had stopped with the dog at the turnaround circle.

"This the place?"

"Yes. I let her go here. She went up through there."

He pointed to an empty and overgrown lot that started level with the street but then quickly rose into a steep incline toward the crest of the hills. There was a large concrete drainage culvert, which explained why the lot had never been built on. It was city property, used to funnel storm water runoff away from the homes on the street. Many of the streets in the canyon were former creek and river beds. When it rained they would return to their original purpose if not for the drainage system.

"Are you going up there?" the doctor asked.

"I'm going to try."

"I'll go with you," Brasher said.

Bosch looked at her and then turned at the sound of a car. It was the patrol car. It pulled up and Edgewood put down the window.

"We got a hot shot, partner. Double D."

He nodded toward the empty passenger seat. Brasher frowned and looked at Bosch.

"I hate domestic disputes."

Bosch smiled. He hated them too, especially when they turned into homicides.

"Sorry about that."

"Well, maybe next time."

She started around the front of the car.

"Here," Bosch said, holding out the MagLite.

"I've got an extra in the car," she said. "You can just get that back to me."

"You sure?"

He was tempted to ask for a phone number but didn't.

"I'm sure. Good luck."

"You too. Be careful."

She smiled at him and then hurried around the front of the car. She got in and the car pulled away. Bosch turned his attention back to Guyot and the dog.

"An attractive woman," Guyot said.

Bosch ignored it, wondering if the doctor had made the comment based on seeing Bosch's reaction to Brasher. He hoped he hadn't been that obvious.

"Okay, Doctor," he said, "let the dog go and I'll try to keep up."

Guyot unhooked the leash while patting the dog's chest.

"Go get the bone, girl. Get a bone! Go!"

The dog took off into the lot and was gone from sight before Bosch had taken a step. He almost laughed.

"Well, I guess you were right about that, Doc."

He turned to make sure the patrol car was gone and Brasher hadn't seen the dog take off.

"You want me to whistle?"

"Nah. I'll just go in and take a look around, see if I can catch up to her."

He turned the flashlight on.